T0200964

By Barb and J. C. Hendee

The Noble Dead Saga—Series One

Dhampir
Thief of Lives
Sister of the Dead
Traitor to the Blood
Rebel Fay
Child of a Dead God

The Noble Dead Saga—Series Two

In Shade and Shadow
Through Stone and Sea
Of Truth and Beasts

The Noble Dead Saga—Series Three

Between Their Worlds
The Dog in the Dark
A Wind in the Night
First and Last Sorcerer
The Night Voice

Also by Barb Hendee

The Vampire Memories Series

Blood Memories
Hunting Memories
Memories of Envy
In Memories We Fear
Ghost of Memories

The Mist-Torn Witches Series

The Mist-Torn Witches
Witches in Red
Witches with the Enemy

FIRST AND LAST SORCERER

A NOVEL OF THE NOBLE DEAD

BARB & J. C. HENDEE

A ROC BOOK

**Published by New American Library,
an imprint of Penguin Random House LLC
375 Hudson Street, New York, New York 10014**

This book is a publication of New American Library. Previously
published in a Roc hardcover edition.

First Roc Mass Market Printing, January 2016

Copyright © Barb Hendee and J. C. Hendee, 2015

For more information about Penguin Random House, visit penguin.com.

ISBN 978-0-451-46931-1

Printed in the United States of America
10 9 8 7 6 5 4 3 2 1

Penguin
Random
House

PROLOGUE

... what are you ... why have you come ... who do you serve?

Magiere lay on the cold stone floor of a locked cell beneath the imperial palace of Samau'a Gaulb, the main port city of il'Dha'ab Najuum and the Suman Empire as a whole. Shackled by her wrists with heavy chains anchored in the cell's rear wall, her wrists had long ago torn, bled, and half scabbed from straining against her bonds. And those three questions repeated over and over in her mind.

She'd heard them pressed into her thoughts rather than spoken by a voice, and they still echoed even now. Her tormentor had asked these on his first visit to her cell, though she never once heard him speak aloud. At times, she awoke thinking he stood inside the closed door, but when she opened her eyes to the complete darkness ...

Magiere was alone until he came again and tortured her without even touching her.

Was that even possible, or did she only think so?

She didn't know anymore.

She lay curled up with her long black hair lying tangled and lank across the floor stones. Strands stuck to her nearly white face, which was smudged and marred with filth. Her falchion and Chein'âs white metal dagger had been taken before she'd been locked away. How many days and nights had she been here?

Hunger, thirst, cold, and pain were her existence, leaving little room to feel anything else . . . except fear for what had become of Leesil. She remembered her husband—and Wayfarer, and Chap, and the few others who were precious to her—but only by memories her tormentor had somehow ripped from where they hid in her mind.

Memories of those she loved had become shadows in the dark. Whether she closed her eyes or not, only Leesil remained clear enough to hold on to . . . along with her hate for the one who'd come again and again.

Hate now kept her alive more than anything else.

A metallic clack echoed in the cell.

Magiere flinched, shuddered, and struggled to the cell's back wall. In the beginning, she'd risen into a crouch and watched the cell door open whenever *he* came. She hadn't resisted her dhampir half when it overwhelmed her in those earliest days—or were they nights? There was no way to tell the difference in the dark.

Her jaws had ached under the sudden growth of her teeth. Her irises had widened until they blotted out the whites of her eyes. And she'd lunged again and again.

Chains creaked and clattered but never broke. Their anchored brackets wouldn't rip from the wall. All she'd done was savagely claw the air halfway to that door . . . and *him*. But now she curled against the back wall, unable to summon her other half so she could at least see in the dark.

Perhaps this time it was just a guard sliding in another bowl of scraps or water.

When the door opened, its hinges squealed. She scrunched her eyes, shielding them with a raised hand against the sudden but dim light of a lantern. The iron door slammed shut before she lowered that hand . . . and there *he* stood.

As always, he was robed in shimmering gray with shadowy but glinting strange symbols upon the fabric. That was all she ever saw of him. With his arms raised waist high, each hand was always tucked into the opposing sleeve, and the sagging hood hid his face as well. He was slender, though tall for a Suman. She'd guessed he was a *he* only because the robe's thin fabric would've exposed a woman's build.

On the floor to his left but back nearer to the iron door sat an oil lantern with its wick turned down low. Perhaps it was the same one as before—and before—though she'd never seen him touch it in any of his visits. And each time she'd stopped screaming, she'd found herself on the floor. When she could lift her head, the cell had been dark and empty.

She'd never heard the door reopen, let alone close, when he'd left, though a few times she'd glimpsed the Suman guards outside. Once, when they'd opened the door to slide in food or water, she'd demanded to know who *he* was. They'd stared at her as if she were a witless, mewling beast, and then they'd left. It had taken a few more times before one apparently understood her.

"No one come you," answered that one in broken Numanese, and then he'd snorted with disgust. "You lone . . . till die."

She'd stared in confusion and shrieked like a beast when he left and the door clanged shut. After several more times, she gave up trying to talk to the guards.

How could none of them remember letting in the one who now stood before her?

The whispers began again in Magiere's head.

. . . no one left to trust . . .

. . . no one will come for you . . .

. . . all are locked away or fled . . .

. . . you are alone . . . forever . . .

Like a chorus of voices that rarely spoke the same words, they never stopped so long as he was there. They scratched and skittered like bugs in her skull until she'd clamped her hands over her ears. She didn't bother anymore, for it wouldn't stop them.

"What do you want . . . this time?" Magiere hissed through clenched teeth.

As if rising out of those whispers, memories came again . . . of home, her long-dead mother, the bloody tales of her birth . . . of her travels, her friends, allies, and enemies . . . of an orb once under her hands but now gone and hidden by someone else.

Her parched voice gained an edge. "I don't know anything more! So why bother? Why keep me alive?"

Out of that noise trying to smother her thoughts, one whisper rose above the others.

For a bargain with my master . . . your master.

Magiere slumped down the cell's back wall. It wasn't the first time she'd asked, heard the answer, and he never explained.

"Then what?" she croaked. "I don't have anything else . . . so what do you want . . . now?"

The gale of whispers waned to a soft breeze. That brief moment was an eternity of relief. Then they rose even louder and whipped into a frenzy.

Magiere grabbed her head as his answer came.

Another scream . . . please.

* * *

Leesil slumped against a cell's left sidewall with his chained hands limp in his lap. The only scant light came from around the edges of a closed peep-window in the cell's iron door, and this wasn't enough to let him see anything.

Somewhere in the dark with him, Chap and Wayfarer—a large dog and a girl in her youth—lay sleeping, each of them chained to a separate wall.

From the first night, Leesil had tried to count passing days by when guards brought food or water. They were the only ones who ever came. Even so, he wasn't certain how long he'd been here. The guards he'd seen changed now and then. What that meant for the passage of time he had no idea, for he didn't know the length of their shifts. What little food they brought was so bad that Wayfarer hadn't touched it for the first few days . . . or had those been nights?

Leesil listened in the dark and heard only Chap and Wayfarer's slow, weak breaths. He wore the same clothes from the first day he'd been imprisoned, and all of it was filthy and stank. All of his weapons had been confiscated.

On the day they'd been arrested, in anticipation of resisting, he'd dropped the pack and travel chest he carried to free himself for a fight. Then he'd realized they were too outnumbered and a fight would further endanger those he cared about. Nearly everything they owned had been left behind in the street.

Only the aging assassin—that butcher, Brot'an—had eluded capture, as if he'd known what was coming.

"A guard should . . . might . . . bring water soon," said a small, weak voice.

Leesil heard someone shift at the back wall—perhaps they were sitting up—as chains dragged slowly across the stone floor. At the scrape and hiss of a sulfur-tipped stick, he shut his eyes against the sudden light. Blinking, he looked to where Wayfarer—once called Leanâlhâm— knelt at the rear wall, her wrists chained like his own. She touched the small flame to a half-burned-down candle already rooted to the filthy floor by melted wax.

"I'll get you out of here," he said for maybe the thirtieth time, though now it lacked any conviction. "I'll find a way."

He told her this every time she lit the candle, and she'd always replied, "I know, Léshil," using the elven version of his name.

This time, Wayfarer said nothing.

As a mixed-blood elven girl only sixteen years old, she had her people's darkly tanned skin, overly large but slanted eyes, and peaked ears. She didn't have their amber irises, though, as she'd been marked at birth with darker ones. They scintillated between topaz and verdant green in bright light. Like Brot'an, she was of the elven people called the an'Cróan ("[Those] of the Blood"), from the far-off eastern continent. Where her people's hair was mostly white-blond, hers was almost the color of her skin. And she was no taller than a human girl.

All of these oddities were supposedly from being one-quarter human.

Leesil was half elven—half an'Cróan—with even slighter peaked ears and slanted eyes. His irises were amber and his hair nearly white-blond, like his mother's. But even in Wayfarer's current state—starved, frightened, and with dark rings around her large eyes— her strange beauty and maybe her frailty had their effect upon men.

On their first night locked away, the cell's darkness became too much for her—as if she didn't have enough terrors already. One younger guard showed pity when she'd cried out and begged for light. That one brought her a candle and a thin cedar stick, along with a small clay jar with enough sulfur paste to replenish the latter. The candle was lit only for meals, or when they thought such would come. They didn't know whether this pity would last long enough for another candle.

And whenever the candle had to be blown out, Leesil listened to Wayfarer's whimpering breaths in the dark. Even his attempts at comforting words didn't stop this, at least not until later, when she grew so weak she couldn't stay awake and dropped onto the floor stones. Now she sat with knees pulled up and her chin upon them as she watched the door without blinking.

Wayfarer didn't look at Leesil or even at the cell's third occupant chained to the far wall. In his guilt, Leesil couldn't bear looking at her and focused on the third prisoner in the cell.

Chap might look to most like a silver-gray wolf, though sometimes his fur had an almost bluish tint in twilight. When standing on all fours, he was taller than such an animal and longer of leg. He lay with his head on his paws, with two manacles for a prisoner's wrists chained to the far wall fully opened and bolted together around his neck.

It was too tight a fit, and Leesil often heard his oldest friend struggling to breathe.

Chap's body was that of majay-hì, descended from wolves of ancient times inhabited by eternal Fay spirits during the supposed mythical war at the end of the world's Forgotten History. But he was different— more—than even this. He *was* a Fay spirit born years ago by his own choice into a majay-hì pup—a new Fay-born in the body of a Fay-descended being.

Chap barely cracked open his eyes, and the candle's light flickered in his crystal-like sky blue irises. He glanced once at Wayfarer before looking across the cell . . . and words rose inside Leesil's thoughts.

—*She is not . . . being given . . . enough water*—

Leesil's throat was too dry to scoff. None of them was getting enough of anything.

He hadn't always cared for Chap dipping into his head to find spoken words in memories with which to speak to him. Now it didn't bother him so much. Chap had to see him to do this, which meant it happened only when the candle was lit.

In the past, Chap had communicated by pulling up any memories that he'd seen in someone at least once. It was his unique talent as a Fay-born in a Fay-descended body. Through bits and pieces of a person's own memories, he made basic notions or commands reasonably clear . . . or just manipulated those unaware that he was doing so.

Learning to use only sound—words—in those memories was a new trick.

—*Ask . . . the guards . . . to bring . . . more water*—

Leesil stared at Chap. "Like I haven't tried!"

"Tried what?" Wayfarer asked weakly, and then her gaze shifted to Chap.

"Nothing," Leesil said. "You should rest while we wait."

Wayfarer didn't move. Chap closed his eyes with a coarse exhale. Leesil dropped his head back against the wall.

Nearly a moon ago, they'd all arrived by ship to seek one of the last two "orbs." Some believed the Ancient Enemy had wielded these devices a thousand years ago in its war on the world. Its living and undead minions now surfaced to seek the orbs for their master, or perhaps just for themselves. The orbs could not be allowed to fall into such hands.

With no warning, Leesil and his companions had all been captured and arrested—except for Brot'an—upon arriving in the empire's capital port. They'd been accused of multiple murders they hadn't committed, and then Magiere, Leesil's wife, had been dragged off separately.

Leesil, Chap, and Wayfarer had been locked up together, but they'd not seen Magiere since.

Chap had attempted to learn what he could by dipping any surfacing memories from the guards' minds. Those men knew only to keep their charges locked up and fed enough to stay alive. All that Chap learned of Magiere was that she was in a cell farther away under separate guard. Worse was waiting for the only hint that she was still alive: the sound of her screaming.

That didn't come often anymore.

Leesil hadn't heard Magiere in five days or nights, at a guess. On the first night, when he hadn't heard her by the time another meal came, he'd felt relieved that she might've finally been left alone. When the next meal came, he was lost for what to feel at all. At the meal after that, relief vanished, replaced with rising fear.

Helplessness was not something Leesil dealt with well. That Brot'an was the only one free didn't help either. If the aging assassin had come up with a way to rescue them, he'd have done it by now. And Leesil kept waiting for any sign that his wife still lived.

A shriek suddenly echoed from somewhere outside the cell.

Chap's head snapped up as his eyes locked on the door.

Wayfarer collapsed in a rattle of chains and clamped her hands over her ears.

Leesil's wave of relief died quickly under anguish.

Magiere *was* still alive, but, as always, only her screams let him know this . . . until this scream ceased more quickly than ever before. He sat up to stare at the door and then looked across the cell. Chap still watched the door without blinking, his ears stiffened upright. Several long, tense moments followed. Leesil wasn't sure how long.

A metal clack echoed in the cell and the iron door squealed open.

Wayfarer thrashed back against the rear wall and then threw herself toward Chap. The chains stopped her, and Chap quickly shifted as far as he could to reach her. She got close enough to bury her face in his neck.

Leesil blinked and squinted as light spilled in through the opened door, and when his sight cleared . . .

A robed figure in light gray stood inside the opening.

Leesil was too worn and shaken to say anything at first.

The figure's sagging hood turned slowly toward all three inside the cell. When the hood's black pit fixed on Leesil, strange whispers began building in his head . . . until he choked, convulsed, and the walls blurred and darkened in his sight. One voice in his head rose above the chaos of the others.

Where are they . . . the devices of my master?

Everything went black.

Leesil thought he might vomit from the sudden pain, and then the buzz of a thousand whispers in his head went silent all at once. When he could see again, he found himself collapsed upon the cold stone floor. He hadn't even found the strength to push up when he saw the hood of the gray robe was turned the other way . . .

Wayfarer lay on the floor, utterly silent and unmoving. Before Leesil cried out to her, he spotted Chap. The dog's ears were flattened as he glared up into that hood, and his sky blue eyes narrowed. Even in weakness, Chap's jowls pulled back in a dry-throated snarl.

"What do you want?" Leesil got out as he pushed up to a sitting position. "Where is my wife?"

Chap still stared up into that hood, and the hood never turned as an answer rose in Leesil's mind.

She is not yours anymore. And until I have what I desire, you will never see the sun . . . or have the freedom of death.

The figure turned for the open door. Only then did Leesil notice that none of the guards had come in. The one that he could see outside in the passage stood facing away as if nothing were happening.

"What are you talking about?" Leesil choked out. "What . . . what do you want . . . from us?"

The figure paused in the doorway, though it did not turn back. The storm of whispers filled Leesil's head like a nest of wasps stirring around the answer.

Ask your . . . dog . . . since I cannot ask him myself.

The gray robe drifted out, and the heavy iron door slammed shut without a guard turning to grab its handle.

Leesil was caught in confusion. He tensed as he heard the outside lock bolt slide home. He looked to Chap. The dog's eyes were still narrowed over a silent snarl as he watched the cell's door. From the look of him, whatever that robed figure had done—could do—Chap hadn't been affected.

"Who was that?" Leesil whispered.

Chap barely lowered his eyes but didn't meet Leesil's.

—I do not know—

"How did he do that . . . get in my head like . . . like you?"

—Not . . . like me—

"Then how?"

Chap remained silent for so long that Leesil wondered if his old friend even knew. He looked to Wayfarer's crumpled form. Before he called to her, he heard her shallow breaths, as if she simply slept. And Chap's answer struck him then.

—*Sorcery*—

Leesil's whole mind went blank and he grew cold. It was one word he hadn't thought would come. That art of magic was supposed to have been wiped out long ago, but it didn't answer his other question.

"You heard something. I can see it. What in the seven hells is that robed one after?"

Leesil waited—and waited—but not a word popped into his head. The dog lowered his eyes and, with one glance at Wayfarer, his muzzle settled on his forepaws.

Chap stared blankly across the floor in silence, not looking at anyone.

Leesil grew frantic. Whatever the robed figure wanted, it might be enough to stop Magiere's torment.

"Chap?" he whispered, and then more sharply, "Chap, what does that . . . man want? Damn you, answer me!"

CHAPTER 1

G hassan il'Sänke slipped through the night back-
streets of the empire's capital. Once a sage in the
Suman branch of the Guild of Sagecraft, he made his
way silently toward the inland side of the guild's local
grounds. As on previous surreptitious visits over the
last moon, he was uncertain what to do when he arrived.

He no longer wore the midnight blue robe of a domin
of Metaology, for that certainly would catch anyone's
attention—too risky considering he was now an outcast
and sought by both the city and the imperial guards. In
disguise, he now looked nothing like the sage of rank
that he had once been.

Beneath the hood of a faded open-front robe, his short
chocolate-colored hair with flecks of silver was in disarray.
Strands dangled to his thick brows above eyes separated
by a straight but overly prominent nose. His borrowed
clothing of a dusky linen shirt and drab pantaloons was
no different from that of a common street vendor.

He turned into the small open market that he passed
through on all such visits and headed into a cutway
between two shops for a less visible approach to the
guild's complex. In part, he wondered whether such

caution was needed. Few people about this late would ever glance his way.

Most of the stalls were closed with their tarp flats pulled down, and all nearby shop awnings had been lowered and shut tight. But he had learned in hard ways to be more cautious than ever before. When he slipped along the cutway, across the back alley, and then neared the next street, a new smell filled his nostrils.

Something rank cut through the alley's stench.

At the slow *click-clop-scrape* coming closer, Ghassan peeked out from the cutway's black shadows. Up the northward stretch of the next street, an old man with a cane of scrap wood shuffled nearer along the sandstone cobble. Wrapped in rags too filthy to show any hint of color in the dark, he dragged his lame foot more than the good one. Of the many unfortunate moments that must have made up this beggar's life, he slowed in turning his gaunt face toward the cutway's mouth.

Ghassan's training was quicker than his caution. With barely a blink, the dark behind his eyelids filled with lines of spreading light. In an instant, a doubled square formed in sigils, symbols, and signs burned brightly. Then came a triangle within that square and another inverted within that, both at the center of the pattern. As his blink finished, he completed his incantation with a flash of thought quicker than spoken words.

The glowing pattern overlaid Ghassan's sight of the beggar's face.

The old man blinked as well. He looked about as if he'd seen something, and then seemed like he was second-guessing upon seeing it no more. With a tired sag of his shoulders, he moved on in his *click-clop-scrape*.

Ghassan waited until the beggar was halfway to the next cross street before silently stepping out. He could have made the old man see someone else in his place, but to wipe his presence from the awareness of one target was much simpler.

Such were the subtleties of sorcery, especially for a master of the third and most reviled practice of magic.

Well past dusk, Chane Andraso stood on deck as a ship maneuvered into dock at the Samau'a Gaulb, the main port city of il'Dha'ab Najuum, one country in the Suman Empire. Arrival after sunset was nothing more than good fortune. Had they docked earlier—considering he was a noble dead, specifically a vampire—he would have had to wait until nightfall to disembark. Now he gazed out over the vast, seemingly endless port with mixed emotions.

He and his companions had sailed south along the coast for nearly a moon. Partly relieved to reach their destination, he struggled to suppress anxiety over what they might face here.

"It's just as I'd imagined," said a breathy voice beside him.

Chane glanced down as Wynn Hygeorht stepped to the railing. She was so short she could have stood beneath his chin. Though in her early twenties, she looked younger, or at least she did to him. For a moment, his gaze locked on her pretty, oval face of olive-toned skin surrounded by wispy light brown hair.

With heat lingering from the day, she had packed away her cloak and wore what she often called her "travel robe." This marked her as a scholar—a "sage"—from the Guild of Sagecraft, specifically its founding branch in her homeland of Malourné, far to the north. Back there, all sages dressed in full-length robes, but this shorter one stopped at her knees. Beneath it she wore pants, tunic, and boots to move more easily. Still, the robe was the wrong color for her.

Not long before, Wynn had worn gray for the order of Cathology, until she had been forced to change orders for a number of reasons. She now wore the midnight blue of the order of Metaology.

Chane was still unaccustomed to this; he would always see her as a cathologer . . . a preserver of knowledge itself.

Wynn looked away from the port and up at him. Her gaze ran over his pale face and red-brown hair. A puzzled frown then clouded her expression. Not wishing her to think he was studying her, he turned his attention back to the port that awaited them.

"Isn't it what you expected?" she asked.

In truth, he had not given this much thought or expected anything in particular. Now, upon their arrival, the place looked too . . . foreign.

His night vision was far better than that of the living. By the clear sky and three-quarter moon, he could see that most of the buildings nearest to the piers were only one story high. Many of the structures beyond peaked high above the waterfront buildings. Some had to be huge, by a guess, especially those set farther and farther into the immense capital of the Suman Empire. Every structure within sight was mostly golden tan sandstone except for heat-grayed timbers and planks or the occasional dyed wall or pinnacled dome with colors faded by the desert sun.

"Do you know where to find the guild's Suman branch?" he asked in his nearly voiceless rasp. He had once been beheaded by one of Wynn's past companions and then brought back to his undead existence for a second time by someone else. His voice had never healed.

"I've a rough idea," Wynn answered as she turned the other way and looked to their two companions down the railing. "Shade . . . Osha . . . the ramp will be down soon. Time to gather our belongings."

Shade, a long-legged black dog resembling an overly tall wolf, stood only a few strides away. With her forepaws up on the railing, she too looked out into the city. Then, dropping to all fours, she padded to Wynn's side.

Chane studied Shade's every movement in concern.

Before this voyage, the dog had been badly injured and nearly killed. Though she appeared fully healed, he still did not want her exerting herself unnecessarily. It was a strange thing for him to care so much for anyone or anything besides Wynn.

Shade, a majay-hì, was a natural enemy of the undead. Yet in recent times she had fought at his side—both with and for him—and not only for Wynn's sake. He could not help his concern for her in turn.

All such thoughts faded as Chane glanced toward the aftcastle door.

The fourth member of their group had turned to readying the last of their belongings. An exceptionally tall elf with long white-blond hair hefted several packs.

From what Chane understood, the word in the an'Cróan elven people's language for the man's name—Osha—meant "a sudden breeze." To Chane, Osha was a sudden and unwanted interloper who had forced his company upon Wynn. Unfortunately, Wynn did not see things this way, which was all the more irritating to Chane.

In grudging fairness, Chane had to admit that Osha was astonishingly skilled with the long, curved bow strung over his right shoulder. His shots struck with more accuracy than should have been possible. Over his left shoulder was a quiver of black-feathered arrows, as well as a narrow wrapped bundle tied to his back.

Osha raised his head with the usual dour expression on his long, horselike face. This softened only whenever his large amber eyes fixed on Wynn.

"All is ready," he answered to her.

Though Osha now struggled less with tongues other than his own, Chane had rarely met anyone as inept with languages. He looked away, scowling for reasons besides those concerning the elf.

Around them, sailors tossed down lines to men on the pier, and Wynn suddenly stepped off to join Osha by the small pile of their belongings.

"Come, Chane," she called without looking back. "You'll need to carry the chest."

Following her halfway, his gaze lowered to a travel chest at Osha's feet. It was much heavier than it appeared, for inside it lay the orb of Spirit. The one called the Ancient Enemy and other names and titles had once wielded that potential weapon in an all but forgotten war upon the world.

The thought of the chest's contents sharpened Chane's anxiety. He had brought Wynn all this way, at her insistence, to reconnect her with past companions, but Magiere, Leesil, and Chap were hunters of the undead and certainly did not accept Wynn's connection to Chane.

They would never accept him either.

More than anything, he feared what might happen should Wynn be forced to make a choice.

"Are you all right?"

Startled, he raised his eyes to find Wynn frowning at him again. He quickly stepped in to heft the chest.

"The ramp is down," he said. "Let us go."

Still frowning, Wynn turned the other way and grabbed her staff leaning beside the aftcastle door. It was taller than her head, with its upper end sheathed in leather over the long crystal atop it. She picked up the last pack and headed for the ramp as Shade closed in at her side.

Wynn let out a breathy sigh, perhaps as daunted as Chane over what they would face in the next step of this journey.

"All right, then," she said without looking back. "Everyone stay close."

Wynn tried to keep a confident air as she led the way down the pier toward the city. Though she'd come searching for Magiere, Leesil, and Chap, the only way she could think to find them was through one Suman sage of Metaology.

Moons ago, she and Magiere had agreed to split up in the search for the remaining two orbs: Spirit and Air. In all, there were five of these devices, hidden centuries before by minions of the Ancient Enemy. Upon learning of the orbs' existence, Magiere, Wynn, and their other companions had soon found themselves embroiled in a desperate search to find them all and keep them from the wrong hands. Three had been recovered—and safely rehidden—leaving only two left to locate.

So Wynn had remained up north with her small group to search for the orb of Spirit. Upon finding it, she'd immediately sailed south to reconnect with Magiere, who, in her search for the orb of Air, had taken her group south to this very port, seeking assistance from Domin Ghassan il'Sänke—at Wynn's suggestion.

The domin had once spent time in Wynn's guild branch.

Unfortunately, he was unpredictable, perhaps untrustworthy, and always had his own agenda. One couldn't even guess what he might do or why. Still, when Wynn and her oldest companions in this search had last been together, she couldn't think of anyone better, let alone able and willing, to help Magiere.

It seemed reasonable that the first person she should speak to would be Ghassan il'Sänke. If anyone might know the whereabouts of Magiere and those with her, it would be him.

As Wynn dodged between passersby on the waterfront, she licked her lips, now drying in the night's hot air. She was well aware that she didn't have much to go on in her search, and she turned her attention to the sights and sounds of the capital.

The air of the waterfront was tainted with spices and dust that mixed with the odors of sea brine and masses of people. She wondered how strong the scents might become inside the city's narrow ways. And if it was this bad to her, it must be so much worse for Shade's nose.

As if that thought called the dog, Wynn felt Shade press up against her thigh. She glanced down and saw the dog's ears were half flattened; Shade never liked crowds.

Most of the dusky-skinned and dark-haired people on the waterfront wore light, loose-fitting cloth shifts or equally loose leggings or pantaloons. Wraps upon their heads were done up in all sorts of mounds, short or tall, thick or thin. Perhaps there weren't as many people as there would be during the day, but there were far more than she'd seen in any port at night during her travels.

Some herded goats or carried square baskets of chickens or birds she couldn't name. Many spoke to one another, but she couldn't follow much of what was said. She read the common dialect of Sumanese quite well and even spoke a bit of it, but all languages in common usage tended to evolve like living things. Her knowledge of it was more scholarly than practical.

A number of people glanced at her or her companions, and she could hardly blame them.

Osha towered over everyone, and though he was dressed in brown pants and a simple tunic, his tan skin and large but slanted amber eyes were exotic in this place. Worse was his white-blond hair, which glowed too brightly whenever he passed under an oil lamp.

Chane wasn't much better, with his pale face and jaggedly cut red-brown hair. Dressed like a traveling nobleman in a well-tailored but well-worn white shirt, dark pants, and high boots, he would likely be fixed upon by any cutpurse around. That is, until they spotted the two sheathed swords at his waist instead of one. Fortunately, his unusual eyes might not stand out as much as Osha's in passing. Once, Chane's irises had been light brown, but the longer he existed as an undead, the more they lost their color. When he grew angry or agitated, they turned crystal clear.

Wynn looked down once more at the tall black dog— or wolf—walking at her side. She buried her small fingers into the fur between Shade's shoulders, mostly for her own comfort.

Who wouldn't glance at all of them?

Looking into the city, she saw no trees or plant life anywhere, only an endless stretch of light-toned buildings. They stepped off the pier's landward end and onto the walkway along the shore.

"You know . . . where go?" Osha asked in his broken Numanese.

It was easier for the two of them to speak in Elvish, he in his an'Cróan dialect and she in that of the Lhoin'na ("[Those] of the Glade")—the elves of this continent. But he often attempted either Belaskian or Numanese, either for practice or to be polite.

In the journey's previous moon, he'd improved a little in both . . . sort of.

"Where *to* go," she corrected, glancing back at Osha following behind Chane. "From what I've read, the guild's Suman branch is a huge compound with numerous structures located on the capital's northwest side. If we stay near the waterfront, we should spot it down an inland street."

Chane frowned, as if he'd expected her to know more—or perhaps because she spoke to Osha and not him.

Wynn turned ahead, taking a slow breath. Dealing with those two and their separate feelings for her, let alone any feelings she had for either of them, wasn't something she could let distract her right now.

A sandstone arch stretched between two buildings like a gate into the city. Wanting out of the crowd and trying to appear confident, Wynn walked through the arch. When they reached the next street parallel to the waterfront, she turned north again. Along the way, she peered up the side streets, looking for one wide enough that it might reveal their destination.

Shade kept pressed into her leg, and when Wynn glanced back, she noticed that Osha was carrying his own belongings on his back and both of Chane's packs in his arms. Wynn carried her own pack over her left shoulder, and Chane carried the chest with the orb—which was heavy—but Osha was burdened with everything else. She would have noticed sooner if she hadn't been so distracted.

And then Chane looked back as well and half turned. "Put one of my packs on top of the chest."

Osha slowed, keeping more than an arm's length behind Chane. "I . . . fine."

Chane moved on with a subtle sneer, and Wynn sighed as she headed onward. She'd hoped the two would've learned to tolerate each other by now. This quietly hostile competition was becoming annoying.

The mainway was almost as well lit as the waterfront by streetlamps hung high at every intersection. As she'd expected, the smells grew stronger, trapped by still air between the buildings. The scent of jasmine sharpened in her nose, though she saw none blooming along the rows of shops and eateries they passed. It thickened even more as she passed a dark-haired woman in a gauzy wrap and bangles of brass around her neck and wrists.

Even the people here overperfumed themselves; without warning, memory-words rose in Wynn's mind.

—*Too many . . . people . . . too many . . . smells*—

"I know," she whispered.

Shade was no ordinary dog as a majay-hì. She was descended from wolves of ancient times inhabited by the Fay during the Great War at the end of the world's Forgotten History. The descendants of those first Fay-born had become the guardians of the elves, first the Lhoin'na and then later the separate an'Cróan on the world's far side. In the lands of the latter, Shade's homeland, majay-hì barred all but the elves from entering their vast so-called Elven Territories. More than this, and due to a plan hatched by her father, Chap, Shade had traveled across the far ocean and the whole central continent to protect Wynn.

Among a few unusual abilities, Shade communicated with Wynn by raising memory-words in her mind.

"We'll find the guild soon," Wynn added, scratching lightly between Shade's shoulder blades. "We'll be welcome there and maybe it won't be so . . . scented."

In truth, she didn't know what kind of welcome they would receive. As a sage, she should be offered shelter for herself and her companions. But of the few Suman sages she'd met, even fewer shared much about the customs of their own branch. She respected Domin il'Sänke's knowledge and abilities but didn't exactly trust him. He had assisted her in the past, but at other times he'd done everything he could to stop her own pursuits.

"Wait, stop," Chane rasped.

Wynn looked back to find him halted before the side street she'd just passed. He jutted his chin up that street.

"This looks best, if we need to go farther inland," Chane added.

Wynn nodded and headed for the side street. From what she saw, there were no street signs or markers pointing toward anything, and she grew worried. In order to find Magiere, she needed to find the domin, and to find him, she needed to find the guild. Then she spotted an elderly man with a heavily lined dusky face coming her way, and she tried her best in simple Sumanese.

"Pardon."

The man stopped, blinked several times, and took in the sight of her companions. Perhaps his eyes widened a little at the huge black "dog," since few Sumans would have ever seen a "wolf."

"Guild . . . Sagecraft?" she asked in Sumanese, hoping either word came out like a question.

He looked over her short-robe and nodded once. Instead of answering, he held up six fingers and then pointed up the way. Before she could nod, he pointed northward and held up four fingers. Wynn smiled—six blocks inland and four to the north.

"Thank you," she said, or hoped it was a close equivalent.

He nodded more slowly, with a smile of his own, and continued onward.

Wynn pressed on along the route she'd been given. Before she'd even finished the final four blocks, she saw a low wall beyond the end of the street.

"There it is," she said, though likely the others had seen it before she had.

She quickened her pace and soon reached a seemingly endless stone wall stretching in both directions. It was surprisingly short and was probably just something to mark the extents of the grounds and keep the public from wandering in. Standing on tiptoes, Wynn pulled herself up to peek over the wall's top.

Around a vast courtyard stood numerous enormous buildings of tan stone with ornately peaked rooftops. The courtyard had been painstakingly cobbled with dark brown and red tiles in an arcing diamond pattern. Paths between buildings were well swept and benches had been placed at comfortable intervals. She felt a little daunted at the sight of it all.

These grounds were far larger than those of the Numan branch, which by comparison looked like little more than a squat stone keep tucked tightly inside a four-towered old wall.

"The entrance," Chane said, pointing.

Following his finger extended along the chest's side, Wynn indeed saw an opening about forty paces to the right down the wall.

"We'll have rooms and supper soon," she assured,

leading the way. Much more important, they should soon learn where to find Magiere.

Upon reaching the entrance, she halted before a set of opened iron gates between two immense sandstone columns. Four men—obviously not sages—were stationed inside the columns, and all four turned to stare at her.

They wore identical tan pants of fine fabric tucked into matching tall, hard boots. Dark brown tabards overlaid their cream shirts, and red wraps were mounded atop their heads. Each had an ornately sheathed curved sword tucked into the heavy red fabric of his waist wrap.

Wynn hadn't expected armed guards. She was staring at them with growing concern when one barked a question in Sumanese. She didn't quite catch it and shook her head.

"Do any of you speak Numanese?" she asked.

All four guards looked over the visitors with a wariness that bordered on fear of a threat.

Wynn's worry increased, though she resisted glancing back at either Chane or Osha. She hadn't heard Chane drop the chest yet, so that was good, but Osha could draw and nock an arrow faster than a man could draw a sword.

Then Wynn heard the sound of packs being dropped on the street stones behind her.

Both men, along with Shade, were far too protective of her. When Shade rumbled at the guards, Wynn clenched her fingers on the dog's scruff. One guard with a close-trimmed beard took a step toward her.

"I speak your tongue," he said, eyeing her robe. "What is your business here, sage?"

His accent was thick, but his command of Numanese was sound, and at least he recognized her for what she was. Still, none of the guards stepped aside, and intuition warned her not to mention Domin il'Sänke just yet. This unexpected "welcome" at the gate left her wondering if the domin might be a questionable figure within his own branch.

"I am visiting from the Numan branch," she answered. "Could you please direct us to High Premin Aweli-Jama?"

Asking to see the branch's highest-ranking sage was presumptuous but safest. For the sake of good manners, Aweli-Jama would have to offer hospitality to a fellow sage—albeit a foreign one—and her companions.

The bearded guard simply studied her. Then his gaze shifted beyond her, likely to Osha and Chane. He twisted slightly, whispering something to the other guards, and then . . .

"Wait here."

Wynn's mouth gaped as he turned away and walked across the courtyard. She watched as he entered the beautiful sandstone building straight ahead with six peaks along the top of its roof. Her view was then cut off as the other three guards positioned themselves across the entrance's opening. There was another strange thing Wynn noted.

Though it was well past dusk, the evening meal couldn't have finished long before, and yet she saw no one walking the paths of this huge complex. There had to be many sages of all ranks staying on the grounds full-time, especially in a place as big as this.

So where were they? Had a curfew been ordered for some reason?

"What is happen?" Osha whispered in Numanese.

"Happening," she corrected. "And I'm not certain." She eased and then squeezed her grip on Shade. "Anything?"

That was all that was needed between them in situations like this. The dog could catch rising memories within anyone in sight and show such to Wynn, so long as they were touching. Wynn waited three breaths, far too long for any sights or sounds to enter her thoughts.

Shade shuddered once beneath her hand and whined in agitation.

At that, one guard lifted a hand to grip the hilt of his sword.

"Easy, sister," Wynn whispered to Shade. "What's wrong?"

—*Nothing . . . is . . . there*—

Wynn's confusion increased at these words called up and then reassembled from her own memories of things heard from others in the past. What did Shade mean?

—*No . . . memories*— *. . .* —*All . . . blank*—

Wynn's breath caught. No one's thoughts were ever completely blank, at least not at all times. Something was blocking Shade from dipping the guards' memories. How—or, for that matter, why? No one here could've known they were coming, let alone what Shade could do.

Movement across the tiled courtyard caught Wynn's attention.

Four people walked brusquely toward the gate, and the guard who had told her to wait led the way. Behind him came a tall man hidden within the gray robe of a cathologer, with the full cowl up and shadowing his face from the courtyard lanterns. Last came a more disturbing pair: a stout man and a spindly woman, both robed in midnight blue, like Wynn, for the order of Metaology.

That the high premin was flanked by two metalogers was troubling, especially after what Shade had claimed. As far as Wynn knew, conjury was favored among metaologers of this branch versus thaumaturgy in the Numan branch.

This time, Wynn did glance back . . . just in time to see Chane whisper an aside to Osha. The chest now sat on the street, along with the packs Osha had carried.

Osha silently nodded to Chane.

"Oh, not again," Wynn moaned under her breath.

Chane must have sensed something, for anytime those two agreed about anything it meant there would be trouble. Osha shrugged his left shoulder, and his bow slipped off and dropped down his arm. He caught it without even looking, but at least Chane hadn't yet reached for one of his swords.

"You will not bring that canine onto the grounds."

Wynn flinched as she turned around toward the gate and came face-to-face—or face-to-throat—with the sage in gray. He was tall for a Suman, and both metaologers still flanked him. The four guards had broken into pairs at both of the gateway's columns.

"Such beasts are not permitted here," High-Premin Aweli-Jama declared, for that was who he had to be.

Of all the things Wynn expected to hear first, that was not among them.

Other than his accent, his Numanese was perfect, and up close it was easier to see his face. He was likely in his mid-sixties, at a guess, and his gray hair was cropped short beneath his cowl. Dark-toned skin covered a slightly wizened and narrow face with slanted cheekbones. He pressed his hands nervously together, though his expression was unreadable.

"Good evening, High Premin," she said politely as she stroked Shade's back. "I am Journeyor Wynn Hygeorht of the Numan branch. This is Shade, who is not a common animal and will harm no one. She travels with me for my protection, as do my other two companions."

Both metaologers were entirely fixed on her, but she'd been the subject of scrutiny many times before. Both were middle-aged, which suggested they each held at least the rank of domin.

"We have come a long way, and we're weary," she added. "If we could only—"

"Why are you here with so much *protection*?" Aweli-Jama asked abruptly. "Your branch's council did not inform us of sending a journeyor."

This grew stranger and stranger.

"I wasn't aware anyone needed to be informed for a passing visit," she answered, still not giving him the real reason she had come. In the brief silence that followed, she listened for the slightest sound behind her. Both Chane and Osha were quiet and hopefully hadn't moved.

Aweli-Jama shook his head in what appeared to be a dismissal.

"Of course not," he answered flatly, as if her comment was pointless. "I meant that if I had been informed, I could have responded with proper regrets to your premin, who might have informed you. At this time, you and your companions cannot be accommodated based on recent and unanticipated concerns for security. I am sorry you have traveled such a distance, but please seek lodgings elsewhere."

Without another word, the high premin began to turn away.

Wynn's jaw slackened until her lips parted. Something here was very wrong . . . from guards posted at the gate to Shade's inability to pick up any memories to Aweli-Jama's refusing shelter to a journeyor sage of another branch. The metaologers turned to follow the high premin as the guards spread out to block the way in.

Her thoughts raced for something to say that might stall the high premin for an instant. She stiffened when Chane's hand settled on her shoulder, for she hadn't heard him close in behind her.

"Do not mention . . . the others," he whispered in Belaskian.

After an instant of confusion, she realized he meant Magiere, Leesil, and Chap, but she had to say something.

"Premin," she called. "I've come to see Domin Ghassan il'Sänke."

That was the last topic she wished to raise openly, but it was the only thing she could think of in an instant. She had to get in there and find the domin.

"May I at least speak with him?" she went on, and then half lied, "He was one of my tutors when he visited Calm Seatt."

High Premin Aweli-Jama stopped abruptly, as did the pair of metaologers.

Chane tried to still his mind amid the overriding sense—the stench—of fear emanating from the Suman sages. It was so strong that the beast inside of him, his inner feral nature, strained at its bonds. Fear made the beast hungry for prey, and Chane bit down until his jaws ached.

When Wynn spoke il'Sänke's name, the sages halted and that stench thickened.

Chane fought to clear his thoughts amid the beast's snarling.

The high premin spun and fixed on Wynn. For an instant, fear was evident on his lined face. This vanished as his expression became outwardly cold and measured.

"Why do you wish to see him?" Aweli-Jama asked with a slight tremor in his voice.

The metaologers had also turned, one eyeing Wynn, who retreated a step and bumped into Chane. The other looked over everyone with her, one by one.

"As I said," Wynn answered, her voice wavering, "he was my tutor during his stay in the north. I wish to pay my respects. It would be rude to come all this way without doing so."

Aweli-Jama's cold expression remained unchanged, though his voice became even and more controlled. "What exactly is your mission here, Journeyor?" His gaze shifted upward. "One that requires a swordsman and a Lhoin'na archer."

This high premin would not know that Osha was of the an'Cróan elves from the eastern continent. Chane had no intention of enlightening him, and instead wondered how Wynn would answer. He pushed that aside, trying to clear his head again so he could listen to how the premin would respond to Wynn's next words.

"No mission, Premin," she replied. "I'm simply . . . journeying to learn about a land and people I've never seen for myself. While I'm here, can I not see my old tutor and thank him for his kindness? Why would you force me to be rude in not doing so?"

The premin studied her long in silence, perhaps trapped by the cultural manners Wynn intimated. His expression remained flat, though the stench of fear had not lessened.

Chane eyed the guards. Behind Wynn's back, he slowly inched his free hand toward the hilt of his long-sword. The two metaologers worried him the most, but if anything happened, Osha could disable at least one while Chane readied to hold off the guards.

"Domin il'Sänke is not in residence at present," Aweli-Jama said, "but as you are a past student of his"—he half turned, sweeping a narrow hand toward the main building with the six-peaked rooftop—"perhaps we can accommodate you . . . until he returns."

The beast within Chane lurched back in wary retreat; the premin was lying about something.

In the past, he and Wynn had used this odd ability of his. She would ask questions, and behind her, keeping his thoughts still, he would squeeze her shoulder when the beast grew wary or outright vicious. For whatever reason, his inner nature knew when it heard a lie. But the question—and its answer—had been too broken, mixed, and vague to know which part was the deception.

"No," he whispered behind Wynn, lightly squeezing her shoulder. Then he spoke openly to the high premin. "We do not wish to be a burden and will seek arrangements in the city."

"There is no need for that," Aweli-Jama countered. "Journeyor, please bring your companions. We will find all of you some comfort."

The metaologers eyed each other. Both stepped forward, with the woman positioning herself behind the premin and the man to his left. Two guards nearest to each side column stepped forward to the edge of the street.

This might have looked like they'd made room for the visitors to enter, but not so to Chane. When Shade growled again, Chane slipped his free hand up behind Wynn to close it on the longsword's hilt.

"Osha?" he rasped without looking back.

"Yes," came the firm answer from behind and off to Chane's left.

He knew Osha had nocked an arrow and would cripple the left-side metaologer first. He disliked assaulting sages, but there was a hidden danger here, and Wynn came before all else.

Chane pulled gently on Wynn's shoulder as he slid his left foot back.

Shade pulled out of Wynn's grip and sidestepped in front of her.

"There is no need for this," Aweli-Jama insisted with a tinge of desperation. "If you will simply—"

Wynn dashed around behind, startling Chane, but he kept his eyes on the high premin. All four guards drew their curved swords. The male metaologer's lips moved as if speaking, though Chane heard nothing.

"Osha!" he rasped.

"No!" Wynn shouted. "Don't hurt them."

No arrow struck either Suman metaologer.

In panic, Chane froze over what to do. He would not hesitate to disable or even kill armed soldiers, most likely city guards, but sages were another matter. At one guard's advance, Shade inched forward a matching step, and her hackles rose with her snarl.

Chane was about to order everyone to run when that first guard paused while looking beyond him. A puzzled frown formed on the man's face.

"Chane, duck and cover!" Wynn cried.

He almost turned—and then her staff thrust out around his left side. The long crystal at its top end was unsheathed, and he swore under his breath.

Chane spun away as he whipped up his cloak's hem to shield his face.

Osha stalled at Wynn's order contradicting Chane. With an arrow drawn back, he had shifted his aim to the darkly robed man with a raised hand. He did not wish to harm a sage, but neither would he allow anyone to harm his Wynn.

The premin's face twisted with alarm as her staff's crystal lanced out around Chane's side.

"Chane, duck and cover!"

Osha froze, knowing what would come next but not what to do about it. And too much happened all at once.

Chane whirled away as he jerked up his cloak. All four guards drew their swords. One made a rush forward quicker than the others. Shade lunged to intercept the man.

Osha heard Wynn's harsh whispers. He did not understand her words, but he knew what they meant. He barely scrunched his eyes shut as her staff's crystal flashed. Brilliant light, like a sudden noon sun, made his eyes sting beneath his eyelids.

"Run!" Wynn shouted.

Amid the sound of running feet, and just before Osha opened his eyes, he heard Chane utter a grating hiss. Wynn rushed for the packs nearby as Chane snatched up the chest, and Osha saw Shade ram a startled guard in the chest with her forepaws. That man went down, but . . .

The male sage in dark blue still had a hand raised and outstretched. Unlike the others, that one did not blink his eyes in trying to clear his sight. He fixed on the dog.

"Shade!" Osha shouted and released the bowstring.

The dog wheeled, racing away after Wynn, as the arrow hit. It struck directly into the sage's dangling sleeve. Force jerked the man's hand aside, and he stumbled back in fright and shock.

As the fallen guard struggled to get up, the other three, the other sage in dark blue, and Premin Aweli-Jama were all trying to clear their vision from the flash of Wynn's crystal.

Osha spun as Shade raced by him. Only one of the packs he had dropped remained on the street stones. Grabbing its strap, he slung it over his shoulder and ran along the wall after the others. Then he heard the premin shouting in his people's guttural tongue.

The only word Osha understood was "journeyor." There was only one person the high premin wanted caught.

Wynn and Shade ran on ahead with Chane following, the chest in his arms. On his longer legs, Osha knew it would not take long to reach them—but even while carrying the heavy orb, Chane was just as fast.

Osha hated working with—fighting beside—Chane, as if it was acceptable for that undead *thing* to be in Wynn's company. There was no other choice—he would always put her well-being above all else, no matter what it took.

Osha heard running feet coming behind him.

Wynn couldn't believe—or understand—what had happened as she ran, panting, along the outside of the low wall. She carried her own pack and one of Chane's. Hopefully Osha had been able to grab Chane's other pack.

She'd clearly understood what the high premin had shouted to the guards.

"Get the journeyor! I do not care what happens to the others, but bring her back alive."

The premin wanted her taken prisoner after she'd mentioned Ghassan il'Sänke.

What had happened here and what had the domin done?

Glancing back, she saw Osha and Chane closing rapidly on her as Shade sped out ahead. Back along the wall, the four guards were coming with swords drawn.

Chane would kill any one of them if necessary. And then what?

She and her companions would be "wanted" by local authorities, if they weren't already. All of Chane, Osha, and Shade's overprotectiveness had pushed everything out of control. If they'd only given her another moment or two, she might have salvaged an opportunity for their greater needs—but no.

The "boys" and her "sister" had done it again.

Fright and fury pushed Wynn faster. When this was over—if they got out of trouble—she'd put all three back in their places . . . *again*. And she couldn't let herself be captured, not even to save one of them.

She had to find Magiere, Leesil, and Chap. To do so, she had to find Ghassan il'Sänke. He was the key to everything.

"Valhachkasej'â!" she swore as she ran. "Where are you, Domin?"

In truth, Ghassan was uncertain what kept drawing him back to survey the guild grounds. Still, he watched its inland wall and the street along it in both directions. This place was now a danger to him.

If a member of the guild or the city guards spotted him, he would be taken at any cost. Still, he could not rest idle. He returned here again and again, as all other avenues in his search had revealed little to nothing. And he had no choice but to keep out of sight.

A moon ago, he had been arrested, dragged before the imperial court, and faced the imperial presence of Prince Ounyal'am himself, the remaining heir to the empire's throne. In that moment, Ghassan had not known how many of his secrets had been uncovered.

"Is your high premin correct?" the prince had demanded before all present. "What is this I hear of a hidden sect among the metaologers, including you . . . Domin? Is it true that all involved but you are dead?"

The questions had shocked him more than being arrested. Too much was becoming openly known by too many, and it was all true.

Ghassan had been part of a secret sect—a subset within his own order.

It was also true that Prince Ounyal'am knew this long before he had asked.

Conjury was preferred among Suman metaologers versus thaumaturgy in the guild's Numan and Lhoin'na branches. Ghassan was well versed in conjury and soundly knowledgeable in thaumaturgy; the opposite could also be said of metaologers elsewhere. But that did not account for what else he had learned, starting half a lifetime ago.

He had been taken in by a few secreted among his branch's metaologers. Among them was a third ideology of magic resurrected for desperate reasons, though its practice was feared and reviled throughout the known world. This sect feared discovery to such a degree that it had no name, for to name it would make it something to be known, sought, and found.

As Ghassan had stood before the imperial prince, he'd known suspicion of "sorcery" was at the heart of everything, including why he had been arrested. For an instant, he wondered if the prince had betrayed him. No one else present knew that the imperial prince was an allied confidant of the sect.

Ghassan decided the prince's question was not a betrayal.

Prince Ounyal'am was trapped as well, and in danger of discovery; his question was a warning.

All had been lost, and the prince himself could do nearly nothing to help. Further revelations and something more shocking had followed. By an amulet gifted to the prince for his protection, Ghassan heard the prince's warning thoughts telling him to escape by any means necessary. And so he had.

Now alone in hiding and searching, he feared for the safety of his people . . . and his prince.

Not long before his arrest, he had been away on a journey and had returned to learn that a "prisoner" of his sect had escaped. It was from this prisoner, long held for many decades, that the sect had recovered sorcery.

That had cost many lives and much sanity along the way.

And Khalidah had escaped his long captivity.

Once of the triad of the Sâ'yminfiäl—"Masters of Frenzy" during the Forgotten History and later known to a few as the "Eaters of Silence"—Khalidah was now as invisible as a thought. His own flesh had been lost in death centuries before. If one met him now, outside of the ensorcelled sarcophagus of his prison, it would be in one's own thoughts.

It would be too late to escape him.

That "specter," for lack of a better term, had killed almost everyone in Ghassan's sect. A monster of a past age, what some would now call a "noble dead," was loose among—and *within*—the people. The nights were the time to fear it most.

Khalidah could survive daylight only while within a living host, but so many days and nights had passed since his escape. Deaths in the capital attested to his continued survival, though there were not enough reports in the empire's greatest city to raise suspicion. As the last of the sect, only Ghassan knew the signs—or lack of such—in a victim.

And the specter could be within anyone—could *be* anyone while hiding in flesh, even someone within the guild or the imperial court.

Despite the sect's precautions to protect the prince, until he replaced his withering and corrupt father, Ounyal'am was in more than just mortal danger.

Ghassan had come to the guild's grounds tonight hoping to attempt infiltration, but how could he enter without anyone knowing? A compound full of sages, including metaologers, was well beyond blanking the mind of one beggar or a handful of patrolling guards.

City guards stood watch at the grounds' main entrance and all smaller locked ones. They patrolled the short wall's inner side at random intervals. They could be managed in small groups with enough foresight, but Ghassan feared conjured protections had also been set in place.

He would not discover those until too late.

The majority of metaologers in the branch had not been part of his sect; this did not mean they lacked skills or power. He could not afford to be caught, especially by them, and a hint of despair took him. Would he truly learn anything of use here, or had he simply grown this desperate?

And again, for the second time this night, a noise disturbed him.

At the sound of running feet and distant shouts, he cared little for a fleeing pickpocket running from a city patrol. Still, he peeked out of the cutway and around the corner of a shoddy tenement . . . and froze. He had seen many astonishing things in his life, but none had stunned him as much as what he now saw.

Wynn Hygeorht, in a midnight blue short-robe, rounded the compound's far corner in a headlong run behind her big black wolf, the majay-hì called Shade. The crystal atop her staff that Ghassan had created for her was fully exposed. She barely hung on to the packs flopping against her shoulders, and their bouncing, swinging weight kept making her swerve and right herself.

Chane Andraso shot around the far corner next, carrying a chest in his arms.

Ghassan almost stepped out and then hesitated. Why were they in flight?

A tall white-blond Lhoin'na appeared next, running after the other three.

Ghassan fixed on that one with a bow in hand and an arrow held to the string. Before he could tear into the elf's mind, four city guards rounded the corner in pursuit.

Ghassan could not stop a hissing groan.

Who else but Wynn Hygeorht could cause this much chaos any time in any place? But by what, why, and how was she here in his city and homeland? Before he regained composure, both Wynn and Shade flew past. As Chane and the Lhoin'na archer followed, Ghassan quickly looked behind into the cutway for anything of use. He grabbed up a scrap of broken pottery and flung the shard across the street at the guild grounds' wall.

There was little time for a proper incantation, even in thought. Glowing symbols, shapes, and signs flashed quickly across his sight as his gaze flickered from the tumbling shard to the top of the wall. The pottery shard struck there, and its fragments scattered over the wall in the grounds.

The lead guard skidded to a stop and turned toward the noise.

Ghassan ducked back, barely peeking around the corner with one eye.

"What?" a second guard snapped, stalling near the first.

"Noise . . . over the wall," answered the first as the final two guards slowed.

"Could one of them have gotten over and inside?" asked a third guard.

And the first began cursing as he glanced up the street.

Ghassan waited no longer to see how they might split up. His own quarry was running wild in the streets and would likely lose him in trying to lose the guards. He crept down the cutway and ran north along the back alley, heading in the general direction that Wynn had to have led the others. He could not help cursing as well.

Wherever Wynn went, there came trouble as well. Better to have her under his watch than arrested or loose to get in his way. And why was she even here? By the time he reached the silent marketplace, he heard running feet, and too many to be only guards. He veered across the market into a cutway on its far side, hoping to get ahead of his quarry.

Wynn and Shade shot past the cutway's far end, and he sped up to lean out just as Chane rushed by.

"Wynn!" Ghassan whispered, loud and sharp.

The Lhoin'na spotted him, dropped the pack he was carrying, and drew the arrow held fitted in the bow.

Ghassan stepped a little farther out, holding both hands in plain sight. He carefully brushed back his hood as he repeated as softly as possible, "Wynn!"

By then, she had stopped, as had her black wolf, and her eyes widened at the sight of him. She did not hesitate and ran to him. Slowing as she approached, her eyes were still wide.

"Domin?" she said on a breath.

Shade rounded in front of her with a quiver of jowls as the Lhoin'na lowered his bow in puzzlement. Chane's expression was beyond cautious, bordering on dangerous, as he stepped in, but Ghassan could not be bothered about some overprotective vampire.

The sounds of shouts and pounding feet echoed from the direction they had come.

"In here, quickly," Ghassan whispered, backing into the cutway.

The instant Wynn hurried in past him, the others had no choice but to follow her.

Ghassan remained near the cutway's mouth as he whispered, "Be still and silent." When he peeked around the corner, only two guards came running up the street.

"Look in all cutways and alley mouths," one said to the other.

Ghassan blinked as the first guard neared. In the dark behind his eyelids, strokes of light spread into shapes, sigils, and symbols. Words sounded with greater speed in his thoughts than by voice as . . .

He finished that brief blink. The glowing pattern overlaid his sight of one guard drawing near, who looked directly at him. The guard blinked as well, slowed, looked more carefully, and then sighed in disgust.

"Nothing here," he called to the other, and then he was gone, rushing on in his hunt.

Ghassan waited, shifting his envisioned pattern to the other guard. That one passed by even more quickly than the first. And everyone within the cutway remained silent until all sounds of pursuit faded up the street.

Turning slowly, Ghassan cast another small ensorcellment, this time upon himself. As the darkness in the alley grew brighter in his sight, he took in the small group he had just rescued, finishing upon Wynn.

"Well," he whispered, "this is unexpected."

Wynn had no idea what to think. Moments before, she'd been desperate to find Ghassan il'Sänke, and now here he was. Had she somehow conjured him with whispered words during flight? Ridiculous. She had simply been living in desperation and uncertainty for too long.

"Domin," she began softly, still wary that roaming guards might hear her. "Where did you . . . How did you . . . ?"

He flipped a hand and shook his head, as if such a thing mattered little. "A better question would be, what are you doing here?" He ignored Chane but fixed his gaze on Osha. "And who is this? Not a Lhoin'na, now that I have a closer look."

Wynn glanced back and up at Osha. Most people would never recognize that he wasn't from this continent. Ghassan il'Sänke was *not* most people.

"This is Osha. He's from the eastern continent," she explained, and then rushed on, putting aside a couple of odd things that had just happened. "We've come to find Magiere, Leesil, and Chap, who I sent to find you, but . . . Why are you dressed like that? Why are there guards on the guild? Where are the people I sent to you?"

She might have gone on, but the domin halted her with a raised hand. "Who?"

Wynn held her breath and then exhaled sharply. The domin had never met Magiere, Leesil, or Chap, but there was no doubt they would've found him. Magiere was nothing if not . . . well, "determined" was the polite word for it. Something had gone wrong.

Before she asked another panicked question, Ghassan il'Sänke blinked slowly with a shake of his head.

"Ah, yes," he added. "I believe I did see them . . . briefly."

That panicked Wynn even more—"see" and not "meet."

The domin, so strangely dressed, nodded.

"I recognized them from the descriptions in your journals," he went on. Then he paused a bit too long. "Your friends were arrested, along with a mixed-blood girl, and imprisoned below the imperial palace grounds. I never spoke with, let alone met, them."

"What?" Wynn gasped.

"Mixed-blood?" Osha repeated. "What you mean?"

Wynn glanced at him and then Chane. Magiere had never actually reached Ghassan il'Sänke, never spoken to him. She, Leesil, Chap, and Leanâlhâm had been locked away, but for what reason?

"How long?" Chane rasped.

He and the domin hadn't parted on good terms the last time they'd all seen one another.

"Perhaps a moon," il'Sänke answered.

"And you haven't seen them since?" Wynn asked.

"No."

Wynn's panic edged toward franticness. Even the dim light from a lantern up the way in the street hurt her eyes. The walls of the cutway felt too close.

"This can't be happening," she got out, and then fell into babbling. "We found another orb, and Magiere was here seeking the last one . . . You were to help her. So we brought ours here and—"

"Wynn!" Chane rasped, and even Shade snarled in warning.

Wynn snapped her mouth shut under the fixed stare of Ghassan il'Sänke.

"This is not the place to speak of such things," he said too calmly. "Come with me. I will take you to a place of safety."

"Safety?" Chane hissed. "Your high premin would have simply sent us away . . . until your name was mentioned. No one is going anywhere with you if—"

"Chane," Wynn interrupted. "We need to speak privately and not here in—"

"No, Chane is correct," Osha countered in Elvish.

Before Wynn could argue, Osha narrowed his eyes on the domin.

"You . . . hunted?" he said in Numanese. It was less a question than an accusation.

Wynn sighed, exhausted and still panicked as she turned back to the domin. Perhaps his own branch's Premin Council was seeking him, but the city guards could hardly be after a sage like il'Sänke.

"Just answer them," she encouraged. "Are you wanted by the authorities?"

Ghassan il'Sänke's eyes shifted to fix on Chane in the cutway's silence.

CHAPTER 2

Brot'ân'duivé—the Dog in the Dark—crouched upon a rooftop outside the great wall of the imperial grounds. He maintained this vigil out of little more than habit, as he had come to accept there was little else to do at present. And so it had been for the last moon.

Much of the time he remained in hiding, for his physical appearance in this land and city attracted much attention. Even cloaked and with his hood up, his height brought curious glances. Up north in the Numan lands, he was half a head taller than most human males. Here he towered over everyone and was easily visible even in a crowd.

Coarse white-blond hair, with streaks of gray darkening some strands, hung over his peaked ears and down his back beneath his hood and cloak. He was deeply tanned, nearly as dark as the Sumans, with lines crinkling the corners of his mouth and his large amber-irised eyes. But the feature that stood out the most, if someone drew near enough to look into his hood, were four pale scars—as if from claws—upon his face. Those ran at an angle from the midpoint of his forehead and slanted down through one feathery eyebrow to skip over his right eye to his cheekbone.

He spent much of his time near the palace grounds, where he watched for anything that might be used to his advantage. Patience was a necessity more than a virtue among the Anmaglâhk, guardians of the an'Crόan people and their vast territory; it was even more so for him as a master among them, a greimasg'äh, or "shadow-gripper."

During the waterfront arrest of Léshil, Magiere, and Chap—and Brot'ân'duivé's own young ward, Wayfarer—he had made the instant assessment that he could not stop it. Instead, he vanished before it happened. This had seemed prudent at that time, for they had been so outnumbered that even he saw no way to extract all of the others alive. Within moments of their being taken away, he had managed to sweep back in and save their belongings left in the street. These he had later hidden well.

Now . . . he had come to question his quick decision.

Among the Anmaglâhk—viewed only as assassins by any human who'd survived to recognize one—he was one of the few remaining masters. But he no longer wore his caste's garb of hooded forest gray cloak, vestment, pants, and felt boots. Instead, he now dressed in simple breeches and a weatherworn jerkin beneath a marred and smudged hooded cloak. His change of attire was no simple disguise, for he was at war with his own caste.

Many of his brethren still served their too-long-lived leader, Most Aged Father, a paranoid madman who was utterly self-serving at the expense of his people. Brot'ân'duivé was determined to stop Most Aged Father and his loyalists at any cost. This was one reason he had traveled halfway across the world in protecting Magiere and Léshil from a team of loyalists sent after them.

Once again, Brot'ân'duivé studied the outer wall of the imperial grounds. He had seldom felt regret in a long life, as he did now over his choice to abandon his companions at the waterfront. He assumed he could soon rescue them, but he could not have known then that a human construction would be able to keep him out.

The wall was taller than any he had seen in his lifetime. It was also taller than any surrounding building, for he had set foot on every rooftop around its circumference. That had taken two days and half of the following night.

Sheer and smooth, as if impossibly made from solid sandstone, the wall offered little chance of purchase for a blade's tip to climb it. And even if this were not so, the broad space between it and the nearest structures was twice the width of the widest street in the capital. Regular patrols of city guards walked the wall's outside and top, and imperial guards with gold sashes manned the interior grounds.

And he had only one lead as to what had become of Léshil or Magiere.

On the day those two were arrested with Wayfarer and the errant majay-hì called Chap, he had followed them unseen to the imperial grounds. Among their captors of armed guards were two of Most Aged Father's loyalists.

Dänvârfij and Rhysís were dressed in poorly cut human clothing; both wore swords of a strange make. The very idea was anathema, as by the caste's creed they worked "in silence and in shadow." But sight of them did not surprise him, for they had been hunting Magiere across the world.

He had waited outside all that first day, but only Dänvârfij and Rhysís had emerged. His initial instinct had been to follow and eliminate them, as he had done

one by one with their team ever since leaving his homeland after being branded a traitor.

That urge was quickly abandoned. This pair was his
only link to what had become of his lost companions.
His second instinct had been to capture one of his enemies and extract information by any means. This was
rejected as well. It was doubtful that even he could
break a seasoned anmaglâhk.

And now the only way he knew that Léshil and the
others still lived was because three times Dänvârfij had
gained access directly through the imperial grounds'
main gate. When she left, she looked close to angry and
frustrated.

An unguarded emotion—let alone expression—was
rare for a true anmaglâhk.

Given that Dänvârfij would have surveyed the grounds'
wall as well, the only reason that she continued diplomatic
attempts was that her quarry still lived. By her expression, she had not gained access or learned where they
were kept.

Eight days had passed since Dänvârfij last appeared
at the main gate. What did her long period of inactivity
mean?

Frustration, like regret, was another emotion Brot-
'ân'duivé rarely felt.

Movement at the gate drew his attention.

He watched as Dänvârfij exited between two dozen
guards standing post at the gate.

She still wore her poorly cut human clothing and the
sword on her hip, but over the distance it was too dark
to see her expression. He had been on the rooftop since
late afternoon but had not seen her enter, and he wondered how long she had been inside the grounds.

Brot'ân'duivé flattened upon the rooftop's edge to

watch her walk past below. He knew the route she would likely take, as he had tracked her twice before. Both times she had lost him before reaching her final destination. Somewhere in the capital hid the remainder of her team.

Counting her, only four of the eleven remained alive.

Slipping his right hand to his left wrist, he pulled the cord on the sheath up his sleeve and slightly tilted his left forearm. A stiletto slid out hilt first to settle in his left palm. He spun the blade outward as he rolled back from the rooftop's edge and to his feet without a sound.

Brot'ân'duivé's patience was gone.

He leaped silently to the next rooftop to get ahead of his prey before scaling down into an alley. At the mouth of that dark path, he watched the street less than seven strides to his right.

Dänvârfij appeared and headed onward at a quick and quiet pace.

The instant she slipped from sight along the street's next block, Brot'ân'duivé stepped out to follow. When he rounded the corner closely, prepared to disable and capture her in the dark, another tall figure dropped from above to land beside her.

Brot'ân'duivé swerved silently in against a shop with its awning tied shut. Both figures headed onward without pause. When they passed beneath a lantern at the next intersection, he recognized the newcomer by his movement and the color of his clothing.

In the last season, Rhysís often wore a dark blue cloak with the hood up.

Two anmaglâhk—loyalists—walked apace in silent purpose.

Brot'ân'duivé shadowed them block after block and deeper into the city's northern side. He had never tracked any of them this far before, and when they turned into a cutway beside a three-story inn, he turned up a side street to reach the alley that would run along the inn's rear. There they were, and he watched as they scaled the inn's back side and slipped into a window.

Brot'ân'duivé slipped his stiletto back up his sleeve and tied it in place with a single twirl of his fingers.

Dänvârfij and Rhysís had not come to this city alone, and he had now found the remainder of his enemies . . . his targets. Two others inside the inn might make easier prey for interrogation, but now was not the time, with all his enemies together.

And if Dänvârfij had gone back to the imperial grounds, then Magiere and perhaps the others were likely still alive.

Brot'ân'duivé regained patience as he waited and watched.

Dänvârfij—"Fated Music"—slipped through the window of their current hiding place with Rhysís directly behind her. The single room they had paid for was small, with only two rickety beds, a bleached wooden table, a cracked washbasin, and two candle lanterns. It served its purpose.

The other two members of what remained of her team waited therein.

She waited before the window, but Rhysís quickly approached the two women sitting on the same bed. Like her, they were anmaglâhk in status, though not so in function anymore.

Én'nish, the youngest of the team, was nearly as tan and white-blond as all an'Cróan. She was also smaller and slighter of build than most. Her size was a deception she used to advantage in combat. She also was—

had been—reckless. More than this, or perhaps the cause of it, she was poisoned by their people's grief madness in having lost her mate-to-be to Léshil's blade.

Dänvârfij had opposed Én'nish's inclusion in their purpose from the start.

The young one had proven to be a survivor when others had not, but she had taken a wound in her abdomen during the last battle with their quarry. And again, it had been Léshil who had done this to her.

Én'nish had not healed well and was less than capable for combat. Rhysís stood towering over her, his hair even lighter than hers, which he always wore loose.

None of them now wore the forest gray clothing of anmaglâhk, as they traveled disguised in human attire. Dänvârfij still could not fathom Rhysís's new affinity for blue clothing. In addition to his pants and shirt, even the cloak he wore was a dark shade of that color.

Her gaze shifted to the final surviving member of their team.

Fréthfâre—"Watcher of the Woods"—sat hunched forward on the bed's edge. She could no longer sit straight without support at her back, and sometimes not even then.

"Well?" she demanded. "Did you learn anything new . . . or useful?"

Fréthfâre held status as shared leader of the team, but she was fit in neither body nor mind and perhaps not even in spirit. Her wheat-gold hair, so uncommon for an an'Cróan, hung in waves instead of properly silky and straight. In youth, she had been viewed as supple and graceful. She was now brittle as she approached a mere fifty years—barely beyond half of what most anmaglâhk lived and notably less than half of any other an'Cróan. The human dress of vibrant red that she wore made her appear all the more fragile.

Once covârleasa—"trusted advisor"—to Most Aged Father, Fréthfâre was nearly useless now. More than two years before, the monster Magiere had run a sword through her abdomen. The wound should have killed her, but a great an'Cróan healer had tended to her. Even so, she had barely survived, and the damage would never be wholly undone.

Dänvârfij, ever respectful in dealing with the ex-covârleasa, had no new information to share this night. She shook her head once in answering another of Fréthfâre's spiteful questions.

"The commander of the imperial guard made it clear that I should not return," she added.

Fréthfâre said nothing and her thin lips pursed. What could she say? What could any of them say?

These three anmaglâhk were all that Dänvârfij had left with which to hunt the monster Magiere, her mate Léshil, the deviant called Chap . . . and the traitor greimasg'äh, Brot'ân'duivé.

A year and a half before, when Most Aged Father had asked her to prepare a team and sail to this foreign continent, she had not hesitated. Their purpose had been direct and clear. They were to locate Magiere, her half-blood consort, and the tainted majay-hì who ran with the pair. Magiere and Léshil were to be captured, tortured if necessary concerning the "artifact" they had carried off from the Pock Peaks, and then eliminated—along with the majay-hì, if possible.

Fréthfâre had not blinked at the last of that, though her team, including bloody Én'nish, had balked. Killing a majay-hì—a "sacred one" of their land—even a deviant one, had never been asked, let alone done. And never before had so many of the Anmaglâhk jointly taken up the same purpose.

Most Aged Father feared any device of the Ancient Enemy remaining in human hands.

Eleven anmaglâhk had left together, but one more had shadowed them across the world.

After the first and second deaths among them and before they knew for certain, Dänvârfij could not believe who that one had to be. Only on a night when she had glimpsed his unmistakable shadow had she acknowledged the truth.

Brot'ân'duivé had been stealing their lives, one by one, ever since.

Out of eleven, four remained, yet they could not stop or turn back. Dänvârfij could not fail Most Aged Father, and in the last port, called Soráno, she had devised a new plan.

She had killed two of the Lhoin'na guardians called the Shé'ith and took their swords and emblems for Rhysís and her to assume their identities. Racing against time, they had beaten Magiere to the Suman capital and used their false authority to have her and the others arrested for murdering the crew of a Sumanese ship.

Dänvârfij had been certain her quarry would be locked away in some constabulary. In such an easily infiltrated location, they could be taken unarmed. Everything had gone terribly wrong.

Magiere and Léshil, along with the majay-hì and the mixed-blood girl, had been taken directly to the imperial castle. At the sight of Magiere, the reactions of the imperial prince, the leaders of the Suman sages, and the imperial counselor had been immediate. All of the prisoners were dragged off and locked away somewhere in the immense imperial grounds.

Dänvârfij had been denied access to or knowledge of their whereabouts.

She had gone back several times with various reasons for speaking to them, only to be denied. Worse, the traitor had escaped being arrested. Nothing had gone as planned, and Brot'ân'duivé now moved freely somewhere in this city.

"Do you think our quarry still lives?"

Dänvârfij regained awareness at Én'nish's question. Not long in the past, the young one had questioned her every decision. Én'nish had become hesitant and too easily stalled by uncertainty.

"I do not know," she answered flatly.

"That is the first thing we must learn," Rhysís countered.

"How?" Fréthfâre asked.

He shook his head, almost impatiently. "If the Suman government will not assist us, and we are certain that path is barred, then we return to proven methods. Capture and extract information from someone who does know."

Dänvârfij grew wary. "None of the local guards will possess such information."

"The imperial guards took our quarry away," he countered.

Dänvârfij stepped toward him. "That is a reckless tactic. Any of them missing will be noticed."

"One of them may know," he countered again, "or know who among their own has such knowledge. Recklessness is all we have left, and this will not be a one-step process."

Dänvârfij fell silent rather than argue further.

With every death and failure among them, her authority had been strained or diminished. To take action against the imperial guards could endanger their own secrecy. If they failed, or succeeded but were uncovered, their current lack of options would not be the worst of their obstacles.

Dänvârfij could not think of anything better and looked to Fréthfâre, futile as that was.

Fréthfâre nodded as well. "As you are no longer welcome inside, stalk the patrols on the outside for a straggler to capture."

Dänvârfij inhaled and exhaled slowly.

Standing in the cutway, Wynn watched Chane facing down Ghassan il'Sänke and decided to take matters into her own hands.

"Chane . . . Ghassan is right. We need to get off the streets first." When Chane's brow furrowed, she turned to the domin. "Where will you take us? Some room at an inn?"

The domin hesitated long enough to set her on edge.

"I have a . . . private residence which is little known," he replied.

"So you are hiding," Chane interrupted. "Why?"

"Chane!" Wynn said in exasperation. She looked back in time to see Osha step in and fix on the domin with an expression nearly as suspicious as Chane's.

She didn't trust the domin completely either, and with some embarrassment she remembered that only a few moments before, in her panic, she had blurted out that she'd not only found another orb, she'd brought it here.

If Chane had not interrupted her, she might have spilled out one more piece of information that she wasn't yet ready to share with Ghassan.

In addition to the orb of Spirit, she'd also brought a small, strange device she had acquired that could be used to track an orb. The problem was that this device was currently dormant, she didn't know how to reactivate it, and at some point she was going to need Ghassan's help to make it work. How soon she decided to tell him of this object remained to be seen.

But he'd protected her more than once and made her sun-crystal staff. If he had a safe place, then that was good enough for now.

Without waiting for more arguments, she shifted the pack on her back, hefted her staff, and turned toward the cutway's mouth with one glance at the domin.

"Lead on."

Ghassan turned without a word and stepped ahead of her, looking both ways along the street.

Wynn followed, and at least this time Shade wasn't arguing, but she heard nothing from behind for a moment. Then came Chane's hissing exhale and two sets of soft footsteps. There had been no doubt. Neither Chane nor Osha would let her simply walk away with the domin, whether Shade was with her or not.

Occasionally, their overprotectiveness was useful.

Il'Sänke made his way inland, eventually turning southward, and along the way he stopped often, though he didn't look about.

Wynn wondered whether he was listening, but she heard nothing herself. After a while, the walk began to feel quite long. The domin appeared to be taking them all the way across the city—or at least that was how it felt when they entered an area with more people out at night.

Fine shops and eateries of tan stone lined streets with plentiful lamps and colorfully dressed women scented with jasmine. After another long stretch, all of this gave way to smaller dwellings in disrepair and people in the streets dressed in rags and too often bare feet. They

passed one building with shuttered windows. A few stag-
gered out its broad front door, which was guarded by two
slovenly but armed men, and they shuffled away in a daze.

Wynn passed close to one of the patrons and saw his
eyes staring blankly ahead without looking at anything.
He stank of sweet-smelling smoke strong enough to cut
through the smells of the city.

"I do not like this," Chane whispered from behind
her. "This place is not fit for you."

The domin didn't look back, but Wynn did. "Snob-
bery won't hide us any better. If the guild branch here
is anything like my own, those guards notified the local
constabularies about us."

In spite of her bravado, the glassy-eyed people unnerved her. She'd read about places where something
called hashish was smoked. What were they called,
something that meant "dream haven" or the like? Had
she just walked past one?

The domin turned down a darkened side street without a single lamp along the way. They continued past
three shabby buildings and stopped in front of the fourth
one. Its front door was crooked in its frame and covered
in turquoise paint so peeled and full of cracks that Wynn
could see the spidering lines in the dark. Broken tiles
lay out front that might have fallen off the roof.

"This . . . safe place?" Osha asked.

Shade started rumbling at the door of peeling,
cracked paint.

Wynn couldn't bring herself to shush them, for she
grew reluctant as well.

Ghassan il'Sänke stepped forward and pulled the
crooked front door open.

Wynn started after him, but Shade slipped in front

of her. The dog planted herself with a growl and wouldn't move. In frustration, Wynn nudged Shade's rump with a knee—and again—until they both followed the domin inside.

It was so dark in the narrow hallway that Wynn pulled a cold-lamp crystal from her short-robe's pocket and stroked it sharply across the fabric. When it glowed with light, she instantly wished she hadn't bothered, and Chane and Osha came in behind her.

The place was filthy and dilapidated. Walls lined with warped wooden planks surrounded unpainted doors no better off than the front one. She heard someone coughing somewhere behind one of those doors, but Ghassan quickly headed for the stairs at the passage's end. They climbed upward, though Wynn shuddered more than once at the sharp creaks of the steps beneath her feet.

When they reached the top floor, the domin headed down the only hallway. Raising her crystal, Wynn could see nothing more than old doors and one open, unshuttered window at the hallway's end. And that was where the domin went. When he stopped before the window, perhaps reaching for its waist-high sill, Wynn looked back past Chane and Osha at all the doors along the way.

"Which one is for us?" she asked.

"None of them," the domin answered.

Wynn was about to turn back when she heard Osha suck in a sharp breath.

She looked up to see his lips parted below wide eyes staring over the top of her head. At a clunk, as if a door had closed, Chane dropped the chest, grabbed her shoulder, and jerked her back behind him. She half fell into Osha, who caught her, as Shade's growl erupted with a clack of teeth.

Even in Osha's grip, Wynn regained her feet and spun about, though he held on when she tried to take a step.

Ghassan il'Sänke was gone.

Wynn lost her voice as she peered around Chane's side. Shade inched back as Chane stepped in and . . . strangely, hesitantly extended his hand through the open window, as if afraid to do so.

"Where is he? Where did he go?" Wynn managed to get out.

Chane swung his hand to the window frame's side and began tracing and feeling, gripping and pushing, all around it. He did the same to the wall on both sides and below the window.

Much as Wynn couldn't see how the domin had escaped, Chane's actions were too bizarre. "What are you doing?"

"There was a door," Osha whispered in Elvish. "He went in . . . and then the door was gone."

Wynn had no idea what that meant, but Shade's hackles were up. The dog backed up another step with a mewling growl like a spooked cat.

"Ridiculous," Wynn said. "He must have hopped out the window when I turned my back and the crystal's light was blocked from—"

The wall around the window swung away.

Osha pulled Wynn close, Shade crouched with a snarl, and Chane hopped back in, pulling his shorter sword.

There in the opening shaped like a doorway stood Ghassan il'Sänke.

Chane leveled his sword at the domin.

With an exasperated sigh and a roll of his dark eyes, Ghassan hooked a boot's toe around the open door's bottom corner. Wynn finally noticed that the passage's end wall had suddenly changed and . . . looked like a door.

Solid and made of dark, stout wood beams, unlike all the others along the passage, it was also iron-banded and had a matching lever handle. From what Wynn could see there was no keyhole in the plate around that handle. She finally closed her mouth with a swallow.

"My apologies," Ghassan said a bit tiredly, raising his hands in plain sight. "The door slipped from my grip. It is heavy and spring-loaded to shut if left open. Please come in."

"What is this?" Chane demanded.

Ghassan took a slow breath with an extended exhale. "As I told you, this place is safe and *clearly* no one will find us here."

And then he simply stood there waiting and glaring.

Chane inched in to tap the door's frame with his sword's tip. The frame still looked like part of the outer wall.

The domin scowled, then scoffed and leaned away when Chane inched his sword through the opening. Shade rumbled even louder, and when Wynn tried to take a step, Osha held her back.

Chane stood staring at whatever lay beyond the door and then turned his glare—and his blade—toward the domin.

"How?" he demanded.

After another extended sigh, Ghassan answered flatly, "That is a longer conversation than I care to have out here. Now, are you coming in or not?" He turned his annoyance on Wynn as if Chane's sword meant nothing anymore.

Wynn pulled out of Osha's grip and stepped closer as Chane back-stepped to reach down for the chest without taking his eyes off the domin. She pushed past both him and Shade for a closer look, and what lay beyond in that softly lit place was as shocking as the hidden door.

Shelves lined three walls and were filled with scrolls, books, and plank-bound sheaves, just like those of the archives below the guild branch in Calm Seatt. Unlike that place, everything here was pristine, without a hint of dust, and all was made of dark but shimmering wood.

Several cold lamps with crystals provided light around the interior. One rested on a round table encompassed by three cushioned chairs. By the lamps' ornate brass bases, they had to have alchemical fluids producing mild heat to keep the crystals lit. All chairs were high-backed, and their finely finished near-black wood was intricately carved in wild see-through patterns.

To one side stood like-carved folding partitions separating another area covered in large floor cushions of vibrant patterns with shimmering embroidery. At the back of the sitting area was an open door to another room, and in there were several beds as lavish as the cushioned sitting area. Clean, fringed carpets defined various sections of the floor.

Though impressive, it all struck Wynn as rather cluttered. The last fixture she noticed left her a bit dizzy and disoriented.

In the rear wall, between the cushioned area and the door to the bedroom, was a window exactly like the one she had faced in the passage moments before. Through it, she saw the same night-shrouded buildings across the same back alley, and she absently stepped in.

This was nothing like any hideaway that Wynn could've imagined. In fact, it looked too well prepared and furnished, aside from that disturbing duplicate window.

"H-how?" she stammered, turning around.

Osha entered with Shade, and Wynn saw that Chane

had already dragged in the chest. He stood with sword still in hand as he faced the domin. Wynn wasn't certain whether or not to call off Chane. Osha glanced about, but, unlike Wynn, he looked openly wary.

With a lift of one eyebrow, il'Sänke finally answered. "A mere glamour to hide this space."

"What do you take me for?" Chane rasped as he eyed the duplicate window set directly inline with the door.

Wynn knew that Chane had learned his minor conjury the hard way—without any tutor or teaching and having to scavenge hard-won texts and knowledge delved alone in secret. Something here bothered him, and considering what she saw, she didn't interfere with whatever he was after.

"This entire end of the upper floor has been hidden," Chane went on, still holding up the tip of his shorter sword before the domin. "And yet the window in the passage's end shows the same view outside. I touched that wall and window, and *felt* them."

Ghassan acted as if the sword were not even there. "What would you have me say that you could possibly understand? It is beyond you. Accept that."

These final two words put Wynn on edge. She wished she was the one asking questions and that Chane was behind her to warn her of lies with a squeeze upon her shoulder.

Then again, Ghassan hadn't actually answered the question.

"Why did the mention of your name almost get us arrested?" Chane asked.

In the hesitation that followed, Wynn fixed only on the domin. "And why are city guards posted before the guild . . . at all?"

* * *

Ghassan barely glanced at Wynn, wondering how much to say. Clearly Chane Andraso was the more immediate problem, though one that could be dealt with. Doing so might also undermine gaining answers—and cooperation—for his own needs. And he was still anxious over the revelation that Wynn had gained another orb.

He did not dare to look again at the heavy chest two steps behind Chane. Wynn's appearance, the orb of Spirit, and her obvious accomplishments meant something more.

She and her companions could be useful to him.

Ghassan had been alone in his hunt for Khalidah since returning to his homeland. Wynn might attract trouble as easily as a melon draws flies, but she had skills and a weapon, which he had fashioned for her, that emitted sunlight. Chane could be unpredictable, but as a member of the undead, if properly motivated, he was a skilled fighter and almost impossible to kill. As for Shade, a majay-hì was a natural hunter of the undead. The elf's usefulness . . . well, that remained to be seen.

So how little could Ghassan say to gain more advantage than disadvantage?

"I was part of a hidden sect among the Suman metaologers," he finally answered.

Wynn's brown eyes never blinked, though she still stared at him, and so he continued.

"We studied certain practices which . . . would not have met with the premin council's approval."

"What practice?" Osha asked.

Ghassan ignored everyone but Wynn. "We had kept a prisoner for a long time that we wished to study and safeguard in secret, since others would not be able to do so. Unfortunately, I was sent to your land because our branch wanted its share of the knowledge you brought back from the eastern continent."

The last reference was awkward, considering he had also done his best to stop her from gaining the orb of Earth in the bowels of Bäalâle Seatt. He had failed and, though she had no knowledge of what had come next, he had hurried for home upon receiving a message that *it* had escaped.

"What sort of prisoner?" Wynn asked.

"A dangerous one who escaped while I was away and . . . killed the rest of my sect."

For an instant, his thoughts slipped back to the night he returned home. All of his comrades lay dead in their subterranean sanctuary, their eyes wide and blank, mouths gaping in final horror—even the best among them, those more skilled than Ghassan himself.

All dead but one . . . and that one other than himself was still missing.

"Killed?" Wynn repeated.

"As I told you, this prisoner is dangerous. Upon its escape, my own peers were not the only ones who died, though the rest of the guild is unaware of the cause of those deaths. There was no hiding this or our sanctuary any longer from High Premin Aweli-Jama. As the last of my sect, I was wanted for questioning. I couldn't allow this, as I am all that is left of those who can hunt the prisoner." He hesitated. "Unfortunately, I *was* caught and taken before the imperial court. By happenstance, it was on the same day that your friends were arrested at the port."

There was a pause then, with so much to take in.

"Why?" Wynn finally asked. "What were the charges against them?"

"Murder. Two foreigners sought the aid of both the

city and imperial guard . . . and they looked like him."
He tilted his head toward Osha.

Osha's expression twisted in alarm. "What you mean?"

Ghassan kept his eyes on Wynn only.

"He means not Lhoin'na," she whispered, shaking
her head. "Anmaglâhk?"

Ghassan vaguely recognized that last term, though
he couldn't remember from where.

"You do not know that, Wynn," Chane put in. "This
continent has a large population of elves, and some are
light-haired."

"True . . . but it is possible the anmaglâhk team
picked up Magiere's trail after she fled Calm Seatt,"
Wynn said, closing her eyes and looking tired. She
opened them again and looked to Ghassan. "We must
get my friends out, and you are going to help us."

Before Ghassan could raise an eyebrow—

"What of this prisoner he hunts?" Chane interrupted.
"I want to know more."

"Not now," Wynn insisted, turning back to Ghassan.
"Can you help us?"

Ghassan remained passive. Gods, fate, ancestral spirits,
or something else entirely appeared to favor him this
night. By all accounts in Wynn's travel journals, Magiere,
Leesil, and their majay-hì were skilled hunters of the
undead. And from what he understood, they were devoted
to Wynn.

"I will do what I can," he assured her. "But it will not
be easy."

CHAPTER 3

L ate the following morning, Ghassan donned a heavier cloak and pulled its hood low over his eyes as he left the hidden sanctuary now shared by his "guests." On the long walk to the mainway leading to the front gates of the imperial grounds, he kept his mind clear for any warning from his senses—physical and otherwise. He didn't need to walk so far for his task, but he wanted time alone to think.

What he would ask of Prince Ounyal'am had dangerous ramifications should anything go wrong. As of yet, the precise words for such a request had not come to him, even as he reached the long expanse of the capital's largest open market.

The mainway to the gates was three times as wide as any other main city street, not that one would guess so at first sight. There was enough room down its center only for a slow-moving wagon—if midday crowds got out of the way.

Ghassan barely noticed the array of fresh foods and imported goods, and the merchants and vendors calling to passersby, including him. The scents of warm bread and olive oil distracted him only once, aside from his stiffening in caution every time someone passed too close. That happened often in the bustling market street. There was not much to eat in his quarters, and he knew he should see about purchasing supplies. For the moment, though, he had other concerns.

Without warning, the crowds ahead began to shift. People moved and cleared a wide path as they looked back along the street behind him.

Ghassan drifted left near a leather worker's tent before he glanced back, though he kept his head partway down.

Two litters, each carried by four strong servants, passed by on their way toward the main gates. Personal guards surrounded both. Though the curtains of the litters were partially open, the guards' purple sashes already told Ghassan who was visiting the palace.

Emir Falah Mansoor, second commander of the empire's military forces, was not often in residence inside the city. Whatever reason he had for visiting now was most certainly *not* at the request of the imperial prince.

Mansoor's solution to any diplomatic problem could always be found at the point of a sword. He was of the old ways in his arrogance, believing in the absolute rule of those below by those above in society. No, the emir had not come to see the prince. More likely any report would be made to Imperial Counselor a'Yamin, now that the emperor himself was bedridden and unavailable.

Ghassan was about to turn away when his gaze fell upon the occupant of the second litter: a young woman with her head tilted down. Though long black hair hid half of her face, he recognized her delicate profile and did not have to search his memory for her name.

Mansoor was blessed with five sons and only one daughter—A'ish'ah. Sons could be useful in holding on to power, but a daughter was useful for purchasing more power. And where else could one find more of this than in an unwed prince of an empire?

Ghassan drifted carefully along behind the procession as it approached the main gate and stopped. He kept his head lowered as he watched in curiosity.

Emir Mansoor rattled and clattered in enameled armor as he dropped out of the lead litter. Then he stood basking in the glory of his own self-importance as he waited to be admitted.

Ghassan focused upon the back of the emir's head and blinked slowly. In that wink of darkness behind his eyelids, he raised the image of Mansoor's face in his mind. Over that, he drew glimmering shapes, lines, and marks from deep in memory.

A chant passed through his thoughts as his slow blink finished.

The prince must surely take a wife now that the emperor nears death. Ounyal'am will have no choice but to marry before taking the throne.

Ghassan grimaced upon hearing Mansoor's conscious thoughts. An instant later . . .

If only the foolish girl had the wiles of her late mother. Even so, she must be made to try . . .

Ghassan took care not to sink too deeply. Searching for more than surface thoughts could arouse a target's awareness. And he didn't care to hear much more of the would-be tyrant's innermost thoughts. What he had heard was no surprise.

Emperor Kanal'am grew weaker every day, at a guess, for no one but the imperial counselor, a'Yamin, or attendants appointed directly by him, had seen the emperor in more than three moons.

At thirty-eight years old, Prince Ounyal'am was the

remaining imperial heir and had yet to take even a first wife. Growing schemes, machinations, and plots among the nation's seven royal houses had reached a fevered pitch.

How many daughters had been thrown at the prince since his father had taken ill? Emir Mansoor now apparently joined the fray, vying for his A'ish'ah to be the future first empress.

Ghassan turned back down the mainway through the crowds before the gate even opened. He had greater issues to consider and a task he could no longer put off. After only one city block, he stepped between two vendor tents and into a cutway. He went on to the alley running behind the shops hidden by the forest of market stalls. When he spotted a line of water barrels, he crouched behind the last one. Once settled, he reached inside his shirt, grasped a rough chain around his neck to pull it out, and then stared at the dangling, unadorned copper medallion that he always wore close to his skin.

Closing his eyes, he gripped its smooth metal. After moments of hesitation, he opened his eyes, dropped the medallion back inside his shirt, and merely crouched there in silence.

Ghassan needed more time to carefully work out his request to his prince. For what he would ask, somehow the words never seemed quite right.

Prince Ounyal'am stood in the reception room of his private chambers watching three servants prepare a formal tea on a table constructed entirely of opalescent tiles. The chamber was furnished with colorful silk cushions on low couches. Amber sateen curtains stretched from the polished floor to the high ceiling, each held back by golden tassels. Besides the servants, the only other person present was Nazhif, captain of his personal bodyguards.

Ounyal'am did not look forward to this morning's impending visit.

Of late, he had entertained far too many royals and nobles. All found excuses, urgent needs, and pressing matters to see him. All happened to bring a daughter, a sister, a niece, or occasionally two or even three for company. So many polite manipulations in anticipation of his father's death had left him mentally weary. And none of these visitors knew he awaited that death more anxiously than any of them.

His reasons were far different from theirs, and ones not even his personal bodyguards knew, except perhaps Nazhif. Unfortunately, he was as much in the dark as every conniving noble with a daughter, etcetera, regarding his father's condition.

Ounyal'am had not been called to the emperor's chambers in more than three moons.

Presumably, his father was weakening further and Ounyal'am was expected to take a wife—at least one. As his first duty, a new emperor had to provide a legitimate heir for the security of the empire.

Ounyal'am glanced down at his simple but fine clothing of loose pants made from raw silk, a pure white linen shirt, and a yellow tunic with an open front. These were the simplest fare he was ever allowed to wear. Every item he had worn since his first step as a child had been tailored to fit him perfectly. How many of these young noblewomen would be eager to join him in marriage if he were not the imperial heir?

He often thought that he knew little of women. His mother had died giving birth to him, and he still sometimes felt the loss of her. She would have both loved him and been honest with him . . . or at least that was how he imagined her.

All his life, he had been told he was handsome, but he wondered how much of this was flattery. Though small for his people, he had fine and delicate features with a smooth dark-toned complexion. He wore his near-black hair sheered at the top of his collar and always combed to perfection. He had often been called "scholarly" by imperial advisors.

Accurate and polite as that description may have been, he knew it was not always a compliment.

He was not the great warrior that his father had been. Once, a brash court official had referred to Ounyal'am as "bookish." As a boy of fourteen at that time, he had been hurt, once he realized what that meant.

Showing his pain had been a mistake.

Emperor Kanal'am did not tolerate impudence, for his hereditary line had lasted more than four centuries. When that advisor's headless corpse fell at Ounyal'am's feet, cut down by an imperial guard before everyone present, that was the last time he ever allowed blood on his hands—his shoes—through his own carelessness.

Everything about him had to be perfect in the sight of all, but this morning's visitors would be especially trying. Mental fatigue made him falter when he saw Nazhif pacing before the archways to an open balcony above the palace's inner grounds.

"Your face betrays your thoughts," Ounyal'am said too sharply, "as if you had sucked three lemons for your breakfast."

Nazhif froze for an instant and then bowed his head. "Forgive me, my prince."

He was a muscular man in his early fifties with a

round face and a peppered goatee. A fierce but ever calm warrior, he had commanded Ounyal'am's personal body-guard for the twenty-four years . . . since the day that headless body had dropped at the young prince's feet.

Nazhif had never failed to protect the prince's heart and mind as well as his life. In some ways, he was the father that Ounyal'am should have had and did not.

Four of the prince's other twelve guards stood out-side his complex of chambers—thirteen guards for the pending thirteenth emperor of an empire. All city and palace guards dressed much the same, in tan pants tucked into tall, hard boots, with dark brown tabards that overlay their cream shirts, and red wraps mounded atop their heads. However, the emperor's hundreds of imperial guards were distinguished by gold sashes, and the prince's thirteen private guards wore silver ones.

Ounyal'am regained his composure, regretting his harshness to Nazhif. No one enjoyed the company of Emir Mansoor. At a knock at the main chamber's outer door, the door opened without invitation.

"My prince?"

Ounyal'am tensed with a flash of more than annoy-ance, though, again, he remained outwardly composed.

"Yes . . . Counselor?"

The door swung fully open, and there stood the imperial counselor, Wihid al a'Yamin, in the outer hall-way among Ounyal'am's four hesitant but watchful bodyguards.

"Forgive the intrusion," the counselor said, "but the emir and his daughter have arrived, and so I thought to announce them with all haste."

A'Yamin, in his seventies, still had eyes and aware-ness as sharp as any falcon housed on the imperial grounds. He habitually dressed in tan pantaloons, a cream shirt, and a sleeveless dark brown robe. His white hair was always covered with a red mounded head wrap—like those of the imperial guards. Perhaps he fancied himself a warrior, though he had never served in any military. His face was lined, and he stooped to appear frail, but this fooled no one.

With the failing health of the emperor, the imperial counselor was the most powerful man in the empire.

"How thoughtful," Ounyal'am managed, as he shifted a few steps for a better view of the corridor. Beyond the counselor and his own four guards stood two of the emir's men. And there was the emir himself, along with his one and only daughter.

Ounyal'am quickly turned his gaze away from A'ish'ah.

"Welcome, Falah," he said, using the emir's given name.

The emir stepped forward beside the counselor and bowed his head. "My prince."

"Enter, Honored Emir," Ounyal'am said, and then looked to a'Yamin. "You may go, though I thank you for your trouble."

"My prince," a'Yamin answered in his grating voice. "The emir serves your father well and has my utmost respect."

Ounyal'am could not help clenching his jaw; of course a'Yamin valued a blunt instrument like Mansoor.

The counselor bowed and backed away before turning down the outer corridor.

"Wait out here," Mansoor ordered his guards, as if the prince's own would ever allow them to enter. He waved his daughter in ahead, which was not customary. Nazhif quickly crossed the chamber to close the door behind them, though he remained inside the room.

Ounyal'am faced the emir and his daughter as a

different discomfort flooded through him: unwanted guilt. This worsened at the sight of her gaze lowered to the ornate tile floor. Of all the noblewomen thrust at him, she was different.

A'ish'ah was agonizingly shy and perhaps pained even more by how she was used. In past visits, she had barely been able to look up at him, much less try to charm him as others did. And this was partly why he dreaded seeing her most of all among the would-be wives.

Delicately built, she was so short that she had to lift her head to meet his eyes on the few occasions she had managed to speak to him at all. Today, she was dressed in white pantaloons beneath a matching split skirt of floor length. Her sleeveless lavender tunic dropped past her narrow hips almost to her knees. True silver embroidery at the tunic's stiff neckline showed beneath her long black hair, and both glimmered in the early sunlight flooding through the balcony's archways behind Ounyal'am.

Emir Mansoor was not known for kindness to his children. He had already disinherited one son for disobedience. A'ish'ah was one more thing Ounyal'am had not needed to worry about this day, but he grew anxious that she might suffer if her father became displeased with her.

"Come. I have had tea and coffee prepared," he said formally, gesturing toward the table settings and cushions waiting in one curtained corner of the large chamber. "Emir, I understand you have a report on the eastern provinces in Abul."

This was a thin excuse at best. Officers seldom reported to anyone but the emperor, and now that Ounyal'am's father was hidden away in his decline, they reported directly to a'Yamin—not to the imperial heir.

"Yes, my prince," Mansoor answered.

Ounyal'am half turned but purposefully paused, as if at a sudden thought. "Emir, the morning has passed too quickly. The family gardener asked me to approve a new bed of hibiscus he is growing for my father's upcoming birthday celebration. Would you mind taking refreshment while waiting?"

As expected, the emir frowned, though he certainly would not decline.

Ounyal'am added, "Perhaps your daughter would care to see the gardens for herself?"

At that, A'ish'ah looked up with sudden fright in her eyes.

Singling her out for any private moment with him would be seen as showing her favor. He had never done so for any of the other young women dangled in front of him. As expected, Mansoor's frown vanished, and he offered a deep nod.

"Of course, my prince," he answered. "I shall wait upon you here as long as needed."

At only a nod from his prince, Nazhif reopened the outer door.

Ounyal'am turned and nodded to A'ish'ah in entreaty. Such favor to her would not go unmentioned later by her father. More so to any competitor seeking an imperial alliance through marriage. But at least for this day, she would have nothing to fear from Mansoor. He would be too elated with false aspirations.

A'ish'ah barely glanced up. As she took a small step toward the door, Ounyal'am turned and led the way as was proper. As the pair stepped out and down the corridor, the prince's four current guards fell in behind, their commander following at the rear.

"Have you seen the gardens before?" Ounyal'am asked.

"No, my prince," A'ish'ah answered softly.

"They are a respite of mine."

The palace was laid out in a large square with the rest of the vast grounds spreading around it. Along the rim of the grounds were buildings, such as barracks, stables, a water house, and the like. The highest walls in the empire enclosed everything. The center of the palace proper sported the great domed chamber where audiences were held. Directly behind that was an open outdoor square in which bloomed the imperial gardens.

The emperor had often called it a shameless waste of water.

Ounyal'am loved it and used his personal stipend to keep it funded.

After turning another corner, he paused for Nazhif to step ahead, open another broad door, and then led the way out into the open-air arboretum.

Indeed, the garden required a good deal of water.

Subtle paths of plain sandstone were lined with chrysanthemums, hibiscus, peonies, and even wild roses brought from the northern territories. Between these were interspersed flowering and fig-bearing trees, as well as three ponds with brightly colored carp, a type of large fish said to have been brought from the unknown continent westward across a seemingly endless ocean. Some of the trees had been sculpted in their growth to form shaded archways over the paths.

Ounyal'am had few vices and refused to deny himself this one.

"You are pleased?" he asked.

A'ish'ah slowly nodded, just once, though her eyes were fully wide. She caught him watching her and dropped her gaze again.

"Few would not be pleased . . . my prince," she whispered.

Such a diplomatic answer was disappointing. It should not have been, but it was, and he strolled on.

Behind him, he heard Nazhif's quickly whispered orders to the other guards. Walking the paths of the garden would make it impossible for his contingent to keep him in their sight. Only Nazhif would follow five steps behind while the others spread out to encompass the gardens and watch all entrances.

Ounyal'am did not like doing this to his men, especially Nazhif, but he needed these moments of release. As A'ish'ah fell in beside him, though a half step behind, he forgot her presence for a moment. His thoughts turned to other matters, for the sight of a'Yamin in the doorway had left him anxious.

Throughout his life he had witnessed the power plays and schemes at court. He had never seen it quite so poisonous as now, when he had become the center of it all as his father lay dwindling in seclusion.

A'Yamin had both the ear and trust of Ounyal'am's father. He also chose who, if anyone, saw Emperor Kanal'am. The imperial counselor commanded the loyalty of the imperial guard in the emperor's absence. And all of this made a number of matters . . . difficult.

Of course Ounyal'am professed concern for his father; to speak the truth would have been unacceptable—and dangerous. The counselor heard everything eventually. And unless Ounyal'am married at least once, he might not be "acceptable" as heir when his father died.

A struggle would then occur.

So long as the emperor clung to life, Ounyal'am was regent only in title. A'Yamin controlled the empire, and he was not a man who easily relinquished ultimate power. The differences in how they would each rule were stark; there was no room for both philosophies.

Ounyal'am was deeply troubled that religion should even be an issue, as he believed it had no place in government. A'Yamin—and his father—looked to the ancient ways of the "old gods." In a forgotten time, one of those was said to have sought dominion over the world. The emperor and his counselor believed that time would come again.

They pined and planned for it and would seek favor and power through it.

Ounyal'am did not believe in any deities, though he kept this also to himself.

He barely tolerated the priests who the counselor allowed at court in favor of even the ones who served the newer gods. A theocracy in serving any gods, new or long forgotten and dead, was abhorrent. He had felt so since youth and the day of blood on his shoes, but before that time, the old religion had seemed little more than a dark fantasy.

Then Ounyal'am had met Domin Ghassan il'Sänke.

Somehow the dark-robed domin had entered this very garden to wait for him. Somehow, it happened on one of the rare days he wanted desperately to be alone and had forced Nazhif and the bodyguards to give him some peace in privacy. At first, he had not known all that this sudden appearance had meant or what—rather than who—the domin truly was.

Other secrets—other confidants among a sect of metaologers—had come much later. Perhaps the domin had taken those years to be certain that a young prince was worthy of such trust.

Ghassan il'Sänke expressed concern about "old and

potent ones" who had brought about the downfall of the nations before a unifying empire had risen from such ruin. That lost era, for the few who knew of it by scattered legends, was often called the "burning time." The domin and his sect feared that such a time was coming once more, but a young prince could do little so long as his father lived. In his youth, he had quietly attempted to hamper efforts by any faction to turn back the empire to an ill-fated past. Thankfully, even in his naïveté, he had somehow not bungled into affairs he did not understand.

Later, under the domin's tutelage, he came to understand a great deal.

Counselor a'Yamin was no fool.

Over the years, a not so young prince of the empire had fewer and fewer allies. There were always reasons for such people to disappear: other duties, a mission . . . a fateful mishap. And now all that was left to him were a small contingent of private guards and an outcast domin of an exposed and eradicated sect.

"Are you . . . unwell, Highness?"

In a sudden flinch, he glanced down and found A'ish'ah watching him. At that, she too flinched, which caused him to feel more guilt. Perhaps his nervousness and hers shook words from her before he could speak.

"I am . . . sorry . . . about my father." She swallowed. "I know what this looks to you, Highness, but he . . . he forced me to come . . . again."

Ounyal'am came to a stop and stared at her.

"And I know . . ." she whispered, even more quietly while staring down at the path, "I am . . . not the one you want."

All those at court "talked" but so rarely said anything, let alone the truth as they saw it. Truth was vulnerability or a weapon to keep hidden for a fatal strike. He was now stunned by how wrong—and right—she was in her openness.

"You have no wish to be empress, first or otherwise?" he asked, thinking she might shrink away even more at his own honesty. Her black hair shimmered like polished obsidian in sunlight sneaking through the branches above. She was so small and delicate standing there that he almost wished she would never answer . . . never put him in a position to hurt her in the slightest way.

"I have no wish to insult you, Highness," she whispered. "Not with false reasons for being here. Not ever . . . my prince."

He was struck mute amid a growing but complicated need to protect her. That had started in her first visit with her father. She had not spoken to him even once at that time, but he had watched her too much. Over all subsequent visits, she became the *only* one he wanted . . .

Because of this, he would never marry her.

His father and a'Yamin had turned the court into a deep pit of vipers preying upon one another, and this would worsen for years to come after the emperor's death. When Ounyal'am could no longer forestall taking a wife—and only one, if he could avoid others—it would be someone cold, ambitious, heartless . . . and worthy of this court. One more viper cast into the pit—and it must be someone who deserved it.

He could never do this to A'ish'ah. Even if she were willing, he would not let her follow him into that pit.

A strange and sudden warmth grew upon his sternum beneath his shirt. He held back a sigh of frustration and turned down the path. In only a few steps, he spotted the aging but talented master gardener ahead, and with a pause he glanced back toward Nazhif.

"Remain here," he instructed his guard. And then to A'ish'ah, more gently, "I will return in a moment."

He hurried away before either could answer, as Nazhif never liked for his prince to step too far out of reach. With his back to them, and only halfway to the old gardener still shearing an herbal bed, Ounyal'am reached inside his shirt and gripped the copper medallion he always wore. As he had been taught, he formed a message clearly in his mind.

Not now, Ghassan. After sunset, I will find a way to be alone.

He released the medallion before any answer entered his thoughts, though he knew the domin would not contact him at midday unless it was important.

Ounyal'am needed at least one moment of peace with the woman who would remain his dream and nothing more.

After the domin left the hideaway for his errand, Osha stood in a patch of sunlight coming through the strange window. And that window was exactly like the false one he had seen in the outer corridor. To see the same view through this window made him question whether it was as false as the other one had been . . . just before il'Sänke had opened the "door" into this hidden sanctuary.

But suddenly, he became sharply aware that—with the exception of Shade—he was finally alone with Wynn again.

The undead Chane lay still as death in the back sleeping chamber.

This was nothing new. That *thing* always fell dormant the instant the sun rose.

Osha had become accustomed to that, though not

comfortable with it. On the voyage to this strange hot and dry land, it had bothered—no, *disturbed*—him that Wynn treated their upside-down routine as normal. For the entire journey down the coast, she had inverted her days and nights to be up while Chane was awake and then to sleep much of the days. If and when she was awake in daylight, she had remained on the busy deck while that *thing* was still dormant.

As Osha turned, he could not remember the last time the two of them had been alone together.

Wynn was crouched in the cushioned sitting area nearby, trying to unfasten her pack's flap. Her wispy light brown hair was unbound, and she kept pushing it back. This morning, she had not yet donned her midnight blue short-robe and wore a loose, spare shirt over the top of her pants.

Shade pressed in against Wynn with a grumble, which usually meant the majay-hì wished to communicate something. Wynn lost her balance and, with an exasperated sigh, turned toward the dog.

"Yes, I know!" she said, and then stroked Shade's head. "Just give me a moment."

By way of answer, Shade tried to shove her nose under the pack's buckled flap.

"Stop that!" Wynn pushed Shade's head away. "We'll find something to eat soon. You're getting as bad as your father."

Shade rumbled quietly at that last comment, exposing her teeth.

Daughters and fathers, sons and mothers—in Osha's life, he had too often seen them at odds with one another. Apparently, this was also so among the majay-hì, the sacred guardians of his abandoned homeland. But still, none of them had eaten since leaving the ship last dusk.

"We passed two small markets last night," he said in his own tongue. "Perhaps something more than travel rations can be found in one of them."

Wynn hesitated and looked up at him. "The domin told us to stay here, out of sight. Unfortunately, he didn't mention how little was left in the cupboards of this place."

She tried to sound conversational, but her manner and words were strained. It pained him, for there was a time when she had been more at ease with him than with anyone else in the world.

Roughly two years before, Osha had accompanied Wynn and her companions, as well as his jeóin and teacher Sgäilsheilleache, into the eastern continent's ever frozen heights of the Pock Peaks. He had helped the best that he could in their search for what he now knew as the orb or "anchor" of Water. At that time, he had been an anmaglâhk in training, and his mentor, Sgäilsheilleache, had sworn guardianship over Magiere, Leesil, Chap, and Wynn.

Osha had stood true to that oath as well, perhaps most especially for Wynn, and this had slowly grown into something more.

Near the beginning of that journey, she had startled him by asking about his life and dreams. No one else had ever done so. Once they began the climb into the snowy peaks, conditions became so grueling that customs broke down for the sake of survival. In the freezing nights within a thin tent for shelter, Wynn had slept against his chest beneath both of their blankets and wrapped inside his cloak to keep warm.

She had been—was—nothing like the humans that he and his people had been taught to hate and fear.

He had scavenged food for her, melted snow and ice for them to drink, and when she felt threatened, she had run to him for protection. It meant something, though he could not find words for it. Later, she tried to teach him to dance at Magiere and Leesil's wedding, and no one had ever paid him so much notice. When he had been forced to finally leave to catch one of his people's living ships waiting in hiding near the city of Bela, she came after him to those crowded docks. When they said a final farewell, and he reluctantly turned away . . .

Wynn ran after him, threw herself at him, and kissed him.

She then ran off through the crowd.

Osha had no choice but to leave for the ship with a journal Wynn had given him to deliver to Brot'ân'duivé. He and Wynn had gone their separate ways. And even now, so long afterward in this foreign land, he could not forget the press of her small mouth.

Too much had happened since that kiss—too much blood spilled, too much forced upon him, and too much taken from him. Through a mix of forced choices, he was no longer an anmaglâhk. The Chein'âs—the Burning Ones—were a race who lived in the heated depths of the world. They created all weapons of the Anmaglâhk. They had called him to them, and then, for reasons unknown, they had stripped his stilettos and bone knife from him and forced new weapons upon him. First, a sword that he never used, would not touch, but always kept bundled in cloth and out of sight. Second, a set of five white metal arrowheads and a matching handle for a longbow, and these he had later reluctantly learned to use.

Osha's peace and sense of place had been shattered not long after that kiss upon the docks. He no longer knew who or what he was; though later, after he, Brot'ân'duivé, and Leanâlhâm found themselves on this new continent, a new thought had come to him when they had reconnected with Wynn.

If he could only get her to recognize what they had once been to each other, then he might find purpose again at her side.

When he was expected to leave Calm Seatt and go with Magiere's group in search of the orb of Air, he had made a secret choice to let their ship sail without him. This weighed on him heavily, as he still regretted having abandoned Leanâlhâm.

But a chance to once more be with Wynn had overridden all else.

Nothing had turned out as he had envisioned. During their separation, many events had also occurred in her life, including the reappearance and intrusion of Chane. Worse, she had come to accept Chane's help and protection.

The very thought made Osha ill, but there was nothing to be done about it. He had tried to get her to speak of their past and what they had been to each other in the Pock Peaks.

She had changed—and so had he.

She accepted his help, even welcomed it, and was always kind to him, but he longed for something deeper again. The more he wanted this, the more she withdrew, and he did not know why. So he continued to throw himself into her purpose to find the final orb and to protect the orb of Spirit they had found in the hope that she might reach out to him again.

Here, right now, in this invisible hideaway, at least he had her to himself—except for Shade.

"Should we go?" he asked.

Wynn glanced up at him in mild discomfort.

"All right, but we need to be quick," she answered. "There's no telling when Ghassan will return."

He noticed that she had begun referring to the domin by his first name. Perhaps in their current situation, this was more appropriate and he should follow her example? Human customs sometimes escaped him.

As Wynn rose, Osha slipped off his cloak and held it out. "Leave your sage's robe behind and wear this instead of your own cloak."

She hesitated, frowning in puzzlement. He waited to be questioned and challenged, but instead she took the cloak from his hand and put it on. He did not bother donning a cloak at all, but again, she did not ask him what he had in mind.

"Come, Shade," she said, turning away from him.

Emerging from the stairwell into the filthy tenement's bottom floor, Wynn headed straight for the front door. She hadn't looked back to see the hideaway's entrance close and apparently vanish. She didn't really want to see the passage's end suddenly become a wall with the same window as in the chamber. There was something wrong about that . . . something more than a mere illusion to hide the door.

Even that was half as unnerving as being alone with Osha and wearing his cloak—which was too long and nearly dragged along the ground. She had also left her staff behind at his insistent claim that it would attract attention.

Well, she wasn't completely alone with him, and at least she had Shade along.

For some time now, Wynn had managed to avoid being isolated with Osha and thereby not given him a chance to dredge up their shared past. Yes, she cared deeply for him, but that was complicated. She had to remain focused on freeing her friends and then finding the orb of Air. And yet, she realized there was some freedom to express concerns now that Ghassan was elsewhere.

As she slipped out the front door behind Shade, she finally glanced back. "Osha? Did you notice that when Ghassan spoke of Magiere, Leesil, Chap, and Leanâlhâm being arrested, he mentioned nothing about Brot'an?"

Osha, in his long stride, closed the distance from behind her, carrying a burlap bag for whatever they found at the market.

"Yes, I noticed," he answered, though she spotted the slight wrinkle of his brow.

"Why is that? Where do you suppose he is?"

Osha remained quiet at first. Wynn had to look ahead twice to avoid stumbling into Shade.

"It has been several moons since we have seen any of them," he finally answered, and Wynn looked up at him again. "From what your domin told us, it is possible that the remainder of the anmaglâhk loyalists followed Magiere." He paused. "Perhaps along the way, Brot'ân'duivé was . . ."

When he wouldn't finish that thought, she did. "Killed?"

Wynn was surprised by how much that notion unsettled her. Brot'an joining their cause had been a mixed blessing. Certainly neither Chap nor Leesil would mourn his loss, but still, the aging greimasg'äh—"shadow-gripper"—had more than once fought his own caste to defend Magiere. His very presence in the past had often given Wynn a greater sense of security, plus . . .

Well, she liked him. She couldn't help it.

"Perhaps he was not with them when they were taken," Osha added.

"Then why hasn't he rescued them by now?" she countered.

She couldn't think of a good reason, and Osha didn't offer one. If anyone could break Magiere and the others out of prison by stealth or force, it was Brot'an. And if he hadn't—couldn't—then . . .

Oh, she didn't want to think what that could mean.

"Wait," Osha whispered.

Wynn froze, looking about.

"The smallest market we passed last night is around the corner, ahead to the left."

Wynn exhaled in sudden tension and turned to him.

"Move quickly through the market," Osha instructed, "and do not linger to be noticed."

Perhaps she was a little overly annoyed at his unnecessary caution. "Between the two of us, you're the one who's going to get noticed! There are not many overly tall, white-blond elves wandering around here."

"That is why I will not be with you."

Wynn paused in confusion, and he went on before she could.

"Shade should go with me as well," he added.

"What?"

"The two of us, together, will draw all eyes. This is also why I asked you to leave your robe and staff behind. You will pass unnoticed, or at least unremembered. Anyone in a midnight blue sage's robe would be sought for questioning . . . after whatever the domin has done."

For an instant, Wynn was again at a loss for words. Osha almost sounded like Brot'an, and that made her uncomfortable, no matter how much she might like the elder shadow-gripper. And perhaps Osha knew it, for he lowered his eyes, not looking at her anymore.

"What good is it for me to pass unnoticed if you are?"

she countered. "We're all going to have to go out in the open eventually. You will stick out no matter what or when."

Osha sighed and raised his eyes. "When I am alone, if I wish, I have . . . can . . . pass unnoticed to most."

She didn't like that any better, though this sounded lonely more than anything else. It made her ache inside. Before she said more, Osha stripped off a short rope around his waist, hidden beneath his tunic's lower half, and crouched before Shade.

"May I . . . please?" he asked her, holding out a loop at the rope's end.

Shade looked up at Wynn and then back at Osha. With a wrinkle of her jowls, she huffed once at him. Osha slipped the loop around Shade's neck and rose up, still looking at the dog.

"If you would perhaps make yourself . . . noticed . . . when we pass through?" he asked, closing his eyes briefly and bowing his head to Shade.

Shade grumbled but huffed consent, but Wynn was a little put out. Obviously Osha had thought this through long before saying anything. It was even more off-putting that Shade went along so easily.

"Stay to the outside stalls," Osha instructed Wynn. "And if—when—others turn to look, do not do so. We will meet you where the market reaches the next cross street, and we will keep sight of you at all times."

With that, he walked off toward the corner, though Shade trotted ahead to the end of the makeshift leash.

Wynn stood there, still fuming. She was so tired of those around her treating her like . . . like she was made of glass! No matter how many times she put them in their place, they just kept doing it.

With a low hiss, she took off for the corner but

paused long enough to peek around it. So much the worse, for she spotted Shade and Osha strolling right between the small tents, carts, and makeshift stalls. And worse again, because people did turn to stare at a tall elf with a bow strung over one shoulder and a huge black wolf on a rope leash.

Wynn ceased watching and slipped along the street side, looking for anything they could bring back to eat. From one outer stall to the next, she paused in searching among what was offered. She slowly filled a burlap sack with plump dates, apricots, flat bread, a brick of cheese, and dried goat's meat. She moved along swiftly in her shopping and, thankfully, also found two leather-capped clay urns of fresh water.

Soon she reached the little market street's far end.

When she looked about and peered down the left run of the next main street, she didn't spot either Osha or Shade until she heard Shade's low huff. Looking the other way to the side street's far corner, there they were. Both barely peeked around the corner watching her. She hurried across but pulled up short at what she saw in Osha's hand . . . instead of on his shoulder.

The bow.

Wynn went straight to him. At least he hadn't pulled an arrow and fitted it. He slipped the bow back to his shoulder, took her burdens without asking, and insisted on carrying them for her.

"Oh, come on . . . both of you!" she whispered.

Not long after, they returned to the end of that upper passage and Ghassan's secret chambers. Wynn lost her annoyance staring at the false window that looked out over the street. Getting back inside the hideaway was something she hadn't done yet on her own. The domin had given her something rather strange to do so.

He had handed her a small stone, the size of a pebble.

Though accustomed to various esoteric tools of metaologers, Wynn had never heard of anything quite like this. Remembering his instructions on how to use the pebble, she dug it out of her coin pouch. It looked like any other she might have picked up off the ground. It was supposed to be used only "just in case." None of them was supposed to leave until he returned . . . unless absolutely necessary.

Well, food was necessary.

From what Ghassan had told her, all she was supposed to do was grip the pebble tightly in her hand until it hurt a little. That it was a pebble instead of something more obvious—more arcane-looking—made her doubt grow.

"Have you tried?" Osha asked from behind. "Do you see the door?"

"No, not yet," she muttered, and stepped closer to the passage's end.

One thing she wasn't going to do was stick her hand through that false window first . . . and see it go through, the way Chane had. Nor was she going to use her mantic sight to see the element of Spirit and, if she could, whatever had been done to the end of this passage. Chane hadn't needed to warn her off from that. It might cost her more than peeking through the wall and getting sick.

"Wynn . . . do you wish me to do this?" Osha whispered.

"No." She gripped the pebble tightly in her hand, until the pressure hurt. That little wave of pain changed everything before her eyes.

The shadow overlay of the door's frame appeared in the end wall. Its wooden planks were . . . ghosts of planks across the view through the window. Low to one side, near the window frame's bottom left corner, was a plain iron handle with no keyhole in its mount plate, as if locking that door was unnecessary.

And apparently, it was.

Before Chane had retired, they'd stepped aside to speak in private. She'd asked what he'd felt when he inspected the passage's end, after Ghassan had vanished through it. Chane said he'd felt nothing but the wall and the window.

Exactly what kind of magic could hide something from touch as well as sight?

This was more than an illusion constructed through thaumaturgy and light.

Wynn hesitated as her free hand hovered near that semitransparent iron handle. Then she grabbed it. The handle felt as solid as if fully there. With a quick twist on the handle, she shoved the door open.

The door became suddenly real as it swung inward.

The window around it—through it—had vanished. She saw the other supposedly real window directly ahead at the hideaway's rear, as if the window had leaped away from her. It was so disorienting that she froze until she heard a creak of metal.

"Stop the door!" Osha ordered.

It was already swinging shut on the force of its springs.

Wynn stopped it with one hand and almost jumped through rather than be caught halfway in. And then she stepped back right into Osha, who was carrying all her purchases. Whatever half-spoken exclamation he started was cut off, for Ghassan stood off to the left near the table and high-backed chairs.

Wynn was caught between hoping the domin had learned something and worrying about being caught outside the hideaway. But he didn't even turn to look at her.

Ghassan stared down at the floor with his hands folded together behind his back, and his expression was both angry and troubled.

"What's wrong?" she asked, forgetting everything else. "Has something happened? Did you find no help for Magiere and the others?"

His left eyelid fluttered. "Not now, Wynn," he half whispered.

He blinked several times as if then realizing he'd spoken to someone. Raising his head, he looked over, and his half scowl vanished in a flattening of his expression.

"Pardon me . . . No, I have not failed, only been postponed," he went on. "I must go out again at dusk, but I will gain assistance to rescue Magiere." Then he looked past her at Shade and Osha as she heard the door finally close.

"What have you been doing?" Ghassan demanded. "I told you to remain hidden unless it was necessary to flee."

"We needed food," Wynn answered. "And I couldn't find anything in here."

Wynn wondered what he had been eating. She was under the impression he'd been staying here for some time. And then she spotted a bag not unlike her own behind him on the table.

"I brought some things as well," he said, looking past her again, likely at the bag Osha was holding. "Bread, goat's cheese, figs, and some olives."

Without a word, Osha went to the table and began unpacking their own food. But now Wynn couldn't stop thinking about Magiere, Leesil, Chap, and Leanâlhâm.

"You'll find help tonight?" she pressed. "Some way to get them out of that prison?"

"I begin to see why your own high premin loses patience with you," he chided. "Still always thinking you know what is most important when you are out of your elements."

At that, he glanced sidelong at Osha and down to the food Wynn had acquired. Shade came up beside Wynn with a slowly growing rumble. As Wynn settled her hand on Shade's back, Ghassan took a deep breath and let it out.

"But yes," he said more evenly. "I will find a way to free your friends."

CHAPTER 4

At dusk that evening, Dänvârfij crouched with Rhysís on a rooftop in sight of the main gates to the imperial grounds. They had been there since dawn.

"I do not believe any guards will leave the palace after dark," Rhysís whispered.

Dänvârfij did not answer. They had held their vigil together rather than in shifts and rarely moved about alone, for Brot'ân'duivé was in the capital somewhere. Only she and Rhysís together stood a chance against a greimasg'äh who had eliminated more than half of their team across half a world. And their task for today—tonight—had been to capture an imperial guard for interrogation.

Should one such emerge alone, Dänvârfij thought it best to have two to track and silently steal away their target. But not a single guard wearing a gold sash had gone farther than the main gates all day. She now second-guessed her strategy, wondering whether she had ever seen a member of the imperial forces alone outside the palace grounds.

Of course they would accompany the emperor or the prince should either have reason to leave, but how often did that happen? Not once since she had arrived in this stinking human city. The emperor was bedridden, and the prince was reputed to love his garden and books and seldom ventured out. What had seemed a plan with some potential had become an exercise in futile waiting . . . like so many other plans of late.

Far too many days and nights had passed since she arranged for the "arrest" of Magiere and Léshil by Most Aged Father's instructions. As of yet, she had not found a way to learn even where her quarry was being held. Failure after failure began to take its toll.

Looking at her hands, Dänvârfij found both unconsciously clenched into fists.

"Remaining after dark will not profit us," Rhysís pressed. "There was little food or water in our room when we left. We need to purchase provisions before the last of the shops close."

Dänvârfij shifted only her eyes toward him. He still watched the gate, his expression flat and emotionless with his uncombed white-blond hair hanging loose around his face. Loyal, composed, and highly skilled, his less than subtle challenge was another sign of failing discipline.

They had been away from home and Most Aged Father's guidance for too long.

Anmaglâhk thought nothing of going without food or water for days. Their task, their mission, their given *purpose* was all that mattered. Rhysís now suggested leaving their chosen watch because one day had passed without success.

He thought of Én'nish.

Not of Fréthfâre, the spiteful and crippled ex-consul to Most Aged Father, waiting to hear of at least one task fulfilled. No, Rhysís thought only of Én'nish, the still wounded member of their team. His growing need to care for her had become a problem, which had started even before she had been so badly wounded.

Dänvârfij's lips parted as anger sparked. She stopped before uttering a word.

Of what remained of her team, Rhysís was the last able member besides herself. She needed him. Half a world away from home, the four of them had no one but one another. Perhaps he understood that better than she did.

"Do you have coin?" she asked him.

He nodded once, though he still watched the gate and walls. He had been resupplying their money by robbing people in alleys and leaving no witnesses.

Dänvârfij looked to the gate and wondered whether Rhysís was correct. There seemed little chance any imperial guards, let alone one, would emerge after dark. Yet simply leaving felt like another defeat after so many others.

"As you say," she whispered. "We will purchase supplies before the shops close. Once we see to the needs of Én'nish and Fréthfâre, we return to our purpose here."

Dänvârfij did not need to look at him again. She heard the soft shift of his cloak's hood from one nod. In this way, she consented to his indirect request without abandoning their task completely. Taking the lead, she slipped off the roof's edge and dropped soundlessly to the back alley's floor.

Brot'ân'duivé lay flat atop a roof three structures behind his quarry. He watched as Dänvârfij and Rhysís dropped into an alley below. He did not move at losing sight of them.

They would not try to gain entrance to the imperial

grounds, so they would have only one other destination in abandoning their chosen post. But other details remained a mystery.

Dänvârfij had changed tactics.

She had spent the entire day on a rooftop with Rhysís. Both had watched the main gates, waiting for something. For what, and why? And was she no longer allowed inside?

Brot'ân'duivé hated being in ignorance of even whether or not Léshil and Magiere still lived. He had sacrificed too much to fail and would accept no outcome other than their eventual rescue.

He froze in stillness, clearing his mind . . . until it was as still and quiet as a shadow.

The last year had taken something from him. Before, he would not have allowed himself to be "rattled," as humans would say. In slow, deep breaths, he shifted across the roof toward the street below, recounting the few facts available to him.

Most Aged Father was aware of the existence of only one orb, or "anchor"—that of Water—but did not even know to call it by its proper reference. He knew it only as an artifact of unknown purpose created and wielded by the Ancient Enemy. He was willing to do anything to acquire it or, short of that, remove it from human hands.

Most Aged Father did not know of the other four orbs.

Brot'ân'duivé did, though he had yet to *see* one.

He knew the one of Earth had been hidden in the dwarven underworld of Dhredze Seatt. Chap had hidden Water and Fire somewhere along the coast of the northern wastes of this central continent. And even now, Wynn Hygeorht was likely somewhere in Malourné seeking the orb of Spirit.

These ancient "anchors of creation" must have unmeasured power if they had served the Ancient Enemy. How much power and to what purpose, Brot'ân'duivé did not yet know. If they had a use in whatever was coming, he would learn it and, if possible, place that use in the hands of one person.

A name had been placed on that individual by one of his people's sacred ancestral spirits, by Léshiâra—"Sorrow-Tear."

Leesil . . . Léshil . . . Léshiârelaohk—"Sorrow-Tear's Champion."

Léshil had been named as the champion of the ancestors.

For this, Brot'ân'duivé had refused to be shaken off, even when Léshil—or especially Chap—had made it clear they wanted him gone or worse. He had protected them all from anmaglâhk, spilled the blood of his own caste, and would not be severed from his agenda.

If such devices would not serve Léshil's purpose, they might still serve Brot'ân'duivé in removing Most Aged Father forever.

In either case, he had to first locate and free Léshil, as well as Magiere and Wayfarer, and even Chap.

Movement in the street below stilled his thoughts and fixed his attention.

Dänvârfij and Rhysís walked rapidly away into the city. Such haste marked a strange desperation that puzzled and restrained Brot'ân'duivé. That Dänvârfij kept returning to her vigil before the palace gates meant that she at least believed Magiere and the others still lived. Brot'ân'duivé's reason and instinct told him that she knew little more of use.

Perhaps she was now embarking on a new strategy, one that might even serve him, and that was all that kept her alive for now.

He could have broken into their inn earlier that evening, tortured Én'nish and Fréthfâre for information, and made them tell him what they knew. But they might know little more than what he had already uncovered, and such drastic action would have ended their use to him.

Brot'ân'duivé remained upon the rooftop until Dänvârfij was well down the way, and then he scaled down the building to follow.

Shortly before dusk, Ghassan again slipped away from his sect's ensorcelled sanctuary. Heavily cloaked, he walked softly through the darkening streets, somewhat relieved to have a few moments to himself. The afternoon had been straining.

Once he and Wynn had put away newly purchased food stores, she immediately began pressing him about his plans to free Magiere and the others. Sharing news of his alliance with Prince Ounyal'am—over half the prince's lifetime—should not be done until necessary. Ghassan had managed to put her off.

In addition, among the most unwanted complications, he had also noticed something unspoken between her and the quiet an'Cróan archer. Wynn seemed almost manically determined to fill every moment with some sort of activity. It had taken Ghassan only a little while to realize she did so in order to avoid speaking to Osha. In the end, she'd asked Ghassan to tutor her in colloquial Sumanese. He had readily agreed, if only to keep her from badgering him further.

And then . . . there was the chest in the second room on the floor beside one of the beds.

He longed to study the orb of Spirit, but it was always

watched, and he knew it was too soon to safely ask Wynn for permission. Trust had to be gained first, and if it was not, there were other ways. More bizarre was the guardian of that chest.

Chane Andraso lay on his back, fully clothed and not breathing, appearing dead for all practical purposes on the bed beside the chest. Ghassan had spent other afternoons of his life in stranger settings—but not many. Once dusk was pending, he donned his cloak while assuring Wynn that he would not be gone long.

The streets were still busy in the early evening, now that the day's heat had subsided. Numerous people conducted business and errands to get out of their homes and into the relatively cooler air. As he began looking for a side street, cutway, or alley with fewer passersby, he was suddenly startled—and then troubled.

The medallion inside Ghassan's shirt grew suddenly warm.

He had not expected the prince to be the one to establish their agreed contact. Caught unprepared, he looked around carefully, and then hurried into a narrow space between an eatery and a tea vendor's shop. He went all the way to the back corners of the buildings and, with one quick look for any nearby watchers, hooked the chain around his neck with one finger. He had barely drawn out the medallion and gripped it before . . .

Ghassan, are you there?

At the soft voice in his thoughts, he fixed his will upon the medallion before answering.

Yes, my prince.

I do not have much time. I am dressing for dinner and found a reason to send my personal attendant on an errand.

Ghassan knew the prince's duties sometimes made

privacy difficult. As they were both pressed for time, Ghassan went straight to the point.

An unexpected change of circumstances has arisen. If we both act quickly, I might gain needed . . . unique . . . assistance to locate and destroy Khalidah.

This would stun his prince at first, and so he waited. Once the prince understood or accepted this, explanations might be easier.

Assistance? I thought all in your sect were dead.

Yes, in all likelihood. When Ghassan had returned from Bäalâle Seatt and rushed to the deep underground chambers of his sect, he had found only bodies . . . but one was missing.

Tuthâna had been the last to whom he had spoken while away, for all wore a medallion tuned specifically to each. He had not found her among the dead, and there could be only one reason for her absence.

Khalidah, amid his escape, had taken flesh again—Tuthâna's flesh.

She was by far the most trusted and most loved among the Suman metaologers, whether part of the sect or not. Her calm demeanor and kindness to others were widely admired, for most knew her as one of the few Suman metaologers who had studied thaumaturgy instead of conjury. She was an extraordinary healer favored by the elite of the imperial court.

Khalidah would have known this. All members of the sect had long been part of extracting the lost secrets of sorcery from him, including Tuthâna. And with her body, that monster could go nearly anywhere.

Ghassan feared she had not lived more than a few days after the escape. She would have been a vessel of transport until that ancient thing shifted to someone far more prominent. And who knew what had even happened to her body.

Ghassan? Answer me!

He gathered himself, for he could not think upon her now. He needed the prince to take a great risk.

There is another—an outsider. A onetime Numan pupil of mine has sought me out. She has the absolute loyalty of the black-haired woman you locked away on the day of my arrest. That woman may be immune to Khalidah . . . immune to possession.

Ghassan paused, waiting for confusion and curiosity—and perhaps hope—to overtake his prince. The silence went on so long that he feared he had lost contact, when . . .

And what does this matter? She is locked away with the others beneath the palace grounds, as I had no choice before the imperial court.

Yes, there were complications, and what Ghassan would ask next would be worse.

Find a way to free them . . . to get them out of the palace compound. I will take over from there.

The next thoughts he heard pierced him.

Free them? I have no authority over the prison!

Ghassan had known this response would come, but it needed to be provoked before he could ask for the obvious and worse option. He waited until the prince continued . . .

I can only condemn, and not even my father would undo this for fear of . . . how it would look before the court. His counselor would thereby advise against it . . . or in my father's seclusion, claim the emperor had denied such a request.

There was the trap in which the prince was caught.

Then you must arrange for an escape . . . and in secret, at least long enough for me to reach them.

The silence was much longer this time, and Ghassan pressed further.

Khalidah could even now "be" someone within the palace or the guild. I do not know his plans, but possibly he intends to reach you or your father. Imagine that thing sitting upon the imperial throne, sustaining whatever flesh in a reign you do not want to imagine. I must destroy him quickly, and I do not even know if I can. I need the black-haired woman.

Still more silence, and still Ghassan waited.

I assume you have a plan for how I am to arrange this?

Ghassan blinked slowly in relief. *Yes, my prince.*

Chane awoke at dusk. He first checked that the orb's trunk was secure, and then left the hideaway's back room. When he reached the open archway, the first person he encountered was Shade.

The dog sat staring toward that "other" window in the rear wall between the cushioned sitting area and the sleeping chamber's outer wall.

Chane simply watched her, though she did not look over at him. Her scintillating blue eyes remained fixed on that disturbing window. Though she was silent, her ears were flattened. He quietly stepped past Shade and then spotted Wynn.

She sat in one of the high-backed chairs and, with one hand, slowly turned and turned a tinted handleless glass cup on the table. Osha stood nearby, and when he looked up at Chane's approach, he appeared dourer than his usual brooding self.

"What is wrong?" Chane rasped. "And where is il'Sänke?"

Wynn did not even start from her silent nervousness. She related that the domin was having difficulty procuring the help he'd promised and had gone out yet again.

"We've been stuck in here all day," she added with an edge in her voice. "I know we've endured long journeys on ships, but this feels more like being trapped. I can't focus on anything until I know we can get to the others."

The others, of course, were Magiere and those with her.

Chane suppressed any reaction; it would have only burdened Wynn even more. But he had questions of his own, and the domin was not here to answer them. As he blew air sharply out of his nose, a habit left over from his living days, Wynn looked up at him.

"Do you need to slip out?" she asked quietly. "You haven't . . . I mean, I don't think you've had . . . any sustenance since we boarded the ship at Oléron."

Osha's horselike face wrinkled in disgust. So much the better, since he stalked off toward Shade, and Chane remained fixed on Wynn.

No, he had not had "sustenance" since before Oléron. He had once promised Wynn that, so long as he remained in her company, he would never again feed on a sentient being, and only upon animals—normally livestock. Now he wondered how much he should say or keep to himself, for that too had changed.

It had started on the night they had procured the orb of Spirit.

In their search for it, they had traveled to the keep of an isolated duchy with no way of knowing what they would find. In the span of a single night, they learned not only of an orb hidden in the keep's lower levels but that an old threat to Wynn—a wraith called Sau'ilahk—had used that orb to transmogrify a young's duke body.

After a thousand years as an undead spirit, Sau'ilahk regained flesh through that body, but only for one night.

Chane's only companion had been Shade when the two of them caught the wraith in the guise of a young duke. Sau'ilahk struck down Shade so hard that Chane thought she'd died in that instant, and he had lost control. Pinning the duke's body to the ground, he bit through the man's neck and bled him to death.

He had not told Wynn of this last part, and Shade had not been conscious to see it happen, so she did not know either.

Would Wynn even understand, considering why he had lost himself in that moment and become that monster she expected him to deny? But since that night, he had not experienced a hint of hunger.

Chane had not felt the need to feed, not even once.

This had been an advantage while on the ship, but if he had been affected by feeding on . . . by draining the duke—the wraith in flesh—unto death, then what else had changed for him? Yes, he was still undead, though the feral beast inside him had grown calm, perhaps watchful in waiting for him to slip again.

Once or twice he'd nearly told Wynn to see if she had any conjecture on this.

But the way she saw him now, and her continued company, mattered more than another secret he kept from her. In time, perhaps the changes in him would fade. Even if that meant struggling again and forever with the beast inside himself, it would be better than telling her. He could not stand the thought—the chance—of her sending him away.

"Shade . . . will you get away from that window!" Wynn snapped, and then more quietly, "I'm sorry. That window is unnerving . . . This whole place is unnerving."

Chane frowned in worry as he looked over his shoulder. Osha now crouched beside Shade, and if they had been staring at the window, they both now stared at Wynn. Shade got up and padded over beside her. Much as Chane expected Wynn to succumb to more guilt for her outburst, she simply put her hand on Shade's back and scratched between the dog's shoulders.

"Have you learned anything more about this hideaway?" he asked.

Wynn closed her other hand around the small glass cup. It appeared to contain water. "No . . . no. I don't suppose you have anything new on that?"

Chane's suspicions remained unchanged. Mere illusion could not accomplish what he had experienced in the passage. Hiding something from sight was possible by manipulating the light playing upon it; hiding it from touch was not and would require physically transforming affected objects. Then there was the great effort it took to permanently emplace such a work of thaumaturgy to respond only to specific individuals . . . or whoever had possession of a linked pebble.

This place was beyond anything he had seen in his limited arcane experience.

"Nothing as yet," he finally answered.

Wynn released the cup and slumped back in her chair. Chane settled in the one to her left.

"Well," she said, "Ghassan tutored me for a while today on useful phrases in commonly spoken Sumanese. I could teach some to you?"

"Of course."

Chane was always interested in languages, though he wanted to speak of more important matters. Then there was the other little change that he'd noted.

Wynn now often used the domin's first name, though in the past, she had generally referred to him as Domin il'Sänke. Then again, Chane wondered whether il'Sänke was still a domin at all. Even if he was not, Wynn would probably always see him as such, regardless of what she called him.

She turned her head toward the sitting area. "Osha, we're going to practice a bit of spoken Sumanese. Do you want to join us?"

Chane scowled. Why did she always feel the need to include that *elf*?

Osha appeared from out of the sleeping quarters, though Chane had not noticed him leave the main room. The gangly elf's eyes shifted once from Wynn to Chane.

"Come sit," Wynn added as she leaned over to dig through her pack by the chair. "The domin wrote a few phrases down to help us if we need to shop at the market."

Osha did not move and, for the first time, Chane wondered what had been going on as he lay dormant. Then he barely heard footfalls on the stairs outside and down the passage.

"Someone is coming," he said, though Shade's ears had already pricked up.

Everyone looked toward the door as it opened, and Ghassan il'Sänke stepped in and shut it again.

Wynn rose too quickly, jostling the cup on the table. "How did it go? Can we get them out?"

Il'Sänke studied her for a moment. "I have gained assistance from someone inside the imperial grounds."

"Who?" Chane demanded.

This domin, now responsible for Wynn's safety as well as being the reason for that need, kept far too many secrets.

"Someone highly placed . . . someone I trust." Il'Sänke's gaze shifted briefly to Chane and then back to Wynn. "Tomorrow night, Magiere and the others will be secretly freed and taken to the front gate. After that, we are on our own. We must be in place and ready for anything . . . including pursuit."

Shade rumbled, lifting her jowls and exposing her teeth. Wynn reached out and touched the dog's shoulder.

"What is it?" Chane asked.

"She wants to know more," Wynn whispered, glancing at him. "I think . . . she thinks this is happening too quickly—too easily."

"I agree," he whispered back.

Wynn turned to il'Sänke. "If our friends have been imprisoned for a moon, we cannot get them out quickly enough."

"I want . . . to . . . see entrance," Osha said from the other doorway. "Plan . . . tonight."

Again, Chane could not help but agree. "So do I. Regardless of risk, we must study the surrounding area if we are to have any chance of success."

His next impulse was to insist that Wynn stay there, but that would only cause a fuss. Also, on second thought, keeping her close would make it easier to protect her, no matter how well hidden this place was.

Il'Sänke inhaled through his nose as if considering options, but then he nodded. "Everyone get your cloaks, pull your hoods low, and follow me—and do exactly as I say. I will show you what we are facing, and then we return and remain here until tomorrow night."

CHAPTER 5

The following night and well past dusk, Prince Ounyal'am paced alone in the entry room of his private
chambers. He struggled to ignore the repercussions of
all that could go wrong in the events he had set into
motion. At a soft knock upon the outer door, he froze
for an instant.

As he went for the door, a voice spoke from beyond it.

"My prince? Commander Har'ith has arrived."

Ounyal'am took a slow breath upon hearing Nazhif.
"Enter," he replied and quickly assumed a cavalier and
almost bored demeanor as Nazhif opened the door and
stepped back.

A tall man in his late forties with narrow, hawkish features entered wearing a broad gold sash wrapped over his
left shoulder and across his chest. He halted after three
steps inside and bowed his head, though he appeared
mildly puzzled.

Har'ith commanded the imperial guard. The prince
rarely sent for him—and certainly not after dark.

"You summoned me, my prince?" the commander
asked.

Ounyal'am let silence hang for two breaths, as if annoyed by such an obvious question.

"I visited my father tonight," he said. "The emperor made a request."

Har'ith's eyes widened slightly, as well they should have. Counselor a'Yamin allowed few, if any, to see Kanal'am, including his own son. Then again, aside from the emperor himself, no one had open authority over an imperial prince.

For an instant, the commander's gaze flickered, as if trying to peer into every shadow in the room. That ended in a start as Ounyal'am stepped to a small side table and picked up a rolled parchment bearing the imperial seal.

"My father expressed concern over the treatment— and security—of the foreign prisoners. You are to conduct an inspection tonight and report to me after my morning tea."

Commander Har'ith blinked and hesitated before taking the rolled sheet. He immediately cracked its seal and unrolled it to view the order. To make matters worse, the commander was well-known as one of a'Yamin's minions, though he would not question a direct order from the emperor, no matter how bizarre.

The order was as brief and succinct as Ounyal'am's instructions, for he had written it himself.

Earlier that evening, after manipulating his way into his father's quarters in the counselor's absence, he had dismissed any servants present. They fled in panic, not daring to question his sudden appearance in the emperor's chamber after three moons. Perhaps he had stood there too long in staring across that room to his father's bed, hidden behind a haze of gauze curtains. Even obscured, the sleeping, decrepit form tucked beneath vermillion sheets left him sickened.

Some palace servants had whispered rumors about his father being seen once or twice wandering the halls downward through the palace dressed only in a long dark robe and hood. Of course, none had said this openly, and none seemed to know where that figure went. Looking upon the withered corpse-to-be, Ounyal'am did not believe a word of this.

How much better all would have been—would be— if he had smothered that wrinkled face with a pillow. But such a thought had filled even him with self-loathing as he stood there in the half dark within sight of his father.

The order had been quite simple to draft. Forging his father's signature was another skill practiced over half a lifetime at the insistence of Ghassan. After he used the imperial seal, he carefully cleaned and returned it to the cabinet, never again looking to the bed. He had waited until the scent of melted wax dissipated before leaving that place.

At some point—there was no way to guess when— the imperial bodyguards on duty outside his father's chambers would inform the imperial counselor of his sudden nighttime visit.

That could not be helped.

"Perhaps you should hasten," Ounyal'am said shortly, affecting a yawn, either sleepy or impatient, to hide his panic. "I will expect you again in the morning."

Har'ith's eyes narrowed slightly. It would seem to him beyond unlikely that the emperor would give a passing thought to the treatment of foreign prisoners accused of murdering Suman citizens, but it was not the commander's place to question—only to obey.

"Yes, my prince," Har'ith said clearly, and with another bow of his head he pivoted on one heel and left.

Ounyal'am followed a short distance behind and took a half step through the door, though Nazhif had reached for the handle to close it. They both stood there in silence, watching the commander of the imperial guard stride off down the passage.

To either side of the door waited two more of the prince's personal bodyguards, both wearing silver instead of gold sashes. But as Ounyal'am looked to Nazhif, his thoughts fixed on two of his guards who were not present.

"Fareed and Isa are in place?" he whispered. "They understand what must be done?"

"Yes, my prince," Nazhif answered quietly. "They will wait until the commander opens the first cell door and—" He finished with only a nod.

Ounyal'am nodded once in return. Only Commander Har'ith had authority over the use of keys to all cells for imperial prisoners. That fact had left Ounyal'am with no choice, and he studied the captain of his bodyguards.

"And the prisoners' belongings, anything that was taken from them?" Ounyal'am asked.

"All has been arranged, my prince."

Likely Nazhif's instincts had screamed at him to stop as he had given Fareed and Isa their orders. There was no other way that any of this could be managed for Ghassan's needs.

Events had been initiated, and Ounyal'am could not stop them now if he wished to.

Leesil shifted where he lay on the cell's floor. When his chains clinked dully upon stone, he opened his eyes a little. Not that he'd actually been asleep in such thirst and hunger. And of course there was nothing to see, as the candle had been snuffed out for a long while.

Wayfarer hadn't spoken all day. By the sound of her slow breaths, she was likely curled up as close to Chap as her chains allowed. Something that Leesil *hadn't* heard made his despair worse than hunger.

Magiere hadn't screamed tonight.

Amid this nightmare existence, that silence brought him no relief. It brought a terror that was eating him alive from the inside.

A soft, short scrape of metal came from the direction of the cell's door.

Leesil jerked his head off the floor as somewhere in the darkness Wayfarer inhaled sharply. Their meager food and water for a day and a night had already been brought some time ago. With one exception, no one entered the cell after that.

The door cracked open with a louder squeal of iron hinges.

Light from a lantern in the passage blinded Leesil briefly. As the opening widened, all he saw was the silhouette of a tall man in a head wrap like those of all the guards. Chap rumbled, but Leesil didn't look away, even as he heard Wayfarer's chains rattle against the floor stones. He squinted warily, wondering what fresh suffering was about to enter.

In two blinks, he made out the man's sharp but overly shadowed features. The guard's attire was much like any other, but as Leesil's vision cleared slightly, he made out a wide gold sash. The man's face looked faintly familiar, and realization came without any shock.

This one had been among those who'd dragged him

into the domed chamber in the palace's heights on the day of their arrest. The man covered his nose and mouth, as if the stench in the cell was too much. He turned his head, eyeing all three prisoners, one by one.

Leesil kept silent, waiting to see what the man wanted, what he would do. Finally the guard lowered his hand and opened his mouth, as if about to speak, but the words never emerged. Instead, a solid thud sounded and he collapsed. His knees struck the floor with an audible crack before he toppled face-first against the stones.

Leesil rolled back to push up the cell's wall into a crouch. What game were these guards playing now?

Another man stood in the doorway holding some kind of club. Though he was cloaked, with his hood down, the bright red scarf wound around his head marked him as another guard. A second, similarly dressed man stood a few paces behind him. The tall guard on the floor appeared to be breathing, though unconscious.

Leesil's eyes adjusted more to the dim light flooding the cell. The first newcomer—the one with the club— was in his late thirties and muscular, with black eyes and a rough complexion. The second guard out in the passage was perhaps ten years younger and more slender. He carried several bundles in his arms.

The first wasted no time and stepped into the cell.

Dropping his club, he pulled the keys from the fallen man's hand. Flipping quickly through the keys, making a tinkling sound as he did so, he pinched a small one before he looked up at Leesil. His expression was tense and reluctant, as if he didn't wish to be here.

"I have orders to take you to the front entrance," he said in perfect Numanese. "Do as I say, and you will be free this night. If you attack me or cause a disturbance, you will bring down the prison wardens and then the imperial guards, and we will all most likely die here. Do you understand?"

Leesil stared hard at the man. "Who are you? . . . Who sent you? . . . Why are you doing this?"

The man just looked back at him, waiting.

Leesil heard Wayfarer's quick breaths somewhere at the cell's far side, beyond the fallen guard. He was desperate for any chance to find Magiere, and to get Wayfarer and Chap out of this cell. What if he led them all into another trap? Was this simply a way to execute all of them and circumvent whatever orders had kept them all alive so far?

"Why should I trust you?" he croaked.

Turning his head, the first guard nodded to the second. Coming to the doorway, the younger man knelt and set down his burdens. The objects appeared to be two heavy cloaks, but one of them was being used as a kind of sack. Opening that cloak, the guard revealed Magiere's falchion, her Chein'âs dagger, both of Leesil's sheathed winged blades, and his white metal bone knife and stiletto. The latter two weapons had been stolen from the dead body of an anmaglâhk.

He heard Chap struggle up, and words rose in his mind.

—They are . . . telling the truth— . . . —They have been sent—

The muscular leader then asked, "Will you come?"

Even without Chap's words, at the sight of his weapons Leesil held up his chained wrists.

"Get me loose. Where's my wife?"

Without answering, the guard inched in and unlocked Wayfarer first, then Chap, and then Leesil—who tried to rush the door.

"Wait," the guard ordered, holding up one hand. "We must prepare."

Turning, he said something to the younger man and handed him the keys. Leesil couldn't follow the Sumanese, but he did make out the first word, "Isa," perhaps spoken like a name. The younger guard took the keys and left the cell.

Leesil didn't want to wait. He fought to hold himself in place, and the elder guard took off his cloak and held it out.

"Put this on and pull up the hood," the leader ordered.

Without his cloak, his sash was exposed. Leesil had never seen a silver one before. To his surprise, the elder guard removed that sash and shoved it inside his shirt. Crouching, he stripped the gold one off the unconscious man and arranged it over his own left shoulder. And as he stepped out of the cell door . . .

"Have the girl don a cloak as well."

"Léshil?" Wayfarer whispered, sounding terrified.

"It's all right," he answered.

He had no idea if anything was all right, but he wasn't about to stop now. The cell was small, without much room to move, now that there was a tall, prone guard on the floor. As he tried to step over the body, he realized that his legs were weak and it was more difficult to move than he'd expected. He put on the cloak and managed to strap on his weapons—and Magiere's as well.

Handing another cloak to Wayfarer, he said firmly, "Put it on."

Rising, she did so, though he had to help her fasten it.

"Can you walk?" he asked.

"I think so," she whispered. "Chap?"

The dog was already beside her, and she leaned one hand on his high shoulders. When Leesil emerged into the passage, he saw no one except the muscular guard who'd set them free.

"You are kept in an isolated area," the leader explained. "So long as we are quiet, no one will come."

Then Leesil heard another cell door creak open, and before he could move, the younger guard called out softly in Sumanese from somewhere out of sight. He sounded distressed.

The elder guard frowned and strode off toward that voice. Leesil tried to dash ahead but stumbled as his legs nearly gave way, and he cursed beneath his breath. Before he'd managed three steps, the younger guard emerged from an open door.

Somehow Leesil found the strength to rush ahead. When he neared that other door, he saw the panicked expression of the younger guard, shoved the man aside, and looked inside the cell. At the sight before him, anguish choked a sound out of him like an injured animal, and he stumbled inside.

A thin heap lay on the floor with filthy black hair stuck to her emaciated face. Her eyes were closed, and he barely recognized his once beautiful wife. She was beyond thin, and her pale, stretched skin looked gray in the dim light. Her chains had been unlocked but she hadn't moved, and both her wrists were torn and bleeding.

"Do you wish me to carry her?" someone asked.

Whirling, Leesil found the elder guard, now wearing the gold sash, standing behind him, and anger replaced his anguish. These men might be assisting now, but they were part of the mechanism that had arrested and locked Magiere away in the first place. They were as much to blame as anyone.

"You don't touch her!" Kneeling down, Leesil touched the side of his wife's face. "Magiere," he whispered. He went on whispering her name until her eyelids fluttered open and she looked at him with no recognition.

Magiere's eyes—irises fully black—went wild. She raised one hand to claw at him. He caught her hand easily, as she was so weakened.

"It's all right," he whispered, trying not to think about what she must have suffered. "It's me. Chap and Wayfarer are just outside. Can you put your arm around my neck?"

She didn't appear to understand, though her eyes cleared slightly as she stared up at him. At least she let him draw her arm up around his neck. In the past, he'd carried her easily. For all her strength in battle, her body was light, and he'd had no trouble carrying her for good distances when she'd been wounded. Now he could barely walk himself.

And he wouldn't let one of those guards touch her.

"Keep your arm around my neck," he urged. "Try to help me if you can."

He managed to pull her to her feet and hold her there. As he made his way toward the cell's door, she supported some of her own weight and struggled to walk. When they emerged, Wayfarer, Chap, and the two guards were waiting. Leesil's anguish returned when the girl saw Magiere and her young face twisted in pain.

Wayfarer barely got out "Oh, Magiere" before she began weeping.

"Quiet," ordered the elder guard, turning to her.

Wayfarer clamped a hand over her mouth but couldn't stop crying.

Leesil had no comfort to give her. The girl barely stood on her own, with one hand braced on Chap's back. Thankfully, the dog didn't collapse himself, and both guards took action, as if every step had been planned.

The younger one covered Magiere with a cloak, tying

it around her throat and pulling the hood up. With little choice, Leesil let him do it. The elder one locked the door of Magiere's cell, led them back down the passage, and locked the first cell as well, with the fallen man inside. Then he dropped the ring of keys outside that door.

"Now what?" Leesil asked.

He noticed the younger guard hadn't removed his own cloak. The hood was down, but he kept the front tied closed.

"As I said," the leader answered, "you were being kept in an isolated area with access in case someone of high rank wished to visit. One floor above us, on the ground level, there is a side door leading out onto the grounds. Once outside, we will take a path to the front gate that offers minimal chance of us being seen."

Leesil nodded, still afraid of too much hope.

"When we reach the gate," the elder guard continued, "you will appear to be visitors escorted out by imperial guards. Keep your hoods up, keep the dog quiet, and you will soon be free." He frowned at the sight of Magiere with her eyes closed and her arm draped over Leesil's shoulder. "If anyone asks, we will say the woman fell ill and you are taking her home." He paused and then asked again, "Should I carry her?"

Leesil jutted his chin down the passage. "Lead."

Ounyal'am paced his outer chamber, waiting to hear that his men had succeeded.

If Isa kept the cloak on—as many guards did at night—and Fareed wore the gold sash of an imperial guard, none of the city guards posted at the entrance would question them. The imperial guards patrolling the grounds were so great in number that none knew all of the others. With the exception of officers, they would simply assume a gold sash marked one of their own.

With luck, the prince's own guards could lead their charges to freedom.

Once outside, the domin would be waiting to take them away. No one would know of the escape until the change of prison guards at dawn, or perhaps not until later. Of course, once Commander Har'ith was discovered, there would be questions followed by chaos. The entire palace compound would be sealed for who knew how long.

Any injuries Har'ith incurred did not trouble Ounyal'am. Possibly no one would be troubled, except perhaps Counselor a'Yamin. That was fitting, considering that the few others of the palace whom Ounyal'am had trusted were gone, one way or another. All that were left to him were Nazhif and his twelve other bodyguards.

This night, he might lose two of them if something went wrong.

Even if a'Yamin uncovered the truth, in part or whole, he would not openly accuse the imperial prince and heir of complicity. If he did, how would he explain that the emperor was no longer capable of giving any orders? To do so would reveal that Ounyal'am's father no longer ruled the empire.

That would remove the counselor from supreme authority, which would then shift to the prince. Counselor a'Yamin would not easily allow that.

Ounyal'am's attempts to reason out of his worry were interrupted. At voices out in the corridor, he stepped close to the front door, listening.

"I must see the prince immediately."

Ounyal'am froze at the sound of Counselor a'Yamin's voice.

"Pardon, Imperial Counselor, but my prince has retired for the night," Nazhif replied, still outside the door at his post, and perhaps with a slip of spite he should not have displayed. "All attendants have been dismissed for the night. My prince will see no one until morning."

"Step aside!" a'Yamin ordered. "Commander Har'ith was due to report to me but never arrived, and now he cannot be found. I was told he had been summoned to the prince's chambers."

Ounyal'am knew that Nazhif would never step out of the counselor's way. The counselor held the power of life or death over nearly everyone in the palace, but he had no authority over an imperial prince's bodyguards, unless that prince was proven guilty of treason.

Still, Ounyal'am panicked at the danger to Nazhif.

How far would the counselor go if thwarted by a mere bodyguard? He quietly gripped the door's handle.

"Did Commander Har'ith come to the prince?" Frustration and anger made a'Yamin's voice tremble.

"Yes, Counselor, they spoke privately, and then the commander left."

"How long ago?"

"Sometime after the prince returned from visiting his father."

The silence that followed was such that Ounyal'am grew more chilled. Had Nazhif revealed this before the counselor discovered the truth for himself? Perhaps that was the point: to put a'Yamin on defense.

"Was Har'ith going to see the foreign prisoners?"

Ounyal'am ceased breathing altogether. That was less a question than a statement to be verified.

"I do not know, Counselor," Nazhif answered. "As I stated, the commander met with the prince in private."

"You have been most unhelpful," a'Yamin said quietly,

"and I will not forget it, as I am now forced to attend this matter personally."

Loud footsteps followed and faded. Ounyal'am waited until they were gone before opening the door. For all Nazhif's calm manner with the counselor, he looked annoyed in silence, which was the same as worried for a seasoned warrior such as him. The other two bodyguards present appeared unsettled. Likely they feared for Fareed and Isa, as did their prince.

"Will he go to the prison directly?" Ounyal'am asked.

The space of two breaths passed before Nazhif shook his head once. "I do not know, my prince, but by now Fareed and Isa should have . . ." And he said no more.

Yes, by now the prisoners should be nearing the front entrance. Even if a'Yamin went to the prison and discovered what was left in one of those cells, it would be too late.

Still, if the two bodyguards were somehow caught, and Ounyal'am could be implicated, a'Yamin might decide it was worth the risk to openly accuse him.

Anxiety overwhelmed Ounyal'am. Ever since meeting Ghassan in his adolescence, he had never allowed the counselor a single weapon to use against him. Treason was one of the few that would be effective against an heir to the empire.

CHAPTER 6

Osha climbed up the back of a two-story building along the main street to the entrance of the imperial grounds. He slipped onto the rooftop and kept low as he crept in behind a wide clay chimney, and then dropped to a crawl around to the chimney's side facing the grounds. There he settled and pulled his cloak around himself to mute his shape against the rooftop.

He had no wish to be reminded of his anmaglâhk training, though that was what served him now in silence and in the shadow of the chimney under a nearly full moon. Tonight he carried only his longbow, quiver, and the knife he'd acquired in his earliest flight across the world in the company of the tainted greimasg'äh. The quiver over his right shoulder now held seventeen steel-tipped arrows along with the five fletched with the white metal teardrop tips forced upon him by the Chein'âs—the Burning Ones. The seventeen were fletched with black feathers from crows, unlike the five adorned with pinion feathers gifted by a rare black séyilf, one of the Wind-Blown.

A part of him could not help feeling relieved to be doing . . . something.

On the previous night Osha had accompanied Wynn

as she, Shade, and the undead followed the domin to this same area. They had hidden behind the eatery in this building's bottom floor and watched the main gate while contriving a plan—or rather a set of options. Nothing that might happen this night was certain. Once they had exhausted the possibilities, Ghassan insisted they return to his sanctuary.

Osha had not slept much since departing the ship, and neither had Wynn. He refrained from suggesting she do so and thereby starting another "spat," as she would call it. Soon enough, they had both fallen asleep in the back room. Upon waking before dawn, he realized they faced another seemingly endless day of inactivity, trapped in that disturbing set of concealed chambers within the worn tenement.

Chane fell dormant at dawn. Shade paced. The domin somehow managed to keep busy. And Wynn continued to fill her time with meaningless activities.

Osha had kept quiet, watching Wynn throughout the long day.

A thousand unspoken words remained unsaid between them.

At least tonight, the stars once again glinted in a clear sky, and he was again useful to her . . . and perhaps to other friends he had thought to never see again. The previous night Wynn had even boasted to the domin about his skills as an archer. It embarrassed him how much this pleased him. In part, he wished he did not care so much about what she thought of him.

Osha regained focus, though he avoided recalculating again every possible outcome for this night. Everyone else had taken their designated positions below, but at the domin's suggestion Osha had placed himself atop this building in clear sight of the entrance and the street below. If all seemed calm and well when Magiere and the others exited the palace grounds, Wynn alone would go to meet them and lead them quickly out of sight.

In recent times Osha could not remember anything that had gone well or as planned.

Down below and one block up the street, Ghassan and Wynn hid in the next side street. If there was trouble, the domin, being the closest, would assist first, but to Wynn's—and Osha's—frustration, he'd never answered concerning *how* the prisoners were to be freed. Osha knew what this truly meant.

Whatever the domin's arrangements, Magiere, Léshil, Leanâlhâm, and Chap were not simply being released.

Somewhere across the street and another block closer to the entrance, Chane and Shade hid as well. They were to be the last fallback at ground level should pursuit occur.

And over all of them, Osha would watch and act from above as the others fled.

Everyone was to meet at a halfway point, which Wynn and the domin had chosen—a small area behind a Suman shrine. Osha had no idea who or what was worshipped in that place, but the large building was impossible to miss. The back of it faced an alley that provided a place to hide. Once any pursuit was evaded, everyone could then retreat to the domin's sanctuary.

In Osha's days as an anmaglâhk, he had listened, though not contributed, to several like strategies. Tonight's plan seemed sound by his limited experience, though Wynn had been adamant—especially to Chane—that they avoid killing any of the guards . . . and thus add more fury to the urgency to recapture the prisoners.

Osha had agreed with this as well, for in all his life he had never killed anyone.

This was one last vestige of his true self to which he clung as he shifted forward to one knee and slipped his bow off his shoulder and into his left hand. He reached to the quiver over his right shoulder, felt for an arrow's end without a wrapped thread ridge, and drew it.

Osha nocked a normal steel-tipped arrow and aimed downward, watching for Wynn as much as for anyone exiting the gate.

Dänvârfij had chosen a rooftop four city blocks away from the imperial grounds' main entrance. Once again, she and Rhysís had watched since late morning, spelling each other for brief rest or the limited nourishment they had brought with them. Her choice for this spot served more than one purpose.

Each day she varied their vantage point, knowing that Brot'ân'duivé was somewhere in the city. Any pattern of habit in surveillance would leave them vulnerable to the traitor. The distance this day did not provide the best view of activity at the gate, but that was not their immediate purpose. She and Rhysís could still spot, track, and capture an imperial guard marked with a gold sash, should one emerge and go off on his own.

Once again not one had come out. After only a two-day vigil she wondered whether they required a new strategy.

Far too much time had passed, and she would face ultimate failure if Léshil and his monster of a mate died beyond her reach. She had failed Most Aged Father in too many ways so far and could not fail in the end.

To return home having utterly failed in her purpose was unthinkable.

Rhysís stiffened upright, lifting his head.

"What?" she asked softly, though she followed his sight line.

All she saw was an empty rooftop with a solid chimney. The subtle motion that pulled her gaze there was a thin smoke trail caught in a bit of light from lanterns hung upon an upper-floor balcony.

Rhysís settled back down. "Nothing," he whispered through his face wrap. "I thought— It was nothing." And he turned his gaze back toward the imperial grounds.

Dänvârfij returned to her vigil as well.

In an exhausted haze of fright, Wayfarer repeated the same words over and over in her mind as she was rushed though the darkness.

I trust Chap . . . I trust Léshil . . . Everything is—will be—all right.

As promised, the two guards led everyone down a passage, up a flight of steps, and outside through a ground-level door. Now they all hurried along the back sides of various buildings nearest to the immense wall surrounding the grounds. Everything was happening too quickly.

Wayfarer cringed at being forced into the open. Part of her wanted to run back inside and hide, even in the horror of the small cell. Worse, she could not wipe that first glimpse of Magiere from her thoughts.

To her, the pale warrior woman she had met years earlier in her abandoned homeland was as savage as any human from her people's tales. And yet, in her way, Magiere was also as honorable and protective as Wayfarer's lost uncle, as well as kind and as caring as her departed grandfather.

Magiere feared nothing. She would charge the most powerful enemy without hesitation for the sake of those she cared for. But the sight of her starved, weakened, and nearly broken had shaken Wayfarer more than anything she had seen since fleeing into this human world. As she hurried to keep up with the others, still bracing a hand on Chap, she must have clenched her fingers too sharply into his fur.

He looked up at her but raised no memory-words in her mind. Of the four of them, he seemed the least weakened. Wayfarer leaned aside, trying to catch a glimpse of . . .

Magiere's eyes were closed as she stumbled along beside Léshil. He still held her left wrist, keeping her arm draped over his shoulders. He too had trouble walking, and Wayfarer wondered—worried—how much longer Léshil could support Magiere.

The elder guard out front stopped suddenly and swung back one hand to signal everyone to halt. The younger one directly behind him looked around in alarm and whispered, "Fareed?"

Was that the elder man's name? Earlier, Wayfarer had heard the younger one called "Isa." Both were nervous— no, *frightened*. And why were they risking themselves to free four prisoners? None of this made sense, and in a world that she barely understood, that made everything so much worse.

"What now?" Léshil whispered sharply.

Neither guard answered, though Isa glanced back. Fareed stood frozen, staring ahead at . . . something. He crept onward, though his hand flashed back again for everyone else to remain in place.

On their left was the back side of a stable; on their right, they were standing so close to the outer wall that Wayfarer could have reached out and touched it. She did not dare look up at it again. The last time had made her dizzy for its impossible height under the bright moon.

Directly ahead of the stable was a long building set so close to the wall that perhaps only one person at a time might pass through the narrow space.

Fareed crept out past the corner of the stable and hurried to the long building's nearest corner. He paused there and turned his head back to look down the space between it and the stable that led out toward the open grounds. Perhaps he was listening as well as looking for something. Then he started forward again, ducking into the narrow passage between the long building and the wall.

Wayfarer lost sight of him in the dark space until his silhouette appeared again at the building's far rear corner. He seemed so far away. And she heard footsteps, though Fareed's shape remained still.

Heavy, quick, and even, those steps were much closer, coming from the left between the stable and the long building's nearer end. When she glanced toward the stable's nearest corner and then looked farther ahead again, Fareed's silhouette had vanished. And everyone else in front of her was in the open between the stable and that next building.

—*Down now*— . . . —*Against the wall*—

Wayfarer held her breath and crouched low with Chap beside her. She barely peeked over the top of his back.

Léshil stumbled once as he pushed Magiere up against the grounds' outer wall. He teetered and tried to pull the sheath lashing on one winged blade. When Magiere slumped and slid down to the ground, Isa stepped out from everyone and drew the curved sword from his waist sash.

A heavyset guard in a gold sash came around the far building's front corner. He immediately turned upon sighting Isa standing before the others. The new guard's eyes widened instantly. He looked all of them over and up and down until his gaze fixed on the space between the wall and the stable's back. He might have spotted Chap, but then Wayfarer found those dark eyes staring at her.

The guard's puzzlement vanished, replaced by shock and then anger. He barked something at Isa in their strange tongue. When Isa shifted a slow step backward, the heavyset guard pulled his own sword and charged.

Chap snarled, and Wayfarer's fingers dug into his fur. She was too stiff with fright to even duck back below him. Just as frightening, Isa did not rush to cut off his adversary. As Léshil finally drew a winged blade, the new guard snarled something more.

And still Isa did not move.

The other man's sword came at his head, and then he stepped back a bit toward the grounds' outer wall. The blade passed so close to his right shoulder that Wayfarer saw his shirtsleeve rustle. He did not raise his sword even then.

At the other guard's slight stumble and quick turn to face him again, Isa merely shifted in another side step, this time toward the stable's end. He paused as if waiting.

Wayfarer almost cried out as Léshil tried to step in.

The new guard suddenly lurched to a halt as a hand came around his head from the right and clamped over his mouth. With his eyes wide again, whatever he shouted was smothered as an arm wrapped around the front of his neck from the left.

The man's head was instantly wrenched sideways.

Wayfarer whimpered at the muffled crackle of bone.

Isa still stood calmly where he had paused. The heavyset guard crumpled and fell . . . revealing Fareed standing behind him.

When the body hit the ground, its eyes were still wide and did not close.

Léshil's brow wrinkled as he eyed both Fareed and Isa. He turned away without a word, sheathed his blade, and crouched near the wall to pull up Magiere.

Wayfarer began panting as she stared at their two rescuers.

Isa was so young but had not blinked at acting as bait to give Fareed a chance to kill an imperial guard with his bare hands. She had seen ugly and cold acts in the company of Brot'ân'duivé that still marred her sleep.

Was this anything like what had caused the tainted greimasg'äh—and even Osha—to turn on their own caste? Was there something that could possibly be worth such viciousness against one's own kind? And who had sent these two for this task?

Fareed approached Léshil, who only then raised Magiere up.

"We cannot be seen again," Fareed whispered harshly. "Move now!"

Léshil appeared unaffected and did not move. He struggled to hold Magiere but glared back at Fareed.

"That guard was *looking* for something," he hissed. "Someone already knows we escaped."

Fareed's impatience was clear. "If he was, the imperial forces will keep the search quiet at first in making an initial sweep. If you are not recovered quickly, they will sound the alarm. Now we must go."

Léshil said nothing more.

—Up now—

Wayfarer shuddered at Chap's command in her thoughts.

—Grab . . . my tail— . . . —Do not let go . . . until we are . . . through the long, narrow gap—

Fareed led the way. Without a chance to think, Wayfarer was rushed into the dark, narrow path between the long building and the wall. She did not look down as she passed the dead body or back as she heard Isa dragging it out of sight. Once inside the back passage, she gripped Chap's tail as if her life depended on never losing it.

They all hurried onward until Fareed halted at the building's far corner and turned to Léshil.

"The gateway is twenty steps more," he whispered, pointing around the building's end.

Léshil returned a sharp nod, and Fareed spun around the corner. No one hesitated to follow, and as Chap pulled Wayfarer out of the passage, she saw the gateway ahead and released his tail. Her mind went blank as she crossed that distance walking on her own power.

The opening in the great wall had to be as tall as three or maybe four men. When she entered it behind the others, she saw a timber gate ahead that filled half or more of the opening's height. And there were more guards, who all straightened at the sight of Fareed. Only one dared step forward to speak with him, and the pair spoke too softly for Wayfarer to hear, even if she could have understood them.

All of these guards wore brown tabards and red head wraps, but not one of them wore a gold—or even silver— sash. Pointing to the gate, the lead guard turned to bark at his companions. The others rushed to slide an immense brace beam, which made a crackling sound as it moved, and then the gate opened.

Fareed ushered Léshil out and into the city without a word, and remained where he stood.

Wayfarer followed, bracing on Chap again. They stepped out into a long, wide street.

Sandstone cobble stretched ahead into the darkness between the quiet buildings. She still did not make a sound—and feared to even look back—until she heard the immense gate close; almost instantly, a loud crack followed as the beam was slid back into place on the inside.

To be free was too much to believe, and when she turned her eyes from the gate to look around—

A cloaked figure stepped out of a side street on the mainway's right.

At first it was difficult to see, until it came far enough to be illuminated by the sparse street lanterns hanging on light chains strung from iron standing poles. Small and slender, it was most likely a woman, and Wayfarer felt there was something familiar about the way it—she—stepped purposefully up the street.

A long, loud horn pealed out in the night.

Wayfarer spun to look back as she heard shouts in Sumanese rising from somewhere beyond the closed gate. She heard grinding and then the *thunder-thump* of the inner beam being slid again. Before she even twisted back ahead—

"Run!" Léshil shouted.

Brot'ân'duivé had taken a vantage point several rooftops behind and to the south of Dänvârfij and Rhysís, and he had watched them throughout a tedious day and into the night. That Dänvârfij still hunted *something* meant that she might yet lead him to a way to retrieve Léshil and the others.

He could be endlessly patient, but after a long day in the heat he pulled a leather flask from the back of his tunic for a sparse sip. The flask barely touched his lips when a shadow rose up on that rooftop up ahead of him.

Dänvârfij was on her feet, fully exposed to anyone else upon the city's heights. She faced away from him toward the imperial grounds. For someone of her training and experience, it was such a rash action.

Something had happened.

Before Brot'ân'duivé could tuck the flask away, he heard a loud horn reverberate in the night. The shadow of Rhysís rose beside Dänvârfij, and he pointed toward the grounds.

Cold calm filled Brot'ân'duivé. He shoved the flask away and jerked the tie on his right wrist sheath. A stiletto slid down out of his sleeve against his palm. For whatever reason, he knew that a moon of waiting was over.

From her hiding place down the main street, Wynn had watched Leesil and Magiere come out of the imperial gate. She'd nearly bolted out to them in a flood of relief, but Ghassan had grabbed the back of her cloak. She'd bitten her lower lip to keep from pulling out of his grasp. Even if he hadn't been forthcoming about his methods, he had somehow achieved what he'd promised.

Wynn waited anxiously as Leesil led the way, but he was almost dragging Magiere along, as if she couldn't walk on her own. Behind him, Leanâlhâm hobbled as she leaned with one hand on Chap's shoulders.

Ghassan made Wynn wait until all four were clear and the gate was closed behind them.

"Now," he whispered. "Quickly, but do not run and attract attention."

Wynn needed no such urging. At first she thought to keep to the street side's shadows, but then she might only startle Leesil. She stepped into the open, walked briskly, and at first no one appeared to notice her. Magiere's head hung with her hair curtaining her face, and Leesil was focused on helping her. Then Leanâlhâm looked up.

Even in the dark, Wynn saw the girl's bright green eyes widen. Any relief vanished as a horn bellowed in the night. Shouting rose beyond the gate, and Wynn heard a thundering clack. Leesil glanced back, said something to Leanâlhâm, and broke into a stumbling trot as he dragged Magiere.

The gates began to swing open again; Wynn forgot Ghassan's warning and ran toward her friends.

Five city guards rushed out of the widening gap.

Wynn jerked her hood back, exposing her hair and face. "Leesil! Here!"

A flash of shock flattened his expression at the sight of her. That was all, and he immediately pulled Magiere along at a faster pace. Chap lunged ahead, nearly jerking Leanâlhâm off her feet, as the guards behind them shouted and drew their swords.

Ghassan suddenly rushed past Wynn.

"This way," he commanded.

As Leesil reached them, Wynn saw his face more clearly within his hood. She choked. He looked sickened, gaunt, and desperate. He could take a good deal of punishment, of suffering, but he looked near the end of his endurance. Magiere was even worse, with her eyes unfocused and barely opened. Wynn caught only a glimpse of Leanâlhâm's face, but never had a chance to look at Chap.

A shriek erupted along the street.

The first pursuing guard toppled in his run and struck the cobble to roll once. A snapped-off arrow shaft protruded from his thigh. He grabbed at it as the other guards veered for the sides of the street.

Somewhere above, Osha guarded everyone, but he couldn't do so for long. And Wynn saw three more guards run out of the open gate.

Wynn! Get on with this—now!

She flinched at that voice in her head, its words coming in every language she knew, and looked straight into Chap's sky blue eyes. This voice wasn't like his trick of pulling broken spoken phrases out of others' memories. She was the only one to whom he could *speak* like this after she'd fouled up a thaumaturgical ritual while journeying with him, Magiere, and Leesil.

Chap looked better than the others, though filthy and lean.

Ghassan ducked in and braced up Magiere's other side. Leesil turned a glare on him, but Wynn regained her wits.

"Follow me!" she half shouted, running a few steps forward.

A snarl, the clatter of steel, and another shriek from an arrow's strike sounded behind Wynn. At this, she knew Chane and Shade had rushed out to cut off the guards, with Osha covering the escape from above. She glanced back and slowed upon seeing the others struggling to follow. Chap had half turned and stopped, leaving Leanâlhâm stalled and waiting on him. He must have heard his daughter, Shade, entering the fight.

"Chap, not now!" Wynn shouted at him. "Come on!"

Thankfully, he saw Leanâlhâm looking back, and he turned to follow. As the others caught up, Wynn rushed into a side street, leaving Chane, Shade, and Osha to deal with any pursuit.

Chane had held back until Leesil dragged Magiere past where he and Shade were crouched. At the sight of the dhampir, hatred almost overwhelmed him. He'd expected trepidation, even anger, over how Magiere's presence might affect his relationship to Wynn—but not this almost physical intensity. He froze in place as his sight widened until the night became brilliant in his eyes. He could feel his teeth begin to change.

Holding his place was all he could do . . . until someone snarled and pulled his gaze.

There was Shade watching him and still rumbling with a twitch of her jowls. She could not sense that feral beast within him straining to go after Magiere. No, she had only seen the look on his face, perhaps.

Chane pushed the fury away and nodded to Shade, once again in control of himself.

Before he could even look back up, the alarm sounded, long and loud. The gate reopened and five guards rushed out. The one in the lead shouted after the escapees. As Shade's hackles stiffened and her ears flattened above bared teeth, Chane pulled his dwarven longsword.

The lead guard's shout broke with a cry of pain. When he tumbled across the street stones, a broken arrow protruded from his thigh.

"Now!" Chane rasped, though Shade had already charged, and he raced out behind her.

Other guards veered away from the first as more arrows cracked against stone, driving them into erratic dodging. Shade launched directly into one guard backpedaling from an arrow's strike. He went down under her weight and his head slammed sharply on the street. The red wrap around his skull did little to cushion the impact, and three more guards rushed out the imperial gate.

Chane bit down against Wynn's instructions not to kill.

If only he could take a few heads, and in the terror of that, Osha could cover their escape. Instead, he charged the nearest guard, let the man take a slash with his curved blade, and blocked it aside with his own.

Chane struck with his fist, and the man's head whipped back under the crack of impact. The guard toppled as his sword fell and clattered. Chane turned as Shade lunged off the top of her own target.

Two more guards came at them. One lost his footing as another black-feathered arrow struck his shoulder and he swerved in a spin. The second took an instinctive glance at the first, and Chane lunged one step and kicked into the second's knee. In a yelp, the guard crumpled, and Chane kicked him in the head to put him down and out.

Only the span of four or five breaths had passed.

Shade shot past Chane in a straight line toward the three new oncoming guards, and he quickly rasped, "Wait!"

Whirling, he peered up the street. Wynn and the others were already gone. Distant shouting pulled him the other way as Shade rounded his legs to watch the street.

More guards high up on the palace wall called wildly down to those in the street, and these wore gold sashes. One ran along the wall top toward the gate, screaming the same few words over and over.

Chane knew imperial guards would soon be pouring out of the gate. It was time for the next step.

"Howl!" he told Shade.

She did not even look up at him. She knew the plan as well as he did.

A manic sound out of the back of Shade's throat pierced Chane's ears.

"Run and lead!" he said.

Shade took off up the mainway away from the palace and out in plain sight.

Chane followed, hoping any emerging men fixed on him and her . . . rather than go hunting for Wynn.

CHAPTER 7

Dänvârfij froze in indecision upon the rooftop. She watched as her quarry came out of the imperial gates, and though their faces were obscured, hidden, or unclear, the deviant majay-hì was unmistakable. Before she could act, an alarm was sounded.

Guards ran out after the prisoners—Dänvârfij's stolen prisoners. Arrows flew down into the street from somewhere high across the mainway. Two unknown figures appeared and hurried off Léshil, Magiere, the quarter-blood girl, and Chap. Even then, Dänvârfij had stalled again at the appearance of a tall swordsman with another majay-hì—a black one fighting beside him.

Three more guards ran out of the gate.

Rhysís as well could only stare.

Within moments, the swordsman and black majay-hì ran down the mainway, obviously trying to draw off any pursuit. Dänvârfij recognized those two who had fought beside an interfering little human "sage" back in Calm Seatt.

Was Wynn Hygeorht somewhere down there as well?

As the swordsman and black majay-hì vanished from sight, six imperial guards in gold sashes rushed out of the gate. How bitterly ironic, considering that Dänvârfij no longer needed even one to interrogate.

"What action do we take?" Rhysís whispered.

Magiere's group was now too large in addition to there being several unknowns among them. For Dänvârfij to attack so many with only Rhysís would be a great risk, and there was no way to know if or when the swordsman and black majay-hì would double back to join their companions.

"Report to Fréthfâre but keep to the rooftops," she answered. "I will track our quarry to their final destination. We can then find a way to separate and capture the ones we want."

In that, they would need Én'nish, despite her near crippling wound. Even in the face of so much effort wasted, Dänvârfij took hope in her quarry's panicked flight.

Magiere had barely been able to walk, but she was out in the open. It was simply a matter of finding a way for her or Léshil to be taken alone. For the first time in a long moon, Dänvârfij breathed more easily.

"Go," she told Rhysís.

He ran silently over the roof and leaped to the next one across an alley. As the imperial guards rushed off to harry the decoys, Dänvârfij slipped over the building's front. She dropped easily to the street and headed after the true prey of this night.

Brot'ân'duivé crouched in stillness at the rooftop's edge, his stiletto in hand with its blade flattened beneath his forearm to hide it from the moonlight. He absorbed the most unexpected events taking place below in the street.

Wynn Hygeorht had a penchant for chaos, though it often hid something purposeful. Yes, he recognized her even though strangely cloaked. Her movements and gait were unmistakable, and the others had not hesitated to follow her. Unfortunately, the surprising young woman too often overlooked and failed to anticipate complications.

Two of Most Aged Father's loyalist anmaglâhk were watching from above as Wynn and the others slipped beyond sight. Dänvârfij had dropped to the street to follow as Rhysís raced across the rooftops deeper into the city, likely to report to Fréthfâre.

Brot'ân'duivé was uncertain what Wynn Hygeorht would do next—or where she would take Léshil and the others. He did not like indecision, especially his own, and glanced toward Rhysís slipping farther away.

A choice had to be made between two different targets.

Brot'ân'duivé flipped his stiletto, bit the blade in his teeth, and swung over the roof's edge to drop.

Osha nocked another arrow and aimed as Chane and Shade fled up the mainway. He understood their need to draw the guards off, but they were heading for a more populated district. How would the citizens react to a howling wild beast if Shade did not fall silent, and soon?

There was nothing to be done. The guards must be lured away, but Osha worried that, with Chane to slow her, Shade might not have enough of a lead.

He turned his eyes on the gate as six men in gold sashes ran out and down the street. He aimed ahead of them and released the bow's string. Ducking low as the arrow flew, he saw it strike the cobble two strides before the lead guard.

That one skidded to a stop, forcing the others to do

so as well. At their shouts to one another in looking about, Osha dropped below their sight on the roof.

He no longer heard Shade's howling, and neither she nor Chane was in sight. The guards below would have to slow in their search without a visible quarry.

Osha stayed low as he crept around to the chimney's back, facing the roof's inland edge. About to drop into the cutway and head for the chosen place to meet the others, he looked back one last time . . . and stalled.

Across the mainway along the rooftop silhouettes, something moved beneath the moonlight, silently running deeper into the city's northern reaches. In less than a breath, it leaped as if vaulting a narrow street or alley somewhere below. The noise of the guards down the mainway had faded, but even so, Osha never heard the shadow land on the next rooftop.

Nor did it slow in doing so.

He did not know *who* the shadow was, but he knew *what* it was by its ways and movement.

Anmaglâhk.

Somewhere in this city, it was still possible that Brot'ân'duivé sought his own pursuits. If he yet lived, there would have been no chance to seek him out—not that Osha wished to—while striving to free the others.

But Brot'ân'duivé would never be seen in the open like that running shadow.

And Osha remembered something the domin had said.

There had been two light-haired elves among those who had captured his long-lost friends. At the time Ghassan had mentioned this, Osha and Wynn had wondered . . . but this was a large continent with its own population of elves.

Osha rose in panic upon the rooftop. Any remnants of doubt vanished.

After all that had been done to cut off Dänvârfij and her team, they had tracked Magiere and Léshil to this city. One of them was now in sight—likely male to judge by its height—and was not going in the direction Wynn's group had traveled.

An anmaglâhk outnumbered would wait and follow or seek others to assist. If this messenger succeeded, more of Dänvârfij's team would soon descend upon the others . . . upon Wynn.

Osha dropped from the roof's edge, landing so hard in the cutway that he had to tuck and roll. Rising with his legs and one shoulder aching, he bolted across the mainway, without even looking for guards, and scrambled up another building to rise and search the night.

And he saw the shadow even farther away.

There was no time for stealth as he raced over the top of the city. Everyone else was in danger, including helpless Leanâlhâm . . . including Wynn.

As he ran, he reached over his shoulder and felt for an arrow without a thread ridge, one with only a steel tip. Gripping that, he hesitated for a half breath. A trained anmaglâhk could hear an arrow coming and evade it, especially in the quiet of the night. He pinched the thread-ridged arrow between his last two fingers and also grabbed a different one—without a ridge—between his first two fingers.

He now held one arrow with a Chein'âs white metal head and one of plain steel.

Osha halted, quickly drew back the steel-headed arrow, and fired.

He aimed slightly low and left to catch his target in the thigh and hobble it. If the arrow hit by chance, that would be enough to halt his target's flight. As the arrow left the bow, he drew back the white-tipped arrow and fired again—the first to mask the sound of the second in flight.

In that instant, Leanâlhâm broke through Osha's thoughts of Wynn.

He had left her to Léshil, Magiere, and Chap. He had believed they of all people could keep her safe from harm, even in the company of Brot'ân'duivé after the loyalists had been cut off. She had not been safe after all, but imprisoned in a foreign land. The greimasg'äh had escaped that same fate . . . and left Leanâlhâm there.

One blink after Osha had fired the first arrow, the shadow lurched to the right.

This did not matter; that was where he had aimed the second arrow.

A bit of white glinted in the dark as moonlight caught on a thin line of metal . . . like an anmaglâhk blade. Wynn was now somewhere below in the streets and unaware of pursuit.

Osha instinctively twitched his grip on the bow.

Beneath the leather wrap in his grip hid another gift of the Chein'âs: a white metal bow handle to match the head of the second arrow. Out in the dark, that arrow shifted in flight as his aim instinctively fixed dead center upon the shadow.

He never heard it strike.

The shadow's silhouette suddenly twitched, convulsed, and toppled. He heard it fall to the roof and slide. Then came the distant sound of cloth tearing. In the silence that followed, Osha remained rigid in place, until he heard the body's impact upon a street somewhere below.

Osha stood frozen and could not lower the bow. A flickering image of Wynn overlaid the one of a shadow convulsing in the dark. Both visions burned into his

mind, and he grew sick, began shuddering, and fought
to keep his feet.

His first kill—which he had never wanted—was one
of his former caste.

> *. . . what are you . . . why have you come . . . who do
> you serve?*
> *. . . no one left to trust . . . no one will come for
> you . . .*
> *. . . all are locked away or fled . . . you are alone . . .
> forever . . .*

That whispering chorus echoed out of memories in
Magiere's head. She was barely aware of being dragged
through night streets she didn't recognize. Even the
pain of her torn wrists, feeling as if they were still manacled, wasn't enough to shut out those whispers.

"Magiere, please!"

That voice was louder than the others. It pierced her
right ear, as if she had actually *heard* it.

"Help me . . . try to move your feet . . . and walk."

It was so familiar, that voice. It taunted her, but she
couldn't place it. Air and strange smells—different from
the cell's stench—rushed across her face and filled her
nostrils. Her arms and shoulders ached as if stretched
to their limits by whatever chains now held her up.

. . . no one will come for you . . .

Those words again scratched and skittered like bugs
crawling in her skull. At their pain, she opened her eyes.

Magiere cringed as a passing light burned her irises.
She shut her eyes in a hard blink. When she opened
them again, strange buildings along a dark street rushed

past her, except for another lantern drawing nearer ahead as she was . . . dragged onward.

"This way," someone half whispered from up ahead, and that voice was also familiar, like the one in her ear. "The shrine isn't far. We'll hide around the back to wait for the others."

What was happening?

Magiere barely turned her head, and Leesil's face appeared so close to hers. He was looking forward to wherever that other voice had come from. She became vaguely aware that both of her arms were over the top of two people who were dragging her along. She didn't look the other way for the second of those two; she looked only at Leesil.

She had dreamed of him amid the whispers for so many . . . how many days or nights? The skin over his face was tight, and he was panting.

"Leesil?" she breathed.

His face twisted instantly toward her, and she shook under his sudden stop.

"Wynn . . . wait!" he called.

His voice hurt her ears after so long hearing nothing but whispers in her head. His bloodshot amber eyes filled with relief.

"I'm sorry," he whispered, and again, "I'm so . . . sorry . . ."

Confusion tangled with hope. Was he truly here to save her? Had he just called to Wynn? No, Wynn was far away, and none of this was real. Anguish killed hope as Leesil blurred in her sight.

"No . . . no, don't cry," he whispered. "Everything is all right . . . everything. We just have to go a little farther."

Her left arm jerked upward and then dropped at her

side. Leesil stumbled as her whole weight shifted against him.

"Ghassan! What are you doing?"

At that other voice—again out in front—Magiere tried to turn her head.

"He must carry her alone, so I am free to act as needed."

This third voice—deep and tainted with an odd accent—came from her left. She didn't have a chance to look as someone else rushed toward her.

Magiere's eyes opened a little wider at the pain from her left arm being raised again. When it came down, it settled on smaller shoulders much lower than those of whoever had helped carry her before. She swallowed the pain as she looked over into . . .

Large, wide, round eyes of deep brown peering up at her out of an olive-toned face hidden inside an over-sized cloak's hood.

"Wynn?" Magiere whispered.

With only a brief half smile, Wynn nodded and then twisted her head to look up the street. It took effort for Magiere to follow that gaze.

There was Chap, and Wayfarer leaned on his shoulders with one hand as the two looked back at her. Despite relief on the girl's haggard face, there was lost panic in her forest green eyes.

Wynn suddenly stiffened. "No! That's not it," she half voiced, her eyes fixed on Chap. "Three more intersections . . . then a right and two more."

Chap must have babbled into Wynn's head again.

"We need to go!" that foreign male voice ordered, now somewhere behind. "I will watch at the rear."

Chap turned off up the dark street, forcing Wayfarer to follow.

"Can you go on?" Wynn asked.

"Yes . . . yes," Magiere answered, looking to her lost husband. That was where she had always drawn strength when she thought she had no more.

"I'll make this up to you." He breathed into her face. "I swear."

What did he have to make up for? He was the one who'd saved her.

No . . . you are alone . . . forever . . .

At that last echo of whispers weakly scratching at Magiere's skull, her hate came back.

Hate gave her strength. Someone had done all of this, someone in that shimmering robe, and someone would die for what had been done to her and those she loved.

Brot'ân'duivé wove swiftly and silently through shadows in the alleys, cutways, and streets as he tracked Dänvârfij. He kept enough distance that even she would never hear him, though she would not have seen him if she looked back.

"Wynn, wait!"

As Dänvârfij halted at the alley's mouth, so did Brot'ân'duivé near its other end. He had so intently focused on the hunt that the voice from far ahead caught him off guard.

Léshil should not have betrayed the others' position so carelessly. By his voice, they were no more than another city block away. Perhaps they were even down the street beyond Dänvârfij. It took only the span of a breath to reassess the situation.

Imperial guards would be sweeping the city, though as yet he had not seen or heard any nearby. When they appeared, and they would eventually, they would not give attention to any nearby altercation as they sought to recapture prisoners. And his own prey might use that complication.

Brot'ân'duivé abandoned the need for the proper place and time. He backed out of the alley and charged up the last side street to round the corner for the street onto which the alley emptied. He stopped at the corner amid the cloying stench of a spice shop, but he did not see either Dänvârfij or the others along the open, empty street. That alone was the only fortune as he crept toward the alley's mouth.

Dänvârfij went still upon hearing Léshil's voice—followed by other voices too soft to hear clearly. Her first impulse was to scale to the rooftops, get ahead of her quarry, and only then drop to the street when she could take either Léshil or his monster of a mate. The others would not dare challenge her for fear she might kill a hostage.

She quickly rejected this notion.

Her task was to track and scout wherever their quarry would hide. Soon enough, imperial guards would flood the streets in a wide search. Attempting to take one of her targets now might prove a wasted opportunity if she had to escape capture herself.

Rhysís was to report to Fréthfâre, and then Dänvârfij was to follow with more information. They were spread thin in number, and it was essential to adhere to set plans. With the pending search of the guards, Léshil and Magiere would not dare move from wherever they next hid.

To know that place was all that mattered. And upon the rooftops, she might be delayed or cut off by any street too wide to leap across.

Dänvârfij cleared her thoughts with regained purpose and stepped out of the alley.

A shadow filled the corner of her sight, and she instantly spun toward it.

There was no mistaking who stood there, even without the garb of his caste. In a catch of breath she thought of all those of her team who had died since leaving their homeland.

Dänvârfij knew she stood no chance against a greimasg'äh, a "shadow-gripper," a master of her caste's ways. Once, she had revered him, lived in awe of him.

Sadness, mournful and infuriating, flooded her.

No anmaglâhk feared death. They feared only failure.

"Traitor!" she called out.

To her dull surprise, his answer was soft, perhaps sad.

"That would be you—and Most Aged Father—to our people."

Hkuan'duv, her own jeóin and teacher, had been a greimasg'äh long before he died while killing Osha's jeóin, the revered Sgäilsheilleache. By Hkuan'duv's teachings and her love for him, Dänvârfij would not allow the traitor to walk away unmarked.

Brot'ân'duivé saw Dänvârfij's expression drain of all emotion. It would have been better for her to hesitate, perhaps flee, and die more quickly that way. When she rushed him, he did not move at first.

Her first strike never landed.

The blade passed a whole hand's thickness from his chest as he twisted and dropped into a crouch. He slammed one palm up into the elbow of her outstretched arm. The other slapped the inside of her forward knee.

Both of her legs buckled willfully instead of just the one. As she came down, her extended arm folded and her elbow slipped off his palm before his strike was completed. She slashed down with her blade as she dropped into a crouch to match his own.

Brot'ân'duivé twisted his striking hand, and her blade slid off his palm as he threw himself into the near building's sidewall. He folded his outer leg before his weight overcame inertia and pulled him down the wall, and he thrust out with a foot.

To his surprise, she intercepted the heel coming toward her head by raising her shoulder. The kick still knocked her back to roll across the street stones. She was on her feet again as he rose up.

He did not close but stood his ground, waiting as she poised for another rush.

He half expected her to charge past him at a tangent, seek the wall to step up, and come down upon him from above. Or perhaps she would finally turn and run.

Brot'ân'duivé had calculated every option available when Dänvârfij came again.

In a flash, her lunging foot slid forward along the ground. It was too predictable, though that was his mistake as much as hers.

He barely sidestepped, twisted, and spun the blade in his other hand, still held hidden beneath his wrist. He drove it toward her right eye as she hit the ground in a hurdler's straddle.

She collapsed forward over her outstretched leg, ducked her head under his thrust, and her right hand struck for his forward knee. He shifted weight to his other leg, taking the blow as she pushed off her rear-cocked leg, shot upward, and thrust her blade for his abdomen.

Brot'ân'duivé speared both hands downward as he dropped his own blade.

One hand turned her blade aside as his other thrust

down along the far side of her head. He let his weight drop with a sudden crouch as his deflecting hand swung up under her blade arm. His other snaked in and folded around her neck.

Brot'ân'duivé thrust up with both legs, arching his back.

A mute but sharp crack of bone answered his effort.

She went instantly limp with her head wrapped under his right arm. Then came the clatter of her blade upon the street. He waited for three calming breaths.

When he let the body flop to the street, he stood there looking at her. Dispassionately, his gaze traced from her open but blank eyes, with large amber irises, to the barely parted lips and then on to the neck, broken and twisted aside at an unnatural angle.

It had all taken too long and left him wondering why he had let it be so. When he turned away, a sharp pain in his left side halted him.

Brot'ân'duivé brushed aside his cloak.

He stared at blood soaking his tunic around a clean slice in the fabric. It was not that he had been wounded. This had happened more than once in his life, but not in recent memory against only one opponent. In fascination, he looked back at the still body in the street.

She had wounded him. Not severely, but still . . .

A strange sorrow overtook him but not for her death.

Dänvârfij, "Fated Music," lay still with empty eyes staring up at nothing. Like all of his people, when she had come of age, she had gone to sacred ground to face the spirits of their ancestors. By whatever one saw in that place—which was never to be spoken of—a new name was taken.

Brot'ân'duivé heard no music in the street or anywhere in this faraway city. For all the loyalists he had killed, he had felt nothing. They had become the enemy, serving a paranoid madman who endangered the people.

His regret was not that he had killed her. It was the waste of what she might have become. In that silent moment, without even the whistle of a bird in the dark, it was as if her name—her life's truer purpose—would never be fulfilled.

Regret turned to an anger he could not suppress. Perhaps that regret had been there all along, for there was one other thing he had almost left behind. He returned to lean down over her corpse. After removing all her weapons, he searched for one specific object, found it, and held it up.

Smooth and tawny and oval, it had been grown from the very tree in which Most Aged Father had lived for perhaps a thousand years. It was a communication device much like one that Brot'ân'duivé carried for speaking to other factions of dissidents among his people. The ones carried by anmaglâhk on a mission had only to be pressed against the trunk of any tree to speak to Most Aged Father.

This was the last word-wood possessed by Dänvârfij's team. Without it, they were cut off from their tyrant patriarch.

Brot'ân'duivé studied the smooth bit of wood. Instead of destroying it, he slipped it through the bloodied slit, hiding it within his tunic. He retrieved his own stiletto, which he had also forgotten. He had forgotten or overlooked too many things this night.

Before joining Léshil and the others, he had one more stop to make, to retrieve a few things he had purposefully hidden.

He left Dänvârfij's body where it lay.

CHAPTER 8

G hassan grew more concerned as he led Wynn and the escaped prisoners onward, enough that he abandoned following, watching from behind, and stepped out to take the lead. It did not help that the silver-gray wolf eyed him with what he guessed was suspicion.

Once the escape had been uncovered, an alarm had been raised inside the imperial grounds. He fervently hoped the prince remained unconnected to any of this. Ounyal'am was one of the few allies he had left, and the prince was the only one with both political power and the placement to use it. But Ghassan had been shocked at the physical state of Magiere.

He had gone to great lengths to engage potential assistance in hunting Khalidah, but this barbaric, pale-skinned woman could not even walk on her own. Now he feared he had risked too much—including his prince—for too little. Worse still, by now the imperial guards would be searching the city for the escapees, and he had not yet reached the halfway point to his hidden sanctuary.

Everyone with him was out in the open. Though few citizens passed by in the streets this late at night, more would have been better in slowing the search by any guards.

"You two, down there," someone shouted.

Ghassan did not look back. Dwellings along this street were built one against the next. There was nowhere to dash quickly out of sight.

"Ghassan?" Wynn whispered from behind him, still bracing up Magiere.

"We need to find another route," he whispered.

He hurried for the next side street but stopped as two men in gold sashes appeared a block ahead.

"There! Quickly!" one shouted to the other.

Ghassan heard Chap snarl behind him, and then a howl carried from afar as if answering him. He recognized Shade's eerie sound. What was the black majay-hì doing? Her noise would call every other guard within hearing.

He blinked slowly, and in the dark behind his eyelids, lines of light spread, but he never had a chance to finish with his gaze fixed on the first guard.

The man suddenly stumbled and fell hard.

There stood Chane right behind him. The second guard skidded to a stop beside his downed companion and turned. Instead of using his sword, Chane struck with his free hand. His fist cracked against that one's face. As that second man dropped, he kicked the first in the side of the head.

Ghassan had no time for questions as the black majay-hì uttered another howl from somewhere. Chane pivoted sharply toward that sound, and his jaggedly cut hair swished over one glittering eye as he looked toward Ghassan.

"Go!" he rasped. "Now!"

Instead of coming to the group, Chane turned and ran down an alley in the direction of Shade's howling.

Ghassan shook his head. Chane was going after the dog? This was a group of bizarre and unexpected loyalties, but Ghassan did not hesitate and fixed on an alley's mouth halfway up the block.

"Everyone run!"

Chane followed Shade's howl, and it ended abruptly. They had had to split up to further divide and confuse the imperial guards leaving the grounds. Only blind luck brought him to two more of those about to close on Wynn and the others. And now Shade was in trouble.

She would not have howled twice in a row to simply keep any guards from following her.

When her last howl ended, Chane lost his only certain way to track her. He bolted down a side street following the last sound she had made. The street did not run fully in the right direction, so he swerved into a cutway, veered again when he reached a back alley, and raced out across another street to where the alley cut through another block.

He stopped completely.

The alley did not go through; it was a dead end.

Something glinted ahead in its darkness.

Chane's sight widened as he let hunger flood him. Near the alley's blocked end stood two imperial guards with their backs to him. Whatever growled beyond them kept their full attention . . . including a snarl and a clack of teeth.

He could not see beyond those guards, but he knew

Shade's sound was spurred by panic and anger. Both men had curved swords in hand, though one withdrew a step at Shade's warning. Why did she not rush them and break through?

Something more was not right.

The one who backed up snapped something at the other, but Chane's Sumanese was still too poor to catch the words. There were no wolves this far south, and these two might be confused about exactly *what* she was.

Chane crept in along the alley's left wall. As he neared, he spotted something more.

A third guard was trapped in the dead end's left corner, and his right sleeve was shredded and stained dark. His wide, unblinking eyes fixed toward something still blocked from Chane's sight—likely Shade. Those eyes twitched toward a sword on the ground just out of reach.

Shade had hobbled one but had to turn to face the other two. If she charged, the third stood poised to snatch up his sword. And if Chane startled any of them too soon . . .

The third one's eyes looked right at him.

Chane raised his sword, tip up, as he charged.

The nearest of the paired guards began to turn. Chane smashed the sword's hilt into the back of that one's head as the second turned in alarm.

As the first began to topple, Shade charged for the second guard. She stumbled as her right foreleg buckled slightly. The third, wounded guard behind her lunged for his fallen sword, and Chane lost self-control for an instant.

The feral thing inside of him almost cut loose.

He slammed his shoulder into the toppling guard, trying to knock the man into his companion, and he heard Shade snarl and snap. The third one crouched, gripping the hilt of his fallen sword, and without thinking, Chane slashed downward with his own sword.

The tip tore into the third guard's jaw and throat as he tried to rise. His head whipped back and he toppled into the rear wall.

At more snarls, snapping, and a sudden scream, Chane spun before the body hit the ground. On the floor of the alley, Shade was atop the second guard trying to get to his sword arm.

Chane rushed in and kicked the man in the head too hard.

The guard's body spun a hand's length on the alley floor, nearly tumbling Shade before she could hop off. Other than Shade's panting and rumbling, the alley went suddenly silent. All three guards had been put down.

Chane dropped on one knee and reached for Shade.

She twitched her head back with another rumble, and he froze. They stood there staring at each other. She finally swung her head and looked to the guard near the alley's end wall—the one he had slashed.

Chane did not look. He knew the man was dead.

He had sworn to Wynn not to kill, but she had not been here. When Shade's head swung back and she made to step around him for the alley's open end, her foreleg gave a little again.

"Are you injured?" he rasped. "I can carry you."

She huffed "no" twice but slowed in looking back at him. She saw what he had done, though it had been to save her. The injury to her head from more than a moon ago might have weakened her more than anyone realized. She had been injured again, perhaps, though she would not let him check for wounds.

Either that, or she did not want to be coddled anymore, or . . .

She huffed "no" once more, though much softer this time.

"Very well," he answered as quietly. "Let us find Wynn."

Wayfarer struggled as her legs threatened to give way even while leaning upon Chap. She did not know how long she could keep this pace as cutways, alleys, and dimly lit streets blurred by in the night. The few people they passed never said a word, and most only glanced their way. The dusky-skinned man continued to stop and look back to whisper to Wynn at the mouths of various alleys. Wayfarer welcomed these brief respites.

She was lost in a haze as to how any of this had come about or how Wynn could possibly be here. At least Magiere's eyes opened more often as she held on to Léshil and Wynn in their flight. And then Wynn stopped and left Léshil to hold Magiere alone as she went to an alley's mouth.

"We're almost there," she whispered, pointing ahead.

Wayfarer spotted a large building with a center spire rising high above its domed roof. Light within that place flickered behind ornate peaked windows of yellow, green, and violet glass panes.

"We'll be well hidden but easy for the others to find," Wynn continued, hurrying back to help Léshil with Magiere. "One last dash across the street. Everyone ready?"

When no one answered, the Suman man stepped out and something about his face was familiar. Wayfarer could not place him, though she was certain she had seen him before. There was no time to remember as Chap started forward and memory-words rose in her mind.

—Not far now . . . and then I will insist . . . that we rest longer—

That was a little comfort.

She clung to his fur as they hurried into the street, and she saw a narrow path along one side of the shrine between it and a smaller building. A few hard breaths later, she followed Chap down the narrow way behind Wynn. Behind the shrine was an alley with room for all to press up against the long building's back, out of sight. Once there, Léshil and Wynn lowered Magiere down the wall, and Wayfarer collapsed to her knees beside Chap.

"We rest now?" she asked.

—Yes—

Léshil suddenly jerked up his head, looking about. Wayfarer's breath stopped as his right hand went to one of the winged blades strapped on his thighs.

A tall form dropped from above, landing in a crouch.

Wayfarer saw only locks of white-blond hair dangling out of a deep, dark hood. She almost scrabbled over the top of Chap as one thought filled her head: *Anmaglâhk!*

Chap spun up to all fours and swerved around her, snarling.

Léshil pushed off the wall and stumbled as he tried to get in behind the dog.

The tall figure rose up, back-stepped, and held out both hands. "No . . . it . . . me," he whispered in broken Belaskian.

Wayfarer spotted the end of a bow over one of his shoulders and a quiver above the other. She was too shocked to even say his name.

"Osha?" Léshil whispered.

Wayfarer's emotions churned like a storm tearing leaves off trees.

Osha had once been her only comfort in a darkening world. He had cared for her after she had lost everything and everyone she had ever loved. He became her only family . . . until he had left her without a good-bye, without even telling anyone what he would do. The ship he was supposed to meet had carried her and the others southward to this land.

And now he was here.

Osha had *chosen* to remain in Calm Seatt . . . with Wynn.

Wayfarer turned numb inside. Osha's hooded head turned toward her. What must she look like after a moon of suffering and near starvation?

"Leanâlhâm . . . I . . ." he barely breathed.

She had no peace to offer him, if he felt guilty.

"Do not call me that," she whispered. "My name is Wayfarer."

How cold her voice sounded to her own ears. After too many unwanted names, this would be the last that anyone would call her—including him.

"Next time," Léshil grated through his teeth, "don't drop on us like some gangly spider in the dark."

Wayfarer could not see Osha's face or eyes in the dark, and he said nothing more at first. His hood sagged as if he dropped his head in turning a little toward Léshil.

"Sorry," he whispered.

Wayfarer understood Osha enough to know that he was upset . . . and by more than Léshil's annoyed chastisement.

Wynn watched both Osha and Wayfarer, uncertain of what had passed in the few words between them. She knew him well enough to guess that something more than mere guilt—at facing the girl—was troubling him. Wynn was about to squeeze past to go see him when Chap lunged around Osha's side with a loud snarl.

"Quiet," Wynn whispered in alarm. "You'll bring the guards!"

His snarl only settled to a low, throated growl, and Wynn spotted someone coming up the narrow space behind Osha.

Osha barely turned his hooded head, perhaps hearing something, but that was all.

Wynn was panicked enough to call out a warning, but Osha didn't turn, as if he knew who had come. And there was only one person tall enough to peer at everyone over Osha's shoulder.

Leesil pulled a winged blade, though Wynn doubted he had the strength to use it.

"Quiet that dog," Ghassan ordered from behind her.

"Please, Chap," Wynn whispered. "Stop it!"

Chap fell silent, though he remained facing Osha with his hackles bristling.

Wynn took in the sight of Brot'an standing behind Osha. The old shadow-gripper carried a large pack over one shoulder and a travel chest in his hands. In the dark, his ashen blond hair looked gray, though some remaining white-blond would have shown in daylight. She barely made out the four scars skipping across his right eye.

Brot'an's gaze passed over everyone in the alley and came to rest on Leesil and the weapon in his hand.

"Do you intend to use that?" Brot'an asked softly.

"Get out of here," Leesil spat. "You left us to those guards on the docks!"

To Wynn's surprise, Brot'an's brow might have wrinkled in the dark. "Yes . . . and no," he answered.

Wynn struggled forward in the narrow space,

hurrying to get between them. "This is not the time, and we're still missing Shade and Chane!"

At that last name, Leesil turned on her instead of Brot'an, his mouth half open.

Wynn flinched away from Leesil's stare and glanced back. In the alley's back end, Magiere was slumped to the ground with her head hanging where she leaned against the building. Wynn pushed past everyone to the narrow path's front.

Peering around the huge shrine's corner, at first she saw nothing. She grew frantic and even thought to go out and search. In a half-conscious step, she froze.

Down the way they had come, part of a building's dark silhouette appeared to bulge for an instant. That blackness separated and stalked out into the street.

Wynn almost ran out as first Shade and then Chane came toward the shrine, but something was wrong.

Shade was limping.

When she reached the shrine's outer wall, Wynn could no longer keep back. She ducked out, scurrying to Shade, and dropped to her knees in relief. She put her arms around the dog's neck and held on for an instant as Chane closed on both of them.

"It is all right," he said. "We were not followed. Most of the guards out so far are to the west, where Shade drew them."

"What happened?" Wynn asked.

Chane hesitated.

—Not . . . now—

Wynn started at those memory-words.

With her hands still on Shade, she peered at the dog. As she was about to argue or ask about the limp, Shade wormed around her and headed for the path leading to the alley behind the shrine. And still Chane said nothing.

Wynn should have told them—him—how much she valued what they'd done. Instead, she rose up to follow Shade and, turning, found both Brot'an and Leesil watching around the corner. Shade slipped past them behind the shrine, and Wynn thought of Magiere.

It seemed Wynn was forever trapped by the hatred, or worse, that so many here had for one another.

Chap and Leesil wanted Brot'an gone. Leanâlhâm—or Wayfarer, wherever that name had come from—felt abandoned and betrayed by Osha, who in turn had his own reasons for hating the anmaglâhk master. Then there was Chane . . . and Magiere.

Ghassan's little hidden sanctuary, still a ways off, would make everything worse, once they were all packed in there.

The domin stepped out from behind the sanctuary before she could enter.

"There are too many to travel together," he said, looking less than pleased. "I will take the escapees and perhaps Osha by another route. You will follow the planned route with the others. If you arrive before me, use the pebble as I taught you. And this time do not leave again for any reason."

Wynn felt Chane hovering silently behind her. On top of everything else, he didn't care for the domin. She had her own different doubts about Ghassan, but she nodded to him.

"Give us a brief head start," she said.

Én'nish sat in the single chair of their small, shabby room with her small hands clenched upon the side of the chair's seat. It was long past when either Rhysís or Dänvârfij should have returned.

Fréthfâre sat on the bed off to Én'nish's right. The two had never felt the need to fill silence with meaningless words and often passed half a day or night without speaking. This did not mean they were content.

Again Én'nish peered around at the faded gray walls and cobwebs in the high corners. A wave of sadness struck her as she thought of home in the vast an'Cróan forests half a world away. When she closed her eyes, she saw its bright green trees, the deeper greens of the underbrush, all splashed with color from wildflowers, fungi, clear streams, and moss-coated clearings. She imagined the taste of proper grain bread baked in communal ovens and sweet juice from peeled bisselberries fresh off the bush.

Self-indulgent thoughts were not suitable to an anmaglâhk.

Én'nish could not stop herself.

"Too much time has passed," Fréthfâre said, breaking the silence.

Én'nish started from her wandering thoughts. "I know."

The two so different in nature were often left to guess what was happening beyond this room . . . this filthy, dark room that stank of humans. Not long in the past, Én'nish had burned with such rage that she was aware of little beside her own hate. And now . . .

She knew fear but did not understand it. Not fear of death, for no anmaglâhk feared that.

Her wound should have healed—had healed—and yet she still could not fight. Her body no longer functioned with the ease she had once known. What would become of her? She had never desired to be anything other than anmaglâhk. She was not like Fréthfâre, whose counsel and leadership was still valued by Most Aged Father.

Én'nish had always been a tool for her caste.

"What should we do?" she asked.

"If you are able," Fréthfâre answered, "then go. Check in with the others and report back."

Én'nish sat rigid in the chair. Since arriving in this city, she had not been given any task. She had been left to feel useless.

"Yes, I am able to . . ." And she trailed off, suddenly cold without the heat of rage. "What is wrong? Do you have a feeling?"

Fréthfâre was given to dark forebodings that often proved true. "Perhaps," she finally answered.

Én'nish wanted to ask for more, but no words would come.

"Go," Fréthfâre repeated. "But be cautious."

After a blink of hesitation, Én'nish pushed up to slip out the window and climb to the roof. She could still walk and climb, but she could not run far. The speed she once so depended upon in battle had abandoned her.

That filled her with regret and self-loathing. She would have given anything for rage once more. Anger had kept her alive and fueled her with purpose.

Without that, what was she?

Bracing, she leaped to the next rooftop and landed soundly on its edge without wavering. It was not a long jump, but for an instant she reveled in this. Crossing that roof and another and another, she leaped again and again. She tried not to think on Fréthfâre's foreboding, but she had not even reached the imperial grounds when she knew something had gone wrong.

The shouts of men rose from the streets below. She flattened to crawl to the rooftop's edge and peeked down. Five imperial guards in gold sashes appeared to be conducting a roaming search. Two more came running, carrying a blanket between them overburdened with something long and heavy.

It looked like a covered body.

The one at the blanket's front began prattling in Sumanese and was harshly questioned by one among the five. Én'nish spoke so little Sumanese that she could not follow what they were saying. By tone and gesture, the five were more than agitated by what the two related. More shouts rose from the south down the street.

All expressions of those below grew more startled as they turned and ran toward those other voices. Cold grew in Én'nish's core as she followed along the rooftops, growing weary as the guards veered into a side street.

Én'nish turned the rooftop's corner and slowed instantly.

Halfway down the side street below, three more guards stood over a body. Confused arguing erupted once more. From above and across that street, Én'nish had to cover her mouth to keep silent.

Dänvârfij, her mouth slack and eyes staring up at nothing, lay motionless with her head at an unnatural angle.

The guards grew more agitated until one pointed back the way they had come. The two carrying the heavy burden laid the blanket down and opened it.

Én'nish's legs shook and then buckled. She collapsed upon the roof, perhaps making noise, though no one below looked up.

Rhysís lay within the unfolded blanket, a broken arrow protruding from his chest. His face was partially crushed.

Én'nish fought to keep her gasping breaths quiet and began to shake.

She had never known his passing would affect her, even after all he had done for her. In fury, the mourning madness of her people had burned so long since the death of her betrothed at Léshil's hands. Én'nish had never considered what Rhysís had come to mean to her.

She had lost him too.

Dänvârfij was gone as well. There was no one of able body left to fulfill the team's purpose. Brot'ân'duivé had won.

Imperial guards still chattered angrily below, but Én'nish could only curl up on the roof, twitching in choked sobs as she begged her people's ancestors to give back her fury.

It did not come back, and she lay there clawing at the roof tiles with her fingernails. By the time she could breathe and push herself up, the street below was empty. There were no bodies to retrieve, render to ash, and bring home.

The return to the inn took far longer than leaving it.

Once there, in halting words, she told Fréthfâre what she had seen.

The ex-covârleasa listened without reaction until she finally whispered, "Dänvârfij possessed our only remaining word-wood."

"I did not see the soldiers find it or take it, and I could not have—"

"You should have retrieved it at any cost! Without it, we . . . are . . ." Fréthfâre sagged as she succumbed to another fit of coughing.

Én'nish waited for that to subside. "If the traitor killed them, he would have taken or destroyed it. Most Aged Father will know when he does not hear from us by dawn. He will know we failed . . . our purpose. He will know the artifact was not recovered."

Fréthfâre's left eye twitched. "Yes."

"We must return home," Én'nish said. "We must

make the report ourselves." Yes, the journey would be long and difficult, but that was the only path to honor their sworn oaths and their fallen. "I will find us a ship headed north," she went on, "and then in Calm Seatt a caravan headed to the eastern coast, where we will find a ship making the cross to—"

"No."

Én'nish grew fearful in waiting, but Fréthfâre remained silent. Én'nish would never abandon the ex-covârleasa.

"This . . . empire . . . on the edge of sands," Fréthfâre finally began, "spans all the way to the eastern coast. There must be merchants and other caravans that make the journey at any time of year. We will travel directly to the eastern shore . . . and then find a ship."

Én'nish considered this as something else occurred to her. "Once we reach the eastern continent, how will we get home? We have no word-wood to call for one of our people's vessels."

Human ships were not allowed in an'Cróan waters. Only a few smugglers took such risk, and most never returned home.

"There are others of our caste in the Port of Bela," Fréthfâre said. "You would not know this. Few would. You will make contact when we arrive . . . as I direct you."

Én'nish was aware that many of their caste ranged widely, but she had not known that any were permanently stationed among the humans. If nothing else, at least she and Fréthfâre could strive to report to Most Aged Father. And yet, even if they fulfilled that much in their failure, what then lay ahead for her?

Eleven of her caste had departed with a joint purpose,

by far the largest team ever sent out by Most Aged Father. All were trained and skilled, but only a crippled ex-covârleasa and one broken anmaglâhk would return.

It should have been the worst of shame and sadness, but it was not, for Én'nish thought of Rhysís most of all. And in acknowledging him too late, she could not even return his ashes to the ancestors.

"We will try to book passage on a caravan tomorrow," Fréthfâre said. "A new purpose for us will begin."

"As this one ends."

"Yes . . . as this one ends."

Prince Ounyal'am paced his chambers and, even at the mid of night, he would not consider sleep. Exhausted, yes, but he obsessed over what Nazhif and others among his bodyguards had reported.

All in all, events could have gone far worse.

Fareed and Isa had relieved two other members of the private bodyguards, as was commonly done at night, and they now stood post outside the door with Nazhif. They had succeeded in their task for Ghassan's need. It appeared they had not been seen by palace forces, or at least none that had been left alive.

Counselor a'Yamin had discovered the escape and the unconscious Commander Har'ith, and quickly ordered a sweep of the grounds before raising a full alarm.

Neither Nazhif nor his men had learned anything more.

Ounyal'am hoped that the domin had somehow taken charge of the prisoners he wanted. If not, and they were recaptured, there would be questions concerning how they had escaped. There would also be answers obtained by any means necessary. Ounyal'am longed to go seek

further information, but, as was his habit, he was supposed to have retired.

Any questions in the night would only draw suspicion. A'Yamin would hear of it.

As Ounyal'am paced back into and across his sitting
room, a high-pitched shout carried in the corridor outside the main door.

"You will stand aside!"

No one could mistake the venom in the voice of
Counselor a'Yamin.

Ounyal'am, in his nightclothes and dressing gown,
reached the door in long strides and jerked it open.

"What is happening out here?" he demanded.

Nazhif, as well as Fareed and Isa, stood evenly in the
path of the counselor, who was backed by three imperial guards. One look at a'Yamin almost made Ounyal'am falter in relief.

The prisoners had not been recovered.

"The foreigners have escaped," the counselor returned. "Commander Har'ith is injured and a member
of the palace guard is dead." As he spoke, he watched—
no, *studied*—only the prince.

Ounyal'am purposely widened his eyes. "An escape . . .
from beneath the palace grounds? How, and who is at
fault . . . among the guards?"

The counselor hesitated, though he did not react to
the implied accusation. "Whatever happened was carefully planned, as someone was lying in wait for the
commander."

Ounyal'am magnified his tone of disbelief, becoming
incredulous. "Lying in wait . . . in the open passages of
the prison? How would anyone have even learned where
the prisoners were secured? Who would have that information to share? Very few . . . I would hope."

At that, the counselor hesitated again but then quickly turned to his own accusation. "I was told that *you* sent the commander there."

"Yes, at the order of the emperor."

Ounyal'am had not wanted to use that tactic, for the counselor would then know for certain he had been circumvented in his seclusion of the emperor. And indeed, a'Yamin fell silent . . . and turned visibly livid.

"My father demanded a report on the condition of the prisoners."

"The emperor . . . demanded?" the counselor asked softly.

"Yes. Though I too found the request strange—rare—I passed the signed order to Commander Har'ith without question. You may consult my father in the morning, as, at his word, I have instructed his guards that he is not to be awakened tonight."

A'Yamin remained silent rather than challenge a prince over possible lies. This led Ounyal'am to believe that his father must still have some lucid moments—in which he might be able to make demands. If so, a'Yamin would remain in a state of doubt over the source of this current crisis.

"I suggest you return to recovering the prisoners," Ounyal'am said quietly, "before you speak with the emperor again."

His attempt at assuming control was not lost on the counselor, who grew . . . flustered.

"And please keep me apprised," Ounyal'am added.

"Yes, my prince," a'Yamin hissed as he turned away somewhat briskly for his apparent age and was followed by his trio of guards in gold sashes. Twice he glanced back, only to find the imperial prince watching from the doorway. And when he was finally gone from sight . . .

"Sleep well, my prince."

Ounyal'am glanced at Nazhif, who bowed his head and, turning, faltered in his first step. Had a brief smile of pleasure barely appeared on the face of his bodyguards' captain? No, certainly not. Ounyal'am closed the outer door of his chambers and leaned against the wall with a long exhale.

No doubt a'Yamin wondered whether he could reach the emperor this night. All knew the imperial guards—especially those who guarded Kanal'am—were in the counselor's favor. But if the imperial prince had given them orders concerning his father, would the counselor dare to even ask, let alone challenge, such?

Not for this night.

Ghassan had best make good use of what time was left, for what it had cost . . . and what it would cost as yet.

CHAPTER 9

After a further trek through the city, Chap reached their final destination by following the domin—along with Leesil, Magiere, Wayfarer, and Osha. Wynn had gone off another way with Brot'an, Shade, and . . . Chane.

Chap was too exhausted to know what to feel at having seen his estranged daughter again—and far too drained to wonder why Wynn's old Suman mentor was not dressed in a proper sage's robe. Perhaps this semi-numb feeling also lessened his disgust at the shabby state of the tenement, from its bleached wood to its warped door. But he could still be shocked.

After entering the building, heading upstairs, and going to the end of a dingy passage on the top floor, Chap watched as the domin grasped something—nothing—to the left of a window looking out over a dark alley.

The window vanished as a door appeared and its iron lever handle was gripped in the man's hand.

Chap instinctively rumbled and stiffened all the way to his hackles as Wayfarer sucked in and held a breath.

"It is all right," Osha assured in his language. "Follow the domin inside."

Chap growled at having no choice. As he stepped

forward, Wayfarer's small fingers clenched in his fur. They entered a cluttered but well-furnished room apparently unseen from the outside. Worse, straight ahead past a doorless opening on the right was that same window.

He saw the same view of the building across the alley in the dark and disliked it even more than the door suddenly appearing in the passage's end. It seemed that the tenement itself was longer when viewed from within this place.

Scrolls and other texts filled shelves along three walls, while several cold lamps with large brass bases provided a little light from their dimly lit crystals. On the left side of the room was a round table with three high-backed chairs of dark wood. Folding partitions separated another space near the doorless opening. The floor was covered in fringed carpets and various cushions.

Chap advanced cautiously until he peered through the opening on the right and found that it was a bedchamber. A small chest sat on the floor near a bed at the room's far end. In a few more steps, the footboard of a second, nearer bed came into his view. With a glance at Leesil, he huffed once and lifted his muzzle toward that room.

Leesil dragged Magiere in there, and Chap followed while trying to comprehend all that had happened this night. It was difficult to accept that they were finally free while facing so many unanswered questions.

Wayfarer hurried to his side, trying to get behind him.

"Be assured that you are safe and will not be found here," the domin said.

Chap twisted around to see the man hovering in the bedroom's open archway. The domin suddenly backstepped, turned halfway, and looked toward the way they had all come.

"Excuse me a moment," he added and walked off.

Chap was not letting that man out of his sight.

He went to the opening, peeked out, and noticed that the main door looked normal from the inside. The domin grabbed its inner handle, jerked it open, and there was Wynn outside in the dingy passage.

She started slightly with her right hand outstretched as if ready to grab the door's outer handle, but she did not get a chance. Strange, since that handle would not be there to see or touch—unless the domin had instructed her about its secrets. Her other hand was oddly clenched in a fist.

"Inside, quickly," the domin urged.

She did so while tucking her fist into her robe's pocket. When her hand came out, her fingers were open and held nothing.

Chap wondered what she had tucked away in that pocket, and then his daughter, Shade, entered next. He numbed all over for an instant, then saw Shade limping, and inched farther out of the bedchamber. She ignored him and padded off to the main chamber's far front side, vanishing beyond the folding partition.

Wynn hurried after Shade, and the undead came in next.

At the sight of Chane, Chap could not hold in a low snarl, which dragged on as Brot'an entered last. However, Brot'an was still carrying a large familiar pack and travel chest. Leesil had dropped both near the dock on the day of their arrest.

Brot'an must have somehow retrieved them later, after his escape.

Chap felt no gratitude for that, though he was relieved. The chest held irreplaceable items, such as Magiere's own thôrhk and the one for the orb of Fire. It was fortunate that Leesil had dropped his burdens that day. Chap did not want to think of the repercussions should that chest have been captured with them and searched.

At least it was safe now.

As Brot'an stepped farther inside, the old shadow-gripper barely glanced at Chap.

Chap didn't know what he disliked the most—the undead, the aging assassin, or this place.

Chane did not look into those crystalline sky blue eyes watching him from the bedchamber's entrance. The majay-hì would be unable to sense him as an undead due to the "ring of nothing" he nearly always wore. The small circlet of inscribed brass on his left third finger hid everything but the physical presence of whoever wore it.

Had Chane not been wearing it, Chap would most likely have been unable to control his savage reaction to an undead—and the same would be true of Magiere once she regained her strength.

Chane had no intention of taking off the ring. Still, he could not help feeling uncomfortable in the situation, so he followed Wynn to the room's other side. At least in that, Chap's sight line was blocked by the sitting area's partition. The tall elf called Brot'an paused to catch il'Sänke's attention, and the two took to whispering. Chane could have heard them if he let hunger rise to heighten his hearing. Instead, he ignored them.

He already knew who was in the bedroom ... who Chap now guarded. What came next was also expected in part.

As Shade settled beside the table of tall chairs, her right front foreleg gave way a little. Wynn was at the dog's side in an instant, dropping down to feel Shade's leg and shoulder. With one hand still on the dog, she twisted on her knees and looked up at Chane.

"What happened?" she asked, almost accusingly. "You were supposed to stay clear of the guards once you drew them off."

Chane was uncertain what to say after promising her that he would not kill anyone—and after what had happened in the dead-end alley.

Shade snarled once and clacked her teeth.

Wynn shrank away as she jerked her hand back.

There was no knowing what Shade had passed to Wynn in that touch—either a few words or even a memory. Wynn dropped her eyes and hung her head. Chane heard her shuddering quick breaths. Of course, she was worried at the thought of Shade being injured again.

"I'm . . . I'm sorry, Chane," Wynn whispered without looking up. "I didn't mean to . . . It was just . . ."

As she lightly touched Shade, the dog settled her large head on her forepaws with an irritable huff.

Chane waited, for he did not believe the matter was settled.

Wynn had once said that any one of them might be lost in seeking their goal. And yet after Shade's last dire injury, Wynn panicked at the dog's slightest wound. Perhaps Chane envied Shade a little in that, though he as well had reacted in kind once the threat to Shade had been eliminated in that alley.

Strangely, Wynn said nothing more, whether or not Shade had told or showed her what had happened.

"Enough," il'Sänke warned, clunking down a large brass bowl upon the table. "Keep your personal issues to yourselves. We must get the others fed and tended."

Wynn nodded and rose, but something more puzzled

Chane as he looked away from her. Osha stood off near that unnerving front door, his expression flat and his unblinking eyes fixed on the floor. Why he had not gone to see the others in the bedroom was puzzling.

Il'Sänke slapped a pile of folded cloths into Osha's stomach, and the elf's eyes popped open as he grabbed the pile in reflex.

"Make yourself useful," the domin ordered. "Take these and go with Wynn. Wynn, you get the bowl and that water pitcher to clean any wounds. Use bed cloths for toweling as needed and report any injuries that require medicinal care."

With a nod, Wynn hurried for the brass bowl on the table.

Chane peered toward the partition. He could imagine Chap standing beyond it, still on guard at the bedchamber's entrance. When Chane turned back, Shade was watching him, but he could not read her expression, so he closed his eyes once in a brief nod to her. That was as much thanks as he could risk in the moment, and she slowly closed her eyes to rest.

Aside from the so-called dhampir, whom he had helped rescue, he was in the company of two majay-hì, natural enemies of the undead. Even more bizarre, one wanted him dead for a final time, while the other had shielded a secret from Wynn—and done so for his sake.

Chane's world grew more complicated with each night because of the woman he loved.

Chap still stood at the bedchamber's entrance, though from his vantage point the only one he could see was Osha. That young one's surface thoughts were filled with something chilling: an arrow in the dark from his bow had killed one of his own.

Chap and those with him had known since first meeting Osha that he was ill suited to the calling of an anmaglâhk. That the young one had fallen from—been forced from—his calling did not change this.

Now Osha had killed for Wynn's sake.

Chap would have wished it otherwise for the once innocent young an'Cróan. All of them except for Wayfarer had committed questionable acts. The necessity of those acts would never lessen their burden.

Wynn broke his thoughts as she came around the partition with a large brass bowl under one arm and a matching, sloshing water pitcher in the other. Before he could speak with her in the way that only they could, she pushed past him into the chamber. Osha followed her, and Chap spun around into the room.

Leesil knelt beside the first bed, where he had laid out Magiere, and covered her with bedding. Wayfarer stood near him, watching only Magiere. When Leesil looked up at Wynn's approach, his gaze quickly shifted past Chap and Osha to the bedchamber's entrance. And his features twisted in a glare, as if he might rush out at someone in the outer room.

"Don't start," Wynn warned. "Everything else waits until we get the four of you fed and tended. Then you need rest, not another fight . . . or argument."

Leesil neither answered nor looked at her again. He turned back to watching his wife, who lay on her side with her eyes almost closed.

Chap understood Wynn, though if Magiere were well enough, the young sage might not have gotten her way so easily. Chane's presence could not simply be ignored.

As Wynn settled on the bedside, and Osha brought her the pile of folded cloths, Chap glanced again at Magiere but then dropped his gaze.

He was supposed to watch over and protect all of them, including Wayfarer.

From the instant they had stepped onto the docks of this city, he had failed. And Brot'an had vanished and remained free. Chane was not the only one who Chap wanted gone—or dead. As to secrets that might have been ripped out of Magiere in a moon's worth of screams, he already knew one she did not have.

Chap had insisted on hiding two orbs without Magiere or Leesil knowing where. What only he knew could never be taken from them, but this was not enough. Something had been taken from Magiere.

When that gray-robed figure had come to the cell, the darkness within its hood had turned toward Chap. It remained fixed on him for too long, as if that one had known him long before that visit. Whatever it might have related to Leesil in that cell, Chap knew by his friend's last question what the robed figure had come for.

How did he do that . . . get in my head like . . . like you?

No, not like him, but there was no doubt that Magiere had suffered worse in being subjected to sorcery. On the rushed walk from the shrine, he had seen snippets of recent memories in her half-conscious mind. He knew some of what she had endured in that cell. Somewhere in her memories was what he had done—hidden two orbs—if not how and where he had done so.

The robed figure could not have taken such information from him. A Fay-born in the body of a Fay-descended majay-hì was not easily overcome, but . . .

How long had it taken that robed figure to learn from Magiere that he knew the whereabouts of two orbs? How long had she been tortured simply to get at him before the torturer came to silently taunt him, face-to-face? And in an act that only Chap knew of, he had done far worse than Osha.

The guide Leesil had hired to take Chap into the wilderness had been left a mindless husk. Without hands of his own, Chap had possessed the man's body with his own spirit—that of a Fay—in order to handle and hide two orbs.

And there was another orb here in this room, in a chest.

He *knew*, for Wynn could not help letting that slip into her thoughts.

Yes, they had all done terrible things, some worse than killing and some worse than what he had done to that innocent guide. In the moon of Magiere's screams, he had done worse in doing nothing.

He would have let her die rather than reveal the location of any orb.

Chap's sins had grown until he now shrank from weighing them as a whole, and this was no time to do so. Someone else in this place was linked to everything since that day on the docks. When he, Magiere, Leesil, and Wayfarer had been mysteriously released, he had recognized the stranger with Wynn.

When Chap and his companions had been brought to judgment, the one called Domin Ghassan il'Sänke had been present in the high glass-dome chamber. And in the streets this night, Chap had been unable to dip a single surfacing memory in that man.

It was as if this domin, no longer dressed as a sage, was not truly present . . . just like Chane . . . just like the gray-robed figure who had come to their prison cell.

* * *

By the time Wynn finished with Magiere and had tended Leesil, Chap, and Leanâlhâm—no, Wayfarer—they were all too exhausted to eat much. She had to stop Wayfarer from drinking too much water and making herself ill. Osha helped settle them in the two beds, but Wayfarer panicked at being left to sleep alone in the second bed. Chap jumped up and settled beside the girl, and Wynn dropped on the floor at the foot of Magiere and Leesil's bed. Osha stood by the room's entrance, facing outward.

It wasn't long before Wayfarer drifted off. In the silence, Wynn realized that since her arrival at the sanctuary Osha hadn't said a word to anyone, at least as far as she'd heard. He hadn't even looked at her unless he had to, and she wanted to ask . . .

Leave him alone.

Wynn looked over at Chap lying on the second bed's edge with Wayfarer fast asleep behind him. Before she could speak . . .

No . . . not until he wishes to speak of it, if he does.

That was even less help, and what was . . . *it?* She grew more worried as she peered at Osha.

There were other important things to discuss, though not in here, so she got up as quietly as possible, but not quietly enough. Osha glanced over his shoulder at her.

His long face lacked any expression, and that troubled her even more. With a quick wave to Chap, Wynn slipped out of the bedchamber, and both Chap and Osha followed. Rounding the partition, she found Ghassan at the table speaking in a low voice to Brot'an. Chane was listening to them from nearby.

There was too much here that Wynn didn't know, from whatever numbed Osha to the core to what had happened to Shade while she and Chane led the guards on a wild chase. Wynn stepped in beside the table and, without greeting Brot'an, faced Ghassan.

"How long will the imperial guards keep searching for us?"

The domin settled back in his chair. "It will escalate, as your companions drew intense interest. At the moment, this does not matter, for while we are in here we are beyond finding."

"Guards not only hunt us."

At Osha's sudden broken Numanese, Wynn swiveled enough to spot him standing beside the folding partition. Before she asked what he meant, his gaze shifted away from her, and his expression filled with anger.

Wynn followed that gaze to the back of Brot'an's chair.

Osha fought a wince as Wynn looked back at him, but he remained focused on that closest chair. It was hard to remain still while so smothered in his self-loathing and loathing for the greimasg'äh.

"What?" Wynn asked quietly.

Osha slipped into his own tongue. "Ask *him*," he rasped, sounding almost like Chane.

Wynn turned toward that nearest chair, but before she could ask anything . . .

"The loyalists followed Magiere," Brot'ân'duivé answered without leaning out into Osha's sight.

Osha looked to Wynn and saw anxiety beneath her calm olive-toned expression.

"So the anmaglâhk really are here in the capital?" she finally asked.

"What is this about?" Ghassan cut in.

It was too much for Osha, and he was not relieved

when Brot'ân'duivé explained. After that, Ghassan turned on Wynn.

"You omitted telling me that your friends are hunted by assassins," he accused. "It makes sense now, but you have no concept of the risks taken tonight by others who—"

"I did tell you!" Wynn interrupted. "That first night you brought us here. Or at least I wondered . . . after you told us you'd seen two people at the palace who looked like Osha. These loyalists—that team of assassins—should have been left behind up north."

"More happened along the way," Brot'ân'duivé said. "But the loyalists may no longer be a concern. I eliminated Dänvârfij this night."

"And what or who is that?" Ghassan demanded.

Osha's stomach clenched as the greimasg'äh explained dispassionately. Osha had not known Dänvârfij well, but even as less than friends they had been connected by death and loss in their lives.

"Fréthfâre is a cripple," Brot'ân'duivé continued, "and Léshil severely wounded Én'nish. Rhysís is the only able one left among the three, and he will have to tend to the other two."

That last name struck Osha hard; it gave him a face out of memory for the one he had murdered.

"Two . . . not three," he whispered.

Wynn's attention turned to him, as did the domin's. Even the greimasg'äh leaned out around the back of his chair, but it was Chane's reaction that fixed Osha for an instant.

The undead straightened with narrowed eyes. He glanced once at Wynn. When he looked back again to Osha, he slowly nodded.

That Chane guessed and approved of what Osha had

done did not help. When Osha looked away, his gaze met that of the greimasg'äh. He felt the sudden urge to add more scars to that old face, if he could.

"We are waiting for the rest," Brot'ân'duivé said.

Osha kept to his own tongue rather than struggle with another in relating the least of what had happened . . . and why it had happened. Wynn watched him as the greimasg'äh translated for the others, and she looked at him with something between sadness and sympathy. Perhaps she knew how sick he felt inside.

However, Osha expected at least the greimasg'äh to question him.

Brot'ân'duivé turned out of sight, settling to face the domin's puzzled frown. "Then only two remain, and they are ineffectual, thus removing any concern."

Osha hoped Wynn saw what else this meant.

If loyalists were no longer a threat to Magiere, Léshil, and Chap, then the greimasg'äh's presence was pointless. Osha bore enough guilt and regret over having left Leanâlhâm in that traitor's care, though the others had watched over her.

Ridding themselves of Brot'ân'duivé might amend that, if not the taint of what Osha had done this night.

"Wynn . . ." Brot'ân'duivé said slowly. "You remained in Calm Seatt to seek another orb. So ultimate success or failure are the only reasons for you to have come here."

Wynn froze at the sudden change of topic, and silence hung for too long. Chane inched a little toward her slightly, shaking his head. Osha knew that warning was pointless.

The greimasg'äh had not asked a question, so he had already guessed the truth.

"Yes, we found another orb," Wynn answered.

*   *   *

Brot'ân'duivé betrayed no emotion at all; Wynn's answer was half of the reasoned assumptions he had already calculated. There was another orb within this place rather than hidden away like all the others, and by count, a final one was yet to be found. He half listened as she summarized the finding of the orb of Spirit.

She finished, "We have it with us in—"

"Shut up, Wynn!"

At Léshil's command from somewhere off behind Osha, Wynn twisted to face that direction. What she would have said or not mattered little to Brot'ân'duivé.

The orb was here.

What mattered more was that whoever took possession of it might partly control the acquisition and use of the other three and the finding of the fifth. That was the true point to consider, and Léshil had grown cunning enough to know this.

Brot'ân'duivé ignored the predictable argument that ensued somewhere behind his chair. It would break the moment Wynn countered Léshil with her own needs and plans. Brot'ân'duivé had grown concerned that this group was now too large, but other factors now weighed against changing this.

He required only Léshil, though to keep the half-blood compliant might require Magiere as well. Then there was Chap, the only one present who knew the resting place of two other orbs. Guiding and controlling Léshil was the way to coerce the majay-hì. And for the fourth orb hidden with the dwarves in their underworld, Brot'ân'duivé needed to reinforce Wynn's trust.

"Leesil, lower your voice!" Wynn finally broke in.

"There's no point arguing over who has what and where. Not until we know why all of you were imprisoned."

Ghassan listened as Leesil, whose name the two elves pronounced strangely, grudgingly recounted being captured. The half-breed and the other prisoners had been dragged to the domed audience chamber before Prince Ounyal'am.

They had been more fortunate than they knew, for Ghassan had been present as well.

In that chamber, they had been accused of mass murder. He now reasoned that the assassins who had done the actual killing, disguised as two shé'ith, had been present as the prisoners' accusers. Most of these details, including some that no one else knew, were of little use at present to Ghassan.

"A few sages were there and one of them panicked at seeing us," Leesil added. "There was also an aging man, dressed in the same colors as the guards, who told the prince to have us locked up."

"That would be Counselor a'Yamin," Ghassan added bitterly. "The sage in gray was High Premin Aweli-Jama."

Wynn's attention shifted to him. "Your high premin was there?"

Ghassan nodded curtly. "But not *my* high premin anymore."

"No trial and not much talk after that," Leesil finished. "We were dragged away and locked up until tonight."

Wynn hesitated and then, "Why is Magiere . . . worse off than the rest of you?"

Ghassan wanted to hear this as well, but the half-breed fell silent and hung his head. The condition of the "dhampir" was a grave concern. The only reason for this night's risks was to gain control over someone who could track an undead.

Wynn blinked rapidly and looked away . . . and downward. Ghassan traced her gaze to the huge gray dog who had followed her out of the bedchamber. When Wynn cringed, clenched her jaw, and then shuddered, Ghassan eyed the one called Chap.

He knew that Wynn had some hidden way to communicate with Shade. At a guess, and by the way Wynn locked gazes with the gray one, the same held true between them. So what had Chap passed to Wynn just then?

"Only by her screams," Leesil whispered as if in answer to a different question than the one Wynn had asked. "That was all I had to know she was still alive . . . for so many days and nights."

Ghassan grew anxious still watching the gray majayhì. It took little effort to quickly raise glyphs, signs, and sigils in his mind's eye. Try as he might, he could not catch a single thought in the dog's mind. When he turned that incantation upon Wynn, she had no true memories to glimpse concerning what Chap might have related. And the last one Ghassan focused upon . . .

Leesil's mind was overwhelmed with one vivid moment.

A figure in a gray robe that scintillated softly with signs, symbols, and sigils filled Ghassan's awareness. That someone had found the dhampir to seek information from her—and her alone. By what had been said or implied, prolonged interrogation in only thought had another purpose beyond gaining that information.

She and her torment could be used as a way to force something out of one of the others.

Before Ghassan could attempt to read more, Wynn stepped up to the table's edge and fixed on him.

"What are you up to?" she asked.

For that instant, she startled him.

"Who helped you get them out?" she went on. "You start answering or—"

"Or what?" he shot back, for his patience had thinned.

When she stalled, he quickly raised another set of symbols and shapes in his mind's eye. As he fixed those onto her surface thoughts, Chane stepped in behind her and dropped a hand on her shoulder.

Wynn's mental presence vanished from Ghassan's awareness, and every sigil and sign he had raised vanished amid his shock.

Chane's other hand settled on the hilt of one sheathed sword. Wynn did not even glance away, as if this were all something familiar to her.

"What in seven hells is going on?" Leesil demanded.

When he tried to step in, Osha raised an arm to block him and nodded to Wynn. The black majay-hì struggled up, shifted away from the table, and stood near Chane, watching.

"Chap?" Leesil asked. "Wynn?"

Ghassan watched her, and she kept her eyes on him as she waved off the half-blood.

"Answer me!" she demanded. "What do you know about the one who tortured Magiere? Chap says it was somehow done without touching her."

The last part was the most telling. None of them greatly concerned him, though he needed to regain control and steer their focus. Only the elder elf concerned him. That one faced him across the table, apparently relaxed but unblinking with his hands in his lap and hidden from sight.

"Ghassan?" Wynn asked.

Perhaps he should have told her sooner. She might

have been useful here and now, but nothing could be done about it. Keeping an academic tone, he looked her straight in the eyes.

"Do you recall me telling you that my sect had been guarding a prisoner?"

"Yes."

How should he do this—slowly in hints or quickly for shock? "This prisoner has no corporeal body but vast arcane knowledge. It . . . *He* survives by entering and taking control of the living. The closest word for it in your language might be a . . . 'specter.'"

No one reacted or said anything at first.

"How long have you known this?" Chane asked.

Again, the answer required more information than Ghassan wished to share. Perhaps the overprotective vampire would be a better foil than Wynn, but Ghassan continued to address her directly.

"My sect held him imprisoned for many, many years. Khalidah once served what you call the Ancient Enemy as the leader of a trio known in records as the Sâ'ymin-fiäl . . . the Masters of Frenzy. Others such as the dwarves of ancient times called them the Eaters of Silence."

All of Wynn's ire faded from her oval face as her mouth fell open. Obviously part of what he related was familiar to her; he knew this and used it. She had uncovered much in her blundering and stubbornness, including those infamous texts she brought back from across the world, which had been seized by her own guild branch.

"Your sect had this *thing* imprisoned?" she finally got out. "Now it's loose . . . and you didn't tell us? It will be hunting *you*, anyone with you, and—"

"You were never in danger while with me," Ghassan interrupted. "And Khalidah now has more desirable prey." His impatience and frustration took hold. "The arrival of your foolish friends, and their own ignorance, drew the specter to where it most wanted to be: the imperial grounds. Any safeguards that I and mine placed there may no longer be enough!"

The gray majay-hì rumbled and looked up, and Leesil immediately lowered his eyes to meet its gaze. Chap's head then swiveled toward Wynn, and she looked to him as well.

Ghassan was at a loss for what any of this meant as Wynn turned back to him.

"How?" she asked. "Chap wants to know *how* you could have protected us."

Ghassan blinked at this phrasing as well as her point of focus. Behind her, the undead's gaze shifted between the others, one by one. Worse still, the elder elf had neither spoken nor moved, and Ghassan could not help a quick glance at Brot'an.

He realized his mistake too late as someone gripped the back of his hair.

"What are you doing?" Wynn shouted.

Ghassan's head wrenched back harder than he thought possible—and then forward and down. His forehead struck the tabletop, and everything blackened before his eyes.

"Chane, stop!" Wynn cried.

Ghassan barely kept his feet as he was ripped out of the chair and whipped in an arch. Snarls erupted from both dogs amid shouts from others. Before he could place any voice, he crashed face-first into a bookcase. His cheekbone struck a shelf, stunning him again, and the grip on his hair shifted quickly to his neck as texts tumbled over his head.

Something pointed, cold, and hard settled at the back of his neck.

"Do not move," Chane hissed, "or look at anyone . . . or I will ram this blade into your skull!"

* * *

Wynn turned frantic amid the chaos. She was about to rush at Chane when Leesil grabbed her arm, Shade ducked in her way, and Chap lunged around her.

"What is that *thing* doing?" Leesil snarled.

No doubt he was referring to Chane, and he'd already pulled the one winged blade still strapped on his thigh. Brot'an was on his feet, and then Chane's voice pulled her attention.

"So this undead, Khalidah, is inside whoever interrogated Magiere. How?"

Chane had his older, shorter blade's tip pressed against Ghassan's neck, but the domin didn't answer him.

"Chane, that's enough," Wynn admonished. "Back away and—"

Be silent and let him finish!

Wynn shuddered and dropped her gaze, though Chap had already turned his head back to Chane and Ghassan. She choked back her anger and sense of betrayal.

Even though Leesil had drawn a weapon, neither he nor Chap had attempted to stop Chane. And they hated him so much that either would have used any excuse to go at him.

What was happening here?

Listen to him . . . carefully.

Again she looked down to find Chap's eyes on her, and when she looked up again . . .

"Wynn, think," Chane rasped, eyeing the back of Ghassan's neck. "All of those years, he and his sect kept this spirit trapped—but how? They would have had to study it, what it could do, and how it could push into another's mind. And he claims he can protect us . . . so *how*?"

Chane glanced back when she didn't answer immediately. Even worse, Wynn simultaneously heard Chap's voice in her head echo Chane's words in her ears.

"Through *sorcery*!"

And still Wynn couldn't speak.

Leesil, and Magiere, and even Chap had each suffered a horrifying encounter with an undead sorcerer called Vordana. A long while back in Magiere's homeland, that undead had trapped each of them in their own phantasm, where they'd lived out their worst fears. Now both Chap and Chane, regardless of their hate for each other, had reached the same conclusion about Ghassan il'Sänke.

Before Wynn could think what to say . . .

"What is . . . sorcery?" Osha asked somewhere behind her.

Brot'an likely knew a correct translation in their language, but she wasn't giving him a chance to complicate matters or take control. She knew only one similar word in their tongue.

"Tôlealhân."

It meant *will-craft*.

Wynn heard Osha shift suddenly—along with the slide of something on cloth or leather. She didn't dare take her eyes off anyone in front of her, and Shade, who hadn't moved or said anything, still stood in front of her facing away.

Someone grabbed the back of her robe and jerked on it.

Wynn stumbled in retreat as Osha jerked on her again. Before she righted herself, he drew an arrow, fit it to the bowstring, and aimed it at Ghassan, though most of the domin was still blocked by Chane. That arrow had a white metal tip.

"Osha," Chane rasped, "if he gets away from me—"

"He dead!" Osha answered.

Any uncertainty or shame Wynn had seen in Osha's face was gone, and again he acted to defend her, along with Chane, with deadly intent. Even if she could stop one of them, she would never stop the other. And after all of this, Brot'an just stood there watching, which worried her more than anything else.

"Enough!" Ghassan shouted, still pinned to the shelves. "If I wished to act against you, then why endanger myself and others who helped free three hunters of the undead? And why again if I could get to the dhampir on my own . . . without any of you?"

Wynn shook her head in confusion. "You broke them out to help you hunt this specter?"

"Magiere isn't hunting anything!" Leesil cut in.

"And why did you come here?" Ghassan snapped back. "Think of the order of events. Wynn told me that Magiere came seeking the orb of Air, and yet your spouse and you were imprisoned. She faced someone with the skill to extract her secrets. One with such power would not need a host of any great importance to infiltrate the imperial grounds. But if need be, he will take such a host. And then do you think any of you will be free to seek another orb?"

Once again the room fell silent, and Wynn began to piece things together.

Whoever had helped Ghassan from inside the imperial grounds would have access to or control over prisoners. It might even be the one who had sentenced them, and yet the crime they were accused of should have led to execution in this land.

Just how high did the fallen domin's connections reach within the imperial grounds?

And should the specter seize someone with that much authority . . .

Wynn tried quickly to absorb all of this. She had been a naive fool again in not seeing the worst possibilities. Still, if what Chane claimed about the domin was even half true, Ghassan was as dangerous as Vordana or worse.

She believed he'd helped her friends because of their own friendship, yet he had gotten in her way more than once in their days at her guild branch. He had made the sun-crystal staff that had saved her several times since then, but he had also followed her in secret into a lost dwarven stronghold. He tried to beat her to the orb now hidden in the dwarven underworld. And he had provided this sanctuary that no one else could find.

Wynn's skin began to crawl as she looked about this place that was hidden to all senses. No, not hidden, but rather it somehow got into the minds of those who came near it and blocked itself from their awareness, even by touch.

"Don't listen to him," Leesil whispered.

That frightened her as well. It was bad enough that Chane and Chap of all people were in agreement here. Then there was Osha, who could take deadly action by merely relaxing his fingers on his bowstring.

"Nothing can be done tonight."

Brot'an's sudden words almost doubled Wynn's fright.

"Regardless of what action we follow next," he stated flatly, staring at Ghassan, "it must wait until Magiere is well. Discussion must be paused, and *he* is not to be left alone. Two at least must watch him at all times."

She looked away in time to see all the pale color drain from Chane's irises. She had to do something fast.

Wynn slammed her shoulder into Osha's side. As his bow veered and his big amber eyes widened in shock, she grabbed his drawn arrow with both hands and pulled it down with her weight.

"Chane, step away—now!" she ordered.

"Léshil? What is hap—?" And a gasp followed this, pulling Wynn's attention.

Wayfarer stood peeking around the partition's edge at everyone.

Even for her weakened state, the girl paled all the more at what she saw. The noise must have awakened her, as it likely had Leesil, and Wynn thought of Magiere also resting in that other room.

"Oh, damnation!" Wynn whispered, and then, "Leesil, get her back in the other room." When he turned on her, she cut him off. "Do it— Chap, you too. Neither of you understand all that's at stake. I'll explain soon. Now . . . just go!"

Leesil still hesitated. He looked so worn and pale, even for his tanned complexion, that only anger and fear probably kept him on his feet. He finally turned away and shooed Wayfarer off around the partition. When Wynn turned back, she was caught by Chap's glare.

I will be waiting.

Wynn cringed but nodded, and as Chap went off around the partition, she looked to Chane, who still held Ghassan at sword point.

"Back away," she said.

He was a minor conjurer, self-taught in his living days, as well as anything else. Perhaps something in that had clued him in more quickly than anyone else. She should have listened to him sooner, but it didn't matter now.

"Chane, please," she added.

His jaw muscle clenched, but he stepped back. The tip of his sword was the last thing to withdraw out of the domin's reach.

Ghassan turned slowly around, poised and composed, as if nothing had happened.

"I suggest you all get some rest," he said.

With the rise of one dark eyebrow and a slight tilt of his head, he nodded once to her. Even that was not going to settle the worst of this as exhaustion took Wynn, but he was not wrong about most of them needing rest.

Eventually, and hopefully soon, Magiere would recover.

CHAPTER 10

The next morning, Leesil opened his eyes to dim light. Lifting his head from where he lay on a bed beside Magiere, he looked out toward the main room and saw muted sunlight spilling across floor cushions outside the bedchamber's entrance. After a moon in that black cell with only a candle, even that much light hurt his eyes. Squinting, he rolled his head to the side and faced a mass of black hair.

Magiere still slept with her back pressed against his chest beneath the light blanket over both of them. She was so quiet, like the long silences between screams when he hadn't known where she was.

He almost pressed his face into the back of her neck to be certain she was really there. And then everything from the previous night came back.

Leesil remembered being roused by loud voices in the outer room. He'd wanted to go and quiet everyone before they woke Magiere or Wayfarer. As he'd rolled carefully out of bed, one oddity caught his eye.

Chap was gone from Wayfarer's bed.

He'd rushed out to find everyone else arguing, and not long after that, everything had come apart. Later, once he'd put Wayfarer back in bed, Chap had sat on the floor between both beds and stared at the doorless entrance until Wynn finally came.

At least she'd been smart enough to come alone, though upon entering she'd flinched again when she looked at Chap. Whatever he'd said in her head must not have been kind or even grateful. Yes, Wynn and hers had gotten her friends out of prison, but what had she dragged all of them into?

Leesil had heard too much in that outer room amid the squabble and near bloodshed, and Osha had sided with that undead. By the time Wynn finished explaining all that had happened since her arrival in the city, Leesil had been even wearier than when he'd dragged Magiere into this place.

And now he didn't want to think about any of it anymore.

Peeling the blanket aside, he forced himself up again, but then he sat on the bedside and hung his head, uncertain what to do.

"Are we still here and . . . not *there*?"

Those weak words in the room's half-light wiped away all recollection as Leesil raised his head. Wayfarer and Chap were still sound asleep in the other bed, and he quickly turned the other way.

There was Magiere with her head upon the pillow. She'd rolled partway to look up at him through half-opened eyes. By her expression, she didn't know how he could be there at all. Part of him felt that same doubt, and he pressed his lips to her forehead. When he sat back up, her pale face was still confused.

"Yes, we're here . . . not in the prison," he assured quietly.

He was still weak, and more so with relief, at the

sight of her beside him, of being able to hold her, touch her, protect her. Until she regained her strength, that was all that mattered.

"Rest," he told her. "I'll see what's around for you to eat when you wake up again."

Magiere latched a hand on his forearm so tightly that it hurt. He didn't pull free of the pain. It was a relief she had even that much strength.

"I'll be quick," he whispered, "and Chap and Wayfarer are right over there."

When he cocked his head toward the room's far side, she rolled hers and saw the girl and the dog asleep on the other bed. Her grip slackened, but he still had to peel off her fingers and gently tuck her arm under the blanket.

"Go back to sleep," he urged.

He waited until Magiere closed her eyes before he got up. As soon as he stepped out, he saw several changes.

On the sitting area's nearside, someone was sleeping atop arranged floor cushions and stirred beneath a blanket. It was the one Wynn called "Ghassan," the one everyone had turned on the night before. The partition was gone, folded up and leaning against the wall near the window. That gave him a clear line of sight to the entire room, though more likely it allowed the others to keep an eye on the domin.

Leesil headed around the sitting area, and there was Osha standing with his back to the front door.

Osha had his bow gripped in one hand even with his arms folded. His horselike face twitched around those big amber eyes of his. He bowed his head once, and Leesil nodded back.

Likely, Osha felt guilty over having left Wayfarer for Wynn. Good, he should, and Leesil wasn't certain the girl should forgive him. When he turned toward the table, he paused.

In the far corner along the front wall sat Brot'an on the floor with his long legs folded and hands cupped together in his lap. Though his eyes were closed, his head was upright, as if anyone could sleep that way. And there was Wynn, sitting in the table's far chair as she stared at a small smoked-glass cup encircled in her hands. The chair's tall back made her look that much shorter.

The one person Leesil didn't spot was Chane. He didn't have time to really look, for Wynn raised her tired eyes, looking almost as worn as he felt.

"Did you sleep?" she asked.

He went over and dropped in the chair opposite her. "Some . . . so now what?"

Wynn took a long, slow breath. "Magiere needs better food than what we have here, perhaps some warm broth or stew—you all do."

So that was how it was? They'd just pretend last night never happened? But he agreed and was eager to do something—anything—after being so useless and helpless over the last moon. He knew no one should leave this strange hidden sanctuary unless necessary, but finding proper food for Magiere certainly qualified for that.

"I'll put on a cloak and find a market," he said.

"You will not."

Brot'an's voice didn't startle Leesil at all, and he countered, "Don't fake concern about us after what you—"

"The imperial guards are searching for you," the aging assassin cut in, and his eyes opened slowly, one always caged in those four scars. "If you are recaptured, you place all of us at risk."

Leesil leaned forward in his chair, about to get up.

"He's right," Wynn agreed. "Even cloaked, you

could be spotted, arrested, and worse. I'm the smallest, and I've already been to the market without mishap. I'm less noticeable than you, and the imperial guards don't know I exist."

Leesil bit down a retort.

"Very well," someone else said. "But be quick, keep your hood forward, and look at no one."

Leesil half turned in his chair as Ghassan il'Sänke ambled toward the table. The domin showed no sign that he felt watched, though Osha had unfolded his arms, his bow held at the ready. And as Leesil turned back around . . .

"Yes," Wynn answered shortly without looking at the domin.

Leesil felt pushed aside and didn't like it. "Take Shade," he instructed.

Wynn glanced aside and down.

He then realized that he also hadn't seen Shade. Likely Chap's daughter was below the table at Wynn's feet.

Wynn looked up and shook her head at him. "No, a black wolf would draw attention, and we even used that once as a distraction."

He'd known Wynn for years, and though she might be right, he could tell when she was lying. Well, at least in part. So what other reason did she have for leaving Shade behind?

— *Chane* —

At that memory-word in Leesil's head, Chap appeared beside his chair. Then Leesil remembered the way Shade had acted concerning Chane the night before. Wynn worried for that monster's safety, and this left a bitter taste in Leesil's mouth.

"Oh, seven hells," he said. "Take Shade, and no one will touch Chane . . . unless he asks for it."

Wynn winced at his tone. Once, that might have been all, but she fixed him with a sharp glance. He didn't care.

"She is correct," Brot'an put in. "A black wolf will call attention . . . and I assume by Shade's condition upon returning last night that this may already be the case."

"I won't be long," Wynn said. "I know the way."

She dropped to one knee and whispered something below the table, likely to Shade. With a guttural whine, the black majay-hì rose into sight and padded off toward the back corner on the opposite side of the sitting area and bedchamber's entrance.

Wynn looked to Osha. "You'll . . . help her?"

Osha nodded once as Wynn donned her cloak and went to leave, and Leesil's eyes followed her to the door. He then turned to where Shade had gone. A long bulk under a blanket lay in the back corner of the main room, and Leesil knew what it was.

Chane—completely covered and dormant.

He heard the front door shut, rose up out of the chair, and turned, but Wynn was gone. He didn't even wonder how she was going to find the door again from the outside to get back into this place. He just studied Osha . . . who had promised to help Shade.

A full-blooded an'Cróan elf and a majay-hì both protecting a dormant undead.

The world had gone mad.

Osha watched Wynn leave. When his head turned back, the disgust on Léshil's face made him look away again. In principle, he agreed with Léshil. But here and now, Wynn and Shade were correct.

They needed Chane—needed everyone—for what

would come. The unwanted vampire had more than proven that the night before.

Osha breathed deeply to gain some calm, but silent tension choked the room more than the stale air or the stench of this human city. Without Wynn present, no one had anything to say to anyone.

Léshil began pushing things around on a shelf behind the table, and the domin went to assist him. With a small water bottle in hand, Léshil grabbed Wynn's cup off the table, downed what was in it, and headed for the bedchamber. The domin frowned as he watched Léshil, but Osha lost his focus in attempting to watch as well.

Leanâlhâm—Wayfarer had not spoken to him since the night before. Thankfully, she was likely still asleep. He deserved whatever anger and blame she might throw at him, but he was not certain he could bear it right now. With no desire to share company with Brot'ân'duivé, but needing to keep an eye on the domin, Osha slipped around the table and headed for the dim back corner.

Shade lay on the floor facing toward the table. Behind her, and covered completely with a blanket, Chane lay as still as a draped corpse.

Osha had seen this many times but had never grown accustomed to the sight. Shade lifted her head and whined, and he looked down. She must have felt the tension as well, as she rarely paid him much attention.

The dog hated being separated from Wynn, even for a short time, but more recently had often assisted Chane. And, strangely, she ignored her father.

Osha had wondered about this but had not asked. He was uncertain whom to ask. Soft footsteps behind him made him turn.

Leanâlhâm—Wayfarer—stood watching him from near the bedchamber's entrance.

Osha swallowed hard.

Her brown hair, so odd for an'Cróan, hung in a tangled mess. In daylight, at the sight of her starved appearance, his guilt welled and he could not speak. When she took a few steps between the remaining floor cushions in the sitting area, she stopped as her gaze lowered and she looked beyond him toward the back corner.

"Wynn cares for *him*," she whispered, obviously referring to Chane.

It had not been a question but a statement, and Osha rocked back on one heel as if kicked in the stomach. Those words could have had any number of meanings, but she had clearly said them to cut him. And worse, he felt he deserved it.

Yes, Wynn cared for Chane. There was nothing Osha could do about that, though he had his hopes concerning her and their past together. But something more stunned him.

Leanâlhâm had never before said anything to hurt him. She had changed in more than name since they'd last parted.

Wynn couldn't help a convulsive shudder, as if shaking off ants crawling all over her, as she left that sorcery-hidden place. Even so, she grew anxious at the thought of leaving.

Ghassan was up and about, Chane was dormant, and hopefully Magiere wouldn't leave the bedroom anytime soon. If so, Wynn hoped Chap would be sensible and keep Magiere in check. Lack of trust would've been a blessing, as opposed to hate. There was so much bad—and spilled—blood between Chane and the others, especially Magiere.

Scavenging the little market took longer than Wynn had expected.

First she purchased a large urn with a tight lid of hardened leather and then found an eatery near the market's back end. The proprietor filled the urn with some kind of stew. Judging by the savory smell, it at least had meat in it, probably goat, but she could not be certain. After she paid the man, she went looking for clean clothing, as she didn't know whether the others had spare clothes in the baggage Brot'an had been able to save.

She took care not to buy anything with a colorful pattern—the plainer the better.

In the end, she purchased three sets of simple muslin pantaloons—what passed for pants in this land—and three lightweight sleeveless tunics, which nearly everyone wore here. The smallest one was ruddy red in color. The other two were larger, one of midnight blue and one of sandy orange. At least her friends would be able to bathe properly and dress in clean clothing. And for that, she found and purchased two bars of sandalwood soap.

Though satisfied with her purchases, Wynn found herself a little overburdened as she headed back for the tenement. She tried to focus on the tasks at hand and not Ghassan's betrayal—that he'd risked himself only because he wanted help in hunting down an undead. And maybe there was more than that. If he'd been honest from the start, she might have understood, even if Chane wouldn't.

She didn't know what would come next, as nothing had been settled the night before. Like Leesil, all she wanted for now was to help Wayfarer and Magiere recover. Magiere was the strongest person she'd ever known, and yet now she looked almost broken.

Wynn couldn't imagine what that had taken—and taken from Magiere.

As she approached the tenement, she slipped into a cutway between a few dwellings nearby and turned down the alley for the back door. When she reached it, she shifted her burdens to free up one hand and tried grasping for the door latch. As she did so, something seemed to wink into her awareness on the left.

Wynn's breath caught in her chest at the sight of Ghassan.

He stepped in on her before she could retreat, and everything around her but him appeared to waver and warp. When she blinked in reflex, everything was as before, as if it hadn't happened.

"What are you doing out here?" she demanded. "How did you get past the others?"

"I have not left the chamber. I am not really here."

"What?"

"This was necessary," Ghassan said, and it sounded like his real voice. "We need to speak alone, and I made you see me so it would be less . . . disconcerting."

Wynn looked all around. If what he said was true, how was he doing this? By what Chane had said and done last night, the domin needed a line of sight to use sorcery.

"You already made your agenda quite clear," she said.

His expression tightened. "Obviously I did not."

She inched back a step, and he huffed in disgust. Then she remembered the pebble.

That was the only answer. It did more than just allow her to find the sanctuary's door. It marked the location of whoever held it—it had to.

"Get out of my head!"

She dropped the clothing, bobbled the urn, wrapped her other arm around it, and rammed her free hand into her pocket. Then she dug for the pebble to throw it away.

"Stop acting like a child!" he admonished. "If I

wished to control you, I would not have let you dig for the pebble, would I? And pay attention . . . I cannot grab that urn if you drop it!"

Wynn froze with her hand in her pocket, now wrapped around the pebble.

"You are not even speaking with me," he added, rolling his eyes. "You only think so because I put all this in your head. And yes, it is because of the pebble. Do you think I would give anyone such an item without always knowing where to retrieve it?"

He had once used the staff he had made for her to track her into that lost dwarven city. Yes, Ghassan thought ahead, and she had better start doing so as well.

She looked up at his narrow features and prominent nose, at the white flecks in his dark hair. She should probably never trust him again, but they had been through a good deal together. He'd once stood by her, believed in her, when no one else in her guild branch would lift a finger to help her.

"What do you want?" she asked, still uncertain. "Is that why you let me go to the market? So you could catch me alone out here?"

"Yes, in part," he admitted. "Your companions must accept hunting the specter before continuing in their search for the last orb. I need *you* to accomplish that."

Wynn's suspicions sharpened again. Though the filled urn was getting heavier in one arm, she wasn't about to let go of the pebble.

"You think I can talk them into doing something they don't want to do?"

"I think you can be sensible," he answered, and if possible, his expression tightened further. "I know Magiere wishes to find the orb of Air. At least the half-blood and gray majay-hì will follow her, however unwillingly.

That is not possible or safe while the specter remains . . . especially if it has access to the palace."

That was only a guess, but before she said so . . .

"Think!" Ghassan commanded. "Khalidah clearly inhabited whoever interrogated Magiere. I do not know *who* that was—is—but with his power, he could have addled the minds of anyone nearby. No one will know the host he inhabits, for he would not be foolish enough to endanger a useful body until finished with it. And if he takes someone of great authority, what would he do with that much more earthly power?"

Wynn didn't like that he was making more sense by the moment.

"As of now," he continued, "there are some on the imperial grounds who can limit or interfere with the search for the escaped prisoners. That will not last if Khalidah takes a more influential host. Your friends will never escape this city until he is eliminated, and if they are recaptured . . ."

He never finished, and he didn't have to.

Wynn saw that conditions would worsen the longer that Magiere and Chane were in close proximity. There seemed no way to avoid that if she was to help Magiere through helping Ghassan.

"You have no idea who is the host?" she asked. "Not even a guess?"

He slowly shook his head. "All of my own died in that thing's escape, but not all of his hosts may have died or even remembered his presence. That is why I needed your friend . . . and the second majay-hì as well."

"What of your prince? It wasn't hard to guess that he was the one who helped you. He's the one who sentenced Magiere and all with her, supposedly to forestall their execution. What if he is now the specter?"

"He is not."

"How would you know?"

"I know," he answered too firmly. "Regardless, Khalidah will not rest until Magiere and those close to her have been recaptured. I do not exaggerate about the influence he could have. All city exits are likely guarded by now, and the search for your friends will grow. How quickly and by how much depends on actions taken. Only when Khalidah is removed can I hope to prove so to those who risked much to help me . . . and thereby free your friends to leave on their search."

Wynn knew Ghassan was exploiting everything to use Magiere and Leesil and Chap and Shade, and maybe even Chane. She also couldn't fault his arguments given how little she knew of how he'd arranged the escape.

She again pondered the secret that she had so far held back from him: the device she'd gained in her search for the orb of Spirit. Once the device—fashioned from a piece of a key used to open an orb—was activated, its wielder could track another orb.

She'd failed in trying to do so on her own with words from a dead language she didn't understand. It was a language from this region in ancient times, and Ghassan was the only one she thought might help with that. It might take more than just a scholar of dead tongues. Soon enough, if she were to assist Magiere, she would require the domin's help.

"You see the truth the others would reject," Ghassan added calmly. "Will you convince them?"

Wynn hated being placed in this position, but she nodded.

"Good," he said.

In another waver of everything, Ghassan vanished

before Wynn's eyes . . . or it appeared so. She still looked all around, just to be certain.

Upstairs and inside the sanctuary, Ghassan slowly opened his eyes as if merely resting in one of the tall-backed chairs. He waited quietly until Wynn arrived, entering by using the ensorcelled pebble as instructed. She eyed him once but then turned her attention to tending the others, starting by settling the half-blood and the strangely dark-haired elven girl at the table. The gray majay-hì sat on the floor next to the girl.

Wynn dished up and passed out bowls of stew.

"Eat slowly," she advised, "and stop if your stomach cramps." At the rattle of a bowl on the floor, she turned to the enormous majay-hì. "I mean it, Chap—small bites only!" An instant later, she made an indignant face. "I am *not* a pest, now . . . Oh . . . just do as I say!"

Ghassan frowned. He wished he knew a bit more about how she communicated with these unusual creatures. It appeared to be slightly different between the black and the gray. The black one was still off in the room's dim corner near the blanket over the undead. Ghassan was poised to launch into a more pointed discussion, as it might be best to push things along before the "dhampir" was well enough to be part of any plan.

Convincing the others might be easier without her, and then she would be more easily swayed.

Ghassan was well aware that Wynn sided with him only under duress, but she was intelligent enough to understand the situation. Her pressing him about the prince had come too close to the truths he was not yet ready to share.

Years before, his sect had noted the doctrinal differences between the emperor and his son, to the point where all of the sect knew they would need to intervene. The empire had to be steered toward a path of reason and not a theocracy rooted in a dead, dark religion that few even knew had once existed. The prince's lean toward the former made him a target for those who found his way of thinking—and his future potential rule—dangerous.

Ghassan had cunningly befriended the heir to the imperial throne during the prince's youth and found him trustworthy to a fault. By introducing the young man to a few of the sect, one at a time, he began Ounyal'am's awakening to his father's destructive beliefs.

It had not been pleasant for the young prince. It had also not been much of a surprise, considering all that the young prince would have seen in the imperial court under his father's rule.

To protect the prince, the sect agreed on something that had been unthinkable before. They created one of their own medallions for Ounyal'am.

Ghassan taught him how to use it, and the prince's quick acceptance was startling. In another life, he could have been a worthy "sage" if not specifically a metaologer.

Another life was not to be had. An imperial prince was a tool to wield against the emperor's ways. And the medallion had other properties that manifested over time as Ghassan continued teaching the prince. If he focused, Ghassan could nearly always sense Ounyal'am's whereabouts, or at least direction.

In the past, this had seemed another way to watch over the prince.

Ghassan could not help dwelling on how much time Magiere had spent under Khalidah's influence ... inside her mind. What if that thing had established a like connection to her? That very possibility had also pushed Ghassan into cornering Wynn.

He needed her to make his case to the others and through them to Magiere. There could be no hint that such influence came directly from him where the dhampir was concerned.

Ghassan reassessed all present, starting with Wayfarer, and Leesil, and then Chap. Osha was no threat, as he was so obviously enamored with Wynn and would follow wherever she led.

At the last, he glanced into the chamber's back corner.

Fortunately, Chane lay dormant. The night before, the undead was the one who had been intellectually, and physically, the most challenging. Ghassan had held back from dealing with that one for fear of alienating Wynn.

Shade sat guarding Chane, but she would also follow Wynn in all things.

Then there was the scarred elder, Brot'an, more dangerous and unpredictable than the undead. Chane's impulsive side was linked to protecting Wynn, while Brot'an's personal motivations were a mystery. For now, he simply bore watching.

Wynn half turned where she crouched beside Chap. "Osha . . . Brot'an, Shade . . . there is plenty of stew if you'd like some. I will bring Magiere a bowl and see if she is awake."

Before she could take further action, Ghassan interceded. "Events are unfolding around us, and we need to make some decisions."

Osha stood off toward the front door, and Brot'an still sat cross-legged on the floor in the chamber's front right corner.

Leesil put down his spoon. "What decisions?"

In turn, Ghassan looked to Wynn, though she looked away.

"The domin believes we have to hunt down this specter," she said, "before we can search for the last orb . . . and I think he may be right."

"Like I said last night," Leesil retorted, "Magiere isn't hunting anything. Not now."

Chap sat up, ears rising. No one reacted, so apparently he was only listening. Brot'an rose from sitting without bracing a hand on the floor and stepped toward Ghassan.

"I agree with Léshil," the elder elf added. "This specter is your problem, not ours."

Ghassan said nothing to this and glanced at Wynn.

"It *is* our problem," she countered, "if this specter inhabited whoever interrogated Magiere. According to the domin, Khalidah—in life—served the Ancient Enemy. If he's been inside Magiere's mind, he might know about the orbs . . . at least that some have been found. Now that she has escaped, he will not stop hunting for her. If he has a host with enough authority, he could have imperial guards or even the military at his disposal."

Leesil dropped his spoon and was already arguing with her as it clattered.

Several times Wynn turned on Chap as well for whatever passed silently between them. In the end, she accomplished what Ghassan had needed and without his involvement or being the source of more ardent resistance.

Leesil dropped both elbows on the table, though his breaths were labored by anger. Chap became still, his large blue eyes shifting about the room, but since Wynn made no reaction, the dog said nothing.

In the long silence, Ghassan wondered whether it was time to reveal his connection to the prince. There were things even Wynn did not know and could not have reasoned out. So, as simply as possible, he began to explain how he had come to know Ounyal'am.

When all remained silent, neither resisting further nor consenting, he was forced to take one more risk. He pulled the copper medallion from inside his shirt.

"My sect created one of these for Prince Ounyal'am, so he could communicate with us and we could protect him."

He shared in short some of what he had told Wynn, including his sense of the prince's direction within a limited range.

Wynn's eyes locked on him without blinking. "What are you saying?"

"Khalidah may have a similar awareness of Magiere. If any of you escape this city and take her with you, you may lead him wherever you go . . . including to another orb."

Wynn pushed up, trying to gain her feet, but her heavy chair did not slide away, and she toppled back into it. "Why didn't you make that clear? There's already an orb here . . . with her . . . in the other room!"

Ghassan remained calm at her foolish panic. "No one can find us here by any means. The sanctuary is secure, even from me while outside of it. That was its ultimate purpose. Why else would I have brought and kept all of you here? But we must destroy Khalidah before you can attempt to leave this city."

"He's right."

Even Ghassan was caught off guard by a new voice. Leesil roughly shoved back his chair to gain his feet as Chap wheeled and lunged off across the room toward . . .

Magiere stood watching from the bedchamber's entrance. She was wrapped in a thin blanket and gripped the doorframe for support.

When the gray majay-hì neared her, he slowed as if

hesitating. He dropped his head, with perhaps only his eyes looking up at her as his ears lowered.

Magiere looked down at Chap as if startled, though that came too late to have been caused by his rush at her. A low whine filled the room, and the canine utterance was pained and pitiful, like a howl caught in Chap's throat.

Magiere's eyes widened in something akin to fright. She dropped to her knees and put a hand against the side of his face.

"No," she whispered. "Don't say that. Even if you could've . . . you couldn't. It's all right . . . Please, you did right."

Ghassan was lost by all of this, and apparently so were the others.

"Leesil?" Wynn asked quietly.

He shook his head as he both stared and frowned at the pair in the bedchamber entrance.

Magiere looked up and across the room as her hand slipped down Chap's neck and around his shoulders, as if she might grab hold to pull him close. He went silent as he buried his face in her neck.

"I take it you have a plan?" she asked, looking first to Wynn and then directly at Ghassan. "And that would be a trap . . . with me as the bait."

Ghassan wondered how long she had been listening.

"No!" Leesil snarled.

He lunged one step toward her, stopped suddenly and turned, and then charged the table straight at Ghassan. Wynn grabbed at him, barely achieving a grip, and Shade came snarling out of the room's back corner. Osha took two fast steps closer and stalled, visibly panicked and confused about what to do.

Magiere kept her eyes locked on Ghassan.

Yes, he mouthed at her.

She looked to Leesil. "We don't have a choice."

He thrashed out of Wynn's grip and turned to her. "Yes, we do! We don't have to do—"

"Leesil!" Magiere cut in.

Chap pulled his head out of her neck to look as well.

Leesil's eyes shifted everywhere as he panted in fury or panic. For one instant, he might have wanted to collapse. Then he turned slowly, and there was cold hate in his eyes as he looked at Ghassan.

"If we can't be located in here, by any means, then we aren't doing a thing until she's recovered. Understand?"

Ghassan nodded. "Of course." Satisfied that he had succeeded, he rose and grabbed his cloak. "I will find out how far the prisoner recovery efforts have progressed," he said. "And how many guards are searching the city—and where. The scale of their efforts may help us estimate the rank or placement of Khalidah's current host."

Brot'an stood up, and then his entire body went still.

Osha glanced at Leesil in alarm, as if questioning whether he should act to stop Ghassan from leaving the sanctuary.

Ghassan paused, waiting. Since the night before, they had treated him as a prisoner to be watched. He had indulged them, but this had to stop. If any of them tried to stop him now, it would be time to show them exactly what he was capable of.

"Let him go," Magiere ordered quietly, and looked at Brot'an. "I mean it. Everything has changed now. And again . . . he's right."

Leesil shook his head in anger—and perhaps defeat. "What if you're spotted?"

Starting for the door again, Ghassan did not dignify the question with an answer.

CHAPTER 11

As soon as Ghassan left the sanctuary, all talk of impending hunts ceased and Wynn turned her attention to making her rescued friends more comfortable. First she found a bucket and several large empty urns stored in various places about the sanctuary. She also gathered the urns she'd purchased at the market. Then she and Osha went downstairs, outside, and walked one block to the west to use a communal well. They filled their vessels.

Though somewhat heavily burdened, they made their way back to the top floor of the tenement in good time.

Rather than using her pebble, Wynn decided to try something else, just to see if it would work. Stopping at the false window, she set down her bucket to free up one hand, then knocked softly.

"It's me," she whispered.

The door opened from the other side and Leesil peered out.

Good. That meant that so long as at least one of them was inside, anyone else could come and go as necessary.

After bustling in, with Osha behind her, Wynn heard

Leesil close the door, and she assumed full charge of the situation.

"Osha, please take two of the urns and this bucket into the bedroom. Then try to hang a sheet in the doorway."

He nodded and went to work.

Piles of blankets, sheets, and any other light pieces of cloth were soon gathered, along with the new clothing she'd purchased, both bars of soap, small pots of medicinal salve, and bandages. She also dug a wooden comb out of her own pack. Wynn then divided up these items. Leaving some of them on the table, she hefted an armload of others.

"Magiere, Wayfarer . . . come with me," she said, heading off for the bedchamber.

By that point, Osha had strung a sheet across the bedchamber's entrance for privacy. Wynn pushed the sheet aside and stepped in. Several large urns of water, along with the bucket, were now set between the beds. As Magiere and Wayfarer followed, Wynn set down her armload of blankets, sheets, and a bar of soap, and she went to check that the sheet curtain was securely in place. Leesil could remain with the other men and take his bath in the outer room, where she'd left him two urns of water, soap, blankets, and clothing.

Shade's nose then poked around one side of the hanging sheet.

Wynn should have thought of the other "woman" in the group, and Shade pushed through to join them. At that moment, Wynn wished Shade might have stayed out in the main room with Chap. A daughter would do well to soften a little toward her father, but this was no time to worry about such things.

Wynn found herself relieved by Wayfarer's quick compliance, for this morning and last night the girl had been standoffish, almost cold. Most of that had been directed toward Osha, though strangely—or not—some of this had spilled over toward Wynn. As to the story behind another change of name for the quarter-blood girl, that could wait as well. Magiere and Leesil, and even Chap, now called her Wayfarer, and that was enough.

Wynn's attention turned to more immediate matters as Wayfarer and Magiere began to disrobe.

Wayfarer looked bone thin and her wrists were badly bruised, but Magiere was now almost unmarked.

Wynn was well aware of how quickly Magiere healed. Aside from being more pallid than before, and malnourished, there wasn't a single wound on her. Even her torn wrists showed almost no sign that she'd been manacled. Disturbing at the least.

Wayfarer stood frozen, naked to the waist as she stared down at her soiled pants. Wynn had expected bashfulness, but the girl looked as if she was in physical discomfort. Wynn peered closer and realized it wasn't a matter of modesty. The fabric of those pants had adhered to Wayfarer's legs in several places after a moon of fearsweats, grime, and bodily filth without bathing.

"Getting them off might hurt . . . a little," Wynn said.

Wayfarer nodded, and as Wynn helped peel off the pants, the girl winced several times, though she never made a sound. When it was done, Wayfarer sat down on the floor and leaned against the nearer bed's side. Wynn was about to toss the ruined pants into the corner and get the salve when she heard a slowly growing hiss resembling that of an angered cat.

Magiere stared down at the girl's marred, reddened legs. For an instant Wynn thought Magiere's irises began to expand; under fury, those irises would swallow any color with pure black.

"No! Do not lose yourself," Wayfarer warned, nearly frantic. She looked down at her own legs. "And please do not tell the others."

Wynn eyed Magiere sidelong. She waited tensely for anything that might go wrong and force her to shout for Leesil or Chap.

With a shudder, Magiere dropped into a crouch before the girl. She reached for a sheet atop the pile of cloth and tore it, shredding it as if it were gauze. Dunking one piece into a water urn, she wrung it out and was about to place it over one of the girl's legs.

Magiere hesitated, her voice strained as if speaking were difficult. "Just . . . let it . . . soak for a . . . short while."

At the girl's nod, Magiere carefully draped the dripping cloth over Wayfarer's leg.

Wayfarer winced, and Magiere paused before placing another soaked rag over the girl's other leg. By that point Wayfarer was shaking from the pain. Magiere reached out, took Wayfarer's face gently in both hands, rose a little on her knees, and leaned in to touch her forehead to the girl's.

"You're strong," Magiere whispered, "so very strong, my girl. And no one's taking me from you again."

As Wynn's eyes began watering, she fumbled about for the bar of soap.

Not long after, Wayfarer removed the damp strips of sheet and managed to wash her own body. Wynn offered to help wash her hair by having her lean over the bucket. Some water was splashed onto the floor, but that couldn't be helped with this makeshift method of bathing.

After that, she dabbed salve on the girl's legs and helped her dress while Magiere took up the soap, knelt by an urn, and began to wash herself. Once she was clean, Wynn helped wash her hair, and then Magiere too dressed in some of the clothing purchased. Wayfarer wore the smaller red tunic and Magiere took the midnight blue one.

When all was settled, the three women—and Shade—left the bedchamber and went back into the main room.

Leesil had finished for the most part, though he hadn't pulled on his new tunic. His hair was still dripping wet but cleanly white-blond once more. He already wore the muslin pantaloons, which fit him quite well. Though thinner than Wynn remembered, his chest and arms were still tightly muscled. He let her tend to him with salve before he pulled the burnt-orange tunic over his head.

Watching him from a few paces away, Magiere said, "That color suits you."

If nothing else, Wynn's three friends were now clean and hopefully a bit more comfortable. Magiere stepped closer to Leesil as Wayfarer sank down into a chair on his left side, and Wynn couldn't help assessing them.

By this point Wayfarer's hair was nearly dry in the warm Suman air. The red of the tunic flattered the girl's tan skin and green eyes, and her brown hair was long and thick. Wynn did not remember her being so beautiful.

However, she had hoped the local clothing would help her friends blend in a little better, and that was clearly not the case.

Magiere's clothing fit her slender frame well, but the lightweight pantaloons and dark blue tunic made her look only more exotic. Her skin was white and her hair was black with bloodred tints in bright light. In this part of the world, that was unusual at best. She would need to wear a cloak with the deepest hood.

At least they had plenty of cloaks.

Throughout all of this, Brot'an sat cross-legged on

the floor near the window, offering neither comment nor assistance.

Magiere settled on the floor directly in front of Way-farer's chair, and the girl immediately reached for the comb on the nearby table. She began untangling Magi-ere's damp black hair, and the sight turned Wynn nostalgic.

In the past, she'd often brushed and braided Magiere's hair. That seemed so long ago. Now she took care of her-self and her own companions, and she glanced toward the main room's dim back corner.

Chane lay dormant beneath a blanket, and so far no one had mentioned him. That was best, though it wouldn't last.

And then there was Osha.

He stood near the front door. His gaze shifted toward Wayfarer, remained there a moment, and then moved to Wynn. He looked away quickly, as did Wynn, and she found Chap watching her intently. Her various worries must have been apparent on her face.

She and Chap had always read each other with a fair amount of ease, and he must have been nearly over-whelmed by so many things in their current situation:

A daughter who refused to acknowledge his ex-istence.

A vampire in their midst—and being forced to accept his help.

A duplicitous domin attempting to use Magiere as bait.

Wynn wished she had a moment alone with Chap. His gaze shifted to Magiere, then to Leesil, and finally to Wayfarer before he looked back to her.

I am glad you are here . . . that you came after us. I don't know what would have happened had you not.

It wasn't like him to share doubt or express gratitude, and that worried her a little. Of the four of them, so far he had appeared the least affected. Perhaps the past moon had affected him more than anyone but she would realize.

Of course, he did look filthy again.

Wynn lifted an urn still half full of water, shifted it to one arm, and then took up a bar of soap as she straightened.

"Your turn, Chap," she announced.

The floor was about to get very wet.

Chap put up only a little struggle as Wynn set upon him. When Wayfarer got up from her chair to come help, the girl clearly found the whole situation unsettling.

Certain aspects of her people's reverence for majay-hì would likely never change. But given the need for normalcy, or the illusion of it for a moment, Chap knew Wynn would be suspicious if he made the enterprise too easy.

Wayfarer lugged over another urn to rinse him. As she tilted it, he jerked out of Wynn's grip and back-stepped when she tried to grab him. Wayfarer's eyes widened just before the pail's contents splashed into Wynn's lap.

Wayfarer sucked a breath. "Oh . . . oh, no . . . oh, my!"

"He's never liked getting wet," Leesil put in absently.

Wynn grabbed for Chap, trying to gain a solid hold. "You . . . you mangy mutt."

"You did that on purpose?" Wayfarer asked, staring wide-eyed at him. "You . . . you are a . . . a bad majay-hì!"

Wynn huffed. "Try chasing him with a brush across the rolling deck of a ship sometime. And if you didn't catch him, he'd be . . . a filthy pig!"

Wayfarer's little jaw dropped at such irreverence, perhaps forgetting she'd just scolded him herself.

Chap merely licked his nose at both of them—his usual flippant response.

In truth, he did not mind Wynn's ministrations. Neither did he enjoy them. Rather, he felt numb inside except for a dull anger at himself. After the shock of being rescued had worn off, and he had learned more of what had happened to Magiere, his sense of failure weighed on him more than ever. Even begging her forgiveness, when she had come out of the bedchamber earlier that day, had not eased this. She and Leesil were his primary charges to protect, and he had failed.

In the past, they had fought side by side when outnumbered or outmatched. Chap had known fear of losing one or both more than once. What he felt now was so much worse. He had not seen the arrest coming or been able to stop it, nor had he been able to take any action once they had all been imprisoned. An entire moon had passed as he'd watched Leesil and young Wayfarer suffer, and Magiere was beyond even his sight. And as he had listened to her screams in the dark . . .

All that Chap could hope was that her suffering would end—and it could end only one way—and not just for her sake but for the secrets he bore concerning the orbs.

She should not have forgiven that, even when he had begged her.

What would have happened had Wynn not come? In his sinking heart, he believed Leesil and Wayfarer would have eventually died as well. He had seen no other outcome but to hope that he would follow them soon. And the orbs he had hidden would never be found again.

But Wynn had come and found a way to save them.

Now Chap found himself suffering a different fear concerning Magiere.

A necromancer named Ubâd, a servant of the Ancient Enemy, had sacrificed one of each of the five races so that Magiere could be born. With the blood of the five in her veins, she could walk into any land in the world unaffected by any safeguards placed for protection. She had been conceived via that bloody ritual to become the Enemy's servant . . . a tool.

Chap, in separating from his kin, the Fay, who existed outside of time but were now and forever linked to the living world, had chosen to be born into flesh. His sole purpose in the beginning had been to keep Magiere from fulfilling the reason for her creation, though he had not known all concerning that in the beginning. And he had used even Leesil's own grandmother to find the half-blood and thereby use Leesil to find Magiere.

She would be unstoppable, should she ever serve the Enemy. That could not happen, and neither could he allow the orbs to return to their maker. The Ancient Enemy of many names could not rise again, no matter what the cost. And now Magiere had been visited over and over by the undead spirit of an ancient sorcerer who had served—perhaps still served—that enemy.

Chap's dread of what might come mixed with self-loathing for his own choices. He kept both to himself, hidden from the others as best he could, but talk of sorcery had raised one of his worst memories, one he could not now banish.

Too long past, in a return to Magiere's homeland, another undead sorcerer in flesh had engulfed him in a terrifying phantasm. He'd found himself running through a dying forest where all life withered around him. Trees and brush wilted and rotted as shadowy silhouettes moved in a wave through the forest. And it was all his fault—his failure.

Spirits were wrenched from the trees and the earth to be swallowed by walking shadows, their numbers growing in the darkness. Nothing was left alive in their wake as they came ever closer. And a lone figure led them, a heavy single-edged sword glinting in her grip.

Magiere's eyes were fully black, unlike the colorless crystalline eyes of the ravenous undead who followed her. Her filthy hair hung in matted tendrils around a deathly pale face, twisted feral around her mouth. Her armor was made of large black scales, as might have come from a massive serpent.

She roared, as if no longer recognizing him, and exposed long fangs amid yellowed teeth. Behind her, those black silhouettes gathered in a horde for as far as he could see among the dead trees. All of their glittering eyes were upon her in waiting.

Chap had sacrificed eternity among his brethren Fay to keep Magiere in the light through Leesil and to keep her from the Enemy's hands and the purpose of her birth. But he saw her standing like a general before this horde.

"Majay-hì," she spit at him.

Sorrow welled and spilled from him in a wail as she looked upon him as her enemy. And when she rushed forward, raising her falchion, the horde surged, leveling all living things in its path. He had stood listless within that phantasm as her blade fell and bit deep between his shoulder and neck . . .

"Chap, what's wrong? Did I get soap in your eyes?"

Chap opened his eyes, not realizing he had closed them.

Wynn studied him as Wayfarer tried to dry him with a blanket, and he had not even felt it. He began to tremble.

Wynn's brow wrinkled. "Chap?"

Are you finished?

"No, you're still a bit wet."

I am fine.

Chap shrugged off the dampened blanket and Way-farer's small hands. Stepping away, he paused at the sight of Magiere trying to comb out Leesil's hair.

For a moon, he had waited for her to stop screaming—for all of it to end. Knowing Leesil and Wayfarer would never have been freed, he would wait for them to pass, giving them what little comfort he could offer. And finally, he would force the guards to kill him.

No one would have ever found the orbs he had hidden.

The life of this world meant more than a paw's count of lives here in this hidden place—but those lives meant something to him. For what he had done—would have done—he should not have asked forgiveness. That Magiere had given it to him so quickly in understanding what was necessary had brought him no relief. It was another shame among many he bore.

And now this Domin il'Sänke wanted them to hunt the undead who had questioned Magiere.

Chap agreed.

In life versus death, this was the only action to be taken. Perhaps Magiere would be safe only once this specter, Khalidah, was destroyed. But could Chap ever again make a choice between the world and those he had come to love?

Wayfarer helped gather up blankets and damp sheets, and then tried using the least damp blanket to mop up the floor. The simple action brought a kind of comfort.

On the inside, she did not exactly feel better, but this short time had comprised nothing more than bathing and dressing and speaking of things that didn't matter and helping to wash Chap. This reprieve made her believe that, in time, she *might* feel better. She might put the terror of that dark cell behind her.

Last night, when she had first seen Wynn, anger like she had never before felt rose up within her.

Wynn had been the reason Osha had abandoned her.

But after the night's flight to this hidden place, Wynn had paid no special attention to Osha, and this left Wayfarer wondering.

Wynn was never impolite to Osha but barely spoke to him either. She had remained focused mostly on caring for the others. This morning, she had returned with warm food and clean clothes, and again turned her full attention to caring for others.

Wayfarer wallowed in guilt. She had judged her old friend wrongly, for Wynn was not to blame.

Osha had made his own choice—and he had not chosen her.

Now he stood near the door, as if uncertain what else to do. When her gaze swept in his direction, she found his eyes locked on her, and surprise filled them.

"Leanâl—" he began, and stopped short, but the damage was done. He kept calling her by that hated name— "Child of Sorrow"—only slightly less awful than the one the ancestors had put upon her: Sheli'câlhad, "To a Lost Way." Everyone else had accepted the final name that Magiere, Léshil, and Chap had given her, but not Osha.

Wayfarer turned away. Why had he been staring at her at all? She knew how little she meant to him compared with . . .

She looked up at Chap's sudden snarl.

The others had begun talking among themselves, and for some reason, Chap was glaring and bearing his teeth at Brot'ân'duivé. Whatever the greimasg'äh had said to anger the majay-hì again, she had missed it. Then she noticed Léshil had turned his head with a hard look toward the room's rear corner.

Shade stood there, seeming to stand guard over Chane.

Tension hung in the air.

Although Magiere was healing faster than anyone, Wayfarer did not see how they would all manage to live in this small, hidden place until Magiere grew strong enough to fight. The prospect was almost unbearable. Perhaps out of habit, she glanced over her shoulder and caught Osha watching her again.

He instantly looked away, and the walls felt too close.

"Léshil," Wayfarer breathed. "I . . . I need . . . some air. Please, even in the alley for a few moments. Please."

He frowned at her in puzzlement; she knew her request sounded foolish and was an unnecessary risk. Magiere, sitting above him in the chair, patted his shoulder, and he got up.

They might not understand what she felt, but at least they understood a simple need: to leave this close and crowded place, even for a moment, after having been imprisoned for so long.

"Of course," Léshil answered. "I'll get us cloaks and take you out back of—"

"No, I . . . will," Osha interrupted in Belaskian. "No one see us, promise."

Wayfarer cringed and ducked her head.

"All right, I should stay with Magiere anyway," Léshil said. "Keep out of sight and knock on the fake window's frame when you come back up."

Wayfarer kept her eyes down. It was right that Léshil

stay with his wife, so she either accepted Osha as her escort or she remained here—and that thought was unbearable.

She could not look at Léshil as he handed her a cloak and tossed another to Osha somewhere behind her. When she turned, she looked at only the door. If Osha wished to offer excuses or pretend he had done no wrong, then that was fine.

Wayfarer had nothing to say to him.

Watching Wayfarer and Osha leave, Leesil almost wished he could go with them. A bit of air might be welcome. However, those two had something to work out, and the sooner the better. Besides, he did want to remain with Magiere.

After washing up and changing clothes, followed by Magiere combing his damp hair, for a short while his world had almost begun to make sense again. Only moments later that feeling vanished as reality took hold.

Brot'an was here, as was Chane. They were all stuck in this place, and when they left, they'd have to hunt an undead like no other they'd ever dealt with. Leesil didn't even see how they could kill something that had no flesh of its own. And all because some fallen Suman sage had more secrets than he'd shared.

Leesil glanced again at the blanketed form beyond Shade in the room's dim back corner.

What was going to happen when that blood-soaked undead rose again at nightfall? Magiere was in no condition to deal with Chane, at least not alone. Brot'an might help if something started. And if Magiere wanted to finish it, Leesil would . . . .

—No—

He twisted his head to look at Chap.

—*Leave Chane alone*— . . . —*For now*—

Leesil couldn't argue without alerting the others to what Chap had said. Turning away, he crouched down before Magiere, who was still sitting in a chair facing the open area around the table. She was a little thin but still beyond lovely, and he *was* grateful to have her back. They simply always seemed to have another battle to fight that couldn't be avoided.

"So, it seems we have another undead to hunt down," he said. "I hope that domin was serious about having a plan."

Wynn came closer and dropped her bundle of blankets into an empty chair. "Well, whatever his plan is," she put in, "it will have to take place at night, as we'll need Chane."

Leesil rose up, unable to hold back. "No, we won't."

"Oh . . . Leesil!" she shot back. "Who fought off guards at the front gates and again in the streets when we were about to be caught? I wouldn't have that orb in the bedchamber if not for him . . . and Shade would have died if he hadn't rescued her. Even Osha is able to work with him." Half turning away, she added over her shoulder, "So spare me your self-righteous indignation. Whatever the past, you—we—will need his help when the time comes."

After snatching up the blankets, she stormed off toward the bedchamber, passing through the sheet that still hung in the doorway.

Leesil glanced at Chap, then looked to Magiere. She was staring at nothing, though her hands were clenched on the side of the chair's seat. Magiere hated Chane as much as anyone, maybe more for her inner nature. She'd once even taken his head, but he'd somehow come back.

Leesil expected her to be as angry as himself, but she was quiet, as was Chap.

Didn't either of them see what was happening here? They couldn't accept help from an undead who had murdered countless people.

Leesil started after Wynn.

"Leave her be," Magiere growled at him.

"Not this time."

Nearing the bedroom, he heard steps behind him and looked back. It was only Chap following, so he kept on. When they passed through the sheet curtain and stepped into the bedchamber, Wynn sat on the floor stroking Shade's neck—which was a surprise.

Leesil hadn't even seen Chap's daughter leave the outer room's back corner—and her vigil there. It was still unbelievable that a majay-hì guarded an undead, but at the sight of Wynn petting the dog, some of Leesil's anger faded.

"If what Ghassan says about this specter is true," Wynn said quietly, "we need everyone we have."

Leesil didn't know what to say to that. How could she justify using one murdering undead to hunt down another?

"I dislike any of us being used as bait," said a deep, quiet voice.

Chap snarled, and Leesil spun to find Brot'an's hulking form inside the doorway.

The aging shadow-gripper too often showed unsettling concern for Magiere's safety. So where was that when he'd abandoned everyone on the docks? Either way, it couldn't be true concern, not from him. Even Chap hadn't uncovered Brot'an's true motives, even now that Most Aged Father's loyalists had been removed.

238 · BARB & J. C. HENDEE

"I don't like it either," Leesil replied. "But the domin says we don't have a choice."

Brot'an blinked slowly. "Magiere is not the only possible bait. Perhaps not even the most effective."

Wynn rose to her feet. "What do you mean?"

"This Khalidah wants to take Magiere alive," Brot'an continued, "or he would have killed her already. So long as she lives, that goal remains attainable. If the domin's sect imprisoned this specter long ago, and all are dead but him, would the specter not want to finish what it started with the domin as a potential obstacle?"

In the following moment of silence, Leesil felt a chill; Brot'an had a way of making the coldest reasoning sound . . . reasonable.

"I've been wondering what you thought of all this," Wynn said, studying the master assassin with a frown. "For the most part, you've been awfully quiet."

"I have been listening."

—*Listen to him*— . . . —*Something is* . . . *missing* . . . *in the domin's plan*—

As usual, Chap was annoyingly right, but Leesil disliked siding with Brot'an.

Wynn let out a tired sigh. "Ghassan is no coward. I can vouch for that. So . . . why use Magiere when he'd be the better bait himself?"

There was little Leesil wouldn't do where Magiere was concerned. He looked up at Brot'an.

"Perhaps we should find a creative way to ask him?"

Osha followed Leanâlhâm—Wayfarer—out the back door into the rear alley. He watched as she leaned against the wall, folded her arms together, and looked away from him.

They were alone and out of sight with their hoods pulled forward and low. There was little chance of anyone noticing them, but that was no longer his main concern.

She had neither spoken to him nor looked at him since leaving the sanctuary, and the weight of his choice back in Calm Seatt was crushing him. Worse, he was painfully aware of not having given enough thought to how that would affect her—had affected her.

Upstairs, when she had come out of the bedchamber with her long hair still damp and lying over one shoulder of her red tunic, he had been startled, as if seeing a stranger. What could he say to wipe away the damage he had inflicted upon her?

Along with her dead grandfather and uncle—the kind healer Gleannéohkân'thva, and the great and honorable anmaglâhk Sgäilsheilleache—she had once treated him as family.

"Lean—" Osha began, choking on that name. "Wayfarer . . . forgive me."

Still, she did not look at him, so he stepped out in the alley to face her.

"I beg you for . . . I am so sorry . . . so very sorry that I remained behind without telling you first."

Her large green eyes instantly fixed on him, as if an apology was the last thing she had expected. Did she think so little of him now?

With a pained expression, she dropped her chin, and though her small mouth opened slightly, she did not speak.

"What can I do?" he asked.

One tear ran halfway down her cheek and drowned him in more guilt.

"*Do?*" she whispered. "I lost my only family. I was driven out by our own ancestors' spirits and then forced to leave all I knew by Brot'ân'duivé. I would have withered and died . . . if not for you caring for me." She choked once. "And you left me with the greimasg'äh . . . without a word."

Osha could barely breathe, as if he again stood in the fiery cavern of the Chein'âs, where his own weapons had been burned off his wrists. That pain, which had almost killed him, seemed as nothing here and now.

"I did not think . . ." he began. "Did not know that you would be so . . ."

"How could you not know?" she nearly cried.

He knew she should lower her voice, but he did not dare warn her.

"You stayed for Wynn," she said flatly.

Osha hesitated. "Yes."

She did not appear eager to continue, but he took no relief when she sank down the wall to sit.

He slowly crouched to face her and, not wishing to spare himself the truth, he asked, "Was it horrible, being left in the care of Brot'ân'duivé?"

"Horrible?" she repeated. "No . . . lonely. Magiere and Léshil are so kind, but they are bonded and must come first for each other. The greimasg'äh was never unkind, though he only saw to my welfare, and that was all."

She looked at him before continuing.

"Our people would find this shocking—perhaps profane—but the majay-hì has been more to me than anyone else, even for how unsettling it is to hear him in my mind. Once, up in Chathburh, when I felt so alone, he stayed up all night with me looking through a book about artisans among the others of our kind . . . the ones called the Lhoin'na."

Osha would have found this shocking in the past. Though he still saw the majay-hì as sacred guardians of his people, he had learned to see Shade as more . . . as Wynn's companion and confidante. Wynn had called Shade "sister" more than once in recent times.

"When we arrived here . . . in this city," Wayfarer went on, dropping her gaze again, "only then did everything become horrible . . . and I would have let myself die . . . if not for . . . for Chap."

The guilt almost broke Osha. "I should have been here . . . should have stopped it."

She raised her chin slightly, perhaps to look at him . . . his legs, his hands, his chest. But not his eyes.

"I am free," she said quietly, "and Wynn has said that she would not have recovered the orb of Spirit without you. That matters greatly to Magiere."

"I will not leave you again," he promised. "I swear." He pivoted to drop and leaned against the wall beside her. "Can you . . . will you . . . tell me how you came by your new name?"

After a short silence, she nodded.

Ghassan's venture outside confirmed exactly what he expected. City guards—mixed with a few imperial guards—patrolled the outer areas of the city, and all exits had been blocked, including the port. Anyone leaving was examined and questioned first.

Whoever Khalidah now inhabited was either in a position of power inside the imperial guard or had the ear of their highly placed officers. Useful as this might seem, the problem was that it still left a number of possibilities.

Even outside the imperial court, there were those who had influence over its policies and actions as well as the imperial guards, such as High Premin Aweli-Jama. Ghassan wished he could converse with the prince and ask who had been making recent military suggestions. But Ounyal'am had not initiated contact, and Ghassan would not risk doing so yet, as he had no idea what was going on inside the palace.

He was still trapped in such thoughts when he arrived at the tenement.

He had used this place for so long now that he no longer gave much notice to the poverty-stricken people along the street. He had also taken to dressing as shabbily as them, to blend in. After pressing the latch on the crooked front door, he stepped inside to find the entryway empty. Closing the door, he paused in the quiet to still his mind.

The hidden sanctuary upstairs had become too crowded, as it was never intended to house so many occupants at once. In this brief solitude, he pondered how soon to reveal more of the plan he had devised. The others could not be given too little, or they might question him, and if given too much, this might invite changes, suggestions, or demands. And how much longer would it take for Magiere to recover adequately?

With a deep breath, he headed onward, but he barely neared the turn upward when someone stepped out around the corner of the stairwell. He halted in the dim passage but had no chance to make out a face inside the cloak's hood. He did not exactly *hear* someone else drop behind him but rather felt the weight through the floor.

The white metal glint of a stiletto appeared in the hand of the one before him, and he recognized the overly tall elder an'Cróan.

"Don't turn around," Leesil said from behind him.

Though slightly shaken—but only at having been caught off guard—Ghassan raised one eyebrow and tried to sound amused. "How dramatic. I assume you wish to speak with me alone . . . though you could have asked."

"We are curious why you wish to use Magiere as bait," Brot'an said. "By our reasoning, you would be the more immediate concern to the specter."

Ghassan dropped his amused tone. "I never said otherwise."

"What?"

Ghassan did not look back at Leesil's one growled word. "We have not discussed all details involved. For that, I needed more information . . . which none of you could acquire."

He waited silently as Brot'an studied him, blade still in hand. The tall assassin half turned, sidestepping out of the stairwell.

"Then we should return upstairs," Brot'an said. "The others will wish to hear anything new as well."

Ghassan disliked being herded like a goat at blade point, but he turned the corner under the stare of those large, unblinking amber eyes.

Once they entered the sanctuary, it appeared the pair of sudden "greeters" were not the only impatient ones. Everyone but Chane was waiting for Ghassan.

CHAPTER 12

Three more days and nights passed, and in that time Magiere began to feel both better and worse. Though physically stronger and relieved to have Leesil again at her side, the spark of hate grew inside her.

She'd always lived in a smoldering state, but this time was different. She'd been made helpless, tortured within her own mind, but didn't remember how. What she remembered was pain, rage, and suffering under those voices in her head, until she could do nothing but cower amid the whispers scratching inside her skull.

Khalidah had taken everything from her.

Leesil thought she'd agreed to hunt the specter so they would be free to search for the orb of Air. He didn't—wouldn't—understand the truth. Rage that burned was a tool, a weapon to be wielded, but the burning inside her had turned everything to ash.

Ashes turned cold.

There was no more heat of rage. There was only cold hate. She wanted to smother Khalidah's life with her hands, no matter what host he used. Perhaps then, hunger and heat would return. She had to believe this. She knew she needed to heal first, but the waiting felt endless.

Only one unexpected effect of their confinement gave her a shadow of peace.

In the early evenings, not long before dusk, Wynn would bring a blanket to cover them both. She would sit with Magiere, as they did now, against the one bare wall of the main room so they could talk. It had been a long time since they'd done anything other than run, hide, fight, and hunt for or hide orbs. And when they'd last met in Calm Seatt, they'd been at odds with each other—over Chane.

Magiere eyed Shade, who lay in the far front corner, and couldn't help wondering why the young majay-hì took such efforts to avoid Chap.

"You'd think she'd miss her own kind," Magiere said quietly, "or at least her father. And what about her mother?"

Wynn sighed. "I don't know everything. Chap took Lily, the white majay-hì, as his mate before we all left the an'Cróan lands. Somehow he gave instructions to send one of their children to watch over me. Shade blames him for having to leave her home, mother, and siblings . . . everything. I understand, though I'd be lost without her now."

The discussion shifted in another direction as Wynn began telling Magiere some of how the orb of Spirit had been acquired on a scholarly investigation to a dark keep on the sea cliffs of Witeny, of how the wraith Sau'ilahk used the orb to transmogrify a young duke's body to take for his own. Afterward, Sau'ilahk had fled with the orb—as the duke and Wynn's group chased after him.

"Chane had to kill him, though I don't know how," she finished. "We were separated by too many opponents. Sau'ilahk nearly killed Shade, and Chane had no choice."

The wraith, like Khalidah, had been a high servant in its real life to the Ancient Enemy. In hearing how Chane had dealt with Sau'ilahk, anger inside Magiere turned to envy that ate at her.

"So you found your orb," Magiere whispered. "Mine isn't even close."

"Find it? No—I practically fell over it. If it hadn't been for Shade and Osha and . . . and Chane, I wouldn't have it at all."

Chane's involvement made Magiere's jaw clench. Much as it seemed he'd been useful, the thought sickened her. Perhaps he'd be useful in putting the specter within her reach, but after that, after Khalidah died in her hands . . .

Wynn was still naive in believing Chane fed only on animals. Magiere knew his nature: a killer, a predator, and a monster.

But was she much different now?

Yes, because she wanted the dead to stay dead.

"You hinted there was more going on when you found the orb."

Wynn's expression became thoughtful. "That's more difficult to explain. It's so . . . tangled in how the orb ended up in that old keep, someone else hunting it besides us, and . . . the method *she* used."

"What about it?"

Before Wynn could answer, something moved in the shadows of the room's back corner, where a cold-lamp crystal's dim light didn't reach.

Dusk had fallen, and Chane stepped out past the table and chairs into the light. After waking, he usually left on some excuse. Magiere suspected he simply couldn't stand the company—and the feeling was mutual.

As he stepped into sight, his gaze fell on Wynn sitting

shoulder to shoulder with Magiere, both of them covered by the same blanket. His eyes shifted to Magiere, and all color vanished from his irises. One of his hands dropped reflexively to his hip but didn't grasp the hilt of his long-sword. Hate was so intense in his crystalline irises that Magiere's entire body responded without effort.

The room grew searingly bright in her sight, and she knew her own irises were flooding black. If she let go of herself, a fierce hunger would wash through her. Her eye-teeth would elongate and strength would flow to her limbs. With a single glance, she gauged the distance to her falchion, which was leaning in the room's front corner.

A flash of surprise crossed Chane's features, and he took a step closer, studying her.

Barely a blink had passed, and Wynn just then noticed him, but she must not have paid attention to his eyes. "Oh, Chane, are you going out? Do you want company? Should Shade and I come with you?"

The offer grated on Magiere, but a much more important realization swept through her, and Chane had seen it too.

If she'd wanted to, she could have grabbed for her falchion and attacked him. Her body had responded, and her strength was *there*.

"Magiere?" Ghassan asked.

When she looked his way, where he sat at the table, he was watching her. Always watching, he couldn't have missed that tense, silent exchange. And he didn't have to ask.

Magiere nodded to him. "It's time."

Near the mid of that same night, Wynn followed Ghassan through the dark streets and farther into the capital's south side. Chane followed behind her, all three of them heavily cloaked, and Shade walked at her side. The dog's black fur made her difficult to spot at night.

Wynn still felt this was all starting too soon.

Magiere needed more time to recover, but she had insisted otherwise, and of course Ghassan was eager to begin. At least for tonight nothing critical or dangerous would happen. Ghassan wished to put only a few pieces into place, and tomorrow he would contact the prince. It would then be too late to turn back.

"How much farther is this other hideaway?" Chane asked.

"Not far," Ghassan answered. "Remember what I said and note the route."

The area around them appeared to be a semiwealthy residential area, though nothing like what Wynn knew in even the most affluent merchant districts of Calm Seatt. The homes here were sandstone mansions with elaborate terraces and balconies. Some were merely large, but others could be described only as . . . huge.

Wynn grew hesitant. The poor, run-down district they had come from seemed a much better place to hide. But they had seen few guards on the move along the way, and none up close—fewer still as they neared this district. Who would think to look for fugitives in a neighborhood like this?

Most of the manors were dark, but street lanterns were more regularly placed here than elsewhere. In going slow, they managed to stay out of direct light as they skirted close to the dwellings or along boundary walls.

Finally they emerged into a large, open area filled with a collection of market stalls more finely draped than the small market Wynn had visited. All awnings and tent flaps had been tied down for the night.

Ghassan slipped behind one wooden stall, and all of them dropped low as he did. Shade pressed up against Wynn's shoulder, and Wynn buried her fingers in Shade's neck fur.

She knew better than to expect Shade to catch and pass memories from the domin. That didn't work on him any more than Brot'an.

"Why pause here?" Chane whispered.

Ghassan pointed through the market to the next street of homes. Most were constructed of tan clay bricks. Near the end of the nearest block stood a slightly smaller and older-looking domicile. It was kept up well enough to fit in with the others. Ghassan stretched out his hand toward that place and turned to Chane.

"Down the front hallway of the main floor, you will find a door on your left and a stairwell leading up on your right. Straight ahead, you will see a back door out of the house, but hopefully you will never need that." He paused. "Take the door to the left, which opens onto a stairwell leading down to a lower passage. Ignore all doors along the way and go to the end wall . . . which will appear as nothing more than a wall."

He pulled his other closed hand out from beneath his cloak and opened it. "Use this pebble to locate and open another hidden door in that end wall, with a cellar sanctuary beyond it."

"How many of these places do you have?" Chane asked.

"Enough," Ghassan answered. "Or so I thought before I returned here. I chose this location because of the cellar. As I explained, we will trap the host down there before dawn, and with the absence of natural light, Khalidah will not realize the time until too late."

Wynn peered at the house. "So the back room in the cellar is . . . hidden by . . ."

She didn't even want to say that word—*sorcery*—though she did wonder and worry again how much skill and power the domin's sect had wielded in secret.

Ghassan ignored her and remained focused on Chane. "Do not forget a single turn or shadow on the way here. You must get the others to this place as quickly as possible."

Chane nodded. "It would have been better if they had seen it for themselves."

"I cannot risk them being spotted in the open until necessary," Ghassan returned. "And they will follow you as agreed."

That didn't reassure Wynn. Having Chane guide Leesil, Magiere, and Chap was almost the most dangerous—no, insane—part of this plan. It brought other concerns to mind as she eyed Ghassan.

"Aside from explaining how Magiere can destroy Khalidah," she began, "you didn't provide much about the specter itself." And Magiere hadn't asked much beyond the *how*. "Chane and I followed you so far, but I expect more. He can't lead Magiere, Leesil, and Chap without being fully informed."

"Here and now?" Ghassan whispered, and, after a sharp exhale, "What do you wish to know?"

"Does the specter need to feed like other undead?"

"Touching a victim in his spectral form does not allow him to draw life. Unlike the wraith we faced in Calm Seatt, Khalidah is more pure *mind* than *spirit*. He cannot feed—spirit to spirit—upon the living. He requires seized flesh, with its own spirit as a conduit, to feed upon life by touch."

The mention of "we" stuck in Wynn's head. She, Shade, and Chane—and Ghassan—had faced Sau'ilahk together the first time. This situation didn't feel much like that one.

"So his touch is as dangerous as Sau'ilahk's while he inhabits a host?" she asked.

"More dangerous," Ghassan corrected. "Even without touch, he can affect a victim's mind."

"We need to tell Magiere."

"I'm certain she has reasoned this for herself."

Wynn wasn't certain. Ghassan kept too many things to himself until pressed to share.

"If Khalidah needs to feed like other undead," she countered, "how did you and yours keep him imprisoned for so many years?"

"He was trapped in a specially constructed and prepared sarcophagus of brass."

"And what of his needs for survival?" Chane asked.

The question startled Wynn. She hadn't considered this before.

"If you knew how to kill him and did not," Chane continued, "then how did he remain functional and aware for so long?"

Wynn wanted the answer for what horror lay behind it. She'd reasoned out one other detail, for there was only one way that the sect's predecessors had resurrected sorcery.

They had extracted its secrets from Khalidah.

If the specter had been trapped for so long, how had it survived? Undead did not die for lack of feeding, or at least not those Wynn had encountered. They withered and fell dormant unless utterly destroyed, and she couldn't see how the latter was possible for a purely mental undead. And without sustenance, Khalidah would've been useless to Ghassan and his kind.

Ghassan eyed Chane in silence. "You have what information is necessary, and there is more to do. Daylight will kill him, like any other undead, unless he inhabits a host. To get Khalidah out of a host is what you—we—must focus on now."

Wynn swallowed hard. The lack of an answer to Chane's question left much to her imagination. Earlier tonight, their task had felt daunting; now it was ambiguous as well. She had viewed Chane and Magiere as the true hunters in their plan, and everyone else would play a support or defense role. But she realized that she, herself, could be pivotal if things went wrong.

What if they couldn't trap and hold Khalidah until daylight?

What if he fled his host before dawn?

There was only one answer: sunlight in the dark.

And there was only one way to create that: the sun crystal that Ghassan had made for her. It was the last line of defense to keep Khalidah from taking a new host, and when Wynn looked up . . .

Ghassan's dark eyes were fixed on her. Had any of what was now happening been part of why he so willingly made that crystal for her? Or did it have something to do with how Khalidah had been kept imprisoned?

"You understand?" he asked flatly.

Unfortunately, she did and didn't.

"Let us return," he added, not waiting for her answer. "Tomorrow, we begin and end this."

As Ghassan rose to lead the way, Chane and Shade followed, but Wynn paused.

The fallen domin had made the sun crystal. It stood to reason his sect would have made the same to deal with the specter, as needed. Yet all had perished because he had been away when Khalidah broke free and slaughtered the rest.

How had that happened?

Late the following afternoon, Prince Ounyal'am sat at the front of the dais in the great domed chamber atop the imperial castle. Living his whole life in the immense palace of wonders, he now barely noticed the intricate mosaic floor.

Its polished shapes of colored marble were arranged in a looping, coiling pattern centering upon the one-step dais three yards in diameter. The entire chamber was awash with tinted sunlight filtering through the similar mosaic of glass panes in the dome above. Four imperial guards stood at attention, one in each corner of the vast room, and two of his private guards, Fareed and Isa, stood directly behind him.

This was the last place Ounyal'am wished to be.

Once a moon, the imperial court allowed public audiences so that common citizens could bring petitions or disputes to be resolved. With his father now "indisposed," Ounyal'am was required to take the emperor's place in these proceedings. Normally, he did not mind.

It was a relief to be useful in serving those of his people he so rarely saw face-to-face. Though he'd never dare say so aloud, he believed—knew—he was a fairer judge than his father, and certainly more so than a'Yamin.

But today he was deeply preoccupied.

The prisoners he'd helped to free had not been recaptured. If a'Yamin had uncovered any hint of the imperial prince's involvement in their escape, the counselor had said nothing. Commander Har'ith had recovered from his assault in the prison and then promptly locked down the city.

Ounyal'am had done his best to assist Ghassan by suggesting to the commander that the imperial and city guards focus their search on the city's outer areas and exits. This was based on the reasoning that escaped prisoners would be desperate to leave. And with the commander's agreement, he then made certain additional other duties were given to the imperial guard based on improved security for the palace.

In truth, he needed to scatter the resources of both the imperial and city guards to give Ghassan room to act before it was too late. And he had not yet heard another word from the domin.

Twice, he had considered initiating contact himself, but he feared interrupting critical actions beyond his awareness. It was better to wait and, when Ghassan contacted him, find some excuse for a few moments of privacy.

Ounyal'am looked slowly around the chamber.

His gaze passed over a number of noble and affluent visitors come to observe the day's proceedings. For as long as he could remember, it had been customary for such families to bring their children to these events so that they could benefit from a firsthand education in the needs of citizens and the reasons behind a final imperial ruling. These families humbly knelt on mats placed to each side of the walkway from the main entrance to the dais.

Ounyal'am had always supported this custom. Young royals and nobles needed to see something of the importance . . . something other than fine food and drink, affluence and influence, and the garish clothing so prevalent at court. Hopefully, they would see that those placed in power over the common people held an even greater responsibility.

Typically, only two or three families per moon brought their children to observe and learn. Of late, since the emperor's "retirement," that had changed, though not for the right reason.

Families from as far as the eastern coastal provinces were in attendance this day. They crowded the floor all the way to the walls, leaving poorer citizens to walk a narrow path to the dais. And all in attendance had brought a daughter, a niece, or a sister of proper age . . . for marriage.

Some of this could be attributed to the celebration of the emperor's birthday in three days, not that anyone expected Kanal'am to be in attendance. But the celebration had to take place, and it proved convenient for nobles seeking an imperial alliance by marriage . . . and later by blood through a firstborn child.

The prince counted no fewer than nine such women—such offerings, such bait—kneeling virtuously beside a well-dressed father and/or mother. What a lovely image they made to uninformed eyes in displaying their interest in the day of "the people's court." And kneeling closest, no more than ten paces away, was the most striking young woman.

Durrah was considered by most to be Ounyal'am's likely choice.

Her family was one of the wealthiest in the empire. Her bloodlines could be traced back almost as far as the imperial line. Tall and well figured, with a mass of dark wavy hair, she was a simulacrum of her mother in spirit and body. Her mind was more like her vicious father.

Durrah's gaze shifted slightly to meet Ounyal'am's, as if she knew whenever he looked her way. The barest smile spread across her dark, full lips before she shyly looked away, but he saw the hard triumph in her eyes at his notice.

Cold, ambitious, and cruel, Durrah was most suited to this imperial court.

He swept his gaze over the other young women who knelt among their families like willing sacrificial offerings. He hoped not to see one face . . . but he did.

A'ish'ah knelt beside her father, the emir, with her head down and her eyes fixed on the mosaic floor beyond the edge of her mat. Her straight hair hung long enough to touch the floor as she knelt so low. Lovely as she was in her long pale yellow tunic over a white silk skirt and matching slippers, Ounyal'am quickly looked away.

The last thing he wanted was to draw attention to her, for the other families would always be watching. They were capable of anything should they fear their own candidate's success was threatened. He knew full well that when he finally had no choice but to pick a wife—first and last—he should pick Durrah. He would not subject anyone he cared for to such a life.

No, not A'ish'ah.

At his nod, two imperial guards pulled upon the sweeping, golden handles of the far doors made of the purest ivory slats. As the entrance widened, petitioners entered under the guards' careful scrutiny. And as always, Counselor a'Yamin led the way with an armload of scrolls.

It had long been the counselor's duty to oversee the petitioners. In truth, Ounyal'am thought a'Yamin had little interest in common citizens and their needs. The counselor merely insisted on being at the center of anything that happened within the imperial audience chamber. He liked to display his position and authority, more so in the absence of the emperor.

"My prince, I present the people's requests," a'Yamin announced, bowing dramatically and holding out the first scroll.

Ounyal'am took it and the proceedings began.

Most issues were typical, such as complaints of overpriced livestock or goods, with the injured party requesting repayment from the seller. In these matters, the prince listened fairly and attentively to all sides.

One man, who had recently suffered from illness, requested a reprieve for taxes on his candle shop. Ounyal'am granted this instantly. And the afternoon crawled on.

One after another, citizens came before him, bowed low—too low for his conscience—presented their situation, and then awaited an imperial pronouncement. There were a few more interesting cases toward the end.

A young man in attendance had become engaged to be married, and the bride's father had paid her dowry in coin seven days before the wedding, as was customary. The would-be groom spent a good deal of the money on improving his home, to ready it for an impending family. The day before the wedding, the bride's father broke the engagement and demanded the dowry be returned. The young man learned that the father had arranged for the daughter to marry a more affluent tea merchant. The would-be bride had agreed, assumingly of her own choice.

"I cannot return the dowry," the young man explained. "I spent much of it in good faith to make a suitable home."

"Yes, but the marriage will not take place," the bride's father insisted. "The dowry must be returned!"

Ounyal'am considered this for a few moments. True, the wedding would not take place, but that was hardly the fault of the would-be groom.

"How much of the dowry remains?" Ounyal'am asked the young man.

"Nearly a third, my prince."

"As you did not sever the engagement and spent the coin to improve your impending bride's new home, you will return a third of the original coin and keep whatever small amount remains."

The young man bowed his head in relief. "Yes, my prince."

However, the bride's father, Counselor a'Yamin, and Emir Mansoor appeared stunned and disapproving. In such a case, it was customary for the entire dowry to be returned. This practice allowed any father to keep his options open without risk.

A'Yamin took a step toward the dais. "My prince—"

Ounyal'am cut him off with a cold stare. He waited until the counselor dropped his less than respectful eyes before all in the chamber. Humiliating the imperial counselor was not wise, but Ounyal'am's bitterness overwhelmed him.

"I see there is one last petition," he said, and he held out his hand.

The counselor shuddered in his stooped fury, but he presented the last rolled paper.

Ounyal'am took it, peeled it open, and scanned it. The last case was more difficult.

Two sisters had recently lost their father, who had owned one of the largest goat farms adjacent to the city. He had been a steady supplier of milk and cheese. Instead of following custom and leaving everything to his eldest child, he had divided it. Half of the livestock had been left to his younger daughter.

Most of the farming equipment was left under the control of the elder daughter, but she was to allow the workers a choice of which sister they would serve. Nearly all had chosen the younger, and neither sister was turning a profit. The elder wanted to assert her legal—traditional—right to full inheritance.

"Can you not hire new workers?" Ounyal'am asked the elder, and then to the younger, "Can you not purchase the necessary equipment?"

"I tried," the elder answered, "but the workers have been with our family all our lives. They know our ways and the goats. With new workers, the goats' milk ran dry. This is harming not only me but other merchants in the city who have relied on my family for many years."

"And I have no spare coin to purchase equipment," the younger said. "Not nearly enough buckets or urns and no wagons to carry such to market. I am failing, Highness . . . failing in the eyes of my father's spirit."

Ounyal'am was struck by an idea he should have put aside. Once it took hold, he could not resist as he gazed around at the nobles, some sitting with their daughters.

"A difficult case," he announced, "and with so many young observers here today, I should use it to assist with your education."

Counselor a'Yamin paled slightly. The emperor had always made every pronouncement alone and without question.

"Lady Durrah," Ounyal'am said, "how would you resolve this dispute?"

Kneeling with her back straight, she bowed her head deeply—properly—to him.

"By our laws, my prince, the eldest sister should have inherited all for lack of a son. The father did not follow his duty by tradition. Because of this, his entire farm is in danger of failing. I would grant the elder sister her proper due."

As Ounyal'am turned his eyes from Durrah, he saw Counselor a'Yamin relax visibly and almost smile. Durrah's ruling was the same as would have been rendered by Emperor Kanal'am. Ounyal'am scanned the chamber as if at random. He hesitated again, and again could not stop himself.

"Lady A'ish'ah . . . how would you resolve this dispute?"

Her eyes had been on the floor, but they flew upward in near horror at having been singled out. He knew he should not have done it, but a part of him longed to hear what she might say.

Everyone waited as her lower lip trembled.

"If the father kept a successful business for so long," she finally began, almost too quietly to hear, "then he could not have been a fool. There must have been a reason for his decision. Perhaps he knew the workers would go with the younger sister, and both sisters would initially fail. Perhaps he thought the farm needed them both . . . rather than just one. Equal ownership is not a tradition, but it is the way that both would thrive."

Ounyal'am grew sorrowful and felt more alone than ever. This was the same answer he would have given, and he turned his attention back to the two sisters.

"You will join the goats, equipment, and workers together and share the farm as equals . . . equal inheritors in both ownership and responsibility."

Both young women blinked. Neither said a word at first. They glanced at each other, and perhaps neither wanted to see their father's last gift be lost. But by tradition, neither had seen this obvious answer.

"Yes, my prince," they both murmured at once.

This time Counselor a'Yamin's face reddened amid quick breaths.

With the petitions now done, Ounyal'am rose out of his chair—or rather his father's—always placed on the edge of the dais for this day. Everyone bowed low and, as imperial prince, he needed to say no polite good-byes. So he simply swept through the vast room toward the open doors with the two members of his private guard close behind.

As Ounyal'am passed A'ish'ah, he fought not to look at her, though the wisdom of her judgment kept ringing in his head. No one else in the imperial chamber would have given the same answer.

The entire ordeal had worn him out a little. Leaving the domed chambers behind, he headed for his private apartments, hoping to rest for a short while.

But as he turned a corner, he caught Fareed watching him intently, and he stopped.

"What is wrong?" he demanded.

"Nothing, my prince."

Fareed had been with him for . . . how long? Perhaps eleven years? The initial decision to appoint him had taken some thought. He was loyal, courageous, and skilled in close-quarters combat, but his face was more expressive than it should be. He also had far more opinions than was wise for someone in his position.

"There is something wrong," Ounyal'am insisted.

Young Isa looked startled, and then uncomfortable, at this sudden exchange.

Fareed's jaw twitched in near anger. "My prince, I . . . I do not understand why you continue to antagonize Counselor a'Yamin . . . over the petty disputes of farm-ers. Did you see the counselor's face? Captain Nazhif hardly sleeps, for he worries. He is on the verge of dis-missing your official taster and tasting your food himself."

Ounyal'am stood frozen. He could not remember anyone ever speaking to him in such a fashion, much less a member of his private guard. Nazhif had certainly never been so bold. But something else struck him more.

"Nazhif is not sleeping?"

Fareed glanced away. "No, my prince . . . please forgive me. I spoke out of place."

Ounyal'am said nothing at first. He considered himself fair-minded and observant, but it had not occurred to him—though it should have—that his spite for the counselor would affect others so directly.

"I will speak to Nazhif," he said and turned down the passage.

As he strode along the passages, the doors to his rooms were just coming into view when his chest began to grow warm. Nazhif stood at attention outside the doors and opened them with a flourish as Ounyal'am approached. Normally, at this time of day Nazhif would go inside with him.

"Remain out here," Ounyal'am ordered and paused to find some excuse before adding, "I wish you to rest, as I may have need of you later."

If Nazhif found this strange, his stoic face revealed nothing. "Yes, my prince."

Ounyal'am entered and finally was alone. Settling on a divan in the curtained sitting area, he let a few moments pass as he found his composure. Only when his mind cleared did he pull out the medallion and focus his thoughts.

I am here.

Is everything well for you, my prince?

He ignored this, for he could not answer in the face of all else. *The imperial guards still hunt for the prisoners. I have done what I can to hinder them. Are you safe?*

A pause followed.

Yes, my prince, but I must ask . . . has anyone unusual offered advice concerning the search?

Ounyal'am's brow wrinkled. *No. Myself, Commander Har'ith, and Counselor a'Yamin made most of the decisions in counsel. I tried to keep as many guards near the city outskirts as possible and the rest . . . otherwise occupied.*

What of the high premin?

This was a strange question. *I have not seen High Premin Aweli-Jama this day, but he has visited more often of late than I remember. Why do you ask?*

Khalidah inhabits someone highly placed and interrogated one of the prisoners repeatedly at length.

Ounyal'am was the one to hesitate this time. He had heard nothing of this, and no one to his knowledge had been allowed to interrogate the foreign prisoners.

Do you need me to find out whom?

No, but I want you to help lure him out.

How?

Tell Commander Har'ith that one of your off-duty bodyguards heard from a friend or family member who spotted strange persons at the southern district's main market yesterday near dawn. Send him there with a small contingent tonight, and do what you can to make certain anyone in a position of power either in the imperial guard or at court hears about it.

Ounyal'am stalled in any reply. After his last order for the commander, Har'ith might view any further order with suspicion.

My prince?

Ounyal'am shook off his worry. *I will attend to it.*

CHAPTER 13

Crouched on a rooftop in the still dark hours of predawn, Osha slid his bow off his shoulder and settled it in his left hand. Lost arrows had been replaced in his quiver with brown- and white-feathered ones supplied by the domin. Among them were the remaining black-feathered ones, though only four of those bore white metal tips.

Beside him, Brot'ân'duivé crouched with an assembled anmaglâhk short bow in hand. The greimasg'äh had not possessed such upon leaving their homeland. Osha did not ask from where the bow had come. There could be no doubt: from the dead body of an anmaglâhk.

The shadow-gripper drew a short arrow from behind his back and underneath his cloak. The arrow had a Chein'âs white metal point, like all other anmaglâhk tools.

Osha turned his attention to the southern marketplace below.

"Wynn, Shade, and il'Sänke should be in place," Brot'ân'duivé said. "Magiere and the others will come soon. Take your position and be certain you can see both me and the house at all times."

Osha remained silent but did not care to take orders from Brot'ân'duivé. The night had already been difficult, and he was on edge.

Before leaving the domin's hidden sanctuary, Magiere and Chap pressed for Wayfarer to remain behind. Osha had agreed that she would be far safer that way, but Wayfarer became visibly terrified at the thought of being left alone—should no one return. Yet she was equally frightened by the prospect of a battle with an undead specter and possibly imperial guards.

Osha hated the thought of leaving her behind, but Magiere—and Chap through her—argued that Wayfarer had no way to defend herself. The others would be too engaged to protect her at all times. Osha could not argue with that logic, but he also could not help dwelling upon Wayfarer alone in that shabby tenement.

For fear of revealing his turmoil, he now kept his eyes downcast.

Once more, his role would be to stand on a rooftop with a bow in his hand. He wanted to protect Wynn—and Shade and the others—but his part in their efforts began to feel cowardly.

It was not prideful to admit he was now good with the bow, as he had worked for that. But any men down below threatening those he protected stood little chance against a skilled archer up above them.

"Did you hear me?" Brot'ân'duivé asked. "Take your position."

Osha did not look at the greimasg'äh. He turned away and rose, preparing for the leap to the next rooftop.

"One more thing," Brot'ân'duivé said.

Osha froze without looking back.

"Putting down a guard is not enough," Brot'ân'duivé continued. "He will still be dangerous and able to call attention from the others. One shot per target—one to finish that purpose completely."

Osha did not flinch, but his revulsion grew for Brot'ân'duivé . . . the tainted greimasg'äh.

"I will be certain that my . . . targets . . . will not endanger anyone," Osha answered.

He rushed the rooftop's edge and leaped before Brot'ân'duivé could say more.

Magiere slipped quietly through the streets with Leesil and Chap. She and Leesil were both cloaked with their hoods up in preparation for the moment to reveal themselves. Her sheathed falchion was strapped on, and her Chein'âs dagger was lashed in its sheath at her lower back. Leesil wore both winged punching blades strapped to his thighs, and she knew he had at least one anmaglâhk stiletto up his left sleeve.

Chap's weapons, as ever, were his teeth and claws, the awareness of a majay-hì, and a natural ability to sense an undead—one that matched Magiere's own.

Crossing a city in the dark was nothing new to them. They'd done so together countless times. What *was* new was the heavily cloaked vampire walking a few paces ahead—and not just any undead, but one of the most bloodthirsty monsters Magiere had ever put down.

Years ago, back in Bela, Chane had left a string of brutalized bodies in his wake.

Had someone told Magiere she'd ever willingly allow Chane to lead her anywhere, she'd have pounded the witless snarker unconscious. And the only reason she followed Chane this night was the hope that he would lead her to something she wanted to kill even more than him: the one who had made her helpless.

She wasn't helpless anymore.

"We are almost there," Chane rasped without looking back.

That nearly voiceless voice reminded Magiere of when she'd taken his head, and yet he'd come back again. His hands were gloved, and inside his hood he wore a leather mask. Around his neck hung a pair of metal-framed glasses with lenses so dark they looked black. Wynn carried the same for whenever she used that new staff with the long crystal atop it, so it was obvious why Chane was so covered up.

So he would survive that same crystal and its light like the sun.

This only made Magiere more aware of how much Wynn and Chane had been through together, about how much they had accomplished. Another orb had been recovered.

Thankfully he still wore his "ring of nothing," as he called it. Otherwise, Magiere and Chap would both be distracted in sensing what he really was.

"You all right?" Leesil whispered.

"Yes," she answered.

But every time she thought of that gray-robed and -cowled figure who had tortured her without a single touch, she grew cold inside to the point of being numb.

She wanted the fire in her guts again. She wanted hunger and rage, even to the rush and risk of those overwhelming her. She wanted what had been taken from her. In that, she might need Chane as well. At least in thinking on him she could feel the hunger that fed her strength.

—*We will . . . destroy . . . the specter*—

As these words surfaced in her mind, she almost stopped. Perhaps Chap had done it unconsciously, but there was a sharp, determined tone to the memory-words he'd called up. He sounded almost as driven and obsessive as she felt.

"Yes," she answered him as well.

Ahead, the street emptied into a large open market-place, all quiet in the predawn darkness. So far, they hadn't spotted a single imperial or city guard, and she wasn't sure exactly what that meant.

Chane halted and pointed ahead with one gloved hand. "There, up the next block. Are you ready?"

Magiere settled a hand on her falchion's hilt, even knowing she needed nothing but her hands and teeth.

Ghassan stood behind a shed between two houses across the street from the one he had chosen. Though the sky was still dark, dawn was not far off. When he peeked around the shed's corner, Wynn did so as well, for she was so short he could see over the top of her hooded head when she crouched a little. And in her hand was the staff, its sun crystal at his eye level and unsheathed.

When he had made that for her, he had not known how useful it would be. He also knew that others had been made as a last means for dealing with Khalidah, and yet everyone of his sect had died but him.

He had never learned how that could have happened. He had seen only their lifeless eyes staring upward where they lay. Every crystal in the sect's subterranean sanctuary had been shattered within the chest that contained them. There had been no resources, let alone the time to make more before he fled that place.

Shade stood attentive and pressed up against Wynn, shoulder to thigh. Every now and then she uttered a half whine.

"What is wrong with her?" Ghassan asked.

"She's just . . . overprotective when she thinks I'm going to do something dangerous."

He raised an eyebrow. "With your penchant for trouble, she must be continuously distressed."

Wynn's head turned upward. Whatever irritated sharp look she gave him was not clearly visible in the dark. When she looked away, and he was about to do the same, she jabbed her elbow into his side.

Scowling, Ghassan had no chance to protest.

"Look!" she whispered.

A glint of gold caught his eye. He spotted two imperial guards stepping into view from a side street. They entered the market, briefly looked about, and turned back the way they had come.

Ghassan frowned. "So soon, and closer than I expected."

"At least we know they're here and looking. Your prince accomplished what you asked of him."

Yes, but it would mean little if Magiere and Chane were pulled into a fight before reaching the house. He needed Magiere to nearly reach the house before being seen and recognized as she and her companions entered.

This required stealth and timing, two attributes Ghassan was less than certain Magiere had in her. But once—if—her task was accomplished, any guards who spotted her would not act without orders. Rather, they would send someone off to report to . . .

Ghassan waited for the one who would come—for the host of Khalidah.

All it would have taken was a slip from his prince to be overheard. Not just about the escapees but about a fallen domin, last of a sect of sorcerers who had escaped from the audience chamber atop the imperial palace.

The old assassin and Leesil had not been wrong, though they had been presumptuous in thinking that he had not considered their notion himself.

Ghassan eyed the street both ways.

The specter would not ignore a chance at catching both of his most desired prey in one place. And wherever it found Magiere, it would expect to find the last of its previous keepers.

Whoever entered that house across the way would be Khalidah's host.

"What now?" Wynn whispered.

"We wait."

From above, Brot'ân'duivé spotted Chane slipping down the street with Magiere, Léshil, and Chap. Lifting his gaze, he focused across the rooftops through the darkness.

He no longer knew what to expect from Osha.

Back in Calm Seatt, he had been caught off guard when the young and most inept of anmaglâhk had failed to appear at their meeting point. And then the ship carried Brot'ân'duivé and the others southward.

Osha had chosen to remain with Wynn Hygeorht—and without a word of warning.

Until then, Brot'ân'duivé believed he could read the young man without effort. Osha had surprised him, and not many in the world were capable of this. Worse, for all of Osha's training under the tutelage of great Sgäilsheilleache, he still exhibited a reticence to kill.

Sgäilsheilleache had killed without hesitation when necessary. He had failed in not teaching his last student to quiet his mind, still his heart, and act as required.

That need would come soon, and Brot'ân'duivé doubted Osha could fulfill it.

For a moment, he slipped into annoyance, for he could not spot Osha on the assigned rooftop . . . not until the young one moved and crept to that roof's edge over the street.

Brot'ân'duivé peered downward as the quartet below came closer, and he firmly gripped his short bow. His task—and Osha's—would be to provide Magiere's group cover should they be discovered too quickly before reaching Ghassan's other hidden place.

The domin's plan would fail otherwise.

Brot'ân'duivé shifted up to one knee, pulled the arrow enough to feel tension in the bowstring, and watched as the group below approached the house. Even with their hoods up, it was simple to differentiate between Chane and Magiere by their heights and movements. He did not spot any guards, but they had to be near if the domin's plan was truly in motion. For an instant, Brot'ân'duivé's gaze locked only on Léshil.

To date, he had explained both his presence and his actions as a determination to protect Magiere and keep the orbs from falling into the hands of Most Aged Father. Magiere understood his reasons and believed him—in part, it was the truth. He had other reasons he kept to himself.

First, he had to learn the power of the orbs, their purpose, and their use. It had been a rare frustration to live in the presence of the orb of Spirit and not open the chest to examine it. If he betrayed such interest, he would have given himself away prematurely.

Chap was ever suspicious and missed little.

Second, Brot'ân'duivé had to make certain at any cost that Léshil survived. The half-blood offspring of a human father and his an'Cróan mother, Cuirin'nên'a, served a purpose.

Many years past, and well before Léshil's conception, a few among the Anmaglâhk watched with great concern as Most Aged Father's distaste for humans became something worse. The return of the Enemy was not in doubt by those who still learned of the far past, but the patriarch set the caste to actions that could bring about dangerous repercussions.

In that forgotten age, humans had been used as tools of the Enemy.

Most Aged Father's obsession with this became a threat to his own people. He began using the Anmaglâhk not as guardians and protectors but as weapons themselves. They were ordered to seed war among human nations, to turn such against one another, and weaken, cripple, or eliminate their potential as weapons should the Ancient Enemy return.

Some among the caste, such as Brot'ân'duivé's one love—the maternal grandmother of Léshil—saw the danger that others did not. Cuirin'nên'a's mother, the great Eillean, had been a founder of a hidden collection of dissidents inside the caste and later among the clans.

Yes, it was Eillean who feared that humans would learn what was being done to them, if not why. They would turn against the an'Cróan for vengeance, and a thousand years of peace, sanctuary, and safety would be lost. Brot'ân'duivé later joined the dissidents by Eillean's consent. It had been through her that he learned of Cuirin'nên'a and, more critically, of Léshil as the dissidents' own instrument to strike the Enemy when it came again.

Cuirin'nên'a had followed in her mother's ways.

She sacrificed much to bring her half-blooded son into this world and train him beyond the caste's reach. So he was born and raised in the Warlands, away from his people, with few influences outside of his mother.

This was necessary for him to remain beyond the influence of any one people, culture, or faction. It would then be easier to keep him free for what would come, and to direct—control—him amid his feelings of being cast adrift in the world.

Cuirin'nên'a was to turn her own son into the weapon that their people might someday need. So it should have been—until he fled . . . with a majay-hì.

Brot'ân'duivé easily reasoned this had been Chap's doing. No one could have known then what hid within one majay-hì pup that a grandmother delivered secretly through a mother to a lonely half-blooded boy. But Chap's act of stealing Léshil away did not change fate.

Even the long-dead ancestors recognized Léshil when he later went to them for his name-taking. Instead of leaving him to choose a name for himself, they put another name upon him linked to one among them.

Leshiârelaohk . . . Leshiâra's Champion . . . the Champion of Sorrow-Tear.

Léshil's destiny was clear, and Chap's plans no longer mattered. The mixed-race son of Cuirin'nên'a would play a pivotal role should the worst come and the Ancient Enemy of many names return again.

Brot'ân'duivé would make certain of Léshil's survival above all else.

He watched the half-blood and the others walk out in the open market, now still and quiet, and he knew Osha had seen them as well. Though the young one had become unpredictable, he would not hesitate to protect his human friends.

About twenty paces from the house, Léshil stopped. Chap halted beside him, and Magiere paused ahead to look back. Léshil reached up and pushed his hood back, exposing his white-blond hair, which caught the light of the lanterns halfway down the block. Chap stood in plain sight, looking both ways as Magiere pushed her hood back.

Brot'ân'duivé remained poised. His gaze shifted between every dark place along the street. This was the moment in which the domin's plan might fail.

Wynn held her breath as Leesil exposed his hair. Her friends were almost to the safe house. She jumped slightly when Ghassan touched her shoulder. Looking up, she followed where he pointed.

Eight imperial guards emerged from a side street in the market. They moved, silent and quick, heading toward Magiere and the others. And worse for Wynn's stomach, this was no accident.

Magiere had been spotted as she and hers had passed through the market.

Panic rushed through Wynn. She and Ghassan were too far away to act yet. Somewhere above, Osha and Brot'an would fire when necessary, but more guards could be coming. Magiere's group had to reach the house at the right moment.

"What do we do?" she whispered.

Ghassan didn't answer . . . as the guards suddenly stopped.

Two of them turned and hurried off the way they'd come.

"That is what we needed," Ghassan whispered. "Two have gone to report that the prisoners have been found. The others are waiting for orders."

The domin let out a long breath, but Wynn didn't share his relief.

"Chane still has time to get everyone into the cellar," Ghassan added.

As if signaled, Chane hurried up the front porch, opened the door, and entered. Magiere, Chap, and Leesil followed him, but Wynn wasn't certain any of them had noticed the guards lurking among the market stalls. And when she looked away . . .

The two missing guards returned to the others. They had not been gone long.

A tall, thin figure in a hooded gray robe stepped out of the shadows behind them.

At least twelve more guards followed after that, and the robed figure raised one arm to halt them. He then strode through the guards already waiting in the market until he was in the lead. Without even slowing, he dropped his arm, and all the guards began to advance.

"Too soon!" Ghassan hissed. "Chane will never get them through the hidden door!"

Before Wynn could respond, one imperial guard cried out and toppled backward in the street. An arrow protruded from his chest.

Another went down as his shoulder was struck.

Shouts erupted as other guards scattered for cover, calling out to one another as more arrows struck. But that gray figure didn't break stride and approached the front door untouched with five men behind him.

"We need to get in there!" Wynn whispered loudly.

Ghassan rushed out, and Wynn dashed after him with her staff as Shade sped ahead of her.

CHAPTER 14

Chane led the way into the house with Magiere and Chap directly behind him. He heard Leesil follow and close the door. As il'Sänke had described, Chane found himself in a hallway aimed straight ahead.

Through the eyeholes of his mask, he barely made out small lamps lining one side of the way. None were lit, and he could not see to the hallway's end. He moved on without a word to the others. At least while wearing the mask he did not have to guard his expression.

The trek through the streets had been more difficult than anticipated. It did not bother him that the three he led all hated him. He welcomed their hatred as it meant he did not have to attempt any false civility.

What did bother him was their unmitigated hypocrisy.

Magiere viewed him as a killer, which he was—or had been more than now. But she saw herself as some paragon fighting the good fight. He remembered how this contradiction had once played out.

On the eastern continent in the dank forests of Droevinka, he had been trailing Wynn in secret as she traveled with Magiere, Leesil, and Chap. Wynn ended up separated from her companions and in danger, and Chane had had no choice but to reveal himself to protect her.

Magiere later stumbled upon them and attacked him.

He managed to step inside her guard, catch her with a fist, and knock her off her feet. As he was about to ram his sword down through her chest, Wynn threw herself in his way, begging him to stop.

He hesitated . . . but Magiere did not and struck upward with her falchion.

The blade's broad end cut into his neck and jaw. He never saw the second blow that took off his head. When he awoke much later in a shallow grave, little more than a pit, he was covered in freshly killed corpses and blood, though his head was back on his neck.

Magiere had not known that was possible—neither had he. It was only accomplished by the arcane intervention of Welstiel Massing, another undead and Magiere's half brother.

During the fight, he had hesitated to kill. She had not, and yet she viewed herself as so much better than him.

It was insufferable.

He kept his eyes straight ahead, for hatred had likely turned his irises clear.

"Where's the door to the cellar?" Magiere asked.

He heard the strain in her voice at having to speak to him.

"The hallway's end, on the left," he answered.

Chane drew the extra cold-lamp crystal from his pocket and brushed it against his cloak. It glowed softly.

"Where did you get that?" Magiere demanded.

His first impulse was to ignore her. "Wynn gave it to me." And he walked on.

As he passed a large archway on the right, he saw a well-furnished sitting room beyond it, filled with low couches, chairs and tables, and framed paintings on the walls.

"How will you get us through the lower . . . hidden door?"

This time it was Leesil who questioned him, but Chane did not answer. The half-blood could pick a lock but knew nothing of the arcane. Il'Sänke had given Chane a pebble and told him how to use it. The outcome depended upon whether or not they had been spotted entering the house.

So long as they had, the plan was fairly simple.

Once Magiere and Leesil were recognized and observed going inside, whoever among the guards saw them would slip away to report. Chane was to lead his group downstairs, open the hidden door, and take everyone into the secret windowless cellar chamber. Wynn, Shade, and il'Sänke were positioned close by outside, and the specter—in whatever host—would come directly for this house and enter. He would never risk leaving their capture purely in the hands of the imperial guards.

And the identity of the specter's host would be revealed.

The domin insisted that Khalidah possessed the ability to easily see and breach the sect's ensorcellment that hid the final cellar door from all senses, and he would enter. Il'Sänke also claimed that he himself would sense when this occurred.

The ease of entering the sanctuary unimpeded would leave Khalidah believing that he was in control as il'Sänke, Wynn, and Shade rushed the house. Brot'an and Osha would scatter any guards trying to stop them.

Acting as bait, Magiere would draw Khalidah farther inside the sanctuary as il'Sänke, Wynn, and Shade closed in from behind. After that, il'Sänke claimed he would be able to hold the specter in place, inside the host's body, and trap him there in the ensorcelled cellar chamber until dawn broke.

Chane would know the moment came only when he had to fight to keep from falling dormant. And what then? He would succumb not knowing whether the others had succeeded. At that point Magiere's task would be to drive Khalidah from the host by making him believe she was about to kill that body. The specter could not remain inside someone in the moment of death, or he might share it, and so would flee the host.

The only safeguard was the crystal atop Wynn's staff. Khalidah would have two choices: to be burned out of existence by the crystal or to flee from the house and burn in the dawn.

During a late-night talk in which Chane had been present, Wynn had asked, "What if the specter leaves the host but tries to take one of us?"

"I will stop him," il'Sänke had answered flatly.

Chane hoped that was not a boast. He and Magiere, and likely both majay-hì, were immune to possession by an undead; the others were not. Wynn might be the safest with her staff in hand, so long as she ignited it, but that would also make her the specter's first target to eliminate or possess. No one had mentioned that, though all of them could easily reason it.

However, nothing better had been offered, and now they were here. From the beginning, Chane had suspected they would end up with a "lure and trap" strategy.

He neared the hallway's end, with a door on his left and an open stairwell on the right, just as il'Sänke had described. Peering ahead through a small foyer, Chane saw the outline of the back door to the house.

"This way," he rasped, turning left.

After opening the door, he led the way through. Upon descending the stairs to the lower level, he found himself in a passage. As instructed, he ignored all other doors along the way and went straight to the passage's end wall. Then he reached into the small pocket inside his cloak to retrieve the pebble. His gloves were so thick that it was hard to feel the tiny stone.

"Hurry!" Leesil whispered.

Chane clenched his teeth against a retort. Magiere hung close at his right shoulder and studied the stones of the end wall. He finally felt the pebble with his fore-finger, pinched it, and began to withdraw his hand.

A loud creak carried in the quiet.

Chane hesitated, thinking it was more of Leesil's fidgeting. When Magiere whirled and Chap snarled, Chane twisted around to look up the passage.

A tall hooded figure in a shimmering gray robe, backed by five guards, stood halfway down the cellar stairs . . . having arrived too soon.

Osha let fly another arrow when he gained a clear shot. Imperial guards scattered and ducked along the street below, scurrying between market stalls up the way or into side streets and cutways, trying to run along the buildings' sides below him.

He had not expected so many and began to worry in counting off the shots—the arrows—he fired. He did not know how many arrows Brot'ân'duivé had scavenged from his previous victims.

Osha had wounded and put down two men. Another three lay dead with shorter shafts upright in their face or chest, and those had not been his targets. The longer this continued, the more likely he could not avoid a kill.

And worse, the robed figure and five guards had breached the house too early. Chane could not possibly get Magiere and the others into the secret room before they were caught.

Osha had no chance to wonder what came next as Wynn, Shade, and the domin rushed from hiding and charged toward the house. He quickly swung his aim in their direction. Two guards ran from cover to follow them. One closed on Wynn from behind, and Osha released his bow's string.

The arrow struck true in the guard's shoulder as Osha drew and nocked another. As he aimed for the guard rushing the domin from the other side . . .

An arrow appeared to sprout from the guard's face, and he fell.

Osha did not look for Brot'ân'duivé or at another of the greimasg'äh's victims.

The men below only followed orders, just as Osha had, first under Most Aged Father and then under Brot'ân'duivé. He had once been ignorant of how tainted—how stained in spirit—both had become . . . and how close he had come to that black stain upon himself.

Osha focused only on protecting Wynn.

He would kill again—stain his spirit even more—if he had to. But only for her, and not for the mad "father" of his lost caste, or for that tainted greimasg'äh.

Brot'ân'duivé's spite fractured his calm as he put down the guard rushing the domin.

Osha's reluctance to kill had slowed the process of clearing the street. Every guard left alive, even wounded, was still a threat. Did the young fool not realize this?

It was no mistake that Osha had been stripped of his place among the Anmaglâhk, dissident or loyalist. That the Chein'âs had done this, and not a superior of the caste, was the only mystery. Osha lacked what was necessary to protect his people.

Another imperial guard broke from cover and charged for Wynn. The black majay-hì snarled but did not break stride as yet. Even Shade understood that *purpose* overrode all else—but not Osha.

Brot'ân'duivé fired again.

His arrow struck the guard in the throat at the same instant a black-feathered one sprouted from the man's shoulder. This time, Brot'ân'duivé hissed a curse at the young one's wasted shot.

He already knew how many arrows he had left. At least one had to be kept in reserve until all threats had been neutralized. He had instructed Osha to do the same before they scaled to the rooftops. Soon enough, whoever commanded the forces below would send one or more up to take out the archers that harried them.

Brot'ân'duivé reloaded to cover the domin's final charge for the door. Five guards had already succeeded in following the gray-robed figure into the house. Eight had been killed or disabled in the street; at an estimate, seven more hid out of sight in the market area.

An order was shouted below. Brot'ân'duivé had learned enough Sumanese to understand.

"Do not let them reach the house!"

Men in gold sashes rushed out around market stalls and from dark places along the street. As il'Sänke approached the front landing, Wynn and Shade were close behind.

Brot'ân'duivé pivoted on his knee, aimed at the nearest guard, and fired again.

* * *

Leesil stared at the tall figure, now at the bottom of the stairs; he couldn't mistake that robe even for not seeing any face in the hood's deeper dark. The gray robe that shimmered with shadowy, glinting, strange symbols was the same as the one worn by the one who'd visited their cell and spoken inside his head.

Leesil heard Magiere's breaths stop, but he didn't dare turn his eyes from that robe. Chap began rumbling and snarling beside him. Everyone stood poised and waiting for . . . something.

The robed one suddenly shifted left.

Two imperial guards rushed down the stairs with curved swords drawn.

Leesil jerked the ties on both winged blades. Magiere and Chane—dhampir and undead—were the ones safest to engage the specter, and Chap was a natural hunter of the undead. That meant Leesil had to deal with the guards.

—*Force them back . . . and do not let . . . that thing . . . touch you*—

At Chap's warning, Leesil drew both winged punching blades. He felt Chap brush by his left knee as the dog charged. He hoped Chap was right about the choice of opponents they each had to face—and that the specter couldn't get into the head of a majay-hì.

Leesil slammed into the first guard before the man made it off the stairs, and he heard Chap rushing at the gray robe.

Chane panicked, for everything had gone wrong too quickly. If il'Sänke had seen the robed man approach the house, then the domin was already on the move with Wynn and Shade. Or had Khalidah finished with them?

Leesil hit the lead guard head-on as Chap charged for the gray-robed figure on the left side of the bottom step.

"Leesil!" Magiere called and started after him.

Chane grabbed her cloak and jerked, but before he said a word . . . the robed one vanished before his eyes.

He was too stunned to move when Chap ended his lunge and nearly tripped off the empty step. Magiere slapped Chane's grip away, but he focused on the second guard shifting position to get around the lead guard— likely to find an opening to attack Leesil as well.

That guard suddenly recoiled and nearly toppled, as if he had rammed into something solid.

"Behind me, now!" Chane rasped at Magiere.

He shifted the pebble to his off hand holding the crystal, and then pulled his shorter blade. In the corner of his sight, Magiere locked eyes on him. He could not look away from the whole passage, but had her irises suddenly flooded black?

"It is invisible to our eyes!" he snarled at her.

Chane lunged two more steps down the passage and set himself, putting Magiere at his back. He could not believe what had happened—not to him. Sorcery, the lost art of mental magic, should not affect him. Or so he had thought by the "ring of nothing."

As the ring masked his undead presence, it also hampered some of his inner abilities. Tampering with his mind—and thereby his senses—should not have been possible while he wore it.

Chane grew warier of how powerful the specter might be. The sound of Magiere's falchion ripping from its sheath brought him back to awareness. He was trapped in a narrow passage with his most hated enemies as his only allies. And the specter had blocked its presence from his—from *everyone's* awareness.

Chane quickly surveyed the whole space before him.

Leesil drove the lead guard back up one more step, slashing with both punching blades. That blocked the other guards above from descending, but this would not last. Then the air before Chap darkened for an instant.

Chane stiffened in a half step, and then Chap looked normal again as he spun to lunge in behind Leesil to help against the guards.

But Chane fixed on what he had seen . . . or almost not seen.

It was as if a shadow had passed between him and the dog, and he tossed il'Sänke's pebble back toward Magiere's feet.

"Find and open the door! The specter is still here."

Sweeping the passage with his eyes, he now knew something to look for, or so he hoped. Something had half blocked his crystal's light for an instant. Could the ring have held off part of whatever the specter had done to him—to all of them?

Leesil slashed forward with one blade while simultaneously shifting to allow Chap in beside him, and both appeared to darken in Chane's sight. Something had passed quickly and close behind them.

Chane tossed the crystal halfway to the stairs and lunged another step while slashing his shorter sword again. He could not draw and use his longer one in this narrow space, and he watched carefully for anything that blocked the crystal's light, even for an instant.

* * *

Wynn almost reached the steps to the front landing when a deep voice shouted in Sumanese.

"Do not let them reach the house!"

She nearly broke stride but glanced back. Imperial guards emerged into the street at a run, and a tall one with hawkish features came at her. She was caught between running onward or stopping to face the man with Shade at her side.

The guard suddenly began convulsing and went down with a short anmaglâhk arrow through his left eye. He didn't make a sound as his back hit the street. Shade wheeled beside Wynn, growling, though she hesitated at running on.

"Do not stop!" Ghassan ordered from ahead.

Too much happened all at once.

At another cry from Wynn's right, she couldn't help but look. An oncoming man toppled, one short arrow in the side of his throat. Another guard tried to grab for her before she even saw him, and a longer arrow with black feathers appeared to sprout in his chest. She'd known this would happen. Seeing it so close was something else. Ghassan had less violent methods, but there was no time here and now. Their defense had to be left to Brot'an's methods—and Osha's.

Wynn took a step to rush on and something jerked her off her feet from behind. She barely kept her grip on the staff. Frantic and choking as her cloak cinched across her throat, she reached over and back with her other hand. She was so shocked that she didn't see Shade coming until the dog leaped right at her.

Somewhere above Shade's snarls, Wynn thought she heard whispering, and then the dog's forepaws hit her in the chest. She felt and heard her cloak tear as she went down on her back. Shade leaped off and beyond her. Then came snarls, snaps, and shouts too guttural to understand.

Wynn thrashed over, still clinging to the staff, and looked back to see three guards beyond the one Shade had put down. They were somehow frozen along the street looking everywhere but at her. Hearing the whispers again, she twisted around toward that sound.

Ghassan stood upon the landing's steps, his eyes fixed above and beyond her, perhaps at those guards. The whispers came out through his clenched teeth.

Wynn could only guess what he was doing. As she was about to grab Shade's tail before the dog disturbed the domin's concentration, she heard . . .

One arrow strike . . . a second and a hacking choke . . . and a third with a shriek.

Wynn pushed up to her knees as the first guard hit the street, dead; he fell forward and shattered the short arrow in his heart. The second one choked and dropped with another through his throat. The third stumbled, clutching a longer, black-feathered shaft impaled through his thigh, front to back.

A shorter arrow sprouted from his neck behind his jaw; he dropped and didn't move.

Wynn felt suddenly so cold. Most of the guards she could see were dead or at least down. Two still tried to crawl away, wounded and bleeding. They were the enemy, but they were ignorant of what this all meant.

Some part of her wanted to scream out for all this to stop.

"Up and run!" Ghassan barked.

Shade grabbed Wynn's sleeve in her teeth and wrenched her toward the domin.

* * *

Magiere eyed Chane's back where he stood between her and Leesil as well as Chap. It would be so easy to finish him. But whatever fire of hate he ignited in her had turned toward something else. It wrapped around that figure in gray who had winked out before her eyes.

Her rage came back . . . and swallowed all reason.

The robe, its symbols, the darkness in the hood that hid his face, and the spindly form beneath all of that had stood still and calm as when he had visited her cell. There was flesh inside the robe that she could tear, bones that she could break.

There was suffering to crush out of him for everything he had done to her.

Chane slowly turned his head, peering about. The crystal's light began to burn Magiere's widened sight, but she didn't see the robe—the prey—she wanted. No one was getting to it before she did, and the burning in her stomach lurched up into her throat.

It was still here—she could *feel* it.

Leesil and Chap still fought the guards on the stairs, but Magiere didn't go to help them. In trying to find that thing some way other than by sight, she almost closed her eyes . . .

Chane lunged to the right, and Magiere's eyes snapped wide.

His hand shot out. His fingers appeared to wrap around nothing, but his grip didn't fully close. She saw his arm straighten as if what he held tried to jerk free.

Magiere fixed on the emptiness in Chane's grip, dropped her sword, and charged. Her fingers closed on nothing, unlike Chane's.

She shrieked and slammed him aside to claw at . . . nothing.

Magiere lashed out wildly beyond Chane's grip, but her fingers—her hardened nails—only gouged the wood of the passage's wall.

Leesil knocked a guard's sword aside with his right blade, and both weapons hit the side railing. He heard Chap snap and snarl but didn't dare look at the dog. Somehow, he had to break through and get everyone out of here.

Reaching the hidden room wouldn't work anymore. The specter in its host was gone, and even that didn't matter. What did matter was never going back to that cell . . . never letting Magiere be taken again.

He heard her guttural shriek like a feral animal somewhere behind him. A shudder passed through him, beyond panic, and he grew still inside.

Leesil rammed his forehead into the guard's face.

The man's head recoiled and struck the next guard up the stairs. Leesil thrust with his legs to topple forward as he shouted, "Chap—over!" As he fell, he rammed the wedged point of his left blade into the gut of the stunned guard beneath him.

The weight of Chap's paws landed on his back as he looked into the gaping eyes of the man beneath him.

The instant Chap leaped off and up the stairs, Leesil pulled his legs under himself.

He saw Chap go at the next guard, snarling, clawing, and snapping for the man's throat, and he thrust upward, pulling his legs up.

He caught the right railing with the sole of his right

boot, and that instant of grounding was enough. A third guard's sword came overhead and down at Chap amid the second guard's screams and the dog's snarls.

Leesil deflected the sword with his left blade as he thrust his right into the third guard's throat.

Chane barely kept his feet as Magiere shoved him into the wall, but when she clawed beyond his grip, her fingers passed by and her hardened nails only tore rents in the wood. He could not comprehend how he had held something and she had missed striking it.

Worse, she appeared to have lost all her reason.

Then something struck his whole body at once.

It felt like a wind coming from nowhere, which had been hardened like stone, and everything darkened before his eyes. Stunned, he found himself—when his sight cleared—slumped down against the wall, and Magiere was trying to pick herself up at the passage's far side.

Whatever had hit him had struck her aside as well.

A shadow darkened Magiere's form. She twisted up to her knees, her mouth gaping and exposing elongated fangs . . . but no scream came out.

Chane grabbed for his fallen shorter sword.

Saving Magiere was not what drove him. If this thing could do all of this to him and a dhampir, what had happened to Wynn? He charged, striking at where he had seen that shadow. In the last instant, he remembered . . .

He could not kill the specter's body, its host, with so many present for it to take instead.

Chane twisted the sword's blade and drove one strut of the crossguard behind his swing. The crossguard went all the way to the wall. As the impact jarred his arm, something else struck his face.

Searing cold pain spread through Chane's skull.

Chap grew desperate to get back to Magiere, and yet he could not abandon Leesil.

She could not be left to face the specter alone, and Chane's help did not count. Neither did the blood in his mouth or what was left of the dead guard beneath him. In a wider space for trained armed men to move freely, these moments of Leesil and Chap holding their ground might not have happened.

And the plan was now worthless. The specter would never be trapped in the domin's hidden room.

Chap looked up once at Leesil facing the remaining two guards above.

—*Drive them up . . . out . . . before more come*—

Leesil would not glance back, but his answer came as he lunged up another step.

"Get Magiere!" he shouted.

Chap started to wheel when his whole body was lifted off the steps. He did not have time to even feel a jolt of shock before he flew sideways into the side rail.

Chane let the hunger rise to eat the pain and cold in his head. When his sight cleared, he saw Magiere on her knees. She looked up at him with eyes—not just irises—flooded pure black.

The sight filled him with fear, not of her, but that she had completely lost herself.

Her head snapped around toward the stairs as something there shattered.

Chane looked in time to see Chap tumble down amid broken pieces of the railing. Leesil's body slammed sideways into the stairway's other side. The two guards above were likewise knocked away.

It was not until Magiere lunged up, grabbed her fallen sword, and pushed past toward the stairs, that one thought broke through Chane's fear.

She had looked before he had heard anything. She had known—sensed—something that she could not see. And in her current state, she might not stop until she killed what had tormented her . . . and Khalidah would flee the host before dawn.

When Magiere reached the stairs, she ran right past Leesil and Chap, who both appeared half stunned while struggling to rise. Partway up the stairs, the final two guards—both still teetering—tried to stop her. She knocked the first aside, and Chane thrashed to right himself as he heard the crack of the man's jaw. She split the other man's chest with her falchion and ran past before he dropped.

Magiere had lost to her dhampir half, and Chane bolted toward the stairs.

He tried to shout at Leesil, though he only rasped, "Get up—now!"

CHAPTER 15

Wynn halted on the house's landing when Ghassan froze in the opened doorway ahead of her. Panting in fright and exhaustion, she tried to shove him out of her way to no avail.

"What are you waiting for?" she whispered.

He didn't answer, so she tried to push him aside enough to see into the house. And when she did . . .

A gray-robed figure stood down the long, dark hallway ahead. The pit of its hood shifted slightly from the domin to her.

"No!" Ghassan snapped.

Wynn thought that was meant for the specter, and then the domin's hand clamped over her eyes, and he shoved her back. Stumbling, she swatted away his hand, but he stood fully in the doorway, blocking her as he stared into the house.

Something mournful, then pained, and finally hateful twisted the domin's features.

Ghassan fixed on a gray robe he had not seen before this night. He could not see what—who—hid within the hood, but he felt something worming into his mind. His will alone could not stop it, and whispers swarmed over his thoughts to smother them.

One voice cut through all of them.

"Oh, so much anguish and hate—both so tiny and pathetic. A morsel compared to the meal I deserve, after what you and yours did to me . . . for so long."

Ghassan tried to block out that voice. In its place, a swarm of whispers crawled over his mind like carrion beetles.

. . . worthless . . . coward . . . where were you . . . when they all died, even her . . .

He lost focus and cringed, fearing that name they might whisper at him.

. . . lovely . . . so truly kind . . . and so satisfying to us . . . your Tuthâna . . .

Yes, she had been the best in nature if not skill of all within his sect. She had warned him from afar to hurry back, when he had lost against Wynn and her comrades in seeking an orb in a forgotten dwarven city. Her warning had come too late . . . to reach her.

Ghassan did not know he had screamed until someone struck him in the side. That sharp pain made him gasp.

"Wake up!" Wynn cried. "Don't let it get to you!"

All Ghassan's pain-fed rage fueled the burning lines, sigils, and signs that filled his view. That fiery pattern overlaid his sight of the gray robe standing serenely in the dark. Then he heard a scream, and shouts, shattering wood and feet pounding upon stairs. The gray hood turned slightly, perhaps looking toward those sounds, as did Ghassan.

The others were below, but at least one was coming up. When his gaze shifted back in less than a blink, he looked into that hood's blackness.

All lines of light shattered to splinters within his sight. Like glass shards, they cut and stung his mind instead of his flesh. He heard a spiteful titter in his head.

"And now there is another that I will take again, though not for myself. She belongs to her maker."

Ghassan lurched back as an unseen force struck his whole body. He saw the gray robe drift up the hallway farther into the dark. He barely grabbed the doorframe's sides as someone rushed up from out of the cellar.

Magiere spun, looking everywhere. No matter where she turned, she did not appear to see the gray-robed figure lingering just beyond her. Something was wrong with her face, though it was not clear in the dark.

Ghassan lurched again as the force upon him grew.

"Get out . . . you petty little pretender."

Wynn began shouting, pulling on him, and all he could do was fix on Magiere. He barely raised and held one sign in his mind's eye for an instant. He uttered one command into her thoughts before his focus broke.

—*Clarity*—

Ghassan stumbled back, dragging Wynn with him, and heard the front door slam shut.

As Magiere charged out of the cellar, her insides burned, her guts ached, and hunger overran all of that. Fed on hate born of fear while she'd been in that cell for a moon, something more had happened to her near the end that she'd told no one.

She'd lost everything except a name that wasn't hers.

Each time her tormentor came, less and less of her life—her memories—remained when he left. She forgot faces, events, places, as piece by piece was taken from

296 · BARB & J. C. HENDEE

her or lost under anger, then panic, and then fear . . .
and then nothing.

The last piece she clung to in the dark was only a name.

By the end she was alone and too weak to move. The
face that matched the name blurred more and more
after each visit. It faded further away in the dark of her
cell and her mind. And she then couldn't remember
Leesil's face anymore.

Even when he'd come for her, her first thought was
to kill him.

She'd opened her eyes when he spoke because she
could hear a voice too close that wasn't in her head . . .
wasn't the torturer's but was somehow familiar. That
terrified her.

When she saw and then remembered him, it made it
that much worse.

After that, Magiere swallowed down that moment
and kept it hidden. She'd locked it in the place inside
where she'd always feared that she was the worst threat
Leesil might ever face. He mattered more to her than
anyone, and she might have killed him if she hadn't
been so weak when he found her.

Magiere couldn't bear this. Each time it slipped into
her thoughts, she wanted to die.

As she lunged out into the main floor hallway and
halted, she didn't think—didn't care—whose flesh was
inside that robe. Hunger sharpened violently, and by
that she knew her prey was close. Though the hallway
was nearly too bright in her fully blackened eyes, she
couldn't find what she was hunting, no matter which
way she turned.

Something moved at the hallway's front end.

When she twisted toward it, dim light well beyond

the open door seared her sight. She saw only a dark silhouette in a doorway and . . . pain cut through her head like a thin, sharp blade. So much pain that it stripped away hunger with one word.

—*Clarity*—

Magiere chilled as the hallway darkened before her eyes.

The fire in her that she'd longed for died with two thoughts.

What had she done now, and where was Leesil?

"Get up!" Wynn shouted to Ghassan.

She'd barely gotten to her knees after he'd shot backward and nearly flattened her. Just before that, she was certain she'd glimpsed Magiere in the hallway. Somewhere in the house, the others were trapped with Khalidah, and who knew what had happened—was happening—in there.

The domin lay on his back, breathing quickly and shaking as if struck. Shade leaped over him and went to the closed door, but it didn't even flex when she hit it with her forepaws.

"Oh, seven hells. Please, Ghassan, *get . . . up!*" Wynn begged as she yanked on his arm.

His eyes snapped wide and did not blink as he looked at her. He lurched upright to a sitting position on the landing.

Wynn looked quickly about, for she'd dropped the staff in her tumble. When she spotted it lying farther back with its butt end overhanging the landing's steps, she sighed in relief. At least the crystal hadn't broken. She reached for it.

"They are coming up!" Ghassan said behind her.

Wynn looked back as she gripped the staff below its long crystal. "Who? I saw only Magiere . . . and that robe."

"We must get inside another way," he said. Strangely, he looked up at the landing's roof.

Wynn never had a chance to follow his gaze, for the staff lurched in her grip. Shade snarled and wheeled from the door. All Wynn could do was tighten her grip, but the staff jerked harder. Her knees skidded and she barely twisted around as she was dragged to the edge of the steps, and she looked into the face of another imperial guard.

Where had he come from?

He held the butt of the staff with one hand . . . and a raised sword in the other.

Wynn did the only thing she could: she gripped the staff with both hands and shoved on it.

She never saw what happened as someone—some*thing*—snatched the fallen hood of her robe and yanked her backward. She heard the hood or robe start to tear as she skidded across the landing. When she pushed up, Ghassan stood over her. Nearer the landing's edge, Shade half crouched with all her hackles stiffened.

A muffled crack made Wynn roll away to one knee, and when she looked beyond Shade . . .

Brot'an rose up and dropped the guard's body. The man's neck was twisted at an impossible angle, and his head flopped as it hit the street.

Wynn didn't have time to turn sick at the sight.

Ghassan pulled her up by her free hand and wrist, and she swallowed hard once.

"Where's Osha?" she asked.

Brot'an stepped up on the landing, ignoring Shade's rumbled warning. "Watching from above, I would hope. Without further arrows, I came down . . . fortunately."

Ghassan too quickly dragged Wynn past Brot'an off the landing and down into the street.

"Enough talk," he commanded. "Wynn, hold on to the staff at all costs."

"What are you doing?" she asked. "We have to get inside."

"We will . . . from above."

"What?"

Nearly lost in frustration, she was about to jerk out of his grip and run for the door.

Ghassan pulled her in and wrapped both his arms tightly around her. Shade lunged off the landing, closing in.

Ghassan ignored the dog and looked to Brot'an. "Let no one out of that door until you hear from one of us."

Brot'an took another step, looking once at Wynn. Shade snapped her jaws at the domin.

Wynn had no idea what Ghassan intended—but she also had no notion for how to get through that door if the specter could drive him out so easily.

"Shade, enough!" she said. "Stay with Brot'an and do as he does."

"Do not let go of the staff," Ghassan repeated.

Wynn never had a chance to respond.

All she heard was another snap of Shade's jaws as Ghassan's arms tightened . . . and her feet left the ground. She should have never looked down.

Shade quickly became smaller and smaller below as Wynn rose higher into the night within the domin's grasp. And it felt like her stomach had been left behind. She really was about to get sick.

* * *

Pain vanished from Magiere's head. Everything around her turned suddenly dark, though she still felt that gnawing in her gut like hunger. The burning inside her began again as she turned.

She heard someone pounding up the cellar stairs but ignored the sound. That thing she wanted to mangle was close.

Magiere bit down against her elongated teeth, trying to stop any further change.

Her other half—her dhampir half—had been forced back, and she couldn't let it take control again. She struggled to keep from losing her hold on reason. If she lost control and slaughtered the host before dawn, the specter could flee completely unseen and take another host.

She had to remember that; all they'd done this night would be for nothing.

"And nothing is what you are . . . but a toy and tool."

Magiere spun at the voice so clear but without the torrent of whispers surrounding it.

"You could be so much more for your making . . . if you let me take you to your maker."

Gasping, she fought to push hunger down again. She had to remember herself more than anything now as she caught the shimmer of something slipping up the stairs at the hallway's right side.

Magiere ran for those stairs, clawing her way upward. She thought she heard footsteps in the hallway below and ignored them. No one else should get near that thing— no one but her—as she took the steps two and three at a time. When she reached the top, she pulled the Chein'âs dagger from its sheath at her back. With that and her falchion in hand, she ran for the first open doorway nearby.

White curtains hung over a single glass-paned window at the room's back. There was a small bed on one side and a chest of drawers on the other, and everything smelled faintly of dust. As she inched inward, she saw no place to hide, but she eyed the window . . . until she saw its latch was still closed on the inside.

Magiere turned, about to leave and search other rooms, and she froze.

The gray-robed figure stood in the room's doorway, though she still couldn't see his face.

It didn't matter as hunger burned again, and she felt her rage rising up.

. . . what are you . . . why have you come . . . who do you serve?

Magiere held her place in that gale of whispers. She was not chained down this time. She bit down on her lip, hoping pain would keep her aware . . . keep her from charging blindly to hack that robe into shreds.

And the robe shifted into the room.

"What did you think . . . to kill me with steel? I have lived a hundred lifetimes and will live a thousand more. How long will you last denying what you are . . . why you are?"

Her head swam and then her sight of the room as well. Everything warped before her eyes.

"You are as trapped as in that cell, alone and helpless wherever you go, until you go where you belong . . . with me."

In her growing nausea, something rose to eat it away. It came up her throat like the fire and hunger, and screeched in her head to drown out the whispers . . .

302 · BARB & J. C. HENDEE

and that one voice. Or had that sound like an animal burst from her own mouth?

Magiere's right hand opened and the falchion fell. She held on to the dagger as the room became less and less dark. On the edge of her awareness, she knew this wasn't entirely due to her dhampir half.

Outside the window behind her, night was quickly fading at the coming dawn.

She lashed out with her empty hand. Hardened nails like claws tore into the gray fabric covered in glinting symbols. The only thought she could hold on to was . . . *Daylight.*

Magiere twisted to fling her tormentor toward the window. Somehow he halted without going through it. The hood turned until its black pit faced her again. When the hint of his voice began to cut into her mind, she shut it out, lunged, and slammed into him.

Magiere barely heard shattering glass as she clawed at her prey.

Leesil ran out into the hallway behind Chane. Chap emerged an instant later, still shaky on his feet, but Leesil had lost sight of Magiere. With Chap limping at his heels, he hurried halfway to the closed front door and stalled to look into the empty sitting room. He looked everywhere, every way, in every shadowed spot and corner. Panic pushed him to something he thought he'd never do.

"Where is she?" he barked at Chane. "Where is the host? You should know—feel them—so where? Now!"

Even in the dark, Chane's eyes glinted like fractured crystals as he looked around. When he turned back, he shook his head. Perhaps he truly did not know.

Leesil wanted to hiss. Instead, he pushed past Chap

and then Chane, looking again into every shadow as he headed toward the back of the house.

Ghassan's feet touched the rooftop. He released Wynn and let her drop onto her knees. Running to the roof's side edge, he looked down.

His first impulse upon shooting up through the air by his will had been to propel them both through the first window he saw in the top floor. He had feared dropping or injuring Wynn, though it was not like him to put safety before necessity.

"What are you doing?" Wynn asked as she gagged and stumbled nearer.

Ghassan ignored her. Down below, the majay-hì was still barking. He wished the scar-faced elder elf would quiet the dog. Then he leaned out carefully to peek down over the roof's eave for the nearest window.

A near deafening crash from the house's rear pulled him around.

Wynn sucked a breath as she turned with him, but Ghassan launched himself across the flat roof by his will. When he reached the rear edge and looked down, Magiere was falling in a shower of shattered glass and flapping gray fabric.

Wynn appeared at Ghassan's side, though she turned and shouted toward the house's front, "Shade, to the back!"

Ghassan gave her no more time than that.

He grabbed her around the waist as he summoned glimmering patterns and symbols across his sight. Thankfully, she kept quiet this time. As she wrapped an arm around his neck, he stepped off the roof and threw his will against the lower ground as they fell.

The ground still came up too fast.

In that blink he could slow their descent only so much, and he still buckled upon impact. Wynn lost her hold on him and collapsed to the ground. At a glance, she appeared unhurt as she braced on her staff and pushed up to her knees. Shade rushed around the house's rear corner, but Ghassan looked only for . . .

Magiere struggled up with a long silver-white dagger in hand, and Ghassan barely recognized her. Completely black orbs filled her eye sockets in a pale face twisted like a monster of pure rage. Cheeks, forehead, and any exposed skin were flecked with red from bleeding cuts. She looked insane, perhaps no longer knowing who or where she was. And her teeth . . .

Ghassan had never seen such in a mouth supposedly human.

The robed figure—Khalidah's host—lay just beyond her and attempted to push himself up. One arm gave way as if injured, and with a grating shout Magiere charged at him.

"Not yet!" Ghassan shouted, for the sun had not crested.

Something in his voice must have broken through her madness, for she froze and hung over her opponent with the dagger held up.

Her target had not even flinched and pushed himself up to his hands and knees. As he turned, half of his hood was torn away.

Ghassan lost his voice at the sight of Counselor a'Yamin in the gray robe. Sharp eyes in a heavily lined face stared back at him through white hair in disarray.

The counselor rose as if something invisible pulled him gently up to his feet. He did not stoop with age anymore.

Ghassan went cold inside. He suspected Khalidah had taken someone highly placed, but he had never guessed how high. And how long had the specter been so close to the prince?

If not for the sect's medallion that Ounyal'am wore, all it would have taken was a whisper from a'Yamin in the prince's sleep. The secret of the tie between an imperial heir and the sect would have been lost . . . along with the prince.

The counselor's eyes narrowed as he took in all those around him, and only then did Ghassan notice that Brot'an had come as well.

"Everyone hold," Ghassan commanded.

He did not know if the specter was more desperate than aware, and he had already been beaten down once. There was also Magiere's bloodthirsty state, and all of this had to end now.

Ghassan grabbed Wynn's free wrist as he blinked for clarity. In that instant, he wrapped his thoughts—his very *self*—in walls of glowing glyphs. His quick incantation slipped out in a whisper under the strain. When his eyes snapped open, he reached for the specter's presence . . .

A'Yamin's old face smiled at him.

Something clawed over the shell around Ghassan's mind.

He began to choke as that shell cut off the air he breathed. Incomprehensible words fought to breach the barrier and get to him like worms boring and wriggling inward. One glowing glyph after another withered and decayed, until the last began to rot before his sight.

A chorus of whispers broke through, and Ghassan could almost make out their words.

He quickly retreated deeper inside himself, building more walls as he fled into his own mind's depths. He used the last of his will to focus and to squeeze hard on

Wynn's wrist . . . or he tried to will it so. He could no longer feel anything at all. And on the edge of Ghassan's awareness, he heard Wynn cry out.

"Magiere, pull him down, now!"

Wynn's arm wrenched downward. She had to brace on the staff as Ghassan dropped to his knees still gripping her wrist. The old man in the gray robe hooked his fingers and tried to charge at her . . . or maybe at the domin.

In one sudden step, Magiere caught the back of the shimmering gray robe, wrenched the old man around, and slashed. The Chein'âs dagger split the robe's front and the vestment beneath it. Smoke rose from the wound.

The host's eyes widened over a gaping mouth.

Normal blades caused little injury to the undead. The white metal weapon gifted to Magiere by the Burning Ones was more than steel.

The host screamed and Magiere slashed again and again.

Wynn's relief turned into horror as Magiere tormented her prey. The dagger's blade raised lines of smoke in every slash, under every scream, until the old man was beyond torment and obscured by smoke.

Wynn had no idea what to do as Khalidah's host writhed. Pounding footsteps came behind her and she looked back to see Osha come around Brot'an. Osha stopped upon spotting Magiere and looked to Wynn as if expecting her to do something.

No one did anything. Wynn didn't dare step into Magiere's frenzy.

Leesil and Chap burst from the house's rear door. Then Chane ran out behind them. Wynn couldn't help looking their way, but in that brief distraction Magiere had straddled the host, pinned his legs to the ground, and grabbed his throat with her free hand.

She struck again, and this time sank the blade into his stomach.

His next shriek turned to choking convulsions.

Ghassan's grip clenched tight so suddenly that Wynn almost collapsed. The sun had not quite crested.

"Magiere, stop!" she screamed out. "Leesil, Brot'an . . . stop her!"

But it was Chap who got there first.

He slammed headlong into Magiere's back, and they both tumbled and flopped over the host's head and across the ground. Leesil came an instant later, stopped short, and eyed Magiere warily as she spun on all fours to look for her victim.

The host's body went still with eyes wide toward the night sky. Limbs twitched as a discoloration in the dark wavered above him. But this wasn't smoke.

"Now, you little fool!"

Wynn regained sense at Ghassan's sharp whisper. She pulled up the dark glasses hanging beneath her tunic and held them over her eyes. There was no time to warn anyone as she thrust out the staff's crystal and shouted aloud in Sumanese:

"Mên Rúhk el-När . . . mênajil il'Núr'u mên'Hkâ'ät!"

White light exploded from the staff's end.

Even with her glasses held in place, Wynn couldn't see anything but the light. The black lenses adjusted, but she saw only smoke rising from the body. Whatever else had been there was gone.

Magiere lay curled away on the ground with Leesil crouched atop her, his face covered in the crook of one arm to shield his eyes. Likewise, Chap hunkered beyond them with his crystal-blue eyes shut tight. Above them, the glow of dawn began to spread.

Wynn wiped the crystal's presence from her thoughts. The bright light died, but how long did they stand, sit, or cower there in silence, unable to move?

Ghassan had released his grip on Wynn's wrist and sat on the ground with his head bowed, and she stood staring at the host's body. Its blackened wounds barely smoked anymore, though its eyes were still wide, its mouth gaping, and it didn't move.

Had the specter been burned . . . destroyed? She believed so.

Brot'an held out a hand to pull up Ghassan, and Osha stepped in toward Wynn.

"You are all right?" he asked in Elvish.

Wynn didn't know and looked to the three beyond the body.

Magiere now curled around Leesil with her face pressed into his stomach as he held her. Chap sat close watching, and though he looked up once, not a word from him popped into Wynn's head. When Magiere fell into this state, only Leesil or Chap or both could ever bring her back to herself.

But this time had been so horrible.

"Where's Chane?" Wynn asked weakly.

He'd come to this fight fully prepared and covered, but who knew what had happened since then. Chane never before had to face both the staff and dawn at the same time.

"He turned back before the sun came," Osha answered.

Wynn sighed in relief. At least he'd made it inside before falling dormant.

"Was he still fully covered?" she asked. "Had he been burned?"

Osha shook his head as if to answer that he didn't know.

Wynn turned and ran for the house, and Shade caught up to her.

Osha stared after Wynn. He had stood on a rooftop and fired arrows into the bodies of men to protect her. He had come after her to make certain she was safe. And even when he stood beside her, it was not him she thought of.

It was Chane.

It would always be Chane.

Magiere didn't really hear Leesil's whispers, and Chap had finally given up trying to chatter into her head. Even the soothing memories he called up from the depths of her mind didn't touch her. The last clear thing she remembered was searing pain before she'd crashed through the window and fallen. Other things . . . what she'd done . . . were not so clear, and that made the scant bits she did remember so much worse.

Pulling back, she elbowed up enough to lift her head from Leesil's lap. The early-dawn light hurt her eyes, and when she looked for the others, there was the body.

That sight left her numb. It had no connection to her. It was the specter she had hated, not this shell.

"Is it dead?" she asked with an edge in her voice.

Beyond the corpse stood Ghassan, pale and unsteady. The domin managed a nod to her, but his gaze quickly returned to the body with something like puzzlement.

Magiere wished she could remember—could have seen what had hid in that flesh—when it finally died.

"We must leave. Now," Brot'an said. "We have lingered too long, and the city is awakening."

Ghassan flinched as if startled and looked up at the elder assassin. "Yes . . . yes." And then he frowned and glanced around. "Does Chane live?"

"He's in one piece," Leesil answered from behind Magiere. "Wynn already went to . . . to check on him in the house."

Ghassan nodded slowly with a long breath. "All of you return to the sanctuary. Wayfarer will let you in."

"And you?" Brot'an asked.

"Chane will be dormant until dusk," Ghassan answered. "This house is safe now, and I will assist Wynn in moving him to the hidden room in the cellar. We will join the rest of you after nightfall."

"You'd sit in a cellar all day . . . for him?" Leesil asked.

"Enough," Magiere whispered.

At his sudden silence, she didn't look back. If Chane hadn't been there for what happened in the passage below the house . . .

"Do you really think you can get Wynn, Shade, and Chane out of there after dark?" Leesil asked. "There are bodies everywhere. This place will be overrun with imperial and city guards soon enough."

That did make Magiere look up.

"No, it will not," Ghassan answered calmly and fixed on Magiere. "Go now. All of you."

Magiere stared at the corpse again, wishing she could have watched Khalidah die and remember it clearly. Leesil grabbed her arm and pulled her up, but some things Khalidah had said began coming back.

How long will you last denying what you are . . . why you are?

CHAPTER 16

Two mornings later, Wynn sat on the floor with Shade in the back corner of the sanctuary's main room watching Chane as he lay dormant. She hadn't bothered covering him yet. The sun had risen, but Magiere, Leesil, Chap, and Wayfarer were still asleep in the bedchamber. The sheet tacked up over the bedchamber entrance was still in place.

For Wynn, time seemed difficult to measure since destroying the specter. Some moments had stretched endlessly while others had passed in a wink. After most of her companions had left the battle site two nights before, she—along with Shade, Ghassan, and dormant Chane—had spent the day in that hidden cellar room where they'd intended to trap the specter's host.

She'd found herself unable to openly thank Ghassan, though she was grateful for his help where Chane was concerned. The domin's assistance in getting Chane down the stairs and into hiding, and then sitting vigil with her and Shade all day, had somewhat restored Wynn's trust in him after all of his deceptions.

Unlike the others, Ghassan seemed to accept Chane as a useful member of the group and did not view him as a necessary "evil." But when Chane rose at dusk that night, Wynn had been unsettled by the ease with which they all left that other house.

The bodies in the street were gone, as was that of the specter's host. No imperial guards were present. Other than the broken shards of glass on the ground, the street and market looked as if nothing had happened.

Wynn's wariness toward the last "sorcerer," a fallen domin of the guild, rose again. But in the face of all that still lay ahead, she'd thought better of asking Ghassan anything as they returned to the tenement sanctuary.

Everyone had been quiet since then, though Wynn still wondered about the bodies. Had Ghassan simply blotted those from anyone's awareness, just as his sect had hidden this place she was in? Or had they been cleared away somehow . . . by someone?

She looked down at Chane, thankful that he hadn't been burned by her staff.

Brot'an again sat cross-legged in the main room's front corner. Wynn couldn't see him clearly beyond the table and chairs in her way, but he was likely sleeping sitting up again. Or maybe he was just pretending. Ghassan had made a bed from floor cushions in the sitting area and appeared to be sound asleep. Only Osha was awake.

He sat in one chair and stared blankly at a glass cup framed between his palms on the table. Since Wynn's return, Osha hadn't said a word to her. She wasn't certain why, but that hurt her.

No one had discussed what was to come next. They were all numb from what it had taken to destroy a thousand-year-old sorcerer. In truth, Wynn couldn't stop dwelling on this. Now it felt too easy, though it hadn't been.

Shade whined softly, and Wynn absently stroked the dog's back as she looked down again at Chane's handsome face. She'd gotten over the sight of him like this, considering he always looked . . . dead. His red-brown hair hung in jagged layers against the pillow, and now he looked peaceful. But again troublesome thoughts wouldn't leave her in peace.

None of them had uncovered the specter's true agenda.

According to Ghassan, it had infiltrated the highest level of the Suman court. Why? What did it want there? Perhaps to influence the empire, but to what end?

This didn't fit its obsession with Magiere to the point of torturing her about why she had come here. But he had been a servant of the Ancient Enemy.

Khalidah was gone, and the truth might never be learned.

The lack of answers weighed upon Wynn as she peered toward the sheet-curtained bedchamber. In there, an orb still lay in its chest. All of the Enemy's minions who'd crossed her path had been seeking one of those. That was why she and Magiere had come here.

Had Khalidah come to the empire for that reason as well?

The thought made her even more anxious.

Patting Shade's head, she whispered, "Stay here." She got up and quietly crept around Ghassan toward the bedchamber.

Much as she didn't want to disturb anyone in there, she felt the need to check.

She pinched aside the sheet curtain to peek in and saw Chap lying asleep before Wayfarer on the far bed's edge. The girl's arm was wrapped over his shoulders. Leesil and Magiere were still tucked away in the nearer bed. Wynn crept in slowly.

She knelt before the chest on the floor between the two beds, pulled the pin in its latch a little at a time, and lifted the lid. Weatherworn hinges squeaked, and she froze, holding her breath. Once certain no one had awakened, she pushed the lid up and drew aside a fold of canvas over the chest's contents.

There it lay: the orb of Spirit.

Slightly larger than a great helm, its central globe was as dark as char, though not made of any stone she'd ever seen. Its surface was faintly rough to the touch, like smoothly chiseled basalt. Atop it was the large tapered head of a spike that pierced down through the globe's center, and the spike's head was larger than the breadth of a man's fist. Its roughly pointed tip protruded through the orb's bottom somewhere below in the chest.

Both spike and orb looked as if fashioned from one single piece, with no mark of separation hinting that the spike could be removed.

Wynn knew it could be through the use of a thôrhk, one of the handles . . . an orb key.

She reached in to brush one such key with a fingertip.

That circlet, broken by design, was made of some unknown ruddy metal. It was thick and heavy-looking, with a circumference larger than a helmet and covered in strange markings. About a fourth of its circumference was missing by design. The two open ends had protruding knobs pointing inward across the break, directly at each other.

Those knobs fit perfectly into a groove running around the orb spike's head. Once inserted, the spike could lift out, thus opening the orb and releasing its power.

Wynn had never attempted such a thing, nor did she plan to.

The previous few desperate years had centered upon locating all five orbs to keep them hidden from the Enemy's minions. Now there was only one left.

She carefully closed the chest, looked both ways to be certain everyone was still asleep, and crept out of the bedchamber. In the main room's back corner, Shade raised her head, her ears upright, and Wynn put a finger over her lips to keep the dog quiet.

There was another arcane object related to the orbs that she'd found.

Wynn inched into the back of the main room. Chane had earlier moved her belongings out of the bedchamber and nearer to his. She crouched to dig into her own pack.

Osha was the only one who appeared to be awake, but he didn't pay her any attention. It was common for her to dig into her own belongings in the morning, and she kept her back to him now as she withdrew a small object wrapped in cloth and flipped the fabric open.

In her hand rested a slightly curved piece of ruddy metal. It looked sound for appearing so old, was little longer than her palm was wide, and about as thick as two of her fingers.

This device had been cut centuries ago from the key—the handle, the thôrhk—created for the orb of Spirit.

Wynn had tried to tell Magiere of its existence, but this wasn't a simple tale and would require a good deal of explaining. During her time at Beáumie Keep in Witeny, she had met some of the most unique people of her life.

Aupsha had been part of an ancient sect following some unknown edicts of a long-forgotten "saint," for lack of a better term. Supposedly that someone had been real and managed to steal the orb of Spirit. The saint's followers and their descendants kept the orb hidden in the mountains above the great desert for who knew how long. Aupsha had been less than open but swore her people wished only to keep the orb from the wrong hands; their purpose was to guard it.

Sau'ilahk, the wraith, killed Aupsha's entire sect, much as the specter had done to Ghassan's. Aupsha had followed Sau'ilahk in secret to Beáumie Keep by using the tool Wynn now held.

Wynn turned that bit of metal over, still studying it.

Aupsha's sect had cut up their orb's key found with it. Somehow they'd fashioned the pieces to track the orb, should it ever be taken from them. Of course, they'd had only one orb and didn't know that what they'd created could track the others as well. After the battle outside Beáumie Keep, Wynn had walked away with the orb of Spirit, the thôrhk to the orb of Earth, and this tracking device.

There was just one problem: she didn't know how to reactivate the device.

Shade had heard words in someone else's memory that were used to activate it, and she had passed them to Wynn. The words were in an ancient Sumanese dialect, so Wynn didn't know their meaning or intent. And that was the trick.

Knowing and intention were required—not mere words, like in a children's story.

It was frustrating, considering how many languages she spoke fluently, aside from others in part. Worse— frightening, even—she would have to tell Ghassan everything. He was the only scholar of this region with knowledge of his language's predecessors who might keep such things to himself.

Wynn's trust in her old teacher had been tested of late. She still didn't fully trust him, but then again . . . she'd been keeping many secrets—more and more—as well.

Shade suddenly pressed up beside her, looking at the device first and then up at her.

Wynn covered the device, but kept it in her grip, and

whispered very softly, "I think it's time we told Ghassan and Magiere about this. I don't see how else to move forward."

Shade sniffed the cloth and her sky blue eyes locked with Wynn's.

—*Wait for . . . night*— . . . —*Wait for . . . Chane*—

Wynn frowned. Why did Shade think they needed Chane before showing or saying anything to Ghassan? Or was it Magiere for whom Shade expressed concern? Either way, Wynn hesitated.

"Very well," she whispered, putting the device away. "Until dusk."

Prince Ounyal'am stood on the dais within the great domed chamber. The clear night was filled with stars that glittered in impossible colors above the imperial palace through the dome's tinted glass panes. Just as unreal were the events occurring in this highest place in the palace.

His father's birthday celebration had gone forth as planned, regardless that most members of the court had not even seen the guest of honor in a season or more. Dozens of servants had spent days and nights transforming this audience chamber into a traditional banquet hall, as was the custom for this event each year. Other preparations had been ongoing for almost a moon.

Low tables were carefully positioned and adorned with silk cloths, silver-gilt plates, and shallow gold bowls with floating flowers from the imperial garden—Ounyal'am's garden. Around the tables newly tailored sitting cushions had been arranged, all made from silk and satin and even sheot'a cloth from the Lhoin'na lands. Members of all seven royal households and many noble ones throughout the empire were in attendance, along with wealthy merchants, prominent city figures, foreign dignitaries, and three members of the Premin Council for the Suman branch of the Guild of Sagecraft.

With the banquet still pending, finely dressed guests strolled the chamber's periphery. Greetings as well as polite introductions passed between acquaintances old and new. And there were always whispers behind one another's backs in new and old ploys. This year the whispers grew too many, too loud, and too distracting, due to the one recent event that changed everything.

Imperial Counselor Wihid al a'Yamin was dead.

Ounyal'am could not cancel the banquet with feigned grief. A number of dignitaries had traveled long distances to be here. And privately he had more reason to silently celebrate. Commander Har'ith was also dead, shot through one eye with an arrow.

The prince's hands trembled slightly as he thought on Ghassan's recent message: a'Yamin had been the specter's final host. It was chilling to think that an ancient undead sorcerer had been so close, acting as the public voice of the emperor.

At Ghassan's hasty request in the night, Ounyal'am had had the bodies near the south-side market removed. Any questions among the imperial guard in this were put off. Ghassan's second request—to remove guards specifically watching for the escapees at the city's outer gates—could not be obliged so openly.

Har'ith's subordinate had already taken his place. There were others now vying for the vacant position of subcommander. While imperial guards were trained to follow orders, Ounyal'am was not their emperor yet, and he had to tread carefully. Still, with a'Yamin dead and the emperor fading, the guards would also avoid questioning the imperial heir, as they could soon owe their positions to him.

Ounyal'am had arranged to call in some imperial guards stationed at the city's exit, for there were many important guests who needed constant protection. As a result, there would also be more reallocations of forces, as well as changes in rotation during the coming days and nights. Ghassan would have to watch carefully for gaps through which to escape the city.

There was no such escape for Ounyal'am.

A prince in an empire without someone to speak for its failing emperor had tenuous authority at best. As he was unmarried and unengaged, there were enough present this night who would use tradition to claim he was not suitable as a regent regardless of being the imperial heir. That would suit them to make certain he first chose one of their daughters before gaining their support.

There were also still those among the court who secretly worshipped the old ways, the gods, like his father. They would soon vie and connive to step into a'Yamin's place, and High Premin Aweli-Jama would be among them. Of course, some of those seeking imperial alliance by marriage would work against attempts to install another counselor.

A'Yamin, or rather the specter, had made as many enemies.

"My prince," said a silken voice. "Salutations of joy from my family to yours."

Shaken from thought, Ounyal'am turned his head slowly to regain control.

Resplendent Durrah bowed her head to him.

She had actually stepped up upon the edge of the dais, creating a moment—the sight—of her on the same level of a future emperor. And no, there was nothing he could do about this for the moment.

Durrah was an eyelash or two taller than him, but

nobles—and especially the royals—admired height in a woman. Thick waves of hair fell down around her strong features: a prominent yet straight nose and high cheekbones. Perfectly decorated in sapphire earrings and a deep azure tunic that fit her shapeliness, she smiled softly, little more than an upturn in the corners of her mouth.

She was considered one of the most beautiful women in the empire.

Ounyal'am did not think so, not when he looked into her eyes.

"Forgive my impudence, my prince," she murmured. "I beg you."

There was no begging in her voice, though there was certainty of a kind.

"I thought to offer myself as your dinner companion this evening," she went on, whispering and thereby having to lean close before all eyes. "I only now found courage to beg so. I do not want you to feel so alone, without comfort, in the loss of your counselor and the commander of your guards."

In presiding over the evening's celebration, Ounyal'am would sit right of center at a lone table placed up on the dais. Near its forward edge, all present could see him beside the empty place for his father.

To the left of that emptiness would sit his aunt, his father's aged sister. The cushion to his own right was reserved for whomever he chose as companion for the meal. This custom had existed for as long as he could remember, but no one in his lifetime had *asked* for the privilege.

Durrah's arrogance was demurely curtained in concern, along with her confidence in her charms, her wealth, and . . . all else she had to offer a man. How could anyone resist her after all? Few would.

Ounyal'am turned his eyes from her.

Pretending to survey the great chamber and everyone within it, he was careful not to let his gaze pause on anyone in particular. Yet it still passed over one small young woman standing alone near the chamber's front doors and its guards. She pretended to sip something from a silver cup and clearly hoped to remain unnoticed as her father, Mansoor, connived and chatted with others nearby.

Ounyal'am's gaze kept moving as he spoke.

"Thank you for your concern, but, under the circumstances, I will dine alone this evening."

He waited a breath to see whether Durrah faltered into further entreaty; she did not.

"Considering the imperial counselor's death," he went on, "I cannot unduly worry my bodyguards. The perpetrators have not been found, and likely they did not act alone but had help from someone inside the imperial court. I am certain you understand."

Ounyal'am did not need to look at Durrah. Some would foolishly take this as suspicion cast their way. Others would try to assure him of their innocence in desperation for favor. What could—would—Durrah say?

Nothing, of course.

In the side of his view, she bowed her head low.

"I wish you only blessings and safety, my great prince," she breathed, hushed like the whisper that charms a reluctant suitor. "More tonight than ever before, on your honored father's birthday."

Durrah gracefully backed off the dais without looking to see her father's angry disappointment.

Offering no reply, Ounyal'am stepped off the dais as well. Suddenly, he could not stand the hypocrisy around him a moment longer. Though he kept his expression coldly impassive, he was bursting inside to do something to quell his panic. He headed straight across the vast chamber toward the main doors, veering at the last moment.

At his approach, A'ish'ah raised only her eyes and not her head. She paled and then lowered her head even more. Her silken dark hair nearly curtained her face, and he was forced to look down at the top of her head as he stepped within arm's reach.

"A'ish'ah," he said softly, and then corrected himself for anyone nearby who might hear. "Lady A'ish'ah . . . it would be my honor to have you dine with me."

Did she shudder? His stomach tightened at having made her so uncomfortable . . . and the object of too much attention. But he could not stop himself.

For an instant, he feared she might find some polite way to decline, and he was unprepared for that.

"Of course . . . my prince," she whispered before regaining her voice. "It would be my honor . . . and my family's."

"Then let *us* begin the feast," he said, turning slowly enough to let her step in beside him.

He wanted to take her hand, but that would have shown too much favor in the eyes of all present. The chamber grew quiet as they walked back toward the dais and the head table.

Nazhif stood behind that table watching, and perhaps a little concerned.

Ounyal'am nodded once to the captain of his bodyguards, and Nazhif quickly stepped around to offer a hand as A'ish'ah stepped up on the dais. One—or rather two—of his other men helped the emperor's aged sister to be settled on the cushion to the left of the empty center one.

Once A'ish'ah was seated, Ounyal'am surveyed the chamber, waiting for all to find their place. And then they were the ones to wait, not sitting until he did. Upon settling on his own cushion, he took another quick glance across the vast room, slowing his visual sweep slightly at Durrah's table.

She was as serene as ever with the wisp of a smile on her full, dark lips. Her eyes held something else, cold as a winter's night in the desert.

Before, he would not have exposed A'ish'ah to such attention, and he was well aware that he shouldn't do so now. But without a'Yamin, things at court had altered, and tonight he felt bold.

For once, he felt like doing as he wished.

With a solemn nod from him, the feast began as he raised a cup.

"Let us drink to the emperor's health," he said with a clear voice. "Tonight we celebrate the day of his birth, and we pray for many more to follow."

Nods, murmurs, and some echoes of his words rose around the chamber. A moment later, an army of servants filed through the main doors carrying trays overburdened with the first course. As always, the emperor's table was served first.

A'ish'ah kept her hands clasped in her lap and did not look up at the golden platter set before her on the table. It contained three roasted pheasants surrounded by herbed oysters in their glistening half shells.

"A'ish'ah," Ounyal'am whispered, hoping to ease her mind with a joke, "please eat something, or everyone will think you are afraid of me."

She raised her head and met his eyes. "Perhaps it would do a few of them good to be afraid of you . . . my prince."

Her words took him aback. So much of what she said took him aback. He never knew what to expect.

"Perhaps," he answered. "But not you . . . not ever."

After another moment of silence, she carefully picked out an oyster for her own plate. Dinner was not such a painful affair. There was little said between them, and he did not care, so long as she would look at him—right at him—time and again.

Halfway through the expected courses, with so many watching, his thoughts returned to the impending intrigues concerning a new imperial counselor. Without a'Yamin, there were a few who had the power to gain access to the emperor's chambers. They could pretend having spoken with him and gained his consent as temporarily appointed. Others would likewise dispute this with their own claims.

Ounyal'am could not stop this without exposing that his father was no longer fit to rule, and the repercussions of him doing that could be even worse. While the emperor lived, Ounyal'am would still be only regent, and any panic he created—over what might be a short window of opportunity—could make some of the vipers even more dangerous.

"Are you well, my prince?" A'ish'ah asked so quietly.

He started and looked over. Her face was awash with genuine concern. Again, he wanted to grasp her small hand.

"I was only thinking on . . . on a little nothing."

At that moment, something—he never knew what—pulled his attention to the main doors. Jib'rail, the new commander of the imperial guard, came toward him. Something in the man's face caused time to slow; his stride was steady, but his eyes were manic.

Nazhif stood only a few paces behind Ounyal'am. He would be watching the commander's approach as well. A few others in the chamber noticed and cast curious glances.

Commander Jib'rail bowed upon reaching the table and spoke in a low tone that would not be overheard.

"My prince . . ." He stopped as if stumbling over the title. "I beg forgiveness for this interruption. Could you please step outside with me for a private . . . word?"

Something in the world shifted. Ounyal'am did not yet know what, only that it had. The moment stretched out.

"My . . . my . . ." Commander Jib'rail trailed off again, as if he had forgotten how to address an imperial prince.

With a quick glance at A'ish'ah, Ounyal'am dared to touch her hand once under the table to stop the worried furrow of her brow. He rose, and though he should have assured all present that there was only some minor matter to attend, his throat was too dry.

Gesturing toward the rear doors, he directed the commander out of the chamber. He followed, as Nazhif did so with two others of his private guard, but only after placing the fourth on watch over A'ish'ah. Once out in the rear passage, Ounyal'am faced the new commander of the imperial guard.

"What has happened?" he demanded, trying to sound sharp rather than anxious.

The imperial guards were renowned for their almost complete lack of visible emotion, but though Jib'rail spoke low, his voice broke when he answered.

"The emperor's breath has stopped." He paused and his voice grew more uneven. "I was on guard at his door when an attendant came to tell me the emperor could not be awakened. I checked his condition myself and then came directly to you."

On some level, Ounyal'am knew what the commander had been about to say, but he still felt unprepared.

"Take me to my father, now," he ordered.

Jib'rail bowed and turned quickly. The following

walk through the palace felt endless, even with Nazhif's welcome presence close behind him.

Three imperial guards stood before the emperor's chamber, where three attendants whispered and fidgeted. All six dropped to one knee at Ounyal'am's approach. That sight made his chest tighten and his stomach roil. He passed them without another glance and went straight for the doors.

"Nazhif, with me. No one else."

He pushed through the doors into the overdecorated sitting room and on to the bedchamber. All was silent but for the sound of Nazhif's light footsteps behind him, which halted when he did.

He peered through the gauze curtains at the enormous bed's foot. Nothing appeared any different from what he had seen on the night he had come to use the imperial seal. The windows were closed, and the room now stank even more of decay. He stepped around to the bed's side to clear his view.

What was left of his once powerful father was a shrunken, wizened form. Thankfully, the eyes were closed, but stillness did not confirm what had been said.

Ounyal'am stood so long, unable to move, until Nazhif finally stepped around him to the bedside and reached out with two fingers for the emperor's throat. The very act was presumptuous, but someone had to verify death.

Nazhif straightened as his fingers came away. "He must have passed in his sleep."

Ounyal'am stared down at the face of his dead father. A wave of unwanted regret passed through him, but how could he mourn?

Emperor Kanal'am had loved no one—perhaps not even himself, let alone his son. He had turned the court into a pit of vipers to match his own corruption. And yet, as a son, Ounyal'am had sometimes harbored a secret hope of someday changing their relationship, if only a little, to something better—perhaps mutual respect if not love.

This was his single stab of regret, as now . . . that could never happen.

Nazhif dropped to one knee. "My emperor," he said. "What is your command?"

Ounyal'am could only stand there and breathe. Though he tried to hold off the repercussions, they crept in upon him. He allowed them in slowly, one at a time.

"My emperor?" Nazhif repeated. "Should this be announced at the banquet?"

Ounyal'am's thoughts tangled in what would happen if he made this public tonight with so many royals and nobles present in close quarters.

"No," he answered. "Swear the attendants and guards to silence. I will return to the banquet and continue the celebration. The mourning horns are not to be sounded until dawn, when all guests are in their own quarters."

Still on one knee, Nazhif nodded. "Yes. That is wise . . . my emperor."

Ounyal'am stiffened at the change of address. Nazhif, the closest thing he had to a friend, was far too good a man to offer empty condolences.

"I will need you most in the coming days," Ounyal'am said. "More than ever before."

Nazhif rose up, though he kept his head bowed. "I am ever at your side, my emperor."

They left the room together. Nazhif stopped to speak briefly to Commander Jib'rail, and then the two of them continued on to the great domed chamber. Ounyal'am did not know how he could go back into the banquet, smile and eat, and pretend nothing had happened.

Tomorrow, everything would change.

Upon returning to the banquet, he managed to make some excuse for his brief absence. Later, he did not remember what it was. He remembered only sinking down onto his cushion beside A'ish'ah and how she'd studied his face in concern. Her eyes missed little.

"My prince?" she whispered.

He could not help cringing for an instant. After tonight, no one would ever again call him "my prince."

A'ish'ah's eyes suddenly widened as she took one glance back toward Nazhif.

She knew, and as he stared back into her eyes, a number of truths hit him.

He was emperor.

He could do almost anything he wished, though for some little things, only if he acted quickly.

The imperial guard was at his absolute command, and in time he could effectively clear the palace of the worst vipers. He could name anyone . . . *anyone* as his first counselor. He could appoint Ghassan if he wished.

His eyes moved up and down over A'ish'ah's face.

He could marry anyone he wished, and he now had the power to protect her.

"A'ish'ah . . ." he began, nearly stuttering for the first time in his life. "After the banquet, I wish to speak with you. Will you walk in the gardens with me?" His tone held a note of urgency, but he did not want to order her, not ever. "Will you?"

As with a moment before, her expression took on a look of understanding. She knew what he was asking.

"Yes, my prince," she answered firmly without looking away from him.

CHAPTER 17

Just past dusk, Wynn stood in the cluttered main room of Ghassan's hideaway with him and Magiere. In her open hand, she held the tracking device made from part of an orb key, and she couldn't quite gauge their reactions at first.

"A sect?" Magiere repeated. "Another one, and it cut up an orb key?"

At that notion, Magiere looked outraged or stunned or something else—Wynn couldn't decide which. Ghassan was another matter, eyeing the device like a treasure he didn't know was possible. And he fixed on the device so long in silence that Wynn grew more uncomfortable.

Everyone else was present, as Wynn didn't wish to explain more than once, and most likely they would all be involved in recovering the orb of Air. Of course, Chane, Osha, and Shade already knew about the device.

Leesil stood one step behind Magiere, glanced away, and didn't look back again.

Chap eyed Wynn rather than the device, as did Brot'an.

Wayfarer remained near the sheet-curtained bedchamber.

Osha kept his distance as well, leaning against a cabinet at the room's front, listening but not looking.

Chane hovered behind Wynn, as if she needed protection, and so did Shade on her left. With eight people and two large dogs, the place felt a tad small.

Considering all the varied reactions around her, Wynn remembered Shade's earlier warning about waiting to tell everyone until Chane was up and awake. Perhaps that had been sound advice after all.

"How does it work?" Brot'an asked.

Of course he would be the one to get straight to the point.

"It is activated by a spoken phrase," Wynn answered, "though in a long-dead language, something Shade heard the last time it was used. She passed the words precisely to me, but I've tried them with no success."

On impulse, she thought it best to show them, so she closed her grip on the device and spoke the words aloud as best she could.

"Nä-yavít, a'bak li-bâhk wihkadyâ, vakhan li'suul."

Nothing happened, of course. She even swung her arm in an arc away from the bedchamber, where everyone knew one orb was stored. She hoped the device might wrench itself back that way, but it didn't.

"See, nothing. It's not the words but their intent, like when I ignite the sun crystal." Her gaze shifted to Ghassan. "I don't know their intent, but I hoped you might."

He shook his head slightly, which made her panic in thinking he was as lost as her.

"You never cease to astonish me," Ghassan said with a sigh. "The things you have asked me to make . . . the objects that find their way into your possession . . . and the places in which you end up. Do you realize how rare a thing you now hold?"

"Of course I do!" Wynn answered. "But it's worthless if we can't reactivate it. That's half the reason I came all this way . . . and you are just as much trouble as what you claim about me!"

Magiere still appeared disturbed that anyone would cut up an orb key. "We don't need it. The keys—thôrhks, handles—can track orbs."

"Not like this," Wynn countered, holding up the device. "Wait until you see."

But if she couldn't make it work again, none of them would see.

Ghassan held out his hand. "May I?"

Wynn hesitated, though this was what she'd come for. With no other option, she placed the device in his palm.

He took a deep breath and released it slowly, as if he'd just gained something by chance that he'd not known existed, or, if he had, how to find it.

"The phrase you uttered," he said, still gazing upon the device, "translates roughly to 'By your bond, as anchor to the anchors of creation, show me the way.' So the intent must focus upon the device's connection to the orbs in recognition of what they are, their purpose, and the nature of the one sought and its individuality. The words spoken must be based on this. Whether such knowledge must be firsthand or general, we shall see."

Wynn's heart sank at first but beat faster with hope. She hadn't been certain even Ghassan would understand a dialect that might be a thousand or more years old. But he'd easily translated it, and that was more than Wynn had hoped to gain.

She reached out. "Let me try again."

Instead, he stepped back, closed his eyes, raised the device out level, and spoke with force.

"Nä-yavít, a'bak li-bâhk wihkadyâ, vakhan li'suul."

His arm instantly straightened and leveled with his shoulder. Seemingly of its own accord, his fist—holding the device—lurched toward the bedchamber's opening.

Wayfarer almost jumped out of the way. Osha quickly crossed to stand before her and eyed Ghassan and the device in a less than friendly manner. The room went silent as everyone stared, for the device had directed Ghassan toward the orb.

After Wynn's own failures with that object, the solution had come so easily that she wasn't sure how she felt. Of course she was elated, but she hadn't expected him to take matters—or the device itself—out of her hands. Glancing up and back at Chane, she found him watching Ghassan.

"How do you turn it off?" Magiere asked, breaking the silence.

"Loss of contact," Wynn answered. "Just let go and it goes dormant." And as she finished, she stepped to Ghassan and held out her hand.

Was that a hesitation—a slight frown—before he dropped it into her palm?

Wynn slipped the device into her short-robe's pocket, though it was heavy enough to make her robe sag. Ghassan eyed her carefully as Chane watched him.

"Yes, that's . . . impressive," Leesil said, though he didn't sound impressed. "But I don't see what good it is if it always goes for the nearest orb."

Wynn took a slow, calming breath. He sounded more like the old Leesil, always free with a sarcastic, unhelpful comment, and she wasn't in the mood.

You do not fully trust this domin.

Chap's words took Wynn by surprise, and she looked into his crystal-blue eyes.

And neither do I, but your urging back in Calm Seatt

*is what brought us here. Tell the domin about the new
clue from the poem, as there is nothing else for us to try.
We—I—shall see what he makes of it, perhaps even what
he does not say in words.*

Wynn doubted Chap could catch a single rising memory in someone like Ghassan. Several years before, Chane had taken a scroll from the library of a six-towered castle guarded by a minion of the Ancient Enemy. It was the same place in which Magiere, Leesil, and Chap—and Wynn—had found the first orb.

Inside the scroll was a poem in a dead Sumanese dialect. The words had been scribed with the black fluids of a long-gone Noble Dead, likely a vampire, and then blackened over with a full coating of ink. Only through Wynn's curse of mantic sight, in seeing the words devoid of elemental Spirit, had the poem been uncovered. Metaphors and similes in the verses hinted at the last resting places of the orbs.

Wynn's mantic sight had certain drawbacks. It made her ill, so she could maintain it for only short time periods. As a result, full translation of the poem had been slow and sporadic. Ghassan already knew about the poem, as he had helped to translate the first section.

The Children in twenty and six steps seek to hide
in five corners
The anchors amid Existence, which had once lived
amid the Void.

One to wither the Tree from its roots to its leaves
Laid down where a cursed sun cracks the soil.

That which snuffs a Flame into cold and dark
Sits alone upon the water that never flows.

The middling one, taking the Wind like a last
breath,
Sank to sulk in the shallows that still can drown.

And swallowing Wave in perpetual thirst, the
fourth
Took seclusion in exalted and weeping stone.

But the last, that consumes its own, wandered
astray
In the depths of the Mountain beneath the seat of
a lord's song.

The "Children" referred to the first thirteen vampires
to walk the world, likely the true origin of Noble Dead
and perhaps created by the Ancient Enemy to guard the
orbs, some of which had been moved from their original
locations. The poem had not been helpful in those cases,
but Wynn remained hopeful that the orb of Air hadn't
moved from where it had been hidden a thousand years
ago. Her mind turned over one verse in particular.

The middling one, taking the Wind like a last
breath,
Sank to sulk in the shallows that still can drown.

Back in Calm Seatt, she'd uncovered another clue
with the help of Premin Hawes, head of Metaology in
the guild's Numan branch.

Wynn looked to Ghassan. "Premin Hawes helped
translate another line that might assist our search."

One way or another, they'd all come seeking the
domin, and there was nothing left to try.

Ghassan raised one eyebrow. "And?"

Wynn closed her eyes, reciting what Premin Hawes had uncovered.

"The Wind was banished to the waters within the sands where we were born." Opening her eyes, she launched into suppositions that she, Chane, and the premin had drawn. "The 'we' most likely refers to the Children, since one of them wrote the poem. We know they were created somewhere in what are now called the Suman territories, though the empire didn't exist then. There were separate nations and not the ones of today."

She paused for a breath.

"So that line must hint at someplace near where the Children were first created as servants of the Enemy. But there is nothing but desert between here and the Sky-Cutter Range, and it stretches from coast to coast across this continent. The only 'waters' are at the coasts, but that goes against '*within* the sands.' Premin Hawes said that much more than nations and people could have changed in a thousand years. Perhaps there was once a body of water in what is now desert?"

Ghassan said nothing for longer than she liked and then glanced away. "Ah, Wynn. What a sage you would have made. I am banished from my guild branch, hunted in my own homeland, and after this I fear you will end up the same."

True enough, yet she didn't have time to worry about it now. "Ghassan! Have you—or anyone—ever read of a recorded body of water in this region?"

Magiere stepped closer and looked less friendly in waiting for the answer.

Slowly, Ghassan nodded. "There was once . . . a shallow salt lake, perhaps large enough to count as a small sea." Then he hesitated. "But that does not help us now."

"Why not?" Magiere demanded.

"Because the 'sand' referenced as covering the lake's bottom was saturated with salt. As the lake dried out, crystals hardened and formed a vast reflective surface. With more heat over time, and wind, it fractured, broke down, and blew for leagues in all directions. Then there is also the distance to reach the dead lake bed."

Wynn frowned. "I don't see the problem."

"Not only is it too far to travel in a single night," he continued, "in the worst heat of the whole nation, but salt crystals in the sand catch and reflect the sun. Anything there in the daylight will die—be cooked—by the sheer heat. Some have tried, and their bones might still be found in the crater . . . if anyone could go there and live to leave again."

Ghassan turned to Magiere. "No one can survive the crossing."

"I could," Magiere said and looked to Wynn's robe pocket. "And that thing can lead me."

"No!" Leesil snapped.

Wayfarer slipped away into the bedchamber. She could not bear to listen any longer. Both beds were still unmade, and she thought to at least straighten the blankets for something to do. Instead, she stood staring down at the chest containing the orb.

"Are you unwell?"

Turning, she found Osha peeking in around one side of the sheet curtain.

His long white-blond hair hung loose, and where it fell down the sides of his head, it divided around his ears, exposing their elongated tips. He was so tall he had to hunch or his head would have banged the opening's top as he stepped inside.

Of any male among Wayfarer's people that she had met, only Brot'ân'duivé was slightly taller than Osha.

"Yes . . . I am well," she answered and looked away.

"You do not wish to hear the discussion?"

"They will argue until exhausted, and then Magiere will do as she wants. I have no say in this or whether I go with them or not. They have not even noticed me gone."

When she glanced back, he was studying her, as he had done too often of late.

Osha stepped closer. "They have not noticed I am gone either."

No, probably not. Magiere, Leesil, and Chap—and Osha's beloved Wynn—had their "purpose," as Brot'ân'-duivé would say. The greimasg'äh would also follow wherever they went, as would Chane and Shade . . . in their devotion to Wynn. The strange domin had his secrets too, and he would follow after Wynn or Magiere.

Wayfarer knew she was merely an extra responsibility to them. Osha at least had his bow and his skills.

What good was she to anyone?

She had been marked by her people's ancestral spirits, driven out to wander beyond her people's lands and be forgotten. This was proven by the name she had taken—the name she had been led to take—upon visiting the ancestors.

Sheli'câlhad . . . "To a Lost Way."

Osha was also a wanderer, for being caught in Brot'ân'duivé's war with his caste, but instead of turning to her in shared loss, his heart had turned to someone else.

The shouting in the outer room grew louder, and Wayfarer could not shut it out. She even heard Chap snarl and then bark, and those sounds made her look for anything to take her thoughts elsewhere.

In the room's far corner, at the foot of the bed she slept in with Chap, was the pile of Osha's belongings. Among those was his long, narrow, cloth-wrapped bundle.

He hated that bundle perhaps as much as she hated her true name. He never opened it unless someone forced him to do so, but a thought—a memory, a little thing she could not quite catch—nagged at her now.

"I want to see the sword again," Wayfarer said without thinking.

Osha did not answer.

She turned, seeing pain and shock in his eyes, as if she had asked for something offensive. Stiffening, she shrank away half a step and dropped her gaze. How would she feel if he ever slipped and called her by that hated name again?

"Please," she began, hesitantly. "Could I see it?"

"You have already seen it."

His tone warned her not to ask again, but now that she had started, she could not . . . would not stop.

"Only for a moment on the ship leaving Bela, and I was not myself then . . . still mourning a lost family and home . . . a lost life." She paused and strengthened her voice. "I did not truly look at it, and I wish to now."

When he did not answer, she again added, "Please," as she raised her eyes.

Osha's mouth tightened. He crossed the room in three long strides and snatched up the long, narrow bundle. Grabbing the cord holding the cloth closed, he opened it in one wrench.

The cloth unrolled in his grip and the blade fell on the bedcover without his having to touch it.

Wayfarer stepped closer, studying the long, sweeping white metal sword. The nearly straight blade was as broad as three of Osha's fingers. The last third swept slightly back from the forward edge in a shallow arc to the point, and even the back of that last third was sharpened. Where the top third joined the blade's lower part, a back barb swept forward toward the tip.

The hilt strut had been fitted with tawny, shimmering wood like that of the living ships of their people, though it was not covered in a weave of cured hide strips. The strut had been bare when Osha first received it, and he had not seen to having it finished. Brot'ân'duivé had done that in the fashion of anmaglâhk stilettos.

When the greimasg'äh had returned to their cabin, having seen to the hilt being finished, it was the only other time Wayfarer had seen the blade. She had not paid attention, for her own suffering had been too great.

The hilt might have been twice as long as the width of Osha's hand. Like the blade curved slightly back, that hilt's end swept slightly forward. Two protrusions extended where the hilt met the blade's base. The top curved forward while the bottom one swept slightly back.

Wayfarer then remembered where she had seen such a weapon, though she had never seen such elsewhere the first time she saw it. The other time had come after Osha had left her and stayed behind for Wynn.

"I have seen this . . . or a drawing of it in a book."

When she looked, the revulsion on his face shifted to confusion. "Where?"

"In the library of a guild annex in Chathburh," she answered. "I was looking through a book written by a people akin to us on this continent, the Lhoin'na. *This* is the weapon carried by their protectors—their Anmaglâhk—called the Shé'ith, only they ride horses and carry large weapons openly for all to see."

Osha slowly shook his head as his expression darkened again.

Wayfarer's thoughts tripped one over another.

"You never told me where the sword came from, only that it was forced on you. Who did this?"

His head dropped as he growled back at her, "Who else works in the white metal?"

She had guessed the Chein'âs—the Burning Ones—must have made it. They were a race that lived in the fiery depths of the world and created all weapons for the Anmaglâhk.

"Why?" she insisted. "Why would they force a Lhoin'na weapon on you?"

Her questions had gone beyond poor manners, but she found it hard to care. She knew nothing of Osha's childhood, his family, or why he had worked so hard to become an anmaglâhk. She knew nothing of his reasons for inner turmoil over this past year. To ask such things was a breach of polite conduct.

"Why?" she repeated.

"They called me again to the fire caves," he whispered. "They took my weapons, the gifts they give to only anmaglâhk." Spreading his forearms, he displayed the burn scars on them and his wrists, and dropped his head as he glared at the sword. "They forced that thing on me, along with the bow handle and arrowheads. I was no longer Anmaglâhk."

Wayfarer tilted her head in thought. Did Shé'ith use longbows as well as swords? She tried to remember the drawings in the book.

"Do you miss being Anmaglâhk?" she asked.

"No," he answered slowly. "I miss knowing my purpose. I thought I had found it. I was wrong."

Wayfarer did not understand what he meant by that. She thought of when she had gone to the ancestors for her name-taking, of the long cruelty of the vision she had been shown, of a place that looked like the forest of her people but was not.

Osha had been given weapons made from the same metal as Anmaglâhk blades . . . but one at least looked like the weapon of a shé'ith.

Wayfarer did not ask permission and reached down to close her fingers on the sword's hilt. Perhaps Osha had a purpose—unlike her—that he did not know.

Chap noticed Wayfarer and then Osha slipping away into the bedchamber. He wondered whether their absences might not be for the best.

"It has to be me, alone," Magiere insisted again.

Chap found it odd that she was now the rational one, and not Leesil.

"Stop saying it!" Leesil argued. "You're more sensitive to the sun than anyone here . . . so no!"

That was not precisely true, though Chap refrained from glancing at Chane.

"Have you ever seen me burn even slightly?" Magiere countered. "Does my skin even take on any color?"

"What about bringing shelters?" Leesil asked, turning to Ghassan. "Thick canvas we could set up when the sun rose?" He sounded more desperate than angry now, as Magiere had dismissed every suggestion he'd made.

"No," Ghassan answered. "The closer we come to that long-dead sea, the more heat rises beyond what the body can withstand . . . even beneath a makeshift shelter."

Leesil opened his mouth again.

—*Enough*—

He spun at Chap's memory-word command. Of course Leesil would not want Magiere going alone after the last orb. As much as Chap pitied the pain beneath Leesil's anger, this had to end.

—Enough . . . repeating— . . . —It has not . . . worked . . . so stop it—

Wynn had been mostly quiet throughout the heated exchange. Like Leesil, she was equally concerned. Unlike Leesil, she knew better than to go head-to-head with Magiere.

Chane had been silent as well, but he cared nothing for Magiere and never put forth an opinion unless Wynn was involved. Brot'an watched and listened, like a reptile waiting in stillness for something useful to come into range, and only then would he strike.

Chap eyed Leesil again, calling up more memory-words.

—Magiere is . . . right— . . . —Remember . . . the wastes—

"Don't try that with me!" Leesil shot back. "I may have been down through most of that, but I remember enough. That wasn't the same as what *she's* got in her head now."

Chap noticed the others' glances. It was still strange to most that anyone responded to him as if he had spoken to either Leesil or Magiere.

And worse when Wynn started, "What is Leesil—?"

Stay out of this.

Wynn's eyes widened at him, but the last thing Chap needed was her getting in the middle.

I will explain what you do not know . . . later.

After obtaining the orb of Fire, he, Magiere, and Leesil had suffered a grueling journey back across the frozen wastes of the far north. Both he and Leesil had nearly succumbed to the elements more than to their injuries. Magiere had somehow placed herself into a state in which her dhampir half did not—would not—recede.

She was nearly feral for most of that journey. She committed unspeakable acts. None of them would have survived if she had not, though in the end she might have perished or remained in that state if not for them.

Magiere had called up a power from within that Chap had feared for so long. Yes, she had saved them when no one else could have done so. She had survived many days that would have left anyone else dead.

She was the only one who could get to the final orb, but Chap was terrified of what might happen if he or Leesil were not there to bring her back to herself.

"What about the device?" Wynn asked quietly. "Magiere may not be able to reactivate it on her own . . . and she will need to."

Chap almost snarled at her for giving Leesil more to argue about.

"I will teach her, as long as it takes," Ghassan said. "It will not be an issue."

The domin was still an enigma—ever helpful, ever useful, and Chap had no idea why. His agenda was as opaque as Brot'an's, but at least Wynn's slip was undercut. And still, none of them truly knew the real risk.

Magiere alone, if she survived to return, might never come back to herself.

Chap would not tell the others, though she as well as Leesil knew this. That as much as anything else was why Leesil was so furious with her and Chap.

"We will travel with her as far as we are able," Ghassan continued. "I know the desert, and I will know when the rest of us must stop. She will not have to travel the entire way on her own."

"How many days?" Leesil asked. "How many after she leaves us behind?"

"Uncertain," Ghassan answered. "I would guess at least three in and three out. She will need to carry water, light rations, and not much else."

"Perhaps it won't take her so long," Wynn suggested. "The device should lead her directly to the orb."

Leesil's expression grew pained again. No one spoke, and this time Ghassan did not openly agree.

Chap thought on what Wynn had not added: everything after that depended upon what Magiere found at the end of her search. Twice now she had found an ancient undead guardian of great power wherever an orb was hidden. If this were the case again, she would be facing the next one alone, and with no one to reason for her.

A harsh rasp broke through his worries.

"The orb of Spirit should not be moved from this place. As secure and hidden as it is, even that is not enough. Someone must remain to guard it."

The tall, arrogant vampire stood beside Wynn. Every time he spoke, his voice grated on Chap's nerves, but he had a point.

"Why should we let that be you?" Magiere asked coldly.

"I cannot travel in daylight," Chane answered, "and I would only slow you down."

Magiere's brow wrinkled as if she was unsure how to respond.

Over the past nights, Chane had made seemingly selfless and helpful offers. Chap knew this undead's past and did not believe either, but there seemed to be no other option.

"Few of us need to go," Chane continued. "Only those who wish to. Wynn should remain here with me."

Wynn looked up at him in surprise, and then a flicker of anger crossed her oval face.

Chap hung his head with a lower rumble this time. The last thing he needed now was another spat. Perhaps Wynn had imagined herself trekking to finish the search with the others, for it was the last orb. Again, Chane had a point. Why risk anyone unnecessarily?

"Chap and I will go," Leesil put in. "And Ghassan, as he knows the region. Everyone else stays here."

An alarm bell rang in Chap's mind, and he quickly focused on Leesil.

—*No*— . . . —*Brot'an . . . comes . . . with us*— . . . —*I would sooner . . . leave . . . the orb . . . with the vampire*— . . . —*As Chane . . . will protect . . . it . . . for Wynn*—

Only Leesil's eyes shifted Chap's way, though he should not have done so with Brot'an watching.

—*Chane will be . . . dormant . . . all day*— . . . —*And neither Wynn . . . nor Osha . . . could stop . . . Brot'an*—

Leesil's expression did not alter. "Brot'an comes too. If we run into trouble with brigands, we'll need someone else to defend us."

Brot'an raised the eyebrow with the scars running through it. Likely, he was not fooled by Leesil's reason.

"Of course," agreed the aging assassin.

"Then it's settled," Magiere said. "We leave as soon as we're supplied."

Late that night, Leesil lay on a pile of arranged cushions on the floor of the cluttered main room holding Magiere with her back into his chest. She was awake as well, and they shared a single pillow and blanket.

Ghassan had taken one of the beds in the bedchamber,

and this seemed only fair as he had spent a number of nights sleeping on the floor or in a chair. Wayfarer and Chap were tucked away in the other bed. Osha slept in there on the floor beside them, and Brot'an had taken a space on the floor on the other side of Ghassan's bed, actually lying down for once.

Wynn and Chane had remained out in the main room, sitting against a pillow pressed against the one bare wall. Shade lay curled up beside Wynn. Until a short while ago, Wynn and Chane had been studying a text together and quietly practicing their spoken Sumanese. At some point, Wynn fell asleep on his shoulder, and he did not attempt to move her. Instead, he sat leaning against the wall studying the text alone while she slept up against him.

The sight had unnerved Leesil, so he'd rolled over and put his arm around Magiere, pulling her closer.

"I don't want you doing this alone," he whispered.

"There's no other way."

With nothing more he could say, he lay there unable to sleep.

"It's the last one," she added after a while. "Then it's all over."

He wanted to believe that. "And we'll go home to the Sea Lion?"

The two of them owned a cozy tavern with an upper-floor home in a small coastal town called Miiska. All Leesil wanted was to go back there, serve drinks and food to townsfolk he knew, run card games, and sleep with Magiere in their own bed upstairs.

"Yes," she promised. "Once I have the orb of Air, as soon as we've found a place to hide it and the orb of Spirit—someplace where the Enemy can't reach them—we'll go home."

She rolled toward him, and he propped up on one elbow, looking down into her face. He never stopped marveling at the beauty of her flawless pale skin, black hair, and dark eyes.

"Only one more," she whispered.

Pulling the blanket up over their heads, she kissed him softly on the mouth.

CHAPTER 18

Half a moon later, Leesil pushed through the flap of a tent he shared with Chap and stepped out into the glare of the great Suman desert. Heat enveloped him instantly, though inside the tent was only slightly less hot.

To the east, west, and south all that he could see was endless hardpack with no vegetation. To the north, there were dunes in the distance, and farther north he could make out the vast Sky-Cutter Range. Those endless peaks separated the continent's north half from its south and, from what Wynn and Ghassan claimed, stretched from coast to coast.

Six days and nights had passed since Magiere had gone on alone, north by northeast.

Leesil had made one last attempt to go with her, and again Chap had gotten in his way, not that Magiere would even listen to Leesil's arguments. Before her departure, Ghassan had taught her how to activate the tracking device and, just in case, came up with a way to strap it to her off hand.

However, though the device worked, it hadn't behaved anything like when the domin had tested it with Wynn in the hideaway.

Magiere's arm didn't lurch outward. Maybe distance mattered, but Leesil saw her arm tremble enough to know she wasn't faking. She had turned north by northeast and raised her arm, shifting it for a guild line. In secret, he'd half hoped the device wouldn't work and she'd have to find another way . . . one that didn't involve her walking deeper into the desert alone.

They were well supplied and, before she left, they'd made certain she carried as much as she dared. In addition to loading her down with a small pack of food and two large, bulging waterskins, Ghassan gave her a stout walking stick and a cold-lamp crystal, for she had to keep moving at night as much as possible. He then tied a piece of white muslin over her head. The cloth draped halfway down her back and reached her eyebrows in the front. He made her take her cloak, claiming that, after the day's heat, she might feel cold at night.

Ghassan didn't understand what Magiere would become just to survive out there.

She wouldn't feel cold—or even heat—when the dhampir consumed her.

She'd considered taking a folded tent, but in the end they'd decided against this, as it would've been extra weight and the water was more important. If she stopped during the day, she had the walking staff to prop up the cloak for shelter.

She'd left at dusk.

Leesil had watched until he could no longer see her in the distance. He didn't want that to be his last memory of her.

Since then, as today, he spent much of his time scanning the empty horizon.

A rustling made him turn his head to look back.

Chap emerged from the tent they shared, skirted the
resting camels, and came toward him.

—*Staring . . . will not . . . bring her . . . sooner—* . . . —
It will . . . only . . . blind you—

Leesil turned back to the desert, with its air rippling
in the heat.

"Get back under cover," he said. "In that fur, it takes
too much water to cool you down."

This was an additional problem. Even when they'd
chanced upon a well along the way, Ghassan had watched
everywhere as the rest of them refilled the waterskins.
Taking a tribe's water was worse than stealing its gold or
property. Leesil could understand that, for it was so hot
out here that any sweat dried as fast as it could form.

How long would they just sit and wait? What could
they do to survive if they had to go after Magiere?

—*It has been . . . only . . . six . . . days*—

Annoyance bubbled up inside Leesil; he could count
for himself.

Cocking his head, he looked toward the other tent for
Ghassan and Brot'an. While setting up camp, neither
had expressed the slightest hesitation at sharing with the
other. At first Leesil found this odd, as not only were the
two men strangers but both were secretive by nature.

Then he remembered that Ghassan had spent much
of his life in a sage's guild, with little day-to-day privacy.
Brot'an had undergone long journeys with other members of his caste and would be similarly accustomed to
shared sleeping arrangements.

Leesil had simply been glad that he and Chap had
their own tent. The past six days would have been worse
had they been forced to sleep beside Brot'an.

When—how—were they ever going to get rid of the
scarred old assassin?

At more rustling in the quiet morning, Ghassan emerged from the second tent and approached. He didn't appear affected by the heat, and his lips were less cracked or chapped than anyone else's. The domin scowled at both Leesil and Chap standing out under the sun.

Leesil ignored this, as he knew the domin now knew better than to say anything about it.

"Any sign?" Ghassan asked, shielding his eyes and peering north by northeast.

"No, but maybe we should start looking for her."

Ghassan didn't answer.

Leesil had mentioned this option more than once. It always led to another argument, but this was the sixth day. He wasn't giving in this time and was about to press his point when Ghassan stepped suddenly beyond him and squinted into the distance.

"What?" Leesil asked.

Ghassan dropped to one knee and began digging in his robe.

Chap inched in before Leesil could as the domin pulled out a roll of leather. Leesil had seen it before. The domin rolled it open to reveal two round glass lenses with studded brass frames. The few tools the man carried were all like this: parts broken down for easy storage that could be reassembled.

Ghassan rose up, placed the crude spyglass to his eye, and peered northeast. Leesil didn't have a chance to ask as the domin turned on him.

"Go now!" Ghassan ordered. "I will get water, a wet cloth, and anything else."

Chap lunged past, his back feet clawing up the hard-packed ground.

"Chap, no—you can't help!" Leesil shouted.

The dog didn't listen and raced away.

"Brot'an, she has returned!" Ghassan called.

Leesil bolted after Chap. If it hadn't been for the dog outdistancing him, it might have taken longer to see where to run. He didn't see anything until he began to grow dizzy with exertion in the heat. Then he saw . . . a figure far out beyond Chap, rippling in the air, and as he closed, he thought it was dragging something behind itself.

Leesil made out the white muslin on the figure's head as he saw Chap slow and circle around Magiere. He knew he probably couldn't carry her all the way back on his own, let alone drag what she'd found. But only he and Chap dared get near her when she was like this. They would have to break through to her before Brot'an arrived.

Magiere didn't appear to see him and kept planting one foot slowly after the other. Panic was the only thing that kept Leesil going in the heat as he came to a halt ten paces in front of her. Chap was panting as he paced, watching her.

Leesil saw her fully black eyes.

"Magiere?" he tried to say, but it came out hoarse and half voiced.

Her pale skin wasn't burned, but it looked paper thin to him; the shadows of veins were visible in her face and neck. Still he waited and watched her trudge as he listened for Brot'an's footfalls. She was thin, as if she hadn't eaten enough. Only one waterskin hung over one shoulder and looked flat and empty.

— *Look* —

At that single word in his mind, Leesil's gaze shifted.

What Magiere dragged was heavy and bulky inside the cloak cinched at the end of the rope. The bulk appeared large and round. She took a few more steps toward him, and he looked at her again.

A thôrhk—orb key—hung around her neck.

He wondered wildly whether it was her own . . . or a different key. He hadn't seen her take one with her, but they all looked so similar. The instant Leesil heard Brot'an's fast footfalls coming from behind, he looked to Chap.

"Now!"

Chap lunged into Magiere's path, and she halted. She wavered as her face barely twisted in a snarl at him. Then came a shudder, and she almost lost her footing.

Leesil lunged one step before stopping himself, and all he could do was watch.

Whatever Chap did—whatever memories he called up in Magiere to wake her other half—took hold. The black of Magiere's eyes receded rapidly like ink sucked into her pupils. A hoarse cry escaped her mouth as her eyes closed and she started to crumple.

Leesil rushed in to catch her. He was so exhausted that her weight drove him to his knees. He got one of his arms around her back and the other beneath her legs as he prepared to lift her.

—*She . . . found . . . it*—

Leesil almost snapped at Chap for breaking his focus. When he looked up, Chap had clawed open the cloak . . . and there *it* was.

Brot'an dropped down on one knee, reaching for Magiere.

"No!" Leesil told him. "Get the orb . . . and bring it with Chap."

A day and a night passed, and Magiere still did not awaken. Chap never left her side. He watched as Leesil tended her, wiping a damp cloth on her face and trying to squeeze drips into her mouth.

It did not work.

Ghassan came with healing salve but was dismissed. Neither manacles nor weapons had injured her, and she would have healed from such on her own. She suffered something else now, and no matter how Chap tried, how often he dipped into Magiere's mind, he never found a single rising memory.

Once, he had understood the workings and limitations of her dhampir nature. In the past year and a half, the depths of it had become a mystery again. She pushed her body through trials it should not have withstood, and this time it had been too much.

This time it was his fault as much as hers.

She understood as he did what the others would not, including Leesil, who was too obsessed with taking all three of them home.

Back in the sanctuary, when Ghassan had announced where the orb might be hidden, in the long moment that followed, Chap and Magiere had privately agreed to this plan before she'd openly stated that she alone could survive the journey. This had been the only way to accomplish what had to be done.

The final orb had to be recovered, and no one else could survive.

Now Chap clung to the hope that Magiere would come back to herself and awaken, though something even more dire distracted him upon her return. Both Ghassan and Brot'an took too much interest in the orb of Air. It was within easy reach of a renegade master assassin and an enigmatic domin skilled in the dead art of sorcery. So Chap had Leesil drag the orb into the tent they shared, and he never let it out of his sight.

Chap seethed at being trapped in this small camp,

and it troubled him more than ever that he could not dip one rising memory in either Ghassan or Brot'an.

Amid the second day, when the heat built again, he grew desperate. Through Leesil, he ordered that cloth of any kind, along with water, be brought for Magiere.

He had Leesil strip her down and cover her in soaked cloths.

When Ghassan later warned they were dangerously low on water, Chap lunged and snapped at the domin. Eventually, that next night, Leesil succumbed to exhaustion. Chap forced his oldest friend to crawl aside and sleep, but he remained lying with his head near Magiere's . . . trying again and again to find some surfacing memory inside her mind.

Sometime in the night, Chap lost consciousness.

When he started awake and realized what he had done, he panicked. Then he grew angry with himself for having fallen asleep. Listening in the dark, he heard her shallow breaths. Had he not awakened, he might not have heard . . .

"Leesil."

At Magiere's whisper, Chap pressed his muzzle against her face. He did not wait for her to try to touch him and lunged across the small tent, ramming his fore-paws into Leesil's side. Before Leesil thrashed awake, gained his wits, and grabbed the cold-lamp crystal, Chap was back to Magiere.

Her eyes were still closed, but when he dipped into her mind, this time he caught fleeting fragments of memories. This was enough to calm Leesil once Chap told him.

By late afternoon the next day, Magiere's dark eyes fluttered and stayed open.

"Leesil?" she repeated in a hoarse whisper.

Leesil sagged in such relief that Chap feared he might

fall ill. Ghassan, now sitting inside the tent, reached back to push the flap open and called out, "She is awake."

Chap wrinkled a jowl and waited.

Brot'an crouched in the opening. "Is she well?"

Ghassan shook his head. "I do not know."

Magiere croaked something and tried to sit up. Before Leesil could, Chap pinned her shoulder with a paw. Then Leesil held her head and carefully gave her a sip of water from a small cup made of carved horn.

"The orb," she whispered. "Where . . . where is it?"

"It's here," Leesil said. "Don't worry."

He said nothing more and made her drink again. The instant he withdrew the cup, Magiere began to sob, shudder, and thrash weakly.

"I saw her burn!" she whimpered. "I didn't know . . . but she was there! I tried to stop it . . . but I . . . didn't . . ."

Alarmed, Leesil grabbed Magiere's face and tried to hold her still as he looked to Chap.

They had both seen her enraged, wild, out of control. Chap had never seen her like this.

"Hush, that's enough," Leesil murmured to her. "Everything is all right."

Chap did not believe so.

Leesil again grabbed the small cup and put it to Magiere's mouth. She drained it and then lay in incoherent fits, whispering words too garbled to understand. Even the flickers of rising memories that Chap caught in Magiere's mind were scattered and broken and told him nothing of use. After a little while, Ghassan brought dried figs and brittle flatbread. She ate as if starving. Though this was another good sign, Chap watched her with growing rather than diminishing concern.

Brot'an remained in the tent's opening as Leesil and Ghassan continued to care for Magiere. When it grew dark outside, Ghassan set the cold-lamp crystal inside a real lamp to amplify it. Partway into the night, Magiere rolled her head and looked up at Chap. She seemed calm and more aware.

"You found the orb," Brot'an said.

Magiere's eyes shifted toward him, but she only stared.

Chap wanted to take Brot'an's face off for bringing that up again.

"Was there a guardian?" he asked.

Chap snarled, bearing his teeth, and did not stop until Leesil nudged him. Magiere rolled her head away, and Leesil twisted where he sat to face the shadow-gripper.

"Get out!"

"Different," Magiere whispered. "Different . . . from anything . . . before."

Chap swung back around as Leesil looked at her. "Not now. It can wait."

Magiere shook her head. "You have to know. I have to tell you."

That was unlike the Magiere that Chap knew. She never needed—wanted—to *talk* about anything. He did not try to reach for what rose in her mind for fear it might shake her even more. Magiere kept her eyes only on Leesil as she began to speak . . .

The first night's trek wasn't difficult. The sky was clear, and the stars and full moon offered some light. Magiere had heard that deserts were hot during the day and cold at night. That wasn't exactly what she found. She'd grown up in the dank, wet cold of Droevinka on the eastern continent. The temperature dropped but still felt warm to her.

Even after the sea voyage to this land, and her time

here, the arid air of the Suman region was still so . . . foreign.

All through that first night, she gripped the tracking device, feeling its pull. It led her farther and farther northeast.

From Ghassan's best guess, she had perhaps three days' travel to reach the crater that had once been a salt lake. When she'd complained about being weighed down with two full waterskins, he'd told her, "You will not have that weight when coming back."

Before she knew it, dawn arrived.

As the sun crested, it was not yet unbearably hot, so she continued for as long as possible, and the first hint of something glittering in the cracked ground caught her eye.

Magiere stopped and looked down at countless crystalline shards around her boots. Each one reflected the rising sun like tiny precious gems. She'd hoped she wouldn't see them so soon, for they marked the fringe of the worst to come.

The light from above and below began to burn her eyes as she went on. Tears started to run down from her seared eyes, wasting precious water. Still, she followed the pull of Wynn's device. By midmorning, the heat on her pale skin grew unbearable, and then the pain in her eyes worsened as the world brightened, became white.

Suffering broke her will, and she felt the burning in her stomach rise into her dry throat as her teeth began to elongate. Her dhampir half came to the defense of her body, and clear thought grew more difficult with every step. Even the device strapped to her left hand began to make her palm sting.

She had to stop and wait out the sun before she lost all control.

Magiere dropped, pulled off her cloak, and used the walking staff to hook the cloak's hood so that the back of it faced the sun. She weighted its hem with whatever chips she could scrape off the ground with the Chein'âs dagger, and then curled up in the tiny shelter, holding the staff upright by locking its base in her folded knees.

The water she sipped from one skin was nearly hot enough to make tea. The figs inside her small pack had almost baked together, and the flatbread crumbled apart in dried bits.

She and Leesil had often longed for privacy in their travels. But now she was so alone without him. No Leesil complaining about, well, everything; no Chap digging through the packs looking for any leftover jerked beef.

Nothing but silence . . . And the heat grew.

She stopped thinking of anything as the sun rose overhead and the cloak shelter couldn't shadow her boots anymore.

Again, the burning began rising from her gut into her throat, and that was the last thing she remembered.

Awareness came back slowly. When she cracked open her eyes, the cloak tent had fallen to cover her body, and she pushed the fabric off her head to find the sky darkened by night.

Everything rushed back to Magiere.

She cursed and grew frantic wondering how much time she'd lost lying there. Her eyes and teeth felt normal, and her head was beginning to clear. She lifted a waterskin. Though still warm—hot—the water gave her some relief, but when she stopped gulping, the first skin felt so much lighter.

She was going through water too quickly. The first skin had to last until she found the orb. Even then, the second would have to be stretched out on the return, when she'd be in even more need as she would be dragging something heavy.

She picked up the cloak and, this time, kept it thrown over her shoulder. Then she took up the staff.

Magiere closed her left hand on the device and prepared to regain her direction toward the orb. She did not need to reactivate it, as it had never lost contact with her skin. While Ghassan had taught her how to activate it, and she'd tried speaking the Sumanese phrase, it hadn't worked. On impulse, she tried again in Numanese and failed, and then again in Belaskian, her own native tongue, or one of them.

"By your bond, as anchor to the anchors of creation, show me the way!"

The device came to life, but that wasn't enough for Magiere. She worried that if she succumbed to her dhampir half, saying those words—let alone remembering them—might not be possible. And she knew she would succumb, eventually, just to survive. That was why she'd asked for the device to be tied to her hand.

Now she simply lifted her arm, swinging it until the device stopped twisting, and she moved on. The night was not as quiet as the last, with the crunch of her footfalls numbing her ears and mind.

At dawn, the heat began building at the first spark of light on the horizon. By midday, her dhampir half had risen so fully that it took her a long time to erect the cloak tent.

As she curled up in that tiny shelter, breathing became so difficult that even her inner nature couldn't keep her from passing out again.

Once night fell, and that other half receded, she awoke weakened and drained. The water began to taste salty. The figs had burst sometime during the day, and all of their inner moisture was gone. She rose, packed up, and went on as before, though at times she no longer knew why.

Something inside of her felt . . . pulled. This made her remember she hadn't checked the device's pull before she'd started out. When she stopped and did so, she was already heading where it pulled her. She tried to remember why she was doing this. Fragmented memories came, many of them in Wynn's voice.

More than a thousand years earlier—perhaps more— something of many names, an ancient enemy, had made the first of the undead: thirteen vampires. Wynn had said they were called the Children. Toward the end of a great war, the Children left into five groups, each group carrying off an orb to faraway places . . . and they no longer needed to feed. The power of the orbs fed them.

The orbs of Earth and Spirit had been moved from wherever they'd been originally taken, so Magiere didn't know where those Children—those guardians—had gone. The orb of Water, the first found, had been guarded by three—Volyno, Häs'saun, and Li'kän—in the ever frigid heights of the Pock Peaks on the eastern continent south of where Magiere had been born. As the centuries passed, Häs'saun and Volyno had somehow perished, leaving only Li'kän, and then she had slowly gone mad, forgetting how to speak.

Magiere had locked Li'kän forever in the cavern beneath the castle where the orb of Water had sat for centuries. Back then, she'd thought this better than exposing her companions to battle with something insane and so powerful that it had lasted so long.

The orb of Fire had been taken to the icy wastes at the top of this continent by at least three of the Children. And again, only one had survived the long wait:

Qahhar. And like the first orb, that one had been placed on a pedestal like a sacred object.

Magiere never learned the names of Qahhar's two companions, only that he'd killed them to keep the orb for himself. His madness wasn't the same as Li'kän's, and he'd proved far more dangerous. The only way she'd finished him was by giving in utterly to her dhampir half.

That had started other changes in her, after she'd torn him apart and swallowed his black blood.

She didn't regret killing him, only what it had done to her . . . sometimes. She became stronger but with less control. It was easier to call up her other self but harder to drive it down again. And more than once, if it hadn't been for Leesil, let alone Chap, there were things she might have done that she couldn't live with later.

And now she was once again getting close to . . .

According to the clues Wynn had uncovered, the orb of Air would still be where it had been taken. There would be another guardian, perhaps more than one. What would it cost Magiere this time to gain the final orb?

She didn't slow, and nothing could turn her back, as she struggled to put one foot in front of the other. As night ended and the horizon began growing lighter, she pressed on, determined to walk for as long as she could. When the sun crested she saw something glittering ahead that was far different from the shards in the hardened sand. It was vast and shone like a mirror.

It seared her eyes, reflecting the rising sun.

Magiere shielded her eyes. For an instant, she thought she was looking out across water. The sun had risen fully above the horizon when she reached the lip of an even deeper depression in the desert . . . and it went on as far as she dared to look. She was at the edge of what had once been a great salt lake.

The device lurched in her hand.

The heat made it hard to breathe, but she let the device pull her onward. Along the edge of that deeper depression loomed the outline of a building . . . or did she only imagine it?

Ghassan had warned her of illusions in the desert.

Magiere closed in on that structure, and it grew even larger in her sight. She stopped to stare blankly at an enormous dwelling, constructed of tan stone, on the shore of the cracked and glassy plain.

Wynn had said the poem suggested the orb lay in the water—or the shallows of such. Yet this dwelling stood on the edge—the shore—of the deeper depression. And if this was another place where ancient undeads guarded another orb, why hadn't she felt them yet? In her two previous encounters, she had long before she was near enough to see them.

Almost immediately, a twinge of hunger was followed by rage that grew with the light and heat of this third day. Yet it was different from her dhampir half trying to strengthen and shield her.

There *was* something undead here.

She dropped the staff and drew her falchion. There were no surrounding walls, no sign that anything living had ever existed here. She walked straight to the heavy doors in the square entry, but there was no lock that she could see. Cradling the sword rather than setting it down, she put a shoulder against one door and shoved.

It grated inward across a stone floor.

Magiere stepped in, and before she even looked about, she heard the door closing on its own. She tried to grab its edge but was too late, for it moved faster than when she had pushed it open. Everything went dark as the searing light was shut out.

She couldn't see anything, even as her hunger increased to widen her sight. With the device lashed to free her hand, she again cradled the sword with that same arm long enough to get the cold crystal out and ignite it. The entrance was at the head of an empty corridor that stank of dust and age.

Magiere knew better. It couldn't be deserted for what she felt. Her fingernails hardened and her teeth shifted as her canines lengthened. They always did when an undead was near enough.

Maybe exhaustion kept her in control or maybe it was something else.

In finding the orbs of Water and Fire, getting near one had somewhat kept her hunger in check and kept her mind clearer. She lifted her left hand, holding the cold-lamp crystal between her thumb and forefinger, and let the device lead her down the corridor.

She passed rooms glimpsed through doorless openings on both sides with little or nothing in any of them. None of those pulled at the device. At the corridor's end were stone stairs leading downward, and she hesitated, raising the crystal high.

Its light couldn't reveal the bottom, as if the steps descended forever into the dark.

Who had built this place and excavated so far beneath it? Where were they? They had to be here, at least one of them.

Magiere stepped through onto the first stair and descended quickly, step by step, and she noticed the walls of the stairwell were no longer straight. They curved to the right. She continued down that subtle spiral, moving faster, anxious and eager to know what awaited her at the bottom.

The crystal's light exposed an opening below, and

she slowed to a stop a half dozen steps above. Beyond the exit was a wide space of darkness. She paused again at the last step and peered into a large, plain room.

As she took in the sight of the few objects awaiting her, she became only more confused.

The first thing she saw was an orb like all the others, with its tapered spike intact, but this one rested inside a hole cut into the top of a simple, flat wooden table. With no battle and no blood spilled, she stood within sight of her final goal.

It felt wrong. Nothing here was like the last resting places of the other two orbs she'd recovered. No tripod pedestal, as if it were an object of worship. No preserved bodies of ancient dead creatures as slaves. No chasm or vast cavern with narrow bridges of stone over fire or ice in the depths.

A simple old table supported an orb in silent darkness within a bare room.

Magiere stepped in, looking left and right along the room's front. At first there was nothing to see, but closer to the table she spotted something on the floor beyond its far side. An orb key lay with a curved sword atop faded but carefully folded cloth, perhaps clothing.

Stepping around the table's left side, she became almost certain the decayed cloth was one if not two separate pieces of attire, perhaps robes or something similar. For as old as this place had to be, the decayed cloth wasn't that old. And even standing so close to an orb . . .

Her jaws still ached under elongated teeth, her fingernails still felt as hard as talons, and she knew her irises were still black. There was at least one undead here—somewhere—and yet her thoughts were clear.

Why had she been allowed to get this far without being attacked or even engaged?

Magiere wasn't going to try for the orb until she found whatever was here. She realized that she needn't worry about the device or reactivating it, so she slit its lashing with the base edge of her falchion. As the lashings fell away, she closed her hand and shoved the device into her belt. In these depths, even her eyes needed light, so she brushed the dimming crystal once down her vestment. As it brightened, something more at the room's rear caught her eye.

A number of paintings on unframed canvases hung in a row down the far wall, and she stepped closer.

Now faded, the paintings might've once been brightly colored. They appeared to be a sequence, from right to left, like a story. Each one was about half her height and their bottoms were at waist level.

The first depicted a collection of small dwellings, possibly a village.

Magiere sniffed it, touched one of the dwellings, and licked her finger. In the six-towered castle of the Pock Peaks, she and Leesil had found some walls covered in words and symbols written in the fluids of an undead. The tip of her tongue tasted nothing like that.

The next painting was of a long oval in various shades of tan that showed sand blowing in the wind: the desert.

The image after that was clearly a painting of the sandstone dwelling she now stood beneath, but there were flowers and palm trees around the exterior. On the far side of this, she made out a group of small people, on their knees, bowing down.

Next came a painting of two tall pale figures, a man and a woman with long black hair, wearing muslin robes. They stood beside a small boat.

The final painting was a large blue oval with gentle waves: a sea or a great lake.

Magiere knew nothing of such things, but the paintings looked rather crude to her. And like the robes on the floor, though old and decaying, they couldn't have lasted since whenever this place had been built. They might be old, but were far newer than the dwelling. She shifted left again to look at the image of the two pale figures.

"Baseem'a!"

Magiere twisted around with the falchion raised.

In the opening to the stairs stood a slender girl about eleven or twelve years old. Her perfect skin was dusky. Silky dark brown hair fell over the shoulders of her undyed muslin dress. Her almond-shaped eyes were wide, almost eager and longing. She did not look at the sword and only stared at Magiere.

"Na Baseem'a?"

Magiere lost some of her hunger in confusion. This girl couldn't have survived in this place if she was alive, but she didn't look ancient. In the long search for the orbs, Magiere had faced two of the Children, and this girl didn't *feel* like one of them.

The girl didn't charge or flee. She didn't display elongated teeth, nor did her irises lose color and turn crystalline. There was only a longing hope in her small face where there should've been rage, fear, or hunger.

"Na Baseem'a," she said, this time with a frantic edge and a shake of her head.

More of Magiere's own burning, hunger, and fury faded. What was happening?

The girl inched closer, still not afraid. Instead, her eyes held disbelief that matched Magiere's.

"Min'a illy?" she said.

Magiere should've taken off the girl's head, but the thought somehow revolted her. She back-stepped when the girl tried to come even closer, until only the space of the table's width remained between them.

Was this undead child all that remained here, the only one to know how this place had come to be and why the orb was still here? Those answers might hold more that could help understand the dangers of the orbs . . . and the purpose they'd served.

"I don't . . ." Magiere began, only then realizing her teeth had receded to normal. "I don't understand you."

"Numan?" the girl asked.

Magiere wasn't Numan, but she'd tried that language first as it was the closest other culture to this region.

"Yes," she lied. "You . . . speak it?"

The girl held her index finger and thumb parted slightly and then pointed to her ear as she nodded. Finally, she pointed to her mouth and shook her head.

"You understand," Magiere ventured, pointing to her ear, "better than you speak it?" And she pointed to her own mouth.

"*Na'am! Iy ayaw,*" the girl exclaimed with a nod and a broad smile.

Magiere grew slightly ill. This felt too much like talking with an abandoned child, but this girl wasn't living. There was only one way any undead could survive alone without feeding. Magiere glanced at the orb. It had sustained her.

"Ghazel!"

Magiere's eyes shifted back.

"Ghazel," she repeated softly, pointing at her chest. "Your name is . . . Ghazel?"

The girl nodded again. Magiere turned halfway and tipped the falchion's point toward the picture.

"You?" Magiere asked. "Are those yours?"

Ghazel's browed wrinkled, and clearly she didn't understand. When she stepped forward, Magiere backed around the table. The girl hesitated and then continued on to the back wall. She slowly swiped her hand up and down one painting after another and then pointed to herself. At the last painting toward the far corner, she crouched to pick up a small clay jar that Magiere hadn't noticed before.

Ghazel turned the jar upside down and shook her head.

Magiere understood. The child had had paint at one time. When it ran out, there'd been no way to get or make more.

What Magiere didn't understand was how the girl had ended up here.

Stepping cautiously to the painting of the two pale figures, she pointed and asked, "Who?"

Ghazel came closer along the wall, as if eager to please. She pointed to the male, and her smile vanished as she whispered, "Mas'ud." She shuddered. Then she pointed to the female, and her voice filled with sadness. "Baseem'a."

She looked up at Magiere with hope and mouthed the name again, not blinking.

It took another instant before that sank in.

Magiere realized the girl mistook her for the woman in the painting. This only confirmed her suspicion that the two figures portrayed were likely the ancient guardians of the orb. Where were they now?

"What happened?" she asked, pointing to the painting. "Where?"

Ghazel looked back and forth between Magiere and the painting with a slight frown.

Magiere pointed to the orb. "How did that . . . get

here?" And she waved her left hand, with the crystal, all around the room.

Ghazel's slight frown vanished. She pointed first to Mas'ud, but instead of pointing to Baseem'a next, she pointed to Magiere. The girl motioned to the orb and acted out carrying something heavy around the room.

She stopped at the painting of the desert and waved her hand across it. First, she patted the painting with the small group of kneeling figures. Then she pointed to the image of the sandstone dwelling. Briefly, she stepped away to act out pounding with hammers and lifting objects in the shapes of large squares.

Ghazel put her finger back on the image of Mas'ud, pointed at Magiere again, and then to the boat. She paused but soon continued, moving her finger to the painting of the lake, sliding it to the center of the waters. She returned to acting out carrying something heavy and heaved it toward the water in the picture.

Again, Magiere understood. Two ancients had carried the orb across the desert, had this large dwelling constructed by slaves, and then took the orb out to sink it in the lake.

What more secure place to hide it? It all matched what Wynn had found in the scroll's poem.

The middling one, taking the Wind like a last breath,
Sank to sulk in the shallows that still can drown.

But where had the boat come from? More than that, how had the orb ended up back in this room?

Ghazel held up both hands, churned them around each other, and said, *"Ahyaan."*

This was one of the few Sumanese words Magiere

had picked up in their travels. It meant "time," and she assumed the girl was telling her that time had passed.

Ghazel pointed to the lake, turned her palm downward, and lowered it halfway to the floor.

"The lake began to dry up," Magiere said, more to herself than to the girl. And how many centuries had that taken? If Ghazel knew about it, had she been here since then?

The girl appeared to grow frantic, and her face suddenly filled with fright. She pointed to Mas'ud, grabbed her head with her small hands, and began rocking wildly around. When she stopped, she seemed at a loss for what to say, do, or show next. She pointed at Baseem'a with one hand; with the other she pointed to Magiere.

Ghazel then ran trickling fingers down both of her cheeks, and her eyes filled with sadness.

Again, Magiere wasn't certain what this meant at first. She looked to the painting of two pale figures and back at the girl, and she understood.

Mas'ud had begun to go mad, and Baseem'a had fallen into sorrow.

Ghazel pointed to Mas'ud again and slid her hand across the painting of the desert all the way to the painting of the village. Without warning, she grabbed the front of her dress and acted out being dragged. She slid her finger back across the desert and then pointed to the painting of the stone dwelling. Touching two fingers to her throat, she snapped her teeth.

Magiere went cold inside. "He stole you from your village, brought you here, and turned you. Why?"

Ghazel pointed to Baseem'a and hugged herself with a wistful expression.

Magiere did not fully follow, but she guessed that as the female had grown sad, perhaps the male had attempted to provide her with company . . . a little girl. Somehow Ghazel had come to care deeply for Baseem'a. It also struck Magiere as possible that Ghazel had never once fed on a human being. The slaves would have been gone long before her arrival, and the orb would have sustained her all these years.

But if the girl had not come here until the lake began to dry, how did she know what had happened before then?

Magiere shook her head and pointed to the boat. "How did you know . . . ?" She pointed to Ghazel as well and tapped the side of her own head.

Ghazel pointed back at Magiere. When Magiere didn't respond, she pointed to the image of Baseem'a and then to Magiere again. She gestured from her mouth to her ear.

Magiere nodded, ignoring the girl's confusion about who she was. Baseem'a had told Ghazel everything.

Ghazel churned her hands, one around the other, and again: *"Ahyaan."*

More time had slipped by. She pointed to the blue lake and again pressed her palm downward, this time all the way to the floor.

The lake had dried completely.

Magiere could imagine other changes that had followed. The heat would've grown unbearable, and all trees and flowers would have died.

First pointing to Mas'ud, Ghazel then slid her finger along the lake, curled her fingers as if taking something from it, and again acted out carrying something heavy. She took it to the table and dropped it with both hands, as if setting the orb where it rested.

When the lake or sea had dried up, the ancients had brought it back. By then, no one could've reached them in the searing heat—at least nothing living could have— but what had become of the guardians?

Magiere pointed to their picture. "Where?"

Ghazel's small face twisted with sorrow. She put her finger on Mas'ud, and then once again put her hands to her head. Only this time she turned her head back and forth violently. Mas'ud had fallen further into madness.

Turning from the wall, she ran across the room, pointed down to the curved sword on the floor, and made a harsh slicing motion.

Magiere stood frozen as the girl knelt beside the robe nearest the thôrhk.

"Baseem'a."

And Magiere understood. The robes were not merely clothing lying on the floor. They were the only remnants of where the ancients had fallen. Mas'ud had murdered his companion.

Ghazel grew visibly frustrated as she attempted to relate the rest. She struggled for Numanese words. "Mas'ud . . . make . . . me." Again, she pointed to the sword and repeated the slashing motion.

Magiere exhaled quietly.

If Mas'ud had been the one to turn Ghazel, she would not have been able to refuse any order he gave her. Wynn had explained this once. The child of the creator was physically compelled to obey any order.

Mas'ud had ordered Ghazel to kill him.

Both ancients were dead, and the only one who knew the orb's current location was a small, undead girl.

Then Magiere remembered something else.

Even the undead needed moisture, fluids to stay functional. How had Ghazel done so after the lake had dried out? As the girl's mouth opened, as if to say something, Magiere waved her off.

"Water?" she demanded.

Her mouth still open, Ghazel tilted her head with a

frown. She hurried to the painting of the lake. Instead of pointing, she gripped its bottom, pushed up, and pulled it off the wall.

Behind it was a crude opening in the stone.

Ghazel looked back as if this should mean something, but again Magiere shook her head. The girl stood there an instant longer and then grabbed the lip of the opening to pull herself up and in.

Magiere sheathed the falchion and followed to peer into a rough tunnel angling steeply downward. The girl waved her in and led the way as they crawled. In only moments, Magiere caught a taint in the air both humid and unpleasant. They kept on for far too long until Ghazel sat up, but her head didn't hit the tunnel's top.

Magiere crawled closer, and the knees of her pants were instantly soaked as a smell choked her. By the crystal's light, water filled a small, jagged fracture in the earth in which they knelt. Even before Magiere raised a wet hand to lick it, she knew it wouldn't help. The water was beyond briny, as if a shovel of salt filled her mouth. This might be all that was left of the lake that sunk deep into the earth. Perhaps it was even part of the source that had once created that body of water.

It was no good to Magiere, though an undead could've consumed it without harm.

She turned to crawl back up the tunnel, hearing Ghazel following behind her.

Once back in the room, the girl rushed past her to kneel by the robes. She grabbed one robe and the orb key and held both out to Magiere.

"You . . . stay . . . me?"

Magiere had never before looked at any undead as a victim. To her own disgust, she couldn't help it now.

Yet that didn't alter what the girl was or that Magiere was here to take the orb.

Once the orb was gone, what would happen to Ghazel?

Magiere gripped the sheathed falchion's hilt with her right hand.

The kindest thing she could do would be to take the girl's head at the neck, quickly. She'd encountered vampires turned against their will before, and dispatching them had never made her pause.

What was wrong with her now?

She'd seen ancients—the Children—like Qahhar walk in sunlight. Though she'd never seen Li'kän do so, that frail-looking but powerful, feral woman had been awake during daylight in the six-towered castle where the first orb was found. But Magiere had also seen "offspring" of theirs perish and burn under the rising sun.

Taking Ghazel across the desert seemed unlikely. And later, what would happen to the girl once she was separated from the orb? Magiere had locked Li'kän away below that castle for fear of what might happen once she was separated from the orb of Water.

If the girl grew hungry, she'd eventually be driven to feed and kill, even if she didn't understand what was happening to her.

Magiere couldn't stand it anymore. She couldn't bring herself to kill the girl, but the only safety for everyone else was to leave Ghazel behind. Steeling herself, Magiere stepped in and took the orb key out of the girl's hands.

The sudden hope in Ghazel's eyes made Magiere look away. She looped the key around her neck and then tucked her hand holding the crystal under one side of the orb.

Ghazel cried out in fright, but Magiere ignored the girl.

Grabbing the spike's top with her free hand, she hefted it off the table and headed for the stairs. She heard Ghazel following with a stream of sobbing cries in Sumanese. Even if Magiere had understood any of it, she didn't dare listen as she climbed upward.

Emerging into the main passage, she didn't slow, but small hands latched on her lower arm beneath the orb.

"Stay . . . you stay!" the girl cried. "Baseem'a . . . stay!"

Magiere stalled, almost looked down, and then jerked free of that grip. With greater speed, she hurried for the doors out of that place, even as the child's scream tore at her ears. The sooner this was over, the better.

Ghazel wouldn't follow into daylight if she'd spent ages alone in this place . . . knowing she couldn't.

The sound of sobs followed Magiere all the way to the door. When Magiere rolled the heavy orb into one arm and grabbed a door handle to pull, Ghazel threw herself against the door with a cry that carried no words.

Magiere shoved the girl aside and wrenched the door open. She ducked out, choked in the sudden heat, and stumbled away from the building.

In the blinding sun, hunger came burning up her throat as the dhampir inside of her rose up to defend her flesh. Her thoughts clouded as she clung to one purpose only: the orb in her arms.

After perhaps fifty paces, she stopped, gagging for air under a wave of guilt and indecision.

Should she go back?

What if she waited until dark and tried to get the child across the desert by traveling only at night and keeping her sheltered under the cloak by day? Might there be something Wynn could do? Wynn had claimed

Chane was feeding only on livestock. Magiere didn't believe that, but was it possible?

No! She was a fool to think of taking an undead into a city.

Still, she stood there, suffering at the thought of walking away and condemning a child to face the slow death of starvation. Her hand clenched on the top of the orb's spike.

"Baseem'a!"

At that anguished cry, she whirled. It was too clear to have come from within the building, and Magiere dropped the orb. Hunger failed and heat won out as she screamed at what she saw.

Ghazel's body caught fire as the girl raced out under the burning sun.

Magiere charged back. "No!"

The girl kept screaming the name of the one she thought had returned to her ... until she fell. On impact, ash rose from her in a cloud amid the smoke and stench of burning flesh. When Magiere reached her, there was nothing left but smoldering, blackened bones that began cracking and falling apart amid the ashes.

Magiere stared down, growing dizzy and sick.

Heat made everything in her sight begin to waver. There wasn't even a wind to scatter the remains and wipe the sight away. When the climbing sun crushed her to her knees, she looked over and saw the staff she had dropped upon her arrival. Somehow, she crawled over and picked it up and then rose to stagger back to the orb. She barely managed to push up the cloak tent to shield herself. But she refused to go back inside the dwelling. She couldn't bring herself to do it.

Magiere lay there, barely shaded, and the sight of a burning child wouldn't leave her mind.

* * *

Magiere lay silent, staring up into Leesil's amber eyes looking for . . . something.

What did she want from him? Understanding? Absolution?

She didn't dare look to Chap for that.

She'd done what she had to, and she still heard Ghazel screaming . . . even in the tent's silence as Leesil said nothing. Or did he want to know the rest after that? Did anything else matter, considering she was here and had brought the last orb?

The girl had died long before on the night that Mas'ud had taken her. Magiere had never felt that she *killed* any undead. She only finished something that shouldn't have become what it was. So why should Ghazel have been any different?

Shifting her gaze, Magiere looked to Chap.

—*It is done . . . either way*— . . . —*And you . . . came back . . . to us*— . . . —*Think of only . . . only . . . this*— . . . —*Nothing . . . else*—

Magiere glanced away. It wasn't that simple. And then she felt Leesil stroke her hair.

"Rest another day," he whispered. "We'll leave when you're ready."

She knew Brot'an and Ghassan were in the tent as well, but she didn't look for either of them. She had no idea what the aging assassin thought, and likely the fallen domin's eyes and thoughts missed little.

But they'd understand even less about this than either Leesil or even Chap.

To all of them, only the orb mattered, for better or worse and in different ways.

Once, she'd thought so too.

CHAPTER 19

Wynn counted the days since Magiere and the others had left. More than a moon had passed. At first the days and nights had felt long, but then the five left behind fell into a routine.

Without much discussion, they all took to Chane's sleeping schedule for the most part, though this surprised Wynn slightly. Neither Osha nor Wayfarer had any interest in spending time with Chane. Wayfarer simply claimed it would be easier if they were all awake together. Then again, perhaps she was afraid to fall asleep when Chane was up, now that Magiere and Leesil—and especially Chap—were away.

Aside from this, much of the tension over Chane's presence vanished.

While Osha and Chane didn't like each other, they had learned to work together without the past glares and posturing. Wayfarer didn't interact with or speak to Chane unless necessary, but if she disapproved of him, she was too well mannered to show it.

They were all in limbo, waiting to learn the fate of departed friends and companions.

Wynn and Shade tended to rise first in the late

afternoon. Since Chane remained dormant all day, this was longer than the rest of them could stay asleep. Before dusk came, one of them would walk to the market for fresh food or anything else needed. Later, they ate supper together, though of course Chane only sipped water or tea.

After that usually came chores.

Wynn attempted to reorganize various texts and scrolls on the shelves. She scanned through all of them, but none held anything related to Ghassan and his sect's practices.

Osha, having acquired more materials, set to fletching additional arrows to replace the ones lost. More than once Wynn glanced at the new steel arrowheads, knowing he still had white metal ones in his quiver.

Wayfarer mended a few items of torn clothing she'd found in the travel chest, though she soon ran out of much need for that. Late one afternoon Wynn decided it was time to act upon something that Leesil and then Chap had asked her to do.

Getting Shade to cooperate was a bit of a bother.

"Make it something not . . . disturbing," she instructed the dog. "Maybe from childhood, just running about with your brothers and sisters."

Shade's jowls quivered with a hiss through her teeth. So far, she had refused to interact with her father, Chap. Any references to the short childhood she'd been driven from, to cross the world to Wynn's side, was something Shade avoided.

"Go on!" Wynn insisted.

Shade turned away with another growl and padded across to where Wayfarer sat at the table stitching up a tear she'd found in one blanket. Shade didn't wait for the girl to notice her approach.

She shoved her nose under Wayfarer's wrist and flipped her nose up, and then the girl's hand slipped over Shade's head.

Wynn took a quick step in whispering, "You obstinate little pain in the—"

Wayfarer sucked air in a squeak, lurched away, and fell off the chair.

She popped up instantly on her knees and stared wide-eyed as Shade turned away with a grumble. When Wynn reached the table, Shade pressed briefly against her leg.

—*My memories . . . not your . . . tool*—

At those memory-words from Shade, Wynn glowered back.

Hopefully Shade had stuck to something nice in the type of memory. And yes, in all the time since Wynn had arrived in the Suman Empire, Wayfarer had stayed close to only Chap. The girl never once touched Shade . . . until now.

Wayfarer peeked over and around the chair at the black majay-hì. Even Osha looked puzzled for a moment, though he wouldn't know what had just happened. It was exactly as Wynn suspected and feared—as Chap and Leesil had needed to know.

Shade had direct Fay ancestry through her father, so she wasn't completely normal for her kind. It appeared that Wayfarer—once called Leanâlhâm—experienced the conscious memories of a majay-hì with a touch.

Wynn wasn't certain what it meant as she thought of the girl's name given by her people's ancestors: Sheli'câl-had, "To a Lost Way." That might have more meaning than the others could guess at, though Wynn had only a fragment . . . a piece of that puzzle.

There was one other person she'd met who appeared

to do what the girl had just done. In the forests of Lho-in'na, when Wynn had gone to their guild branch in her search for the orb of Earth's last resting place, she'd met a lone woman in their forests.

Vreuvillä—"Leaf's Heart"—was a priestess of ancient ways, a Foirfeahkan.

That term was so old that even her people, the Lhoin'na, could not accurately translate it. She lived in the wild with the majay-hì packs of that land. Like Wayfarer, Leaf's Heart was notably short for her people. And though the girl had green eyes and the priestess's were the normal amber, they both had hair far too dark for either a Lhoin'na or an an'Cróan.

And apparently both could catch the memories of a majay-hì, though Leaf's Heart was supposed to be the last of her kind.

Wynn thought again of the meaning of Wayfarer's final name given by her people's ancestral spirits.

. . . *to a lost way* . . .

Chane sat up in his usual corner, having risen again.

Wynn looked to the window at the back of Ghassan's ensorcelled hideaway. Dusk had come and she hadn't even noticed. For now, she kept what she suspected to herself.

Sometimes, to pass the nights, Wayfarer, Osha, and Chane worked under Wynn's guidance to learn a little of the most common dialect of Sumanese. Even if Magiere acquired the orb of Air, there was still the matter of hiding it—and the orb of Spirit as well. There was no telling how long they would remain in the south. She also suggested Wayfarer stick to conversing with Osha in only Numanese or, if need be, Belaskian.

Twice Chane went out at night, and Wynn assumed he needed to feed on livestock in secret. However, he never grew unduly pale as he had before when hungry. When he came back, he was not flushed as he'd normally been after feeding.

She wanted to ask about this, but something held her back.

They managed to get through the days and nights. Every once in a while, Wynn succumbed to self-indulgent petulance over having been left behind to wait in ignorance. These bouts did not last long, and then one afternoon ...

Wynn counted off another day as she, Osha, and Wayfarer began discussing what might be needed at the market. Without warning, they heard scraping outside the sanctuary door.

They all looked at one another, then at Chane, who was still dormant in the back corner. In a flash, Osha had a dagger in hand and stepped around to put everyone behind him as he faced the door. Wynn froze, but Shade didn't begin to growl, and this brought a hint of hope.

An instant later, the door opened.

Ghassan came through, followed by Brot'an, Chap, Leesil, and Magiere. The last two carried something heavy between them, hidden inside a large canvas cover.

"You are back!" Wayfarer cried, rushing around Osha and straight to Chap.

Wynn's full attention turned to the bulging canvas Leesil and Magiere set down. She looked up at Leesil, not able to even ask. He nodded once, and she remained frozen in place.

They had the final orb.

A flood of questions filled the cluttered room. Wynn noticed that Ghassan and Leesil answered most, and Magiere was too quiet. Wynn wondered what horrors

Magiere had faced to attain this last orb. At least she *looked* all right, with no serious burns or injuries.

Still, Wynn couldn't help feeling that this final task had cost Magiere something.

Leesil exclaimed that he was starving, and so Wynn hurried to put a meal together. As soon as she was across the room, crouched down, digging in their stores for bread and cheese, Leesil came in behind her. One look in his face told her that he'd sent her off alone for a reason.

"What's wrong?" she asked.

He glanced toward the corner where Chane lay dormant, and then back to her. He appeared uncomfortable, which wasn't like him.

"Do you . . . remember . . . how when we first came to stay here, you'd sit with Magiere so the two of you could talk?"

Of course she did, and she nodded.

"Tonight," he said, "once we've eaten and settled, could you . . . could you do it again?"

Wynn hesitated. "What is this about?"

Leesil's discomfort visibly grew. "Something happened out there, and I'm worried she needs to talk to someone . . . and for once that someone isn't me." He paused. "Will you do it?"

"Of course. I'd do anything for Magiere."

He nodded with a slow exhale and rose up to head back to his wife.

Later that evening, not long past dusk and after another orb had been settled in the bedchamber, everyone was occupied in some fashion. Wynn piled cushions against the front wall and drew Magiere aside to sit next to her.

"I've been hoping all evening to hear what happened . . . from you," Wynn whispered. "Can you tell me?"

Across the room, Chane sat sharpening the shorter of his two blades. Shade lay on the floor beside him.

Magiere watched them both for a moment and then looked to Wynn and nodded.

The next morning, Magiere took Wayfarer on the short walk to the market. She wore a light cloak with the hood up and forward, and she made certain Wayfarer did the same. As Ghassan had promised, there were no imperial or city guards searching the streets. To Magiere, it seemed that she and Leesil were no longer hunted.

It felt strangely normal to walk in the city and head out only to buy food. After talking late into the night with Wynn, she had begun to feel more like herself, or at least less like a traitor to herself. Wynn never saw the world in black and white, right and wrong, but in variations of gray to be constantly reexamined. Magiere had never fully understood that before.

The crowded market lay up ahead.

"What is our next step?" Wayfarer suddenly asked.

Magiere took a deep breath filled with the scents of fresh bread, roasted meats, people in the streets, and other simple things in the air.

"Restock the cheese . . . again," she answered. "Chap finished it off last night."

Wayfarer stopped walking. "I meant with the orbs. Now that they have all been recovered . . . now what?"

Magiere stopped as well. This was the last question she'd have expected from Wayfarer.

"We need to find places to hide them," she answered carefully, "where they will never be found by anyone again, especially the Enemy's . . . servants."

"Wynn told me . . ." the girl began, "told the rest of

us that the wraith went to great lengths to gain the orb of Spirit. He even abandoned the orb of Earth upon finding it, as he did not want it. Once he had the orb he sought, he used it to alter the body of a young duke."

One of Magiere's hands clenched nervously to hear Wayfarer speak of such things.

"So," the girl continued, "it would be wise to move the orb of Spirit someplace where no undead can enter."

"Well . . . yes," Magiere finally agreed.

"No undead can enter the lands of the an'Cróan," Wayfarer added, looking up into Magiere's eyes. "The same should follow true for the lands of the Lhoin'na. What if Osha—and I—took the orb of Spirit to them? It would be safe and beyond the reach of any undead."

Magiere couldn't help the fear, which always came in anger. "You and Osha, take an orb to—"

"He is more than he appears," Wayfarer interrupted. "And once the orb is in that land, we would be safe there as well until . . . whatever is next."

Magiere stared down at her, unable to say anything.

Aside from such a dangerous notion, she knew something had gone wrong between Wayfarer and Osha, and Osha and Wynn, and even that linked to Wayfarer's sudden eagerness to get involved.

Magiere grabbed Wayfarer's hand, pulling her along. "We'll talk about this later."

That night, once again Leesil lay on a pile of cushions on the main room's floor, holding Magiere against his chest. Ghassan and Brot'an had taken the bedchamber to get some rest. Chap lay curled up near one of the bookshelves on another of the large cushions.

Wynn and Chane had taken Shade out to do her

nightly "business." Osha and Wayfarer were engaged in some kind of board game with draughts that Osha had bought at the market.

In a sense, Leesil had Magiere to himself for a short while. Part of him almost couldn't believe the final orb had been found. The exhausting, bloody, seemingly endless searches were at an end. Tilting his head down, he pressed his face into the top of Magiere's hair.

"What are you thinking?"

"We may have a hiding place for the orb of Spirit," she whispered.

He tensed, for that wasn't the kind of answer he'd wanted. "Where?"

"Somewhere safe, though we need the same for the orb of Air. We shouldn't hide two in the same spot. I know Chap did that, but only he knows where they are, and we shouldn't try it again."

None of this was what Leesil wanted to talk about. "Any ideas?"

"Not yet." Magiere rolled onto her back, looking up at him. "I'll think of someplace . . . or Chap will . . . or Wynn." She touched his cheek. "And once it's done, we'll go home. Promise."

He almost couldn't believe they were this close to being done. He brushed the side of her face with his fingers as he whispered, "Home . . . finally."

EPILOGUE

Another large ship docked that night at the teeming port of the empire's capital. Once the ramp was lowered, only one passenger disembarked. He was tall and well formed but with a face so pale that it glowed briefly within a deep hood as he neared a dock's lantern.

Not a bit of other flesh was exposed. Beneath his cloak, he wore black gloves, a leather-laced tunic, dark pants, and high riding boots. A wide leather collar of triple small straps was buckled around his throat.

No one here would have recognized the man known as Duke Karl Beáumie, for that was who had once inhabited this flesh.

Sau'ilahk, first and highest of the Reverent, servant of il'Samar during the Great War, walked the pier now trapped within that dead flesh. He gazed upon the imperial city, which had not been here during his living days. It had also been many years since he had returned to this land in his centuries as a wraith. Now he could actually sniff its air.

It smelled as wretched as he felt.

Upon gaining this living flesh, which he had sought for

so long, the body had been slaughtered by another undead on that same night. This was not the homecoming he'd long envisioned—immortal perhaps but still undead. It was not fair, and his god . . . his Beloved . . . had hissed at him in spite for the last time.

Stepping off the pier, Sau'ilahk had one purpose in mind: to find the one who had done this to him.

When he found Chane Andraso, he would make that undead watch as he finally took the life of Wynn Hygeorht. Even then, he would not finish Chane. That lowly vampire would be left to suffer such a loss for a thousand years . . . or until his suffering grew too much, and he ended his own existence.

Sau'ilahk reached the port's main archway and entered the city. There were few people out in the streets, and not one bowed a head to him, let alone prostrated themselves before him. How he longed to grab one at random and feed, for he had nearly starved for lack of life while on the vessel. Only once did he drain the life of a sailor during a night squall—after which he dumped the body overboard. Any more than that would have raised suspicions among the crew.

He was still learning about his new existence and how this body worked.

Though he had been killed—drained—by a mere vampire, he had awoken as something else. He had not burned in the dawn, as expected, nor did he thrive on blood. He could still feed by touch, though he did so in flesh instead of spirit. He no longer knew what he was.

Now he was loose in a large population that ranged between opulent wealth and desperate poverty. A few night wanderers passed by, from sailors to merchants to commoners. It had long been his intention to purchase fine clothing. What he now wore had been scavenged. Any coin he had procured had been needed for the journey itself, and he had not come all this way out of nostalgia.

It had taken more coin back at the port of Oléron on the southern, coastal end of Witeny to learn where Chane—and Wynn Hygeorht—had gone. They had stolen the orb of Spirit from him. It was hard to know in any given moment whether that mattered more to him than vengeance.

A soft shuffling caught his attention, and he turned.

A ragged beggar crouched at the mouth of a cutway between a tea shack and a lamp shop. At the sight of Sau'ilahk, the bony man raised a chipped pottery cup.

"Coins for mercy?" he asked.

"Of course," Sau'ilahk answered quietly, stepping closer. "But I do not wish for my purse to be seen."

He slipped into the cutway while stripping off his right glove. Turning to face the opening to the street, he backed deeper in as he dug into his pouch. He raised one silver coin into plain sight, and at the sight of that, the spindly man followed. And when the street's lights no longer touched him . . .

Sau'ilahk released the coin.

The beggar's eyes widened—their eyes always filled with fright over a coin that might be lost in the dark.

Sau'ilahk grabbed the beggar's throat with his gloved hand, and the man's mouth gaped for a scream. He clenched that hand, choking off his victim's air. He rammed his bare hand against the man's chest, tearing aside the filthy shirt to gaunt flesh beneath, and then . . .

Euphoria made Sau'ilahk's eyelids flutter as his prey shuddered, unable to even choke.

Sau'ilahk took all of the life he felt in that decrepit form in his hands.

When it was over, melancholy followed as he dropped his prey's shriveled husk. He wanted more and stooped to pick up the coin he had dropped . . . along with any lesser ones in the beggar's fallen cup. But he stalled upon exiting the cutway.

There was a chance that even in a near empty night street a lone beggar might have been noticed and then missed. He turned back the other way for the alley at the cutway's rear.

"Another dead one."

Sau'ilahk halted upon entering the alley, pivoted to the right, and looked for whoever had spoken. Light from the street at the alley's far end revealed a small form stepping closer. Something looked wrong with its shape even before it drew near enough for him to see a small girl in a tattered nightgown.

Closer up, he saw the blood running down her front.

Closer still, he saw the alley's cobble *through* her.

The ghost child stopped at arm's length and looked up at him. Likely her visage was that of the moment after her death. Something had severed her throat.

"You cannot bother me," he said.

"I would never . . . old one."

The young voice was too articulate for her age. At the creak of wooden wheels on cobble, Sau'ilahk turned the other way.

Down the alley's other length came something long and narrow with a bulk atop it. It was rolled on two large side wheels and guided by two tall shuffling figures. When it stopped, he made out two heavily muscled men. Curiosity kept him in place.

The men rocked the rolling litter forward, tilting it until its front end clacked on the cobble. Lashed to the litter was a preserved corpse now held erect by its bonds.

His hands, folded and bound over his chest, were bare, exposing bony fingers. He was dressed in a long black robe. Where his face should have been was a mask of aged leather that ended above a bony jaw supporting a withered mouth, likely more withered in death than in his last moment of life.

Stranger still, the corpse's neck was wrapped in hardened leather, not like Sau'ilahk's own, but rather to keep the head upright.

There were no eye slits in his mask.

"You may call me Ubâd."

Sau'ilahk looked down and found the ghost girl standing beside him. It was she who had spoken, and not the corpse.

"A mere necromancer," Sau'ilahk said with disdain, looking back to the corpse. "And not a good one in having joined his dead."

"Do not assume too much, Reverent One," the child ghost taunted, still speaking for the corpse. *"I know of you, Sau'ilahk, no matter what flesh you have stolen."*

Discomfort raised tension in the back of Sau'ilahk's neck. How did this one know who he was in not knowing the body he inhabited? And how had this lowly necromancer come to be waiting for him?

"What do you want . . . corpse?" Sau'ilahk demanded.

"Oh, not yet. We wait for another."

Sau'ilahk took a step, ready to tear the corpse apart. Soft but steady footsteps made him hesitate and look back the way the ghost child had come.

A lone cloaked and robed figure came down the alley. Something in its sure gait flooded Sau'ilahk with caution. He raised a hand, preparing to summon an elemental servitor to attack it.

A chorus of whispers filled his mind. From out of them came one clear voice in his thoughts.

Lower that hand, old . . . friend.

Sau'ilahk froze in confusion. That voice and the way it reached him . . . It took a moment for his memory to catch up. It had been so very long since he had last heard it . . . with his own ears.

"Khalidah?"

Caution turned to wariness as the leader of the Sâ'y-minfiäl—"Eaters of Silence"—stepped closer. That triad of sorcerers had been the lesser and baser of Beloved's tools so long ago. How could that liar of liars still exist?

And then Sau'ilahk sensed a living body where the shadowed form stood.

"Show yourself!" he snarled, his hand still raised.

"I think not," Khalidah countered, this time with a real voice. "Like you, flesh suits me once again. Unlike you, I will keep mine whole and vital for now."

Again, Sau'ilahk was lost. He did not remember the sound of Khalidah's voice, but he knew the voice he heard was not the right one.

"How long have you—?"

A brief while, Khalidah answered again amid the whispers. *Taking flesh was such relief after so long. But I am certain* you *understand this.*

Sau'ilahk hesitated, for there was much here he did not know. "Why are you here? How did you find me?"

"I can find all that is dead," the ghost girl answered instead. *"Even those who serve il'Samar."*

He glanced down at the child and hesitantly looked to the corpse. Il'Samar was yet another name for Beloved. So these two thought to bring back any wayward ones to their god?

"You will not call *me*," he warned Ubâd. "Take that mind-twister in his new flesh, if you wish. Gift him to Beloved, but I—"

Oh, my my, you are still such an ignorant . . . priest!

Sau'ilahk spun back at that voice in his mind.

"We have no desire to serve Beloved," Khalidah said aloud. "Have you not had enough of that yourself? Have you not had enough of our god's broken promises? Oh, yes, I know you have."

"We will take from Beloved what it took from us . . . ," said the little ghost, though Khalidah finished, "And the way to kill a god is with its own tools."

Sau'ilahk looked between the two. "You have found . . . all . . . of the anchors of creation?"

"We know how to get them," Khalidah answered. "But more than that, we know where Beloved's newest and most cherished is now."

"The dhampir will serve us just as well as the orbs," the ghost girl added.

Khalidah turned in the dark, heading back up the alley.

Be prepared, oh, petulant priest. I will find you again when the time comes for Beloved to die.

Sau'ilahk heard a low, breathy laugh up the alley.

Khalidah's silhouette slipped into the far street, rounded the corner, and vanished. The attendants leveled the litter and rolled it off behind him, and the little ghost girl was suddenly gone.

Sau'ilahk had known disappointment and despair for so long that he was almost afraid to hope . . . to kill his god.

Khalidah walked the street with a narrow smile, malicious but hopeful. After having gone so long without flesh, since his escape from the sect, each body he had claimed was a marvel as well as a minor struggle.

This newest one was not yet fully his own, and he paused near a tea shop closed for the night.

As a poor place, it had no glass in its windows, which were shuttered tight. It did have a worn brass sign dangling before those shutters. He could not help wanting an amusing peek, so he grabbed the sign's bottom edge. As he turned its dimpled surface, he caught a better reflection of his current face.

"I *see* you," he whispered. "And you see me, do you not . . . domin?"

Khalidah grew joyful at a scream rising from deep within his thoughts.

Ghassan il'Sänke stared into his own face warped by the brass sign. He watched another smile accompanied by another low laugh, neither of which was his own. And he screamed again in the dark of his own mind as Khalidah walked away in his flesh.

New York Times **Bestselling Authors**

Barb & J. C. Hendee

THE NOBLE DEAD SAGA

Dhampir
Thief of Lives
Sister of the Dead
Traitor to the Blood
Rebel Fay
Child of a Dead God
In Shade and Shadow
Through Stone and Sea
Of Truth and Beasts
Between their Worlds
The Dog in the Dark
A Wind in the Night
First and Last Sorcerer

Available wherever books are sold or at
penguin.com